The Jefferson Allegiance
The Presidential Series

Bob Mayer

Copyright

http://coolgus.com

THE JEFFERSON ALLEGIANCE by Bob Mayer
COPYRIGHT © 2011 by Bob Mayer

ISBN: 978-1-935712-71-8

THE HISTORICAL FACTS

If a book be false in its facts, disprove them; if false in its reasoning, refute it. But for God's sake, let us freely hear both sides if we choose." Thomas Jefferson. 1814.

In May of 1783, the Society of the Cincinnati was founded. A leading member was Alexander Hamilton, and the first President of the Society was George Washington, before he was President of the United States. The Society of the Cincinnati is the oldest, continuous military society in North America. Its current headquarters is at the Anderson House in downtown Washington, DC. Besides the Society of the Cincinnati, Hamilton founded the Federalist Party, the first political party.

"Can a democratic assembly . . . be supposed steadily to pursue the public good? Nothing but a permanent body can check the imprudence of democracy. Their turbulent and changing disposition requires checks." Alexander Hamilton. 1787.

Thomas Jefferson was not allowed membership in the Society of the Cincinnati.

"Your people, sir, are a great beast." Alexander Hamilton. 1792.

In 1802, President Thomas Jefferson, well known for his strong opposition to a standing army, established the United State Military Academy, the oldest Military Academy in the Americas. In 1819, he founded the University of Virginia, the first college in the United States to separate religion from education.

In 1745, the American Philosophical Society (APS), the oldest learned society in North America was founded. Thomas Jefferson was a member for 47 years and its President for 17 years. He subsequently established the adjunct United States Military Philosophical Society

(MPS) at West Point with the Academy Superintendent as its first leader. The APS has its current headquarters in Philosophical Hall on Liberty Square in Philadelphia. The MPS appears to have disappeared.

"I am not among those who fear the people. They, and not the rich, are our dependence for continued freedom." Thomas Jefferson. 1816.

Besides the APS and MPS, Jefferson founded the Anti-Federalist Party.

"The mass of mankind has not been born with saddles on their backs, not a favored few booted and spurred, ready to ride them legitimately, by the Grace of God." Thomas Jefferson. 1826.

THE 4TH OF JULY 1826

"Is it the Fourth?" In debt, dying, and with only his favorite slave as companion, Thomas Jefferson still had one last duty to discharge.

"Yes, it is, sir," Sally Hemings said, *"but it's still dark. Dawn is a half-hour off."* She wiped a cool cloth across the wide forehead of the man who owned her. Not tenderly like a lover, but with the touch of a favored servant, an occasional confidant, and primarily with the suppressed and paradoxical hope of freedom at the price of her master's passing. She put the cloth back in the bowl and walked over to the drapes. She parted them and looked out into the darkness, seeing the oil lamps scattered around Monticello flickering in the pre-dawn gray.

"Is he here?" Jefferson's voice was a rasp, barely audible.

"He's been here for a week," Hemings replied, irritation creeping into her voice. *"He's waiting in the Parlor."*

"It's time."

Her eyes went wide at the implication. *"Are you sure, sir?"*

Jefferson didn't have the energy to speak again. His thinning gray hair—still holding a touch of red—was highlighted against the pillow. He made a slight twitch in the affirmative.

Hemings escorted in a frail young man with black hair and even darker eyes. His hands shook. He seemed afraid to approach the ex-President's alcove bed as if by doing so, he might bring to completion the act he was here for. Jefferson's eyes were closed. He whispered something and Hemings and the man had to come closer until they were both hovering above the President.

"Poe. It's time." Jefferson nodded toward the headboard ever so slightly. *"It's there."*

Edgar Allan Poe's tongue snaked across his dry and cracked lips, deprived of alcohol this long week, a sign of how serious he took this event. *"Yes, sir."*

Poe reached behind Jefferson's pillow and retrieved a leather bag. Something inside rattled, and Poe glanced inside, and then closed it. He held the bag with his shaking fingers.

"Sir—"Poe paused.

Jefferson's head twitched in the affirmative once more.

"Sir, where is the rest?"

"Safe," Jefferson whispered. "With an old enemy who became a friend. He will pass what he has on to the head of the Military Philosophical Society, whom you must contact. You must go to the Military Academy next."

"I understand, sir. But the Military Academy. I do not think I--"

Jefferson wasn't listening. "Hide it."

"And what is the Key phrase that unlocks it, sir?" Poe asked.

Hemings watched him lean close, his ear almost brushing Jefferson's lips. Jefferson whispered something that she couldn't make out.

Poe straightened and nodded. "Yes, sir." He glanced at Hemings, who tilted her head toward the door, wishing her master would not exhaust any more of his strength.

"Sir, you look well," Poe said. "Perhaps— "

"Leave now. Before it is light," Jefferson ordered, a surge of strength putting force behind the words. "We have enemies. The Cincinnatians are everywhere."

Poe swallowed hard. He reached down with his right hand and placed it on Jefferson's. "It has been the greatest honor, sir." He took the leather bag, and Hemings escorted him out of the bedroom, to the rear door, where a saddled horse awaited. He leapt onto it and galloped off into the darkness. She saw that he was reaching into his saddlebag for a bottle as soon as he was on the road.

She returned to the bedroom. Jefferson had closed his eyes and for a moment she wondered if he had passed, but noted the slight rise and fall of his chest.

His lips parted and he said something. She moved closer. "Excuse me, sir?"

"Do you remember Paris?" Jefferson asked.

"Oh, yes, sir."

"Maria," Jefferson whispered, a forlorn smile creasing his lips. "I should have followed my heart, not my head." His last breath rattled through his throat, and then he was still.

Sally Hemings slid the blanket up over the slack face of the third President of the United States.

* * *

"Independence forever."

Five hundred miles to the northeast, the dawn came slightly earlier to Quincy, Massachusetts, than it did to Monticello in the hills of middle Virginia. John Adams needed assistance to hold up the crystal glass to give his toast to the fiftieth birthday of the country he helped found, and of which he had been the first Vice President and second President. Even that minor effort exhausted him and he barely wet his lips with the alcohol as the others in the room drained their glasses. He slumped back on the bed, his gaze raking over those hovering around his bed.

He thought it a strange group, reflecting the diverse life he'd led. Politicians, judges, businessmen, writers, thinkers, even clergy. Come to pay reverence to one of the few *remaining Founding Fathers of this young country. Over the years many had forgotten that despite his speeches against the Stamp Act in the 1760s, and his fight for the Declaration of Independence in 1776, that in 1770 he'd defended the British soldiers accused of firing on the crowd during the 'Boston Massacre.' His arguments to a Boston Jury had been so persuasive, that six of the accused had been acquitted. The law, always the law, was his guiding force.*

His gaze fixed on a man hovering near the doorway to the bedroom in a mud-splattered uniform. "Let me speak with Colonel Thayer alone," he ordered. The crowd shuffled out with many a curious glance, leaving the officer standing alone.

He nodded Thayer toward the mantle above the fireplace. "There. Behind the painting."

Stiff and sore after his hard ride from West Point, New York, Thayer walked over. In an alcove behind the portrait of a young woman was a packet wrapped in oilskin.

"Beautiful, isn't she?" Adams said.

"Yes, sir," Thayer replied as he took the package and slid it into the messenger pouch draped over one shoulder.

"Abigail," Adams whispered to himself. "I miss you so."

Thayer didn't react to the comment. He spun on his heel like the Superintendent of the US Military Academy ought to, and made for the door, a soldier on a mission.

"Philosopher." Adams mustered the energy to call out, causing Thayer to halt and spin about on his heel once more, stiff at attention.

"Sir?"

"To be used only as a last resort. When all other means have failed. Do you understand?"

"Yes, sir."

"Split the disks you have there with two other Philosophers. Jefferson will send the next Chair to you with further instructions. Make sure all the Philosophers who follow in your footsteps understand. It's a very, very powerful thing you are guarding. A dangerous, but necessary thing Jefferson and Hamilton did so many years ago."

Thayer nodded, his face grave. "I understand very well, Mister President."

"Power cuts both ways, Philosopher."

"I know, sir." Thayer paused. "And the remaining seven disks?"

"In the Chair's hands," Adams told the young lieutenant colonel. "You'll be contacted. The Chair is always a civilian." The voice was slight, drained.

"What, sir?"

"Always a civilian in charge."

"Yes, sir."

Adams dismissed the soldier, his old hand fluttering in farewell. "Godspeed."

Thayer left and the others came crowding back in. Adams turned his head and saw the morning light streaming in through the window. "Fifty years," he murmured to himself, closing his eyes. "We never thought what we created would last this long. The United States. At least now it can start over if need be."

3

His body shook and he felt the darkness closing in. He thought of the first time he saw Abigail. And then of all the time he had spent apart from her, working to make this new country come alive. He felt it had been worth it, but there was still much he regretted.

"Mister President?" Someone in the crowd leaned close.

He struggled to open his eyes. Too tired to even turn his head, he shifted his eyes, peering out the window. He saw Thayer on horseback, galloping away, the pouch bouncing on his back. John Adams, the second President of the United States, drew in a hoarse breath and spoke for the last time: "Thomas Jefferson survives."

CHAPTER ONE

The Present

Gentle swells of snow-covered ground were graced by thousands of sprouts of stone that would never grow, arranged in perfect lines, as if the dead were frozen on parade. It was a formation at parade rest. Forever. The man standing at attention was a comrade in arms, vaguely sensing his life to be a mere formality before he too joined his silent brethren. Although he couldn't quite grasp the birth and depth of that feeling and raged like the warrior he was against the hand he'd been dealt, some of the cards still face-down. The white covering made Arlington National Cemetery look peaceful, a blanket covering the violence that had brought most of the bodies here over the years.

Colonel Paul Ducharme was uncomfortable in his Class-A uniform. A black raincoat covered the brass and accouterments, which adorned his dress jacket, and a green beret covered most of his regulation, short, thick white hair. He was one of those men who ironically lost none of their hair to age, but, alas, kept none of its color. He absently touched the twisted flesh high on his cheek, just below his right eye, not aware of the gesture. His hand slid higher, pushing back the beret and rubbing the scars that crisscrossed his skull. Finally, realizing what he was doing, he shoved the beret back in place and moved forward. Always mission first.

His spit-shined jump-boots crunched on the light snow and frozen grass underneath as he marched forward. It was after official closing time, but Ducharme had entered through Fort Myer, parking in a small, deserted field adjacent to the cemetery. His old friend, Sergeant Major Kincannon, had given him access. Kincannon was somewhere out in the night, shadowing, a dark presence full of laughter and potential, and inevitably, violence.

1

Ducharme checked his guide map to pinpoint his location in the 624 acres of cemetery. He considered the place full of historic irony, given that it had originally been the estate of Mary Anna Custis, a descendant of Martha Washington. Custis married US Army officer Robert E. Lee, West Point graduate—the only cadet who ever graduated the Military Academy without a single demerit, a fact so odd that Ducharme, another link in the Long Grey Line, could never forget, nor could any scion of the Long Gray Line. Through the marriage she passed the estate—and her slaves—to Lee.

Their old mansion, the Custer-Lee House, now called the Arlington House to be politically correct, dominated the grounds, looking straight down Lincoln Drive toward the Lincoln Memorial across the Potomac. Thus, General Lee's former house now looked toward the statue of the leader of the country he'd rebelled against. And come so close to defeating. If only Lee had not ordered that last charge at Gettysburg on the 3rd of July 1863. Ducharme's studies of that great battle had whispered to him that Lee only ordered Pickett's Charge because he too had had trouble thinking clearly, sick from dysentery and exhaustion after years of battle. When the body failed, the mind could produce tragic results. Whether his studies were right or wrong were shrouded in the fog of history and would never be answered. As many never were.

Ducharme looked to his left and studied the mansion on top of the hill, which reminded him once more of General... Ducharme frowned and forced himself to keep from looking at the map for the name. In his mind appeared a picture of an old man with a large white beard, dressed in a grey uniform, sitting on top of a white horse. *General Lee.*

Good, thought Ducharme. His therapist would have been proud. But there was no statue of Lee at West Point, their mutual alma mater, even though Lee had done the most with the least in combat against the greatest odds of any Academy graduate. Such was the cost of loyalty to state and betrayal to country and institution.

West Point did not tolerate betrayal.

Just as randomly, yet also connected, that name triggered, unbidden, Plebe Poop—relatively useless information he'd been forced to memorize his first year at West Point: *There were sixty important battles in the Civil War. In fifty-five of them, West Point graduates commanded on both sides; in the remaining five, a graduate commanded one of the opposing sides.*

Probably why the war lasted so damn long.

Ducharme moved forward, his march going from the regulation cadence of 60 steps per minute to something much slower, as if the bodies in the ground were reaching up and wrapping their shadowy arms around him to whisper in his ear and hold onto him.

During the Civil War, the Union seized Lee's land and began using it for a pressing need: burial sites for the thousands of war dead. It had seemed darkly appropriate to someone in the Union to surround General Lee's house with Union dead.

Ducharme hunched his shoulders, bitterly resenting the pounding in the back of his skull. It was worse than it had been in a while, and this journey had a lot to do with it. Stress, the therapist at Walter Reed had warned him a few years ago after he'd woken from the induced coma, was something to be avoided. He'd shrugged it off, telling her a Special Operations soldier's constant companion was stress, and then he'd gone overseas on another deployment, into the land where the beast that raged in his chest felt at home once more. But she'd said there were other kinds of stress. He knew now she'd meant this: the unbearable stress that is closest to the heart. The beast had kept it at bay, but its true calling was now a half-world's plane ride away.

Ducharme stopped at the fresh grave and stared down at it. There was no official marker yet, just a small plate indicating the plot designation. He glanced at the number on the plate and the number he'd written on the margin of the map. On target as always. He was surprised to feel little, neither sorrow or guilt, both of which he had anticipated, but he was learning that he could not anticipate how he would feel any more. Everything was new and everything wasn't good.

This was—with a sharp intake of breath, Ducharme realized he couldn't recall the name of the man buried here. He couldn't remember his cousin's name, his brother-in-arms for over two decades. A low hiss escaped his lips as he placed his hands against the back of his head and pressed in a panic. He shut his eyes and his forehead furrowed as he forced himself to enact the memory strategies he'd been given in rehabilitation.

He could see his cousin. Numerous images in a variety of places around the world. Roommates in Beast Barracks at West Point, bonding under the bombardment from screaming upperclassmen. Drunk on the beach during summer leave in Florida, between Plebe and Yearling years, trying to convince some sorority sisters to come back to their motel. The monotony of Airborne school at Fort Benning. The thrill of graduating West Point, throwing their hats into the air. The harshness of being Ranger buddies. Serving together in Iraq. Afghanistan. After all that, to die so senselessly here in the United States under circumstances Ducharme was determined to ferret out because the beast had been whispering to him ever since General LaGrange's call to come home.

"Charlie," Ducharme said, sinking to his knees. "Charlie LaGrange."

Uttering the name cracked the emotional wall inside his chest, and he felt as if he'd been punched in the heart.

"What the hell happened, my friend?"

He was losing control. Routine. The therapist had pounded into him that routine was a route back to stability and even memory. Reaching under the black coat, Ducharme drew out his silenced MK-23 Mod O pistol from a holster in the small of his back. He slid the magazine out of the handle, pulled the slide back, removing the round that had been in the chamber. He placed those on the frozen ground. Then, staring at the mound of dirt, his hands moved quickly, field-stripping the gun by feel, laying the pieces out in order next to the magazine and bullet. He was done in a few seconds. He paused, his breath puffing out into the cold air, and then just as quickly re-assembled it.

He continued to disassemble and reassemble the gun, hands moving in a flurry of action, eyes on the grave as if he could see the occupant. The repetitive action was focusing his mind. On the fifth attempt, the slide slipped out of his cold hands to the frozen ground and he came to an abrupt halt, breathing hard.

Ducharme bowed forward, head almost touching the ground. "I'm going to uncover what happened, Charlie. I'm meeting your father in just a little bit to find out what he couldn't tell me on the satellite link. I'll get to the bottom of this. I swear."

The words were taken by the chill wind of the winter storm and blown across the stones, broken, splintered and then gone. Ducharme felt the beast restless inside him even as he was surprised to find that tears were flowing. He straightened, wiping the sleeve of his coat across his face. He knew the man buried here would have laughed at the tears, cracked a joke. Easy-going Charlie LaGrange, always could be counted on for a laugh, up until he died in his car four days ago. According to the General, the police had labeled it an accident, but something was wrong from the cryptic way the General had contacted Ducharme and recalled him from Afghanistan. The fact the General had sent Kincannon to meet him at Andrews Air Force Base raised more questions than it answered, because it was apparent the General had not confided in the sergeant major, yet sent him as added security. Against who or what, had yet to be revealed.

Ducharme reassembled the gun one last time, slowly, methodically, making sure there was no moisture on any of the moving parts that would cause it to freeze up in the cold. Bad form, and possibly fatal. He put the round back in the chamber, not approved for amateurs, but he was no amateur, and slid in the magazine. He was slipping it back into the holster under his coat when he heard the crunch of footsteps on the frost. He swung around, weapon at the ready, finger on the trigger.

Four tall silhouettes were backlit by the glow of Washington.

Ducharme removed his finger from the trigger as he saw they wore Dress Blues and three had archaic, but more than effective, M-14 Rifles at the ready. The fourth had a pistol in his hand. He stepped forward and raised the pistol in a sure grip. The other three, despite the ceremonial garb, spread out tactically.

The lead man spoke. "Sir. We demand you respect the grave of our fallen comrade."

Ducharme lowered the pistol.

The man warily walked toward him, weapon still at the ready. "What's your purpose here, sir?"

"Visiting," Ducharme said.

"Cemetery's closed after dusk, sir."

"I returned from overseas just an hour ago." He nodded toward the grave. "I'm visiting a friend."

In the light reflected through the snow he could see the man's face. "May I see your identification card? And please holster your weapon. My men have live ammunition in their rifles."

Ducharme slid the pistol back into its holster and pulled out his identification card. The man held up a mini-mag light and flashed it on the card, then briefly at Ducharme's face, causing him to wince.

"Colonel," the man nodded at him.

Ducharme made out the crossed rifles on the man's lapels indicating he was branched Infantry. Three gold bars and three gold rockers on the sleeves indicated his rank. The rows of ribbons on the Dress Blues, starting with the Silver Star, topped a colorful tale of combat and bravery read only by those who knew what the little pieces of cloth meant.

"Master Sergeant." Ducharme gave the man the respect he was due. "What are you and your men doing out here?"

"Our duty, sir." He nodded over his shoulder. "We're the off-shift for the Tomb. We had an incident of vandalism on a recent grave by those extremists who protest our deceased heroes in the name of their God over gays in the military. It *will* not happen again."

The determination in the Master Sergeant's voice indicated it absolutely would not happen again. They were the Old Guard, the 3rd Infantry, and the oldest unit in the United States Army. And God help any who tried to cross their line.

Another figure loomed out of the darkness, and the Master Sergeant reached for his pistol as the other three Old Guard swung their rifles about.

"At ease, men," the newcomer drawled. "Just a friend of the Colonel."

"Sergeant Major Kincannon." Ducharme introduced the newcomer. He was a tall, whipcord of a man, his face lined and wizened, indicating many years spent out in the elements. His voice was laconic and seemed on the edge of finding something to laugh at. He was also one of the most effective and ruthless killers in Special Operations, a man born in violence and never far away from it.

"We got to go, Colonel," Kincannon told him. "The General will be waiting for you."

"Give me a minute," Ducharme said.

"Roger that," the Sergeant Major replied. He went over to the Master Sergeant and engaged him in quiet conversation.

Ducharme knelt at the foot of the grave and reached inside his jacket and shirt to a chain that hung around his neck. The pain in his head was almost unbearable; a jackhammer full of deep, twisting shadows he dared not even try to shed a light on. He pulled on the chain until a small leather pouch appeared along with his dog tag. He opened the drawstring and emptied two bulky rings into his palm. One had a smooth black stone of hematite, the other a single diamond set in the center. Ducharme reached underneath his coat, feeling for the knife secreted in the center of his back. He gripped the rough handle and drew out a six-inch long commando knife. It wasn't a large, gladiator-type Rambo knife. Thin, both sides of the blade were honed razor sharp. It was designed for one purpose: killing.

Except Ducharme stuck it into the frozen ground, the blade slicing into the grave, parting the frozen soil. He dug a shallow hole. He placed both rings into the hole, and then covered them up, tamping the dirt back into place. He slid the dirt-stained knife back into the sheath. Ducharme stood and looked down at the marker. He came to attention and saluted.

"I will get the truth."

Ducharme was surprised to feel the pain in his head subside, as if high tide had been reached and it was now washing away, leaving clean sand, waiting for the sun to rise. Not likely.

He turned and walked toward the Sergeant Major. "Take me to the General."

Kincannon nodded, his rawhide, weather-beaten figure stiff in the blowing snow. "The General told me to give you something right after you came here." He reached inside his long black coat and pulled out a small package wrapped in cloth.

Ducharme unwrapped the cloth, recognizing it as oilcloth, a waterproof fabric that had been superseded long ago. Inside was a circular piece of wood with a hole in the center and a card taped to it. Ducharme recognized the name on the card instantly: his uncle, Peter LaGrange—the General. The disk was old. Etched on the rim were letters. Ducharme tried to read if there was a message, but quickly concluded there was just the 26 letters of the alphabet, randomly positioned. On one flat side the number 26 was lightly carved.

"What is it?"

"No idea, sir."

Ducharme rewrapped the disk in the cloth and slid it into his pocket. He moved forward. "Why did the General want you to give this to me now, when we'll be meeting shortly?"

"That ain't the sort of question I'd be asking the General," Kincannon said. "He tells me to do something, I do it."

"He say *anything?*"

"No, sir. Just told me to give that package to you."

"Let's go."

* * *

Across the Potomac River in Washington DC, the growing darkness and thick swirling snow almost obscured the dark red object resting on the copper plate capping the Zero Milestone, due south of the White House. Drawing closer, the old man, pale in the freezing January cold, blanched as he realized he was looking at a human heart on top of the waist-high, stone marker. Rising steam fought with climate, and the warmth won, indicating that the heart still yearned for its owner. The man halted, startled as much by the living voice as the newly dead heart.

"Did you bring me flowers?"

The old man turned in the direction of the sensuous voice, in one hand holding a half-empty bottle of cognac, in the other three roses. A short, wraith-like figure followed the voice, her long black cloak matching the darkening heart behind him. Her face was hidden by a hood, all but her piercing eyes and the look. Perceptive people would recognize the look; that this was a person without a soul, without a conscience. The man was perceptive. His fate was sealed, but like all mortals, he refused to accept it.

"You are not Lucius." His shock caused him to state the obvious.

"I was sent in his place. I assume you brought the Jefferson Cipher rod and your disks." She came to a halt a few paces away. "Should I call you the Philosopher Chair?"

The wind blew cold across the man's scalp, no longer covered by his once thick hair. It hurt for him to stand tall, his body bent with the years, but he did so to face her. "You assume incorrectly."

"About which?"

"I do not have the rod or the disks."

"But you are the Chair." A statement of fact, but he felt compelled to respond anyway.

"Yes."

"The Philosopher you were to meet gave me his disks."

"You lie."

The woman pulled back her hood, revealing short blonde hair and an angelic face, incongruous with the absolute darkness in her eyes. She cocked her head slightly and stared as if he were some crossword puzzle to be solved: difficult, but one she would still do in ink, then discard, to move on to the next challenge. "Where is the Cipher rod and your disks?"

"Where is your master, Lucius?" he demanded.

"I am here in his stead."

He shook his head, glancing at the heart. "I am to meet Lucius and negotiate a deal. Things have gone too far. We must work out a compromise to keep the truce and--"

"I don't make policy," the woman cut him off.

The Chair looked left and right, his guts now as cold as his skin. A dim set of headlights made their way down 15ᵗʰ Street, but the brutal winter storm was keeping almost everyone at home or inside. They were inside their own enclosed snow globe.

"No one is coming to rescue you," the woman said. "The compromise I offer is a quick and honorable death in exchange for the location of the Cipher rod and your disks. And the names of the two remaining Philosophers." She drew back her cloak and revealed a short, Japanese-style sword strapped to her waist. She drew the wakizashi in one smooth motion as she came within striking distance.

The man tried to stand tall in the face of the weapon, but his legs trembled. "So you don't have the disks."

"I will find them," she allowed, signifying he'd called her bluff. "The Philosopher who was to join you here died bravely and without giving up his secrets, but I know there must still be a way to find his disks. President Jefferson would have prepared for such a possibility. I will grant him his genius."

The old man held his ground and met her gaze, even as his heart pounded wildly in his chest. On her coat was a bronze eagle medallion dangling from a small tricolor ribbon. "You are an apprentice to the Society of the Cincinnati? I didn't know they allowed women into their ranks."

"I will be the first."

He shook his head. "Behind the times as always. Our first woman was elected in seventeen eighty-nine."

"Not as a Chair, I'm sure," the woman said. "Not to the inner circle of your Philosophical Society. I will be on the inside of the Cincinnati."

"You're wrong," the Chair said, desperate to gain time. "We've had women in our inner circle. Our first female Chair was in nineteen-oh-four; the President's daughter, in fact. You're on the wrong side."

"I'm on the side I choose. The side that gives me what I want."

"And what is that?"

"This." She brought the blade close to her lips, almost kissing it.

Coldness spread through the Chair's body.

She extended the sword, holding it steady at eye level. "The location of the Jefferson Cipher rod and your disks, and the names of the last two Philosophers. I will make it easy. You will depart this mortal coil peacefully."

"But is it really the Cipher you seek, or what the Jefferson Cipher leads to?" He was trying to buy time with his babbling, which shamed him, but he couldn't stop it.

Her face was expressionless, as if carved out of unblemished white marble. "I was ordered to find the Cipher."

He leaned over, putting the bottle down along with the roses.

She looked down. "What are those?"

"All these years we have been in opposition, and you still know so little."

"I know enough to have met you here. And to have already interdicted the Philosopher who was to join you here. It is I who holds the power here."

"You hold the sword, not the power." He gave a bitter laugh, beginning to accept his fate, an inch at a time, much as he would accept the sword. "On the wall of the Thomas Jefferson building in the Library of Congress is inscribed the appropriate adage for this stand-off: 'The pen is mightier than the sword.' It has been so for a long time. The power you seek—" he shook his head—"it's the core of our Republic. Its very existence has kept the country in balance for over two centuries. You will not gain it with violence."

"I've found violence to be quite effective," the woman said with flat affect. "Where is the Cipher?"

He stood once more. "You know I will never tell you."

She cocked her head once more. She wasn't solving a puzzle now; more inputting data like a computer and then processing it.

"What is your name?" he asked, still stalling for time, giving inches but not feet. Yet. Despite the blizzard, there was a chance someone would see them.

She gave a low laugh; one that would have been appropriate in a bedroom with lights dimmed, but produced goose bumps in this situation. "The Society gave me a code name—the Surgeon."

"An odd designation." He could not help but glance at the heart on the Milestone.

"Four cuts to take the chest," the Surgeon acknowledged. "But he experienced great pain before the end. I've studied the body and I know what causes pain. You don't want to go down the same path he did. He spun a story about where his disks were and who his two fellow Philosophers were, but I knew he was lying and that cost him dearly."

"How do you know he was lying?"

She stared at him. "One of my surgical specialties was facial reconstruction. There are forty-three distinct movements your facial muscles can make, which result in slightly over ten thousand possible facial expressions. I have learned to read many of these expressions, which you cannot control. Yours tell me there is some truth in what you say, but ultimately you are lying. Just as he did and he suffered for it. As you will now."

She took at step closer and there was a flash of steel. Pain shot through him as the tip of the blade cut through his coat and shirt as smoothly and easily as if through butter, leaving a thin red line across his chest, not even an inch deep. Yet. He took a step back in shock and she took a step forward--a macabre dance of torture. Even as he was registering the pain from the first strike, the blade darted forward, tip piercing straight through flesh and muscle. Well over an inch. The Chair froze in agony as the sword skewered him in the shoulder, and then just as quickly, the Surgeon pulled it out of him. Despite the pain, he focused his mind on what had to be done.

"A non-fatal blow," the Surgeon said, looking at his blood on the blade as if it were another curiosity. "Unless you bleed to death. Which will take longer than you have. Where is the rod? Where are your disks? Who are the other two Philosophers?"

He covered the puncture wound, blood slowly seeping through his fingers. His legs gave out and he collapsed to his knees in the snow. The Surgeon stepped closer, sword at the ready. Something was alive in those eyes now. Something worse than the flat darkness. A flame of desire that would put the great lovers of history to shame.

"Never," he said. "You're wrong."

The Surgeon pulled the sword up for another strike.

"You've been lied to," the Chair cried out.

"It is *you* who lie," the Surgeon said.

He raised his hand up to protect himself, and with one blow she sliced off his fingers, causing him to cry out, the fingers tumbling to the snow, a part of him and no longer a part.

"Who are the other Philosophers?" the Surgeon asked as she leaned close.

He said something and the Surgeon put her free hand in his thinning hair, jerking his head up, and putting the edge of the blade against his neck. "Who?"

He whispered two names and she pressed the blade harder. A warm trickle of blood ran down his neck. "Who follows you? Who is your successor?"

McBride shook his head. "Never."

The Surgeon shrugged. "We already have a very good idea of who it is. We are taking steps in that direction. Where are your disks and the rod?"

He clamped his mouth shut. That was another thing he could never say. She removed the sword from his neck and jabbed it once more into his shoulder, twisting the steel. He felt it, but distantly, his nerves over-loaded.

"The disks."

She leaned close once more, her eyes intent on his face. He whispered something. She let go of his hair and stepped back. "The names are true. The location, however, is a lie. And like the Philosopher I just killed, you will continue to lie while you fight for time. Time you no longer have."

She drew back the sword.

"In the name of God, mercy, please," he cried out.

A cold smile crossed her face, amused by the pathetic attempt to reach something inside her that had died long ago. "That won't work." Her eyes locked into his. "The disks?"

"You're so wrong," the Chair said.

She lowered the sword and leaned close, her red lips next to his ear, her warm breath on his skin. "The Society calls me the Surgeon. But you can call me Lily."

He looked up at her. "Please, Lily."

Her arms moved and the last thing he saw was the flash of steel slicing through the falling snowflakes.

* * *

Evie Tolliver walked into the crowded restaurant and looked neither to the left nor the right. She stood calmly, waiting for the maître d' to seat her, seemingly assured of the place and time. She was a woman of average height, but uncommon carriage; the type of body that suggests dance classes or, more likely, years of stern warnings to stand up straight. Her age would be more difficult in today's world of dermatology and expert hair coloring, but the few spots on the hands clasping the book and battered old leather briefcase suggested mid-forties—along with the self-assurance that comes with experience.

At least it appeared that way. It was a good show. Her thick, dark hair had just enough silver to make it fierce. The cheekbones, high and wide, were her only real genetic gift of youth, giving her skin an extra ten years of grip against everyone's Newtonian battle. She had the bold, blue eyes of the black Irish, bespeaking a legacy of bold adventure and high romance. A good story, perhaps.

She was dressed simply; loose linen slacks, plain top, long black leather coat and the kind of jewelry a person who traveled accumulated over a lifetime; each piece special, with a story and worn every day, but of little interest to strangers. Good bag, but years out of style. Leather boots—not stylish, but well-worn and comfortable. A bland exterior, more like a wall, to keep strangers at bay and outside interest to a minimum.

In reality, Evie wasn't as calm as she appeared. Her chest ached. Something wasn't right with McBride—he was not a man who was late. Worse, giving her his briefcase earlier in the day had been completely out of character. After being seated at a table near the wall, she glanced at her watch and then reluctantly opened the old briefcase's clasp. His sleek, ultra-modern personal laptop was in its usual spot—a computer he used to compile his articles, and a journal no one had ever read other than its author, as McBride encrypted everything he put on the machine. He joked it was a book he was

11

writing, the Great American Story, but had always added that it would never be published—never *could* be published for some reason he never explained.

Something metallic glinted in the depths of the bag. She opened the briefcase wider. In the bottom of the briefcase was an iron rod a quarter inch in diameter and eight inches long, with brass knobs on each end. Evie was jolted when she recognized it and she could tell it was authentic, but she also knew it wasn't one of the two known originals—one in Monticello, where she had seen it safe and sound less than three hours ago, and the other locked securely in the Smithsonian.

Looking further, she spotted a thick envelope. She pulled it out. It was addressed to her in McBride's flowing script with a note in parentheses indicating she should open it if he were late—a strange and foretelling postscript. As she fingered the envelope, her mind was in turmoil as questions tumbled over each other: *Why did McBride have a previously unknown Jefferson Wheel Cipher rod? Where were the disks that went with it? And most importantly, why was he late?*

She slid a finger under the flap and broke the seal. Reaching in, she pulled out a piece of parchment folded over something round. Unfolding the parchment revealed a single, aged wooden disk about two inches in diameter and a sixth of an inch thick. She ran her finger around the rim of the disk, feeling the letters that had been carved into it, knowing its connection to the rod that was in the briefcase. The number "1" was etched very lightly into the flat side of the disk.

There was writing on the parchment. Four lines scrawled in McBride's flowing handwriting:

FIND THE CIPHER, FIND THE ALLEGIANCE
ONE PHILOSOPHER CHAIR, THREE PHILOSOPHERS
YOU ARE NOW THE CHAIR
A PHILOSOPHER WILL MEET YOU HERE

CHAPTER TWO

Outside the restaurant, Ducharme was growing impatient. The General was late, something very out of character. Kincannon was down the street, waiting in the black Blazer with tinted windows, and maintaining surveillance of the street and sidewalk traffic.

Ducharme was outside because he'd already checked the restaurant and had not spotted the General; and he disliked crowds. His irritation beginning to border on worry; he entered the restaurant once more, ignored the maître d' station, and took a left toward the less crowded bar. He found a seat that gave him perfect vantage of the door, dropped his black raincoat over the back of the seat, and ordered a neat scotch without looking the bartender in the eye. The lack of warmth would cause the bartender to pour light, but Ducharme easily accepted that for full door coverage.

He took a sip of the scotch, and saw the lone woman at a table just to the right of the door. He stared at her a moment too long. He'd just come back from a long tour in Afghanistan, and he had forgotten about lone women. That was a big part of the problem over there and in Iraq—too many lonely, driven men, and the wrong crusade.

Then he saw that she was looking at the door, and realized she also was waiting for someone. She sensed his stare and turned her head, and her strikingly blue eyes locked onto his. He recognized the look for what it was: pure interest from someone who is interested in things and people outside of themselves. A rare trait in his experience.

He wondered what she saw in him: the uniform? Did she know what all the glittering badges and little strips of cloth lined up on his left chest meant? Was she gauging his height, a little over six-three, or was she wondering about the tan that no amount of sun-block will prevent in the high arid mountains on the Afghan-Pakistan border, and so out of place in winter-time

Washington DC? Maybe she was comparing the grey of his eyes against the white of his closely cropped hair and trying to guess his age?

But then, in the corner of his eye, he spotted movement as the door opened and a man dressed similarly to him entered. Not the General. Much younger. Yellow oak leaves on his shoulders. A major, two ranks below Ducharme. Ducharme stood. The man scanned the room and locked onto Ducharme immediately. He downed the rest of the drink and dropped a ten on the bar even though it was undeserved.

Ducharme moved forward. The major was nervous. Not good. He was talking with the maître d', who led him to a table. Moving quickly, Ducharme took the seat facing the door before the major could take that very seat being offered to him. The maître d' frowned, but Ducharme couldn't give a shit.

"Where's the General?"

As the man took his coat off, he revealed the crossed arrows of Special Forces on his greens, and his ribbons indicated he was no lightweight.

"The General told me to let you know he'd be late and to start dinner without him," the major said. "I'm his aide de camp."

There was no 'sir' in the sentence, either leading or following, and Ducharme felt a slight surge of irritation cross his worry. Special Forces was a tight community, always with a disdain for traditional Army way, but etiquette was etiquette, and he didn't know this guy, and this guy didn't know him well enough to so readily discard it.

* * *

The waiter was hovering and Ducharme ordered the special. The major ordered off the menu, something complicated, with heavy sauces. The major looked blatantly at Ducharme's ribbons and badges after handing the menu back to the waiter, and began talking about his time in Iraq, with just enough jargon, and just loud enough, that nearby diners got quiet, trying to listen in.

Ducharme was embarrassed and surprised that the General would have such an aide-de-camp. He tried to change the subject, to find out what had really happened to Charlie LaGrange, only to be deflected. Ducharme fidgeted in his seat, looking over the major's shoulder toward the door. If allowed his druthers, he'd be dressed in a black turtleneck and jeans. He didn't like his identity being linked with this blabbermouth.

"How long did the General say?" Ducharme cut into another story of derring-do and the major frowned.

"An hour. Give or take."

Bullshit. Ducharme had to bite back the word. The General didn't deal in 'give or take.' Ducharme leaned forward to find out what the major was really doing here when his cell phone buzzed, indicating an incoming text message.

Something *was* wrong. Ducharme had the tingling he got in combat right before everything went to shit. He brought up the incoming message. His body stiffened as he read the words:

*PENNSYLVANIA AVE AND 19*TH *ST*
BE QUICK. P.S. BRING PACS
SEE THE ELEPHANT?

He excused himself and headed for the restroom. He had to pass the woman's table, and she now had the book open, but her eyes were straying toward the door and he felt a mirroring sense of anxiety in her. He saw that the book was a biography of Hannibal, and realized that she was the General's elephant. He also saw that she had ordered the special. Third, he realized that she was more striking than he had thought.

"You have an affinity for Carthaginian generals?"

She smiled warily, and said in a voice he liked way too much: "I'm really reading the latest *Twilight* book. I just put the dust jacket on for appearances."

"I have a little Hannibal trait in me."

"Don't like to delegate?"

He smiled. "Among other flaws. Have the Romans seen the elephants yet?"

She nodded. "But Hannibal is still wandering around Italy without taking the main objective."

"Rome. After Cannae. So much for a battle of annihilation ending a war. You know what soldiers mean when they ask if you've seen the elephant?"

She nodded again. "Whether you've been in combat." She gave him a long, hard looking over. "I know those ribbons don't come from riding a desk."

"You know the military?"

She nodded. "Full bird colonel. Special Forces. Ranger. No current unit patch on left shoulder below those tabs, which indicates either you're in transit between assignments or your assignment is one you can't advertise. On your right shoulder the Special Forces patch—which means you served in combat with the unit.

"Distinguished Service medal—one step below the Medal of Honor. Silver star. Bronze star with V for valor. Purple heart with cluster—sorry about that. Some of the newer ribbons I'm unfamiliar with it—I'm assuming they represent deployments in Iraq and Afghanistan. Master parachutist. I don't know the wings above your right pocket."

"British." Ducharme was impressed. "I did a few jumps with the British Special Air Service."

She understood. "The SAS. Who Dares Wins."

"Who are you?" Ducharme asked, his surprise morphing into suspicion.

"Just a woman minding my own business and reading a book. Do you like to read, Colonel Ducharme?"

She had the advantage of his nametag. "Yes. Miz...?"

"Tolliver. Evie Tolliver."

The name suggested something to Ducharme, someone in the past.

"What do you like to read?" Her eyes floated over to the door once more.

"Military history and strategy and tactics."

"Of course. Do you ever read anything outside of your province?"

He put one hand on the back of her chair and the other flat on the table, adjusting his position so he could see the major and the door. He bent over until his mouth was close to the side of her head. Ducharme whispered: "'It was a night when kings in golden suits rode elephants over the mountains'."

"Cheever."

"Glock," Ducharme said.

"What?" Evie was startled.

"Silenced nine millimeter pistol. The fellow I was with has it at the ready under the table. Waiting for someone?" Ducharme asked as he straightened. "Is he—or she—late?"

"He is," Evie said.

Ducharme was impressed she didn't stare at the major, taking his word about the gun. "And he's usually never late, is he?"

"Never."

"And he left you a note."

"Yes."

"Come with me."

Without protest or hesitation, Evie tossed a twenty on the table, put on her coat, closed the book, and followed him toward the kitchen. Ducharme led her past startled chefs and out the back door into an alley.

Snow was falling as Ducharme edged into the alley, Evie close behind. He drew his Mod-23 pistol and took a step forward. Glancing over his shoulder, he saw Evie looking at the gun with a frown, as if disapproving or perhaps jealous and wanting one herself. He also saw the red dot in the center of her chest, and he slammed her against the brick wall as a sub-sonic bullet missed by less than an inch, chipping brick from wall. Ducharme rolled, pulling her to the ground, his body on top of hers, firing rounds as fast as he could pull the trigger down the alley toward the unseen gunman, his suppressed gun emitting only the sound of the slide going back and forth. A deadly battle played out in near silence.

Ducharme tensed, feeling exposed on the ground, waiting for a bullet to slam home. But there were no further shots as flashing lights suddenly lit up the alley from the street entrance. Ducharme helped Evie to her feet as the doors on a dark sedan opened and four men piled out, weapons in hand.

"FBI! Drop the gun!" one of the men yelled.

Ducharme carefully put the gun on the ground, and then raised his hands.

A black man in a dark suit underneath a long overcoat held up a shiny badge in his free hand. On his head he wore, of all things, a fedora, which rated in usefulness only slighter better than the Green Beret Ducharme wore.

The man came walking down the alley, wary, weapon at the ready, as the other three ran by, after the shooter. He looked at Evie. "Are you Doctor Tolliver?"

"Yes."

He shifted his gaze. "Colonel Ducharme?"

"Who's asking?"

"Special Agent Burns." He holstered his weapon. "I need both of you to come with me. If you please," he added in a tone that indicated he didn't care whether they pleased or not.

"I've got to get some place," Ducharme said.

"Pennsylvania and nineteenth?" Burns asked.

Ducharme tensed. "How did you know?"

"We read it off General LaGrange's cell phone."

Ducharme took a step back as if punched in the chest. "Is he all right?"

"He's been murdered." Burns didn't pause, looking at Evie. "Mister McBride has also been murdered."

CHAPTER THREE

Lily removed her heavy, armored cloak, draping it over a chair. The khaki pants were serviceable and fashionable, and fit her compact five-foot-four frame. The black turtleneck accommodated her shapely upper body. Her short blonde hair framed a face more befitting a nun's habit than an armor-cloaked killer.

She removed the wakizashi from its sheath and gently placed it on the desk, next to the half empty bottle of cognac and the three roses the Chair had carried. She found disinfectant, poured it onto a towel, and thoroughly cleaned the blade with it. She let it sit for a few minutes, then took a silk cloth and carefully wiped the blade dry. Turning it under the desk light, she checked the edge for damage. There was none, not that she expected any, given the quality of the blade and the weakness of flesh, muscle and bone against steel that had been folded so many times by hands skilled in the perfection of such weapons.

She pulled back her left sleeve to the elbow. The skin on the inside of the forearm was marred with six scars, each about two inches long. The scars were poorly healed, red raised ridges marching down her arm, an incongruity for someone who held an MD, and a harsh contradiction to the unblemished beauty of her flesh.

She grabbed the handle of the short sword with her right hand. Slowly and precisely, she drew the sword across the skin, just below the last cut. Skin parted easily to the razor-sharp blade, and blood flowed. The hand holding the sword was steady as a rock. Then she did it again, another slice. Done, she sheathed the still bloody sword and rolled down her black sleeve.

Lily was from a long line of military veterans, but was the first female in the line of service. While her friends received dolls and clothes for their birthdays, she'd received knives and guns. Her father had rigged an old sea bag in the backyard as a punching bag for her and her brother. Instead of the mall, her father had taken her to military surplus stores. For her 15th birthday, her father had given her the Special Forces Medical Handbook and the Special Air Service Tracking Guide. She'd never realized she was different from other girls. Now she was so far out of the bell curve it wouldn't occur to her to realize there was a different reality.

Her four years at the Air Force Academy had honed the harsh discipline of her childhood into a martial zeal bettered by none of her peers. Still, being a woman in a male-dominated institution, the brutal hazing of the first year, coupled with the sexual harassment inherent at the Academy, had appeared to present more obstacles than even that discipline could overcome.

Early one Sunday morning, when her roommate was away on a team trip, someone snuck into her room. Feeling hands groping her, she'd reacted, smashing his head against the metal frame of her bed, and then dashing for the rack where her rifle and bayonet were displayed. Cursing, the upperclassman had come after her.

She'd drawn the bayonet and held it in front of her. In the darkness, and dazed from the head slam, the upperclassman never saw it, running right onto it. His screams as the blade penetrated his bowels woke the entire floor.

The Academy, reeling under Congressional scrutiny from numerous sexual harassment complaints, listed the event as a training accident. The upperclassman graduated after a stint in the hospital, and Lily was told to forget about it and be happy no charges were brought against her for assault with a deadly weapon.

On the plus side, she was never harassed again.

On a deeper level, Lily replayed the moment of the bayonet in her hands penetrating flesh and blood flowing over the blade and her hands, again and again; relishing the thrill it had given her. She had never felt so alive.

She succeeded so well at the Academy that she was one of the select few tapped to go directly to medical school. She believed surgery was one way she could recapture that feeling. It was a futile attempt at control of her newly unearthed impulse.

After medical school, she'd been assigned as a flight surgeon for a transport squadron, but her sense of duty and the drive inside her caused her to volunteer to work on the ground, as far forward as she could go. She'd ended up near Fallujah during some of the worst of the fighting.

Patients in the forward operating center were brought in and treated without regard to what they were—American military, Iraqi civilians and even insurgents were all triaged together. Lily saw an opportunity. Every badly wounded insurgent that came under her scalpel died. In the confusion of war, it was weeks before anyone caught on.

When the commanding officer became aware of what was happening, it was too late. He couldn't charge her without creating a publicity fiasco. A board was quietly convened, a psychological evaluation hurriedly churned out, and she was discharged.

Her family had served in every US war, with her participation in the Gulf being the most recent, although her living male forbearers didn't hold a parade for her when she returned from overseas. She returned to the United States disgraced by the military she had given her life to, but also aware that the hunger inside her needed to be fed.

Leaning back in the chair, she looked at the large painting that dominated the wall. A portrait of Larz Anderson III, whose wife donated their house to the Society of Cincinnati. History was made in the Anderson House. A secret history. A portion of it was open to the public who trickled through, looking at the abundant collection of Revolutionary War documents. The open portion was like the sheath on her sword, hiding the edge underneath. This wing of the house was never on the tour, and entry was limited only to the chosen few of the inner core. Lily had been granted access just a month earlier in her first meeting with the Head of the Society, known only as Lucius.

She looked down at the glowing screen of her laptop. She tapped the keyboard, accessing the secure satellite up-link. She was hooked into the Society's network, which saddled on top of the military's Milstar Internet, and her transmission was encrypted by the latest technology from Silicon Valley— so advanced, that even the military had not yet begun to field it. The encryption allowed her access to be safe from the National Security Agency's screening program that monitored all Internet traffic, even its own.

Like night follows day, the NSA had enacted a program called Carnivore as soon as there was an Internet to monitor. For years, fools had been sending emails unaware that a few choice words would tap them as a danger. A poor actor who typed-- *I bombed; I died on stage*--was snared by Carnivore's database which counted alert words per sentence.

She was using such a high-speed system for something very simple. Googling.

She typed in: *cognac three roses.*

She stared at the results, all-pointing in the same direction. She quickly read the top three entries, collating the information in her brain.

She paused in thought for a few moments, glanced at the door, and then typed in *head heart.*

The first three entries weren't useful, but she paused as she read the fourth. She accessed the entry and scanned it. She knew it was connected, but she had no idea how. As she was puzzling over this, the heavy wooden door creaked open, and an old man in an archaic butler's uniform nodded his head. She cleared the screen and shut the lid on the laptop.

Leaving the wakizashi behind, she followed the servant down the heavily carpeted and dimly lit hallway. On the wall were portraits of prominent

Society members, the angled lamps highlighting them providing the only light. All of those portrayed—exclusively male—were recognizable. A who's-who of American political history: George Washington, Henry Knox, Alexander Hamilton, James Monroe, Andrew Jackson, Zachary Taylor, James Buchanan, Grover Cleveland, Benjamin Harrison, William McKinley, Theodore Roosevelt, William Howard Taft, Woodrow Wilson, Warren Harding, Herbert Hoover, J. Edgar Hoover, Franklin Delano Roosevelt, Harry Truman, Richard Nixon, and the next-to-last two portraits which flanked a set of double doors were of Ronald Reagan and George Herbert Walker Bush.

There was a puff of air, and sensors searched for traces of explosives or dangerous chemicals. There were also imaging machines trained on her, penetrating her garments, searching for hidden weapons. She knocked on the intricately carved wood and waited.

The voice that replied from beyond was low and deep. One that was used to power and respect as a right. "Enter."

She went into a cavernous room and squinted in the darkness. The only light was reflected through the windows from the streetlamps outside. There was a large desk directly in front of her. On the other side of the desk was a single high-backed chair, but it was hidden in the shadows and all she could make out was that it was occupied. As she had been trained as a Plebe at the Air Force Academy, she marched up to it, halted three paces in front, and snapped to attention.

She bowed her head slightly instead of saluting. "Reporting as ordered, sir."

"How did the meeting go?" Lucius asked.

"Sir, as of this evening the Chair of the American Philosophical Society and one of the Philosophers are dead. I have the names of the remaining two Philosophers."

A long silence, then a click as Lucius turned on a lamp, shooting a cone of light onto the desk. Several white chess pieces were directly under the lamp. A king, a queen, and several pawns—the motif was Revolutionary America, as the 'king' was clearly George Washington and the queen, his wife Martha. Some of the pawns were only roughed out, not yet finished.

Lucius's aged hand broke into the light, picking up one of the smaller blocks, an almost finished pawn in the shape of a Minuteman. His other hand held a file. He scraped the file against the piece, the sound loud in the room. "It is very difficult to acquire pure ivory these days," Lucius said.

Lily, as she'd also been taught at the Academy, remained silent.

The file scraped along the side of the piece. "Some of the few remaining expert ivory sculptors use power tools, but I prefer the traditional. You cannot achieve the fine details with power tools. The emphasis has switched from quality to quantity in order to mass-produce trinkets for tourists. A waste of an elephant's life."

The file rasped across the ivory. Then the hands paused. "You were directed to get the Jefferson Cipher, not kill."

There was movement behind her in the darkness. She tensed, but dared not turn her head. *Had she blundered?* With her thumb she began to twist the Air Force Academy ring that adorned her left ring finger. The rough face of small diamonds shaped in a dagger ran across her skin.

"I was given a mission, sir," Lily said, swimming carefully into dangerous and uncharted waters, but pressing on anyway. "There were no parameters placed on how I was to accomplish it. I was told I had complete freedom of action. I took the most direct means for success given the current tactical situation. I was told the Philosophers were our enemy. I needed to use extreme force to try to get them to speak. Their deaths were an inevitable result of that application of force."

The file began moving again. "Do you have the Cipher?"

"No."

The file was placed down on the desktop, and the hand reappeared with an awl. The tip dug into the neck of the tiny ivory soldier. "Then you have failed, and your use of extreme force was futile. Not just futile, but dangerous."

"I have the names of the last two Philosophers."

The hands were steady as the awl dug deeper. "Your killings will bring unwanted attention to the Society. In two hundred years there has been a gentlemen's agreement between the Philosophers and us. How could you--"

She dared to interrupt, her thumb twisting the ring on her finger even faster. "Sir, I am no gentleman. In all those years, the Society has never gotten its hands on the Jefferson Cipher. I thought new tactics were in order. If I am to be the first woman allowed into the Society, I must bring something original to it, and I have done so as you've indicated by your own words—something new. I will find the Cipher. I have enough clues to direct me to a place I must visit. I believe the rod and some of the disks will be there. And I will pay a call to the other two Philosophers."

She watched as the awl continued to work the ivory, bringing form to it.

She swam on. "Even if I do not find the Cipher, the deaths will throw the Philosophers into turmoil. It is a win-win situation for us."

"What exactly do you think you will be winning?" Lucius sighed deeply, the sound absorbed by the sheer size of the room and the thousands of volumes of books that lined the shelves along the walls. "You are overly optimistic. And underestimate our foes. You killed a few tired, old men. Do you feel proud of that?" The awl stopped moving and the fingers turned the piece to and fro under the light as he examined it.

Pride had nothing to do with it, she thought. "I killed our enemies. No matter what form they take, they deserve no mercy."

"Things always stand at a careful precipice," Lucius said. "Your actions—" he fell into silence, and Lily waited for her fate to be spelled out. Her thumb stopped twisting the ring and pressed hard against the diamonds set in the top, the pain refreshing.

"There are a few things you know," Lucius finally said, "but many things you don't and some you probably will never be privy to unless—" He put the pawn down and his hands disappeared. A few seconds later he placed a diamond-encrusted Society medallion on the table—"you rise to a position to wear this, which is highly unlikely. You came to us from the outside and are largely ignorant of our ways. The bottom line is that the inner sanctum of the Society believes it is our solemn duty to serve our country and protect it in times of need."

The chair creaked as Lucius once more picked up the file. "Membership in our Society was originally limited to those officers who served no less than three years in the Continental Army or the Navy during the Revolution, or who had been killed in the line of duty. Subsequent membership required an ancestor who met those qualifications. The only reason we accepted you is because you are nine generations directly removed from an officer who fought with Washington, and we have bent the rules further than ever before to grant you this apprenticeship. Most in the inner sanctum disagreed with me over your appointment." The file rasped away, and small white powder floated in the air around his hands. "We extend a few honorary memberships, usually to Presidents whom we favor and whose policies are in line with our goals."

"What does the Jefferson Cipher have to do with this?" Lily asked. "The Chair indicated it was just the first part of something larger. If the threat was the Chair and the Philosophers, then I have eliminated half of that threat and I will take care of the rest."

"They were just caretakers," Lucius said. "And they will be replaced. They are always replaced, just as someone will replace me in this seat when I am gone. You can also be easily replaced."

Lily almost smiled at the implied threat, and she began calculating her tactical options against whoever was behind her and Lucius.

"You were given a simple job, a test," Lucius said, anger in his voice. He turned the pawn, filing away. "You may know military tactics, but you need to understand the historical and political framework of our centuries old stand-off with the Philosophers."

Lucius pointed the tip of the file at her. "The Federalist Party grew out of the Society of the Cincinnati. It was populated by the true heroes of the Revolution, the men who fought for our freedom. They knew that pure democracy is a sham, since only a small percentage of the population is

23

willing to put their lives on the line to defend the country. Many of the so-called Founding Fathers never approached a battlefield, instead hiding behind desks and arguing with each other over how to pay and supply those who protected them, often short-changing the soldiers in the field while sitting warm and comfortable in the cities, their bellies full. Our Society founders knew the mass of the people were not to be trusted because they were ignorant. They can be trusted even less now." The file was switched out once more for the awl.

"Our enemy, the Philosophers—the three Philosophers and the Chair—came out of the Anti-Federalist Party led by Thomas Jefferson. He would rather see the country plunged into chaos and another Revolution—even against our own leaders—than be secured from foreign enemies by a strong central government. Like many of the other politicians, Jefferson never saw combat, except to flee Tarleton's raiders while he was Governor of Virginia during the Revolution. His constituency thought so much of his cowardly actions that he was never again elected to office in Virginia."

Lucius waved the awl as Lily attempted to speak. "But, whatever their martial frailties, Jefferson and the other members of the American Philosophical Society were not weak men. Do not confuse being misguided with weak. And they were smart, very smart. The military members of the Philosophical Society have always been brave men, however misguided their allegiances have been.

"For over two hundred years our Society has fought to keep our country strong and to protect it from enemies, both foreign and domestic, but primarily we have tenaciously maintained a fragile balance with the Philosophers over the way the Federal government operates to keep it from spiraling into the anarchy they desire."

A small piece of ivory fell from the pawn onto the desktop, and Lucius paused as he examined the piece under the lamp. Lily remained still, waiting for the old man to get to the point and just tell her whom she could kill.

"I don't understand the connection to the Cipher, sir."

"The Cipher leads to the Jefferson Allegiance, which was forged as a necessary compromise during the early battles between the Federalist and anti-Federalists. It is the same threat that has been the wild card behind the scenes of our country for over two hundred years."

"What is the Jefferson Allegiance?" she asked.

Lucius sighed even as the awl continued to dig away into the ivory. "Concern yourself with the Cipher. Fifty years after the signing of the Declaration of Independence, upon their death, the first two Philosophers broke apart their Cipher Wheel—the original one, Thomas Jefferson invented—and spread the disks out: nineteen to the first military Philosopher, who further split six out to each of his subordinate Philosophers, and the last seven and the center rod to the Chair. I doubt you will find them all in the same place. The Cipher holds the key to the location of the Allegiance."

"It would seem prudent, sir," she said, "for there to be a way to find the rod and disks even though the owners are dead. A back-up plan must exist so that the Philosophers can reconstitute themselves, as you indicate they will do. And for the Cipher Wheel to be put back together so that they might recover the Allegiance. There must be clues."

"I'm sure there are," Lucius said, "but the clues lie with the Philosophers, not with us. Two of whom you killed," he added pointedly.

"I will find the clues. It would help if—"

Lucius cut her off. "I will not tell you what the Allegiance is, except that it is so powerful a thing that within my lifetime it toppled a President—a man we supported-- when he was confronted with it."

"Sir, do you wish me to continue my pursuit of the Cipher?"

A long pause played out as Lucius put the awl down and picked up a piece of cloth. He buffed the Minuteman pawn, and then inspected it. Lily could still feel the presence behind her. And she could sense in the way predators could, that it was someone like her, who would kill her at Lucius' command without the slightest hesitation or feeling of remorse. That threat would have to be dealt with first, then Lucius. Although she suspected Lucius was not as defenseless as he appeared.

Finally Lucius spoke. "You cannot bring those you killed back to life, and we care little for them anyway. It will take the new Philosophers time to learn of their new positions, understand their duties, and regroup. You do have the initiative and it is a military maxim to always exploit such an advantage. What is your next step with the clues you have from the Chair?"

"I'm going to Baltimore to look for the Chair's disks, with a stop in Annapolis first to deal with one of the two surviving Philosophers." She felt a warm surge of anticipation at the thought of the detour to Annapolis.

Lucius put down the cloth. He placed the pawn on the desktop, and his hand rested on top of the piece's tricorner hat. To Lily it appeared perfectly formed. Lucius pressed and with a sharp snap, the head tumbled off. "I sensed the ivory was not pure. An inner defect. Go now."

Lily spun on her heel as she had also been taught as a plebe at the Air Force Academy a decade previously, and she marched to the double doors. There was a shadowy figure standing to the right, but she ignored him, keeping her eyes facing front.

* * *

The doors slammed shut and a short silence filled the room before recessed lights came on, filling the room with a soft glow. A man stepped forward from the shadows near the door and approached Lucius. He was short and stocky, his skull completely hairless. He moved gracefully on the balls of his feet, the sign of someone who had trained his body and stood fast more than once inside the ropes of a boxing ring. His nose had been smashed a long time ago and never fixed, a choice that said much about his lack of concern for appearances and other, darker things deep inside his head.

"Your Surgeon is dangerous, Mister Turnbull." Lucius swept the ivory scrapings off the desk into a small garbage can. "You did not suspect she would be so aggressive, did you my old friend?"

"I suspected."

Lucius leaned forward, revealing his own ravaged face to his old comrade. The skin along the right side was red and puckered, the right eye missing, the results of torture inflicted many, many years ago in Korea. A favored son of the Society, Lucius had been brought into the inner sanctum right after the war and stayed in the shadows, nursing his wounds, and gaining knowledge and power as the decades went by until eventually the diamond medallion was passed to him. No one in Washington knew his real name. No one ever would.

Everyone who mattered in Washington did know of his power and his reach.

"'You suspected,' Mister Turnbull?"

"Dangerous can be good as long as it is controlled."

"And if it can't be controlled?"

"Then it is eliminated," he told Lucius. "Because we brought her in recently, we have excellent deniability."

"She does not strike me as stable."

Turnbull shrugged. "She's a psychopath. I read her discharge evaluation from the Air Force. I had my contact approach her, offering her what she covets most—victims."

"Despite her moniker," Lucius said, "she's acting more like a hatchet than the scalpel I would desire. Two murders. It will be hard to keep this quiet."

Turnbull nodded. "Hard, but not impossible. Unfortunately, the FBI already has a high-ranking agent investigating. I'll keep him under wraps and control the investigation. I think she might be correct in some ways. It *will* take the new Philosophers time to pick up the reins and realize their responsibilities. During the transition they'll be weak and vulnerable. It's an excellent opportunity to end this stalemate once and for all."

"Are you getting optimistic?" Lucius asked. "Unusual for you."

"Realistic, sir. I've always been a pragmatist."

"Pragmatism is not necessarily a good trait," Lucius said. "It lacks belief and faith."

"It is a belief and faith of its own," Turnbull said. "Like you, I believe in the higher good."

Lucius nodded. "You have never failed me. What about the two Philosophers who are still alive?"

"As she said, they will be dealt with."

Lucius thought about it for a few moments, before nodding. "Proceed. But you will gather some operatives and follow her. Help her if she is succeeding. However, if she appears to be failing or is about to be caught, eliminate her."

"Of course, sir." Turnbull turned to go, but Lucius held up a hand.

"Do you believe we can finally get the Allegiance? After all these years?"

"It's worth trying."

"I hope you are right."

"I am, Sir."

Lucius leaned back in the chair. "I'm curious, Mister Turnbull. Why were McBride and LaGrange in Washington?"

"A good question."

Lucius's voice took an edge. "That is not an answer, Mister Turnbull."

Turnbull stared at the old man. "I contacted them and arranged a meeting between them and you."

"You lured them to the Surgeon." Lucius stiffened. "Why did you not tell me?"

"My duty is to protect you from some of the harsh realities of what must be done."

Lucius frowned. "Too many times in the past the Philosophers have stymied us with the Allegiance. We need it to be done with, once and for all. We must have the Allegiance."

"I agree, sir."

Silence played out in the office for several long moments. Lucius finally spoke. "What else have you put in motion that you are shielding me from?"

Turnbull accepted his hand had been called into play. "The next generation of Philosophers. One has been eliminated and two more should be eliminated tonight. We will get the rest. So even if we don't get the Allegiance, it will not pass on and will be lost forever."

"But you didn't use the Surgeon for this, did you?"

"Two freelance contractors through a cut-out. There's no way it can be tracked back to us."

"Loose ends, nonetheless."

"I will clean up the loose ends. As I always do."

"As you always do," Lucius acknowledged. He picked up the head of the broken pawn. He abruptly tossed it to Turnbull. "You may go," Lucius ordered.

Turnbull quickly left through the double doors. He walked down the hall and into the office where the Surgeon was strapping on her wakizashi.

"Did you arrange the head and heart as I instructed?"

The Surgeon nodded. "Yes, sir, but Lucius seems to not—"

"I protect Lucius," he said.

"The head and heart will signal—" she began as she slipped on her heavy cloak, but he cut her off.

"'Will signal'?" He snapped. "Are you looking further than you should? Do as ordered, apprentice. Know your place and I'll do the thinking." He held up the pawn's head. "Remember what Lucius said."

The Surgeon snapped to attention. "Yes, sir."

"I will provide you with support. If needed." He handed her a card with a phone number on it and a password. "Use that to requisition whatever you need from any government agency. I will cover you as best as possible with the FBI, but that can only go so far. If you're arrested, my reach will be limited."

"Yes, sir."

"Also, there's another job I might need you to do. I will let you know when and where." He reached into his pocket, pulled out a pair of photos and gave them to her. "These two men. They've done some work for us. They work as a team. When they're no longer needed. . ."

"Yes, sir."

"All communication between us will now be via burst text, using the encryption keys on our satellite phones. Do you understand?"

"Yes, sir."

He stepped close to her and placed a hand lightly on the arm she had cut. He pressed harder, blood oozing through onto his fingers. He looked down at his hand and saw the blood. She gave no indication she felt a thing. "Make sure you do, Lily."

27 JULY 1803

President Thomas Jefferson waited, no doubt in his mind that Alexander Hamilton was late to prove a point. Hamilton always had to prove a point, even if there was none.

Jefferson was alone in an office in Philosophical Hall on Independence Square in the heart of the nation's largest city: Philadelphia. Jefferson tipped his chair back, placed his feet on the desk and stretched out his long legs. The ride from Washington had been made in darkness and thus in difficulty, the carriage driver unable to see all the ruts and holes in the road from the United States new capitol to the original capitol.

Thinking of the city he'd come from, Jefferson looked up at the painting of its namesake on the wall. Good old George. Gone less than four years now, one would think the man a saint the way the papers and people still went on about him. Jefferson gave a fond smile, remembering how Washington, in the early days of the Continental Congress, had protested loudly that he did not wish to be Commander of the fledgling Colonial forces, yet somehow had managed to put on his old French & Indian War uniform every day when he came to protest not becoming that which his clothing clearly demonstrated he dearly desired.

Watch what a man does, rather than what he says, Jefferson thought. And Hamilton being late said much.

The door to the room swung open and then slammed shut. Hamilton strode across the room as if he owned it. The way he walked into every room.

Jefferson got to his feet. "Mister Hamilton." He extended his hand.

Hamilton barely shook the hand, then, without a word, went to the other side of the table and sat down. A breach of etiquette in the presence of the country's President, but Jefferson knew Hamilton felt brazen, having been the instrument three years ago to swing Congress to vote Jefferson into office over Burr, when the two had been tied in the Electoral College. It had not been a sign of support for himself, Jefferson knew, but Hamilton's intense distaste of Burr that had been the deciding factor.

"Shall we get to business?" Hamilton said.

Jefferson sat down. He'd considered how to approach this on the ride from Washington. "As you know, I was not present during the drafting of the Constitution."

Hamilton tapped the top of the desk irritably. "And? Is that your excuse for your recent unconstitutional action regarding the Louisiana Purchase?"

"No," Jefferson said. "I make no excuse. You are quite correct. It was unconstitutional."

Hamilton sat up straighter, his eyes narrowing, suspecting a trap. "You admit as much?"

"I just did." Jefferson held up a hand to forestall his long-time opponent. "I'll give you my arguments so you can ignore all the tripe in the papers. And then I'll tell you what I have learned from my own actions, and what I propose, and why I ask for your assistance."

The line between Hamilton's eyes got even deeper, but he nodded.

"Briefly then," Jefferson began. "New Orleans controls the Mississippi. He who controls the Mississippi, controls all our country's river traffic west of the Appalachians. When I took office, we thought New Orleans was under Spanish Control. What I quickly discovered was that Napoleon, in secret, had gained control of New Orleans from Spain in eighteen hundred. Learning of this, and fearing loss of access to the port, I secretly sent emissaries to Paris to negotiate the purchase of New Orleans."

Hamilton started to speak once more.

"Please," Jefferson said. "Hear me out, good sir. I know I did not have the Constitutional right to be doing such negotiations in secret. However, I felt the importance of New Orleans and the danger of an Imperial French presence on our country's borders superseded my executive limitations, and time was of the essence. I was acting for the greater good."

Jefferson quickly went on. "I also knew, through my own sources, that Napoleon was in trouble. He was building a fleet of barges to invade England. That was his focus. However, the slave revolt in Haiti was draining his resources, troops and money. The slaves, hard as it might be to believe, were defeating his forces. As they continue to do to this day. I fear the end is close in Haiti, and it will be the slaves who prevail.

"Please believe me when I say my ambassadors only went to Paris to purchase New Orleans. We offered Napoleon ten million for the city and river rights. When Napoleon's man countered with an offer of the entire Louisiana territory for fifteen million, my ambassadors were astounded, to say the least."

Hamilton finally got some words in. "I had not heard this about New Orleans. The report was your people went looking for it all."

"No, sir," Jefferson said. "But even you will admit it was too great an offer to refuse. It was an offer that ended the French presence on our boundary and doubled the size of our country at less than three cents per acre."

Hamilton snorted. "But you don't have the money. Is that why I am here? You finally agree with me on the national bank?"

Jefferson nodded. "Yes. We must have one to finance the purchase."

Hamilton could not hold back his triumphant smile.

Jefferson continued. "I've already directed Treasury Secretary Gallatin to contact you and ask for your help."

Hamilton shook his head. "Gallatin will want to issue stock for it. He's already—"

Jefferson quickly cut in. "No stocks. We'll have a debt as you wish. Gallatin doesn't like it, but I've already given him the order."

Hamilton's smile faded, wary. "Then what do you want of me? Absolution of your illegal act in making the purchase in the first place? I could have my people in Congress move to impeach you."

It was Jefferson's turn to snort. "You think that would get far?"

Hamilton leaned forward. "Then why did you have me come here in the middle of the night and meet in secret?"

Jefferson placed both hands on the table. "I am not blind to what I have done. I am aware I overstepped my Executive authority. Only two other men have worn the title of President of the United States. General Washington—" Jefferson used the term he knew Hamilton preferred for the late President, as the two men had served together for many years in uniform—"was a great man. You and I know the nation and Congress would have voted him President for life if he desired it."

"I wanted him to be President for life from the very beginning," Hamilton countered.

"That argument was defeated during the writing of the Constitution," Jefferson said. "And, besides, you know that General Washington wanted no part of staying in power. He desired to go back to Mount Vernon and Martha, and live the rest of his days in peace."

"He was tired of the heavy burden he bore," Hamilton acknowledged.

Jefferson saw his opening. "I bear that burden now. And there will be those beyond me who will bear it. Perhaps you. I circumvented Congress on the negotiations for the Louisiana Purchase. It made me recognize that this office that I hold is at the whim of any elected Caesar in Presidential clothing."

Jefferson could hear the crowing of roosters in the distance as dawn came to Philadelphia, and he waited to see how Hamilton would react.

"What are you proposing, then?" Hamilton asked. "You're pointing out the obvious: that the checks and balances written into the Constitution aren't adequate to prevent the Republic from failing. It is flawed. I said so then, and subsequent events have proven me correct."

"You are correct. And I know what you and your Cincinnatians are up to. I have the votes in Congress to outlaw you and your group as enemies to the state. The bill is already drawn up and my people ready to present it. President Adams got his Alien and Sedition Act passed; I have no doubt I could resurrect the Sedition portion and use it on your Cincinnatians."

Hamilton leapt to his feet. "How dare you threaten—"

"It is not a threat, Mister Hamilton. It is a negotiation. Please sit down."

Hamilton did not do so, but he stopped yelling. "What negotiation? What do you want?"

"I want there to be a secret check on power run amok, primarily by the President, but also to prevent a group like your Cincinnatians from toppling the freely elected government or gaining undue influence. To maintain the country as we envisioned and wrote into the Constitution and Bill of Rights."

"And how do you propose such a secret check be enacted?"

"We've already agreed that the Constitution, as currently written, is not sufficient to keep the country on course. Our country has just doubled in size. The United States will grow more and more powerful. As it does, the office of President, by nature, will attract the power-hungry. At a distance, the people have a limited ability to identify Presidents with sufficient emotional stability to 'know thyself.' Thus, the office of the President is run by the personality of the man holding it. You've seen what I just did with the Purchase.

"At the same time, business will grow. Money will be consolidated in the hands of a powerful few who control that commerce and industry. Your Cincinnatians. It is a repugnant inevitability. That's a very dangerous thing for a Republic. We don't want our country to go the way Rome did."

Hamilton slowly sat down. *"You want a new Amendment to the Constitution?"*

"No," Jefferson said. *"I'm not stupid, Mister Hamilton. Presenting that admits my own malfeasance in the Purchase. As I said, this must be done in secret. I want you and I, as heads of the two parties, to agree to an Allegiance. The Jefferson-Hamilton Allegiance. We will take this Allegiance back to our parties and get just enough members we trust to sign it in secret to pass, and then I will sign it into law. No one is to speak of it. It will be hidden away. But it will be law and it will be the final check on the President and the power-hungry rich who do not have the country's best interests at heart."*

Hamilton was silent for a few seconds. *"What is this Allegiance you wish to put my name to?"*

"Did you know this chair I am in," Jefferson said, *"is the exact same one in which I was seated when I wrote the Declaration of Independence?"*

"Show me this Allegiance," Hamilton snapped, but Jefferson knew his reference to the classic document he had penned was now in Hamilton's head.

Jefferson walked over to a bookcase and picked up a piece of parchment. He brought it back. Hamilton unrolled the paper. It only took a few seconds to read. *"I do not want my name on the title of this."* He looked up. *"So this is why you founded the Military Academy last year? I thought that a most strange move for you."*

"I dwell in reality," Jefferson said. He waited a moment. *"Does that mean you agree to the body of the Allegiance?"*

Hamilton hesitated. *"In exchange for not attacking the Society of the Cincinnati? And establishing the national bank?"*

"Yes."

Hamilton grabbed a fountain pen, dipped it in the ink well, and signed his name at the bottom. *"I will bring it back to you with the signatures needed."*

"I know what you're thinking," Jefferson said. *"You're thinking what you hold is no great matter. That it would never be enacted. I hope that is true. But it is the ultimate*

check against a President who seeks to be King, and against your Cincinnatians or any group like it."

Hamilton rolled up the parchment. He tucked it under his arm and stood. "When I bring it back, and then your people and you sign it, what is to be done with it?"

"Let me worry about that. I will have people appointed to be caretakers. People that can be trusted with such power, desiring none of their own. People that can keep a secret."

Hamilton laughed. "Remember what old Benjamin said about people keeping secrets. Three might if two are dead."

Jefferson met his adversary's eyes. "Let us hope it does not come to that."

Hamilton gave the half-smile that Jefferson had always interpreted as the man thinking he held the winning hand. Perhaps he did, Jefferson allowed as Hamilton departed. But there was more to Jefferson's plan for the Allegiance than he had told Hamilton.

Jefferson laughed. And given Hamilton's insistence, it had a new, simpler name:

The Jefferson Allegiance.

CHAPTER FOUR

Deep inside FBI headquarters on Pennsylvania Avenue, Ducharme stared without expression at the two men across the table from him. They had been asking questions for a half hour, and in that time he had not uttered a single word in response. While they prattled on with their useless inquiries, he was trying to concentrate. To understand what was happening. As he had been programmed to do in harsh military training, he separated emotion from mission and kept the beast raging in his chest on a leash, as this was neither the time nor the place to let it out.

The door behind the two officers opened, and Special Agent Burns walked in holding a bulky manila envelope. Burns leaned over and whispered into the ear of one of the agents who had been asking the stupid questions.

Reluctantly, and with angry glances, the two junior men left. Burns stared at Ducharme for over a minute. Then he said in a voice that was level and emotionless. "They told me you haven't said a word."

Ducharme returned the gaze.

"I'm in charge of this investigation."

Ducharme remained silent.

"You've been advised of your rights, correct?"

Ducharme said nothing.

Burns sat down across from Ducharme, pulling out a small spiral notepad. He flipped the cover open. "You are Colonel Paul Ducharme, United States Army. Apparently. According to your identification card and uniform. However, when I queried our Army liaison on the highest priority, I was told you don't exist. That means you're not who you say you are, or you're deep in covert operations."

Ducharme said nothing.

"If you are covert ops, you were trained not to say anything when interrogated," Burns added. "Probably Level Three SERE training at Fort Bragg. Correct?"

Ducharme crossed his arms over his chest. He'd gone through the Survival-Evasion-Resistance-Escape training at Bragg years ago. The FBI were amateurs compared to the 'interrogations' the instructors in SERE put the high-risk-of-capture students in Level Three through.

Putting down the notepad, Burns reached into a coat pocket and pulled out a switchblade, which he flicked open. He began to slice the skin off of an apple with one long, slow, spiral, as he glanced once more at the notepad.

"I checked out your gun. MK-twenty-three pistol, but one that is specially modified—a military Special Operations version, the Mod O. Built-in laser sighting, trigger pull's been lightened, serial number gone, top of the line suppressor. Those big, bad forty-five caliber rounds. A lot of punch even when subsonic. Not something you pick up at your local gun show. In fact, the modified MK-twenty-three is illegal outside of Special Operations." A piece of apple skin fell to the table.

"The vehicle your Sergeant Major was driving—he's downstairs, by the way, also not saying anything—is interesting. Armored, bulletproof windows, tamper sensors, modified turbo engine for power, more weapons in the rear locker along with night vision goggles, body armor, and other specialized equipment. You could be in big trouble having those automatic weapons in your truck. The registration of the vehicle is to a front company we believe is part of a cover wing of the Activity, an organization in the Department of Defense that isn't supposed to exist."

Ducharme waited for Burns to tell him something he didn't already know.

"You knew General LaGrange." Burns said it as a statement, not a question. He had almost the entire skin off the apple. It fell to the table. Burns jammed the blade of the knife into the apple, and held it in one hand while he opened the manila envelope and slid a file folder and several other objects onto the table. He turned a page in his notepad and began reading it. "Lieutenant General LaGrange, US Army retired and brought back on active duty as Special Assistant for National Security Affairs. Very high level. The calls are already coming from a lot of big names. Deep shit, my friend, deep shit."

Burns pulled a photo out of the file folder and slid it across the table. Ducharme stared at the photo trying to make sense of what he was seeing. Given his history of violence, he could stare at the photos without expression. "That's General LaGrange's heart?"

"We believe so. He's the only body we've found tonight missing one."

"Whose head?"

"James McBride. Retired editor from the *Washington Post*. Know him?"

"No."

"Heard of him?"

"No."

"Not many people outside of DC have. He was behind the scenes, though, of pretty much every major story the *Post* broke for over fifty years. Including Watergate."

"That was a long time ago. Somebody still sore?"

"People in this town have long memories. He had a lot of enemies."

Burns said that with feeling. He must top someone's shit list, Ducharme thought. "Not me."

"Didn't say that. You feeling guilty?" Burns asked. He cut a piece out of the apple and popped it into his mouth.

"Yes." The answer jumped from Ducharme's mouth, surprising him.

"About?" Burns was staring at him hard while he chewed loudly.

"My Uncle's murder."

Burns blinked. "LaGrange was your uncle?"

Ducharme regrouped from the unusual burst of emotion. "Why did you pick up Evie Tolliver?"

"Professor Evie Tolliver, the curator at Monticello. She was waiting at that restaurant for the other victim, McBride. She knew him. She had McBride's briefcase."

"She a suspect?"

"No. She was in the restaurant when that murder occurred. Who shot at you in the alley?"

"I have no idea. Did your men catch the shooter?"

"No."

"What about the man in uniform in the restaurant with the gun?"

"No."

"Not very efficient."

Burns stiffened for a second, then gave a lazy smile. "We'll find them."

"I doubt it." Ducharme looked closer at the photo. The White House was barely visible through the falling snow in the backdrop of the photo. From the angle, the stone monument holding the grisly trophies was somewhere to the south of the building.

Burns looked at his notepad. "Where were you at eighteen-forty-four hours?"

"Arlington Cemetery."

"Can anyone confirm that?"

"Sergeant Major Kincannon. And several members of the Old Guard."

Burns nodded. "Kincannon has said nothing, but the Old Guard already did. We tracked the GPS in your Blazer back to there and the time stamp confirms it."

"Then why are you asking?"

"Being thorough."

36

"Being redundant."

"You received a text message from General LaGrange directing you to meet him at nineteenth and Pennsylvania where we found the General's body inside his vehicle. It was his last communication." Burns checked a notepad. "It was sent at eighteen-forty-four hours. Took you a while to 'come quick' since I met you at twenty-forty-eight."

"If you check my phone, you'll also see I didn't receive the text message until exactly two hours after it was sent, at twenty-forty-four."

"Why the delay?" Burns asked.

Ducharme shrugged. "I don't know." But a disturbing thought wormed its way into the back of his mind.

"What does 'brings pacs' mean?" Burns asked.

The worm crawled into Ducharme's frontal lobe. "The message is a repeat of one that was sent a long time ago."

Burns waited, and then tapped the table top with the handle of the switchblade. "Explain."

"It's from the last written order George Armstrong Custer gave at the Battle of Little Big Horn," Ducharme said. "He dictated it to his adjutant who gave it to Trumpeter Martin to carry to Major Benteen. It said: *'Benteen, Come on. Big Village, be quick, bring packs. P.S. bring p-a-c-s.'*"

A slight smile graced Burns's lips. "'Come on, boys, we got them on the run?'"

"That's a Western myth," Ducharme said. "No one knows what Custer said after he sent Martin off with that message, because every man with him died. People think the Seventh Cavalry was wiped out, but almost half of it survived under Reno and Benteen. The most Medal of Honors ever awarded for a single battle in our history were given to troopers under their command for their actions the night after the massacre when men volunteered to crawl under fire from the hill they were making their stand on to retrieve water from the Little Big Horn for their wounded comrades."

"You sound defensive of Custer," Burns said.

Ducharme's voice was sharp. "I served in the second Battalion of the Seventh Cavalry Regiment of the first Cavalry Division during Operation Iraqi Freedom. I'm proud of the lineage of the unit and the men who served with me."

"So they gave out a lot of medals to put spin on a massacre."

Ducharme bristled. "They gave out a lot of medals to soldiers who risked their lives to save other soldiers. The worst of times can bring out the bravest in people."

"The military and medals." Burns shook his head.

Ducharme realized he was being baited and ignored it, already having started to slide into Burns's pit.

His barb not being taken, Burns pressed on. "Why would LaGrange send you such a message?"

Ducharme sat back in the seat, feeling a tiredness that went beyond the physical weariness creeping into his muscles. "General LaGrange was—" he closed his eyes for a moment in pain. "General LaGrange was an expert on military history, so he specifically picked Little Big Horn and Custer. Sending a message from Custer means he felt there was a good chance he was doomed. I believe the text of the message explains the time lag on the text message. General LaGrange set his phone to send two hours after he wrote it. When he knew, like what happened to Custer and his message to Major Benteen, it would be too late."

Burns was staring at him strangely. "That doesn't make sense if he wanted your help."

"I think he wanted to face whatever it was by himself," Ducharme said. "Then he wanted to meet me if he survived—or if killed, for me to find him and—"

Burns leaned forward. "And what?"

Ducharme fell back into silence.

"This is my case," Burns said. "You're not overseas any more."

"Right."

"Things didn't work out too well for your uncle," Burns said. He cut another piece off the apple.

"They didn't for Custer either," Ducharme said.

"And LaGrange knew that."

"Yes."

"Want a piece?" Burns offered a slice on the point of the switchblade.

"No."

Burns popped it in his mouth and chewed loudly. It was irritating, which was exactly why Burns was doing it.

"Both men were tortured before being killed," Burns said.

Ducharme looked down at his hands, and realized they had tightened into fists. With great difficulty he unclenched them. "Someone wanted them to talk. General LaGrange wouldn't have. I don't know about McBride."

"You sound sure of LaGrange. I thought everyone talked under torture."

"I am sure of the General. And everyone talks under enough torture applied long enough," he corrected. "The killer was in a rush. Also, with torture, even though everyone eventually talks, you can't believe what they say. It's a paradox—when the torture is extreme enough to make someone talk, they'll say anything to stop it, especially what they think the torturer wants to hear, whether it's true or not. That's why it's ineffective."

"Interesting." Burns took a moment to digest that. "You often provided LaGrange with backup in Washington DC?"

"Never before. But we served together."

Burns stared at him. "And now you serve with…?"

"I can't tell you that."

"The Activity?"

"I can't tell you."

"Why do you call LaGrange, 'General' all the time if he was your uncle?"

"We always called him the General."

"'We'?"

Ducharme sighed, and felt the pounding in his head worsen. "His son, Charles, my cousin, was also my best friend. He didn't call General LaGrange, 'dad,' he called him 'the General.' And it was out of respect."

"'Was'?"

Ducharme stiffened. "You a fucking echo? Charlie was killed in a car wreck four days ago. That's why I was at Arlington."

"I'm sorry." Burns ran a hand across the stubble on his chin as he made a note in his pad.

"Do you have anything on *his* death?" Ducharme asked.

"I'll look into it," Burns said. The FBI agent pulled two wooden disks out of the manila folder and slid then across the table. "Seen these before?"

Ducharme took the disks. One had the number "26" etched in it—the one Kincannon had given him—and the other had "1" on the side. "You know I saw one of them since you took it off me."

"Tolliver was carrying the other one in McBride's briefcase," Burns said. "What are they?"

"Never seen anything like them before. Ask her."

"I will." Burns picked the disks up. "They look—feel—old."

Ducharme pointed at the photo, trying for misdirection. "What's the monument the body parts are on?"

"The Zero Milestone," Burns said.

"This placement wasn't done by chance," Ducharme said.

"It's a message," Burns said with a nod. "I've got people working on it." Burns slammed the blade into the desk top, leaving the knife there, handle quivering. He turned toward the mirror on the side of the room and crooked a finger. "What does 'See the elephant' mean in the message?"

"No idea."

"Bullshit."

Ducharme didn't respond.

"So you never met Tolliver before?"

"No."

"But you were waiting for LaGrange in that restaurant, and she was waiting for McBride. Not coincidence."

"Brilliant deduction."

The door to the room opened, and Evie Tolliver was escorted in.

"Professor Tolliver, meet Colonel Ducharme. Again," Burns said. "Take a seat."

Evie sat to Ducharme's right, giving him a curious glance as Burns spread photos over the desk: the head and heart on top of the Monument; a headless body lying in the snow; LaGrange's heartless body in the driver's seat along with others of the two crime scenes.

"We've got two murders," Burns said. "Two bodies mutilated. And you two are connected to the victims. I want some answers."

"What are the questions?" Ducharme asked.

"Don't push me," Burns snapped.

Ducharme stared at the FBI man. "OK, what are the fucking questions?"

Burns's fists clenched. "That asshole thing—nice."

Ducharme nodded. "It's a technique."

"It's not working."

"I think it is." Ducharme shrugged. "It's called frustration and I don't know anything more about this than you. Just wanted to share the feeling." Evie was staring at the gruesome photos, not with shock, but with detachment, which said a lot about the woman. Or anyone for that matter. Tension was coming off her in waves, though. It was costing her a lot to keep her emotions under control.

"Do you see something?" Burns asked her.

"I think there's a message here," she said, tapping the photograph of the Zero Milestone.

"'Think' or know?" Burns prompted.

"Interesting the way you phrased that," Evie said. "'Think or know?' What's the difference?"

"Pretend you have the podium, professor," Burns said with visible impatience, his fingers lightly drumming on the desk.

"Head and heart," Evie said.

"We know what they are," Burns fairly growled.

Evie frowned. "No—the symbolism. It's from a letter."

"What letter?" Burns asked.

Evie shook her head. "It makes little sense. But—" her voice trailed off.

Ducharme spoke up. "Who wrote the letter?"

"Thomas Jefferson." She reached into a pocket and pulled out a silver cigarette case.

"No smoking," Burns said.

Evie ignored him and flipped open the lid. She pulled out a piece of gum and popped it in her mouth. "I quit a while ago. Nicotine gum."

"The letter," Burns prompted.

"In spring, seventeen eighty-six, while serving as US Ambassador to France, Jefferson met a married woman named Maria Cosway. We don't know for sure if he had an affair with her, but he certainly was in love. When she left for England with her husband, he sat down and wrote her a rather remarkable letter that has come to be known as the Head-Heart Letter. Where his head argues with his heart over missing her, and whether to pursue the relationship."

Burns looked confused. "And what does that have to do with the murders?"

"I have no idea," Evie said, but Ducharme had a sense she was holding something back. "It just popped into my head. And McBride had a fascination with Thomas Jefferson. I'm not fond of coincidence. Except, I don't know how your General LaGrange," she added, glancing at Ducharme, "figures into things."

Burns held out the disks. "What are these?"

"Wooden disks."

Burns looked from her, to Ducharme and then back at her. "Two wise guys. Are you going to help me or not?"

"We are helping you," Evie said. "We're not suspects in this, yet we freely came here."

Burns tapped the disks. "These come from a Jefferson Cipher." He glared at Evie. "You know that. Being the curator at Monticello. Where are the other twenty-four?"

"No idea," Evie said.

"There was something else," Burns said, grabbing a photo of what at first appeared to be just snow-covered ground. "Something was pushed down into the snow next to the tracks of Professor McBride. A couple of things, actually. As near as we can tell, it looks like the imprint of the bottom of a bottle and some flowers; three of them—roses, as there was a petal left in the snow. Mean anything to either of you?"

Ducharme shook his head and glanced at Evie as she answered: "If it was a bottle of cognac, then I have an idea."

"Thomas Jefferson put them there, I suppose?" Burns said.

"No." She looked at Ducharme. "Did General LaGrange graduate from the United States Military Academy?"

Ducharme nodded. "Yes. I did too."

Evie tapped the photo of the imprints. "Since nineteen forty-nine, on the anniversary of Edgar Allan Poe's death, a man goes to Poe's grave in Baltimore and leaves a half-empty bottle of cognac and three roses on the grave. He's known as the Poe Toaster."

Burns sighed. "You're just full of useless information, aren't you? What the hell does Edgar Allan Poe and a grave in Baltimore have to do with two murders within blocks of the White House, and a two-hundred-year-old letter from Thomas Jefferson?"

"History," Evie said. "Poe is the perfect connection between the University of Virginia, where McBride got his advanced degree from—and

Jefferson founded—and the United States Military Academy, where General LaGrange graduated from—and Jefferson also founded."

"How is that?" Ducharme asked, intrigued.

Evie leaned back in her seat. "Edgar Allan Poe attended both schools, and he was briefly a confidant of Thomas Jefferson while he was at UVA."

"I don't see the connections *now*," Burns said pointedly.

"I don't either," Evie agreed, "but it's there in the facts. As Sherlock Holmes said: *'When you have eliminated the impossible, whatever remains, however improbably, must be the truth.'*"

"Now you're quoting a fictional detective," Burns said.

Evie leaned back her chair and stared at the FBI agent. "As a detective, did you know that Poe is considered the originator of detective fiction, predating Conan Doyle and his character Holmes?"

"No, and thank you for sharing that worthless piece of trivia," Burns said.

Evie sighed. "Stop with the condescension, Special Agent Burns. Trivia is insignificant fact until you need that fact. I prefer any truth over the significant lies most tend to wallow in." She paused. "McBride was meeting General LaGrange at the Zero Milestone for a reason. He was not a man for idle actions or words."

"Nor was General LaGrange," Ducharme said. He looked at Burns. "What else do you have from the crime scene?"

"*I'm* interrogating *you*," Burns snapped.

"You don't seem to have much at all," Ducharme noted. "Professor Tolliver just gave you more than you have in your folders."

Evie spoke up. "What else *don't* you have from the crime scenes?"

Burns blinked. "What?"

"The killer took the roses and bottle of cognac from McBride," Evie said. "Was there anything missing from General LaGrange's murder site?"

Ducharme grabbed the crime scene photos of his uncle's murder scene. It took only a few seconds to spot it. He slammed a fist down on the desk, the beast surging inside his chest. "The General's ring is missing. His Academy ring. He always wore it. He was proud of that ring." He looked at Evie. "West Point was the first school in the country to start the tradition of class rings. We take our rings very seriously." He turned to Burns. "Who the hell is this killer?"

"We'll catch her," Burns said confidently.

"'Her'?" Ducharme folded his arms once more over his chest and stared at the FBI agent. Burns finally stopped tapping his fingers on the table. "We believe the killer was a woman. The tracks in the snow from the perp indicate that."

"What kind of weapon?" Ducharme asked.

"Blade. Very sharp. One blow to sever the head. The heart was cut out with precision, again with something very sharp, but not a scalpel. A knife or something like it, about two inches in width. It was also used in..." he paused, glancing at Evie, then continued—"the torture. We've got a couple of penetration wounds in non-vital areas. Surface cuts in areas where the bleeding wouldn't be fatal."

Burns slid a photo across the table. "McBride has defense wounds on one hand." Burns tapped the picture. "The perp sliced off all his fingers. He must have been holding up his hand to try to stop a blow."

"Most likely done by the killer out of frustration." Ducharme looked up from the picture toward Burns. "You know what a bitch being frustrated can be when you're trying to get information. Was the blade double or single-edged?"

"Single-edged."

Ducharme nodded toward the switchblade. "You know edged weapons?"

"Yes."

Ducharme glanced at Evie. She was looking at the photos once more. The conversation wasn't disturbing her. Not visibly. Strange woman.

"What type of weapon do you think?" Ducharme asked.

"Some kind of short sword."

"A professional," Ducharme said.

"How would you know that?" Burns asked.

"I'm a professional. Plus, an amateur wouldn't have gotten to General LaGrange. The hand being cut on McBride, though, indicates some level of emotion. The killer probably didn't get all she wanted from McBride either."

Burns was about to say something when there was a knock at the door. He got up and cracked it open to talk to someone.

Ducharme couldn't hear what they were saying, so he turned to Evie and was about to ask her something when she pressed a finger to her lips and shook her head. Ducharme turned back as Burns returned to his chair and stood behind it.

"You must have powerful friends for someone who doesn't exist," he said to Ducharme as he pulled the switchblade out of the table and snapped it closed. "I've been instructed to let you go." He reached into his pocket and pulled out a card. "If you think of anything that could help our investigation, anyone who might have done this to your general, give me a call. If you don't mind," he added, his voice dripping sarcasm.

Ducharme stood and took the card. "My gun."

Burns reached underneath his coat, retrieved the MK-23 and handed it over.

Ducharme checked the chamber, and then slid it in his holster. "And where's my truck and Sergeant Major Kincannon?"

"Both waiting outside the front doors," Burns said. "Pretty high-speed ride. Modified at the hanger in Lakehurst?"

"Nice try." Ducharme took a step for the door, but paused. "Is Ms. Tolliver still being held? You said she wasn't a suspect."

"That's the interesting thing," Burns said. He looked at Evie. "I think you have even more powerful friends than Colonel Ducharme. I've been ordered to get you immediate transportation to wherever you want to go, and to assist you in any way possible." He grimaced. "And to apologize for any inconvenience I might have caused you, Ms. Tolliver."

Ducharme folded his arms, staring at Burns, who was pissed. That apology had cost him. Who was powerful enough to force Burns to eat crow?

Evie shook her head. "There's no need for you to apologize. I want to help catch Mister McBride's killer." She looked at the table. "May I have the disks and the other contents of Mister McBride's briefcase, please?"

"They're evidence."

"It's two hundred years old," Evie said. "Surely it's not important to your investigation."

Burns crossed his arms over his chest. "That doesn't mean giving you evidence from a double homicide to take with you."

Evie faced him squarely. "Colonel Ducharme and I had the disks and the briefcase, not the victims. And since we're not suspects, it's not evidence."

A twitch crossed Burns's face. "You can have the disks."

"I want the briefcase and everything that was in it."

The two stood toe to toe. "We tried turning on the laptop," Burns finally said. "Everything in it was encoded. Not password protected, but encoded. A very sophisticated program that is basically an electronic one-time pad. I'm told by my experts that a thumb drive with the decipher code is needed because it's a randomly generated pattern."

"And?"

"Do you have the thumb drive?"

"No."

Burns waited, then sighed and stepped back. "They'll have the briefcase, with the computer, ready for you at the front desk."

Ducharme turned to Evie, impressed. "Would you like a ride, or would you prefer the FBI give you one?"

"Thank you," Evie said and left the room.

Ducharme looked at Burns. "What are you going to do now?"

"Conduct a double homicide investigation," Burns snapped.

CHAPTER FIVE

Burns paused before entering the observation room. He pulled a worn, laminated card out of the sweatband of his fedora. The hat—and card—had been given to him by his mother when he graduated the FBI Academy. She'd been a fan of the old movies, when the G-Men wore fedoras and took down the bad guys with tommy-guns blazing. He'd been slightly embarrassed then, but over the years he'd grown to love the hat and the words on the card:

I will support and defend the Constitution of the United States against all enemies, foreign and domestic; that I will bear true faith and allegiance to the same; that I take this obligation freely, without any mental reservation or purpose of evasion; and that I will well and faithfully discharge the duties of the office on which I am about to enter. So help me God.

He squred his shoulders and slid the card back into the sweatband, and then entered the observation room behind the one-way glass. He was surprised to see that the two detail FBI agents were gone, replaced by a short, rough-looking older man, obviously someone with more rank than a field agent. He had a bald head, a smashed nose and ice-blue eyes. Those eyes pierced right through Burns.

"I'm Assistant Director in Charge, Turnbull. I'm your liaison to the National Security Council. General LaGrange was an important person." Turnbull pointed at the screen of a GPS monitor. A dot moved out of the interrogation room and down the corridor toward the elevators. "The transmitter is broadcasting clearly," Turnbull said. He had an open file on the desk.

"Where are the two officers who gave me the transmitter?" Burns asked.

"I'm handling this," Turnbull said. "But you lead the murder investigation."

"Then what are you handling?" Burns wanted to know. He received no answer. "You're letting me take point so you don't catch any shit. This goes wrong, it'll be my hit. It goes right, you'll grab the credit anyway."

"There will be no credit," Turnbull said. "We've got the story under wraps. There won't be any news of it in the newspapers or on TV." He smiled without humor, putting a finger to his lips. "This is hush-hush."

"Right."

"You're one of our top profilers from what I understand."

"Don't believe everything you hear."

"I didn't hear it," Turnbull said. "I just read it." He held up the file marked "Top Secret, For Official Use Only," on the cover: Burns's personnel folder.

"How did you get that?" Burns winced as soon as he asked the question. An ADiC could get anyone's file.

Turnbull flipped up a couple of pages. "You have a degree in psychology. Interesting. I suppose that helps you as a profiler."

"At times. Experience is the best teacher."

"What do you make of that Thomas Jefferson, Edgar Allan Poe bullshit?" Turnbull asked.

"I don't know."

"Think we have a serial killer on our hands?"

"I doubt it," Burns said.

"Why?"

"These murders were very controlled and efficient with no physical evidence left by the killer other than footprints in the snow. Although the killer tortured the men, I think it was most likely a result of trying to get information from them, not for some sick pleasure, although there might have been some secondary gain."

"'Secondary gain?'"

"Some sense of satisfaction, perhaps even arousal, that the killer isn't consciously aware of. Or perhaps she is and she's using some other justification to cover her real motive of enjoyment. But this isn't just about the killing. There's a higher purpose to these murders."

"That doesn't mean she's not a serial killer. Tolliver and Ducharme figured out she's taking trophies—the ring from the General and the flowers and bottle from McBride. That's indicative of a serial killer, isn't it?"

"Sometimes," Burns said. "Or she could be gathering proof."

"'Proof?'"

"Proof of death. That she actually did the murders and was taking trophies to show someone else. Or they could be—" Burns paused.

"Go on," Turnbull prompted.

"The scene at the Zero Milestone was staged," Burns said. "Maybe a message being sent. The killer could have taken the items she did as part of something larger."

"Interesting. So what's going on?" Turnbull pressed.

Burns gave him a bland look. "Tell whoever you're reporting to, that you'll know what I know, as soon as I know it. OK?"

"Don't push me," Turnbull said. "You follow orders."

"I follow my oath and my orders."

The room was still for a while.

"Who does Ducharme work for?" Burns finally asked.

"We're still trying to ascertain that," Turnbull said, "but probably the Activity, as you noted. A rather innocuous name for some very wicked Special Operations types the Pentagon uses for their dirty work around the world. They're not supposed to operate state-side."

"They're not supposed to exist," Burns said.

"True," Turnbull said. "Strange, isn't it." It was not a question.

Burns thought about it. "This doesn't make sense."

He waited, but again, there was no more forthcoming. Turnbull turned to the small TV and pressed play. The interrogation room appeared, Ducharme and Tolliver alone in it. Ducharme turned to her to obviously ask a question, but she shook her head and pressed a finger to her lips.

"A secret keeper," Turnbull said.

"Not the only one."

"She's full of useless information." Turnbull was staring intently at the screen.

"Perhaps," Burns said, but he thought otherwise. Tolliver was one of the most intriguing people who'd ever sat across from him in an interrogation room. As was Ducharme. "The head and the heart," he said.

"What?" Turnbull was still staring at the screen, fiddling with the controls.

"The head and the heart of the two victims might be more than just from a letter by Jefferson. Their deaths have drawn Evie and Ducharme together. The head and heart."

"Ducharme seems more analytical than passionate," Turnbull said.

"It's a veneer," Burns said. "He's wound tight. Losing his best friend four days ago, and then his best friend's father tonight has hit him hard. And it seems a stretch that the two deaths are coincidence."

Turnbull was still looking at the tracking screen. "Ducharme is moving and I'm willing to bet he's got Tolliver with him. Weird, isn't she?" Turnbull said it without any passion or particular interest. "How do you see her as the head? Because it's full of bullshit information?"

"Actually, my sense is she's cold and suppressed only externally when dealing with people she doesn't know. She's a cauldron of emotion underneath. She learned the control somehow, and not in graduate school.

Makes her almost dissociative, which is a dangerous state for her to be in. The memory thing is interesting. How she can bring up apparently disparate facts that are actually somehow connected."

"'Interesting'?"

"Yeah. Where's her file?"

"Don't have it yet," Turnbull said.

"You've got my file and information on Ducharme, but you don't have Tolliver's?"

"Odd, isn't it?" Turnbull said.

"Not the word I would choose."

"One has to be careful about word choices," Turnbull said.

"Only with certain people."

"So they'll be heading to Baltimore soon."

Burns was surprised for a second, and then nodded. "Yes. Ducharme isn't the type to let go of something. He served with General LaGrange. He strikes me as one of those people to whom honor is very important."

Turnbull closed Burns's file.

"What else do you have on Ducharme?" Burns asked.

"I don't have Ducharme's classified file yet," Turnbull said. "But he had a life before going into the military that I was able to access. A rather interesting life."

"Interesting in what way?" Burns asked.

"He's from New Orleans, but his family history stretches back to the original French occupation of Haiti in the eighteen century. He's descended from a long line of soldiers, gangsters, and men of violence."

"That's an interesting genetic stew," Burns said.

Turnbull shrugged. "Aren't they all the same?"

"Not necessarily," Burns said.

Turnbull stared at him for a second, then stood. "I have a quick reaction force available that's already moving to Baltimore. Just in case. You let me know what else you need. Everything comes through me. Every report goes to me. You talk to no one else about this. Got it?"

"Yeah." Burns paused. "What about the disks?"

"What about them?"

"They've got to be important."

Turnbull shrugged. "As Tolliver said—they're old. Probably keepsakes."

Burns shook his head but didn't respond to that. "If Ducharme and Tolliver aren't suspects, why have we tagged them?"

"I think they'll lead us to what we want to find."

"The killer?"

"Of course."

* * *

Navy Captain Kevin O'Callaghan finished his thirty minutes on the treadmill precisely ten minutes before midnight. That gave him enough time to shower, put on his robe, and go to his desk to review the latest intelligence briefing from Naval Special Warfare Command for exactly one hour, so he could be in bed at 1 AM, to get his four hours of sleep, which was the maximum he would allow himself. He considered four hours a luxury given that was the total amount allowed during the five days of Hell Week during SEAL qualification. The fact his Qualification was twenty years in the past wasn't something he dwelled on. The fact he didn't have to be anywhere until ten in the morning wasn't even a factor.

He'd considered cutting the run short, given the importance of the meeting he had the next day with Admiral Groves at Annapolis, but he had always made it his mantra to do things exactly according to routine, no matter what the circumstances, and that had stood him in good stead throughout his years in service, and saved his life more than once.

Still, as the last minute counted down on the display in front of him and sweat trickled down his forehead, his mind kept mulling over the implications of the meeting. The Admiral was sick. He'd attended the funeral of the Old Man's wife eight months ago, and everyone attending had seen the spirit fading in the Admiral's eyes.

The treadmill beeped, and O'Callaghan hit the stop button. The machine came to a halt and he grabbed a towel and wiped the sweat from his naked torso. Despite the mental discord, he felt great for forty-two. Almost as fit as when he was active in the field and not riding a desk at the Pentagon. No booze, eating right, and working out—it all paid off. He went into the bathroom and turned on the shower, waiting for the hot water to clear the pipes from the water-heater of the town house.

* * *

Crouched in the crawl space underneath the Georgetown townhouse, the man was whistling quietly. An old Irish song—The Wild Colonial Boy. Appropriate for an O'Callaghan, he thought. He checked the glowing face on his watch as the gauge he'd planted on the copper pipe spiked. Exactly on time. Third night in a row, exact to the minute.

The man admired punctuality. Particularly in others. Made his job so much easier. It had worked with the car crash. The seat-of-the-pants effort at the restaurant—not so well, but he blamed that on his partner trying to get inside information instead of just doing the job. They were at fifty percent, and he wanted to put another win in the plus column, before they reported back to their employers.

He whistled the chorus to the song, the sound barely going three feet, as he grabbed the live wire he had cut with a rubber-gloved hand. He watched the gauge in the glow from the mini-mag light he had clenched between his teeth. The temperature was rising.

* * *

O'Callaghan stuck his hand into the water and adjusted the knobs. Just right. He stepped into the shower, his mind on the meeting. Admiral Groves had been cryptic, but hinted at matters of the highest urgency.

O'Callaghan shrugged—he'd find out what it was about when the Admiral told him what it was about. One thing two decades in uniform had taught the SEAL was to never try to guess what was on the mind of a higher-ranking officer.

* * *

Just right, the man thought. He pulled the gauge out and stuck the wire into the small hole. There was a spark, a loud humming, and then a crack as the main circuit breaker went.

* * *

O'Callaghan went rigid as the water poured over him, the electricity it carried surging through his body and connecting with the water in the base of the shower. His taut muscles were frozen for several seconds, and then the lights went out.

O'Callaghan collapsed, crashing through the glass around the shower and hitting the tile floor. He didn't move again.

* * *

The man placed plumber's cement over the tiny hole, holding his thumb in place for twenty seconds to allow the hole to seal. He pushed the wire back into place, insuring the connection was solid. Then, making sure he had everything he'd crawled in with, he slithered toward the back wall. The electrical box was there, close to the wooden trap door leading to the space under the back deck.

Reaching into a pocket, the man pulled out a fresh breaker. He opened the box, removed the burnt one and replaced it. He flipped the breaker. There was a hum as electricity flowed once more. The man pushed open the wooden door, then backed out of the yard, making sure he left no tracks.

* * *

In the bathroom two floors above, the lights flickered back on. Revealing Captain Kevin O'Callaghan lying motionless on the floor in a pile of broken glass. His skin was cut in numerous places, but there was very little blood, indicating his heart had stopped beating before he fell through the glass and hit the floor.

CHAPTER SIX

"So I assume you *would* like a ride?" Ducharme asked Evie as they exited the Hoover Building. She had a death grip on the battered leather briefcase. The black Blazer with dark-tinted windows was in the no-parking zone beyond the car barriers, a familiar figure leaning against the door.

"Sergeant Major Kincannon," Ducharme said.

"Colonel Ducharme, sir." Kincannon looked at Evie and tipped an imaginary hat. "Ma'am."

"Please call me Evie."

"Evie." Kincannon grinned warmly.

"Hurt anyone in there, Kincannon?" Ducharme asked.

The Sergeant Major spread his hands wide in innocence. "Who, me? They asked a lot of stupid questions. Weren't worth answering or getting upset about. But we *will* find who took out the General." The edge was back in Kincannon's voice.

"Who exactly do you work for?" Evie asked as she opened the passenger door.

Guess she's accepting the ride offer, Ducharme thought.

She paused. "That was all real, wasn't it?" Evie asked.

"Yes." Ducharme's beast wanted to howl, to rage, to destroy. He snapped the leash, his face flat, giving no sign of the internal struggle. "It's as real as things get."

Evie got into the passenger seat. She pulled out her silver cigarette case and took out another piece of gum. She caught Ducharme's glance. "Quitting isn't that easy."

"Quitting anything we're addicted to is hard," Ducharme allowed. "Why was your friend McBride meeting my old boss?"

"Which exact part of the government do you work for?"

"You don't have a need to know."

She laughed. "You have no idea how many times I've heard that bullshit line."

"As the curator of Monticello?" Kincannon asked mildly from the back seat.

"Not exactly."

Ducharme waited along with Kincannon for her to be more forthcoming, but she didn't oblige. He had yet to pull away from the Hoover Building, because he wasn't sure what his next step would be. Burns was right. This was indeed deep shit. But there were two things Ducharme was certain of: he would find his uncle's killer before Burns did; and he wouldn't be arresting her.

Evie finally spoke. "I don't know anything about your boss, LaGrange, so how could I know why McBride was meeting him?"

"General LaGrange was the Special Assistant to the National Security Council," Ducharme said. "Which is a fancy way of saying he was the military's adviser to the Executive Branch on counter-terrorist operations. And he wasn't my boss." Out of the corner of his eyes, he could see Kincannon following the conversation.

"I don't see a connection," Evie said. "McBride had nothing to do with terrorism or counter-terrorism. He was a newspaper editor. After he retired from the *Post*, he was adjunct history faculty at UVA. I have no idea if McBride knew LaGrange, but if he did, he never mentioned him to me."

"And you would remember if he mentioned it?" Ducharme asked.

Evie nodded.

Ducharme checked his watch. He put the truck in gear and pulled away from the curb.

"Were these murders a terrorist act?" Evie asked.

"Possibly," Ducharme said. "General LaGrange was a high-level target."

"And McBride?" she asked.

"Maybe he was in the wrong place at the wrong time," Ducharme said.

"I don't think so," Evie said.

"Don't think what, exactly?"

"That he was in the wrong place at the wrong time. Or that it was terrorism. Conspiracy, maybe, but not terrorism."

"Conspiracy by whom?" Ducharme asked.

"I don't know," Evie said.

She was lying. He was sure of it. The look in Kincannon's eyes in the rearview mirror indicated he knew it, too.

"So you believe in conspiracies?" Kincannon asked.

Evie sighed. "There's what you can see and what you can't see."

"Speak plainly," Ducharme said.

"'When all government, domestic and foreign, in little as in great things, shall be drawn to Washington as the center of all power, it will render powerless the checks provided of one government on another, and will become as oppressive as the government from which—'" She paused as Ducharme cut in.

"What the hell are you talking about?"

"Those words aren't mine," Evie said. "They were written by Thomas Jefferson. Let me continue with President Jefferson's words: *'But while our functionaries are wise, and honest, and vigilant, let us move compactly under their guidance, and we have nothing to fear. Things may here and there go a little wrong. It is not in their power to prevent it. But all will be right in the end, though not perhaps by the shortest means.'"* She looked at Ducharme. "The question is what exactly did Thomas Jefferson mean by this last sentence?"

"I assume you're going somewhere with this?" Kincannon asked amiably. "That there's some connection between Thomas Jefferson and these killings?"

Evie nodded. "The Founding Fathers, particularly Jefferson, understood true power. He also understood politics, which means maneuvering for power. Jefferson was a brilliant man; perhaps the most brilliant amongst the men who founded this country, and they were a most interesting and frighteningly intelligent group, although they naturally had their personal foibles.

"John Hancock was a smuggler, a black marketer. He was also the only person to actually sign the Declaration of Independence on the fourth of July, in seventeen seventy-six. Perhaps that's why his signature is so large: he had all that blank space to work with. Or perhaps it was because his signature matched his ego.

"Benjamin Franklin was carried to the convention hall in a chair carried by four prisoners. Not because he wanted to appear regal, but because he suffered from gout. Thomas Jefferson died deeply in debt. Most of them drank way too much—after all, you couldn't really trust the water in those days so wine and beer were the staple drinks. As good an excuse as any. And the sex scandals—" she shook her head. "Thomas Jefferson and Alexander Hamilton, two most mortal enemies, both threw allegations of affairs and sexual scandal at each other. Hamilton even started the New York Post in eighteen-oh-one as a venue to spread his spin. The Fourth Estate is called that for a reason. McBride was one of the leading members of the Fourth Estate in our time."

Evie fell silent, and Ducharme waited. And waited. But she seemed to have dried up as a font of 'useless information' as Burns had labeled her. Ducharme drove the Blazer toward the center of Washington DC. He could see the Washington Monument ahead and slightly to the left.

Things stayed blessedly silent as he took a right onto 15th, heading back toward the White House. He looked to the left. No flashing lights. No crime scene tape. Nothing around the Zero Milestone to indicate the murders that had taken place.

"They're covering up the killings," Ducharme said.

"That's the government," Evie said.

"I'm the government," Ducharme noted.

"Not *that* government," Evie said. "Come on. You're in black ops. You know there are so many layers in the game, no one knows them all."

"And how do *you* know that?" Kincannon asked.

Evie twisted in her seat and looked at him. "Once upon a time, I wasn't just a curator. Maybe I'll tell you the story some day."

"I'm all yours," Kincannon said, his voice inviting. No response. "Why the Zero Milestone?"

She looked out the window. "The Zero Milestone was created after the First World War, by people advocating the building of roads across the country. It's inscribed on all four sides. I'm not sure of the exact wording, but two sides indicate it was the start point for the first and second transcontinental motor convoys conducted by the Army.

"Did you know," Evie directed at Ducharme, "that General Eisenhower, then a lieutenant-colonel and one of your fellow West Pointers, was part of that first convoy that departed from the Zero Milestone for California? And the difficulties they had crossing the country—along with his later experience in Germany with the autobahns-- led him to start our Interstate Highway system while he was President?"

"Fascinating," Ducharme deadpanned. "What's the significance of the Milestone for our killer?"

"There might not have been one for our killer," Evie said. "I think McBride and LaGrange were going to meet there. You might consider the Zero Milestone the center of the country, symbolically."

"So these murders—" Kincannon left it hanging.

"Cut to the core of the country," Evie said. "Someone was sending a message."

"Where do you suggest we go to find the killer?" Ducharme asked, tired of circling, the beast wanting to strike.

Evie shook her head. "Unfortunately, the killer isn't the priority."

"The rest of the disks," Ducharme said, not asking.

She reached into the leather bag and pulled out her wooden disk. "I have number one."

Ducharme took his out. "Number twenty-six. I assume there are twenty-four more?"

"Correct. And we need to find them."

"Why?"

"They lead to something."

"What?"

"We'll know when we find them and read the message."

Lying again, Ducharme thought, glancing in the rearview mirror for a tail. Nothing. Which was wrong. He pulled into a parking lot and put the Blazer in idle. He pulled out his MK-23 and slid out the magazine, checking it and the weapon. Something wasn't right; years of living with weapons told him that. He stared at it for a moment, and then began thumbing the stubby .45 caliber rounds out of the magazine while Evie and Kincannon watched.

Ducharme got to the bottom of the magazine and noted that the last one was lighter than the others. He re-loaded the gun, keeping the round out. He slid the light bullet into his pocket. "Interesting. Our friend Agent Burns put a tracking device in my gun."

"Why?" Evie asked.

"To follow us," Ducharme said.

"We have to figure out why LaGrange and McBride were meeting," Evie said.

"OK," Ducharme conceded. "Besides the Poe thing—West Point and the University of Virginia—what do you think the thread is between McBride and LaGrange?"

"The Poe thing is in the past," Evie said. "In the present, yesterday, they obviously had a common enemy."

Ducharme nodded. "I think they were worried about their meeting being compromised."

"What makes you say that?"

"McBride's roses and the bottle were a meeting safe signal," Ducharme said. "He was probably going to place them on the Milestone. LaGrange would see them and know it was safe to approach. And if McBride had been doing the same thing at Poe's grave every year, then it was also an annual situational safe signal."

"Safe from who?" Evie asked.

Kincannon answered. "From whoever killed them."

"Why cognac and three roses?" Ducharme asked.

"Poe was a heavy drinker," Evie said. "Alcohol killed him at a relatively young age, although amontillado would seem more appropriate. The roses are thought to represent the three people supposedly buried under his monument: Poe, his wife Virginia, and his mother-in-law, Mary Clemm. You said 'annual situational safe signal,'" Evie noted. "It makes sense."

"You know what a safe signal is?" Ducharme was surprised.

"Yes. The Poe Toaster is reported in the news. If he didn't show up on Poe's birthday it would be reported in the news. And if the Toaster showed up on a day other than Poe's birthday and left the roses and cognac, it would also make the news. An indirect means of signaling when either side doesn't want to directly contact each other."

"I don't think they teach safe signals in civilian colleges," Ducharme noted.

Evie sighed. "They do at the Farm. So following the logic, the killer knew they would be meeting at the Zero Milestone ahead of time."

"Hold on," Ducharme said. "The Farm? You were CIA?"

"Once upon a time," Evie admitted.

"What the fuck?" Ducharme said. "Researcher?"

She gave him a look of disdain. "Field operative. I speak Farsi, Russian and German. Spent six years overseas, two in the Middle East, two in Turkey and a year and a half in Russia. They *appreciated* my memory in the Agency, by the way."

"Well, I'll be damned," Kincannon said. "How do you go from that to Monticello?"

"Long story for another time," Evie said. "Not important right now."

Ducharme ran a hand across the stubble on his chin. "Why do you say the killer knew about the meeting?"

"General LaGrange was killed *before* he made it to the Zero Milestone," Evie said. "Which means there's a very good chance they were going there to meet the killer or someone the killer knew. But they were betrayed."

Ducharme mulled over other aspects of the murders. "What about the head-heart letter by Jefferson? Why would the killer want to infer that letter?"

"I'm not sure the killer wanted to infer the letter," Evie said. "I think it was a lure."

Ducharme was confused. "What?"

"The killer couldn't be sure LaGrange got a message to you or that McBride got one to me. But arranging the head and heart like that, would definitely be sending a message to us. To me at least."

"I don't follow," Ducharme said.

"Perhaps I'm wrong," Evie said.

"And if you're right?" Ducharme asked. "What's the purpose?"

Evie shrugged. "To draw us out into the open."

"Why?"

"No idea.

Lying once more, Ducharme thought.

She spoke. "Let's consider the letter itself. It's a love letter. Sort of. Let me think." She pulled out her iPhone and played with the screen.

Ducharme looked over at her. She stared unfocused at her iPhone, lost somewhere in her own mind. He glanced in the back seat. Kincannon had his eyes closed. Rest when you can—a mantra of Special Forces.

When Evie spoke, her voice was low as she read. *"If our country, when pressed with wrongs at the point of the bayonet, had been governed by its head, instead of its hearts, where should we be now? Hanging on a gallows."* She looked up. "The thrust of the letter was that one should trust one's heart over one's head. Jefferson was in love with Mrs. Cosway. He'd broken his wrist trying to jump over a fountain in Paris in an attempt to impress her just a month before he wrote the letter."

Ducharme was surprised. Thomas Jefferson, the one carved into Mount Rushmore, the one whose Memorial looked solemnly over the Tidal Basin, jumping a fountain to impress a woman?

Evie went on. "Jefferson was trying to use his head to discipline what he believed was his misbehaving heart. If you read it closely, there's also a great deal of Jefferson's political philosophy in it and his thoughts on how things should be conducted in the United States. A political letter inside a love letter, so to speak."

Ducharme rubbed the scar under his right eye, trying to alleviate the constant irritation. "If the letter was politics inside love, perhaps what the killer did was politics inside hate."

Evie looked at him in surprise. "Interesting."

"Maybe it's even simpler than that." Ducharme pulled his hand away from his face. "You really think McBride was this Poe Toaster?"

"McBride was fascinated with Edgar Allan Poe. He had those specific items for a reason."

"So the killer probably also knows that the flowers and bottle was a signal. What was your relationship with McBride?"

Ducharme watched Evie, expecting anything from a snort to a slap, but there was nothing. Kincannon's eyes opened to slit.

"He was my mentor when I did an internship at the *Post*, while I was in grad school," Evie said. "He was my student at UVA after he retired. When he graduated, he taught part-time in the history department. I teach a class there as part of my curator duties. He was my friend."

She reached in the briefcase and pulled out a metal rod. "The disks go on this." She unscrewed one end of the rod and slid on the disk. Then she took Ducharme's and slid it on. "We have disks one and twenty-six. We need twenty-four more disks." She frowned. "But—"

"What?" Ducharme asked.

"There should be two ciphers. Identical. If we only have one—" her eyes got the faraway look for almost a minute before she spoke again. "OK. If there's only one Cipher, then there are two messages on it. One is an initiating Key phrase once we have all the wheels. The wheels are turned to that twenty-six-letter Key. Then we look at the other rows to find the true message."

"Ingenious and simple." Ducharme was used to dealing with encrypted messages. Jefferson had invented a simple but effective means long before the era of electronic ciphers. It had limitations—you had to have the actual cipher, not something you could carry around in your pocket. And the Key.

But still—a metal rod and wood disks cipher that were pretty much unbreakable.

"What kind of message will it yield?" Kincannon asked. "Obviously it's important, but what twenty-six letter message could be that important?"

"No idea," Evie said, her eyes sliding away.

Ducharme glanced in the rearview mirror and met Kincannon's eyes. The Sergeant Major nodded ever so slightly.

"What's strange," Evie said, oblivious to everything around her, "is that there are only two original Jefferson Cipher Wheels known to be in existence. One at Monticello, and one in the Smithsonian. I checked and the one at Monticello is still there. And if someone had stolen the one at the Smithsonian, I'd have heard about it."

"These are from a third."

"Yes. And it's definitely an original made by Jefferson himself. I can tell from these markings on the rod."

"That you, the Curator at Monticello, didn't know about."

She didn't say anything for a moment, and then spoke. "LaGrange and McBride were meeting this evening at the Zero Milestone, but given they were using a safe signal, they were worried they might be attacked. They wouldn't have brought their disks, and they sent one to each of us. The question is why were they meeting now? And here in Washington? Why not in Baltimore at Poe's grave?"

Logical. Analytical. Always thinking. There was definitely something different from the norm with Evie, Ducharme thought, beyond the fact that she had CIA in her past. It was as if the murders earlier in the evening had not occurred. "LaGrange was assigned to the National Security Council. He lived here. Maybe they were meeting someone else in the area."

"Why now?" she repeated her first question.

Ducharme shrugged. "I don't know. Either the meeting was planned a while ago, or they just decided to do it."

"McBride gave me his briefcase and told me to meet him at the restaurant yesterday afternoon. So it was a short notice thing."

Kincannon summed that up. "Something happened yesterday that made them decide to meet. So the killer also knew they were going to meet. So—"

Evie completed the thought for him. "—the killer did something yesterday to make them contact each other. Such as set up a meeting."

"And they were very worried about the meeting," Ducharme said.

"Why do you say that?"

"They sent us the two disks and sent both of us to that restaurant."

Evie nodded. "They did. You know, Poe wrote the *Purloined Letter* and—" she fell silent and went into one of her states again. "The real question is what is the connection forged by Jefferson, the person from the past who reached out from the grave to bring McBride and LaGrange together?"

"And put them in their own graves." The beast reared up in Ducharme's chest. He took a deep breath. Let it out. Forced himself to relax. His head was pounding, a steady drumbeat of pain and anger. "I know the Poe connection, but what is Jefferson's tie to the two of them?"

"Thomas Jefferson not only founded the University of Virginia," she said, "but also the Military Academy."

"You told Burns that, but Sylvanus Thayer was the father of the Military Academy," Ducharme responded.

"Thayer wasn't even the first Superintendent," Evie shot back. "He was the third."

Kincannon spoke from the back seat. "Don't fight the lady, Duke. She's ahead of you in points already."

Ducharme ignored him. "Washington. He founded West Point. There's that big-ass statue of him on the Plain in front of the Mess Hall. There is *no* statue of Jefferson at the Academy. We had to memorize every damn statue at the place as Plebes."

"Jefferson founded the Military Academy in eighteen-oh-two when he was President," Evie said in a calm voice.

The date was right. Ducharme realized he'd never connected the date with the President at the time.

"Few people would think Jefferson founded the Military Academy," Evie added. "He was opposed to a standing army."

"So why'd he do it?" Ducharme asked.

"Publicly, because a standing army was a reality of having a country," Evie said. "Jefferson didn't want the officer corps to be full of favored sons and sycophants. He felt if they had to have an army, they needed a professional officer corps that swore allegiance to the country, not to a particular party or a particular President." She took out her cigarette case, and in the reflected glow from the streetlight he noticed something was inscribed on the cover.

"What's that?" he asked, indicating the writing.

"McBride gave this to me." Evie gave him a sad smile, a surprisingly honest pain in her eyes. Not info-robot ex-CIA agent now, just a hurt woman, missing her friend. "It's actually a misprint from the inscribers. It says: 'A blood of patriots and tyrants.' It should be '*the* blood'. It's from a famous quote by Thomas Jefferson: *The tree of liberty must be refreshed from time to time with the blood of patriots and tyrants'.*"

"So McBride and LaGrange were patriots." Ducharme said.

"Yes." She grabbed another piece of gum, deep in thought. "What are you going to do about the tracking device?"

"Keep it for now." Ducharme told her. "Throwing it away will just let them know we know. Better we play that card when it's to our advantage."

"The killer is headed to Baltimore, of course," Evie said.

Ducharme glanced at the GPS and drove toward the Beltway and the Interstate north. "Poe's grave?"

"Yes."

"Why?"

"There's probably something hidden in his grave."

"The other disks?"

"That would be the logical conclusion." She turned to him and gave a cold smile. "Except the tyrants are going to make a mistake."

* * *

Deep inside the Anderson House, Lucius stared across the polished desktop as Mister Turnbull walked in. The only thing on his desk was the chess set: on one side George Washington commanded in white versus King George in black on the other.

"May I?" Turnbull indicated the chair across from Lucius.

Lucius nodded.

Turnbull sat down and glanced at the board. "You haven't started a game?"

"I have not yet found a worthy opponent. Too bad you don't play."

Turnbull held up his hands, two slabs of meat covered in old scars, incongruous with the deftness of his cunning. "This was the only game I played."

Lucius gave the ghost of a smile. "I don't believe you played when you were in the ring. I saw you fight at the Academy."

Turnbull lowered his hands. "That was a long time ago."

"It's just a different ring now."

"The contractors took out Admiral Groves's replacement. The Surgeon is on her way to see the Admiral as we speak."

"And McBride's replacement?" Lucius reached out and placed a finger on top of a blue-clad pawn.

Turnbull grimaced. "The contractors missed. And—" he paused.

Lucius toppled the pawn over.

Turnbull continued. "There was someone with her. A Colonel. Named Ducharme. LaGrange, his uncle, was his surrogate father."

Lucius became still. "Was there a mistake in killing LaGrange's son?"

"Perhaps. He seemed the obvious successor, but with LaGrange, obvious wasn't always the way to view things."

"So Tolliver and this Ducharme are now together."

"Yes. The FBI picked them up, but released them."

Lucius reached out and picked up Martha Washington. "Curious. How much do they know?"

"Ducharme—not much. I think Tolliver is more clued in. They had two disks and the cipher rod. And McBride's computer, which was encrypted."

"Can you break the encryption?"

"No. A one-time method that requires a thumb drive with the decrypt. We gave it back to her."

"In hopes she knows where the drive is." It was not a question. They'd worked together enough years to be past such questions.

"And they still need to find twenty-four more disks," Turnbull said.

"Your contractor failed and in doing so united two of our enemies, giving them the chance to succeed in both tasks."

"Giving us a chance to achieve our original goal of getting the Allegiance," Turnbull said, "and finding out McBride's secrets."

Lucius smiled and placed Martha Washington back down on the board. "You should play, Mister Turnbull."

Turnbull stood. "I will make the appropriate move."

22 AUGUST 1848

President Polk figured it had to be a hell of a lot hotter down south for the Mexican President than even Washington in the summer, although some might question that. A head of sweat dripped off Polk's nose and onto the copy of the Treaty of Guadalupe Hidalgo which he had been reading one more time, savoring the terms, as if he could feel the actual growth in the United States that the Treaty decreed.

Polk was staying in the White House, an insane decision for anyone who had survived a Washington August. But there was work to be done, and even the specter of yellow fever couldn't persuade Polk to head to the cooler mountains as most Washingtonians with means had done. He could hear the mooing of cows from the large open pasture to the south of the White House, and the occasional rattle of a passing carriage, but otherwise the capitol was still.

Polk turned his chair to a map, his most prized possession since coming into office. He had made four promises when elected to office and the map represented two of them:

-Acquiring some or all of the Oregon Territory.

-Purchasing California from Mexico in order to have access to the port of San Francisco to open trade to the Pacific.

Drawn in fountain pen on the map by his own hand were the successful results of those two promises: the Oregon Territory and a huge chunk of land including Texas and the southwest from the Rocky Mountains to the Pacific Ocean, encompassing all of the California Territory.

It was the second largest expansion of the United States since Jefferson had purchased the Louisiana Territory. It was Manifest Destiny and Polk had done it, stretched the United States from Atlantic to Pacific. That he had done it with blood via a war some considered imperialistic wasn't something he concerned himself with.

Polk leaned back in his chair and barely noticed as he wiped the sheen of sweat off his forehead. He looked over, irritated, as his secretary cracked open the door and stuck his head in. "Sir, there are some gentlemen here to see you."

Polk waved. "Send them in." He stiffened as he saw former President John Quincy Adams leading three men into the room: General Zachary Taylor, who was getting altogether too popular for winning the war Polk had instigated with Mexico. There were more than whispers that Taylor wanted to run for President under the banner of the opposing Whigs.

There was also a tall, rangy freshman Congressman named Lincoln, who had been a minor thorn in Polk's side during the run-up to the war. The press had dubbed him 'Spotty' Lincoln for the resolution he had tried to get past Congress, demanding that Polk "show me the spot" where American blood had been spilled that precipitated the War with Mexico, claiming it had happened on Mexican soil, not American. The resolution had failed, and Polk was determined to crush Lincoln's political career.

Lastly, there was old General Winfield Scott, who had opened the way to the 'Halls of Montezuma' as the press liked to dub it.

Polk stood, focusing on Adams. "Sir, what brings you here?"

Adams had a black, wooden tube in his hand, which he placed, to Polk's chagrin, right on top of the Treaty of Guadalupe Hidalgo. "Let me be frank," Adams said. "You began this most horrid of wars by direct provocation of the Mexicans. Generals Taylor and Scott, while supporting you publicly, verify that privately."

Polk glared at the two generals, but they seemed impervious.

Adams continued. "You used the war to further your Imperial goals, which is inconsistent with our Constitution. And you are a front man for the Cincinnatians."

Polk slammed a fist onto the map. "We now stretch from sea to sea. We won the war. We—"

Adams cut him off. "Mister President, I don't care what the immediate results are. You manipulated the military for the agenda of a select few. As Congressman Lincoln noted, you declared war the way a monarch would, not a President."

"I dealt with the problems I inherited with the office," Polk argued. "Texas was annexed by Congress four days before I took office. The Mexicans had already promised war if that happened. Conflict was inevitable."

"Not if you had used diplomacy instead of the army," Adams countered. "You sent General Taylor and his troops into disputed territory without consulting Congress."

"This is true," Taylor said.

"Indeed it is," echoed Lincoln.

"But Congress voted for war," Polk said.

"On the basis of a fake 'causus belli'," Lincoln said.

Scott finally spoke up. "The army is sick of such a war. We lost more men to disease in that God-forsaken place than the enemy. It cannot happen again."

"How dare you all—" Polk began, but Adams cut him off.

"Read this, sir." He picked up the wooden tube and screwed off the end. He pulled a scroll out and unrolled it on top of Polk's map.

Polk leaned over and read the few sentences. Startled, he looked up at Adams. "What—"

"*Look at the signatures,*" *Adams commanded and Polk obeyed. Before the current President could say anything, the former President continued.* "*The War is done. The treaty ratified. You've had your glory. You have a year left in office. You will not start another war. You will not violate the treaty to grab more land from Mexico or cross swords with the British in the Oregon Territory. You will not run for election again. You will tell your fellow Cincinnatians they have what they sought and that is enough.*"

Taylor spoke up. "*Or else we will enforce the Jefferson Allegiance as you have just read.*"

"*Do you understand?*" *Adams asked.* "*You will abide strictly by the Constitution for the remainder of your term. Clear?*"

Polk weakly nodded, slumping down into the chair where just minutes ago, he had been reveling in his achievements. What they had just dictated meant he would be the first President not to seek re-election since the founding of the country. It was unheard of. But so was the document he had just read. He numbly watched as Adams rolled the scroll and stuck it back in the tube. The men turned and marched out of the room leaving the President alone.

President Polk grabbed the map and tore it to shreds.

CHAPTER SEVEN

Church bells tolled, signaling the end of one day and the start of a new one. Lily sat in her van, scanning the immediate area, searching for the two black vans that had followed her to Annapolis: the 'assistance' promised to her by Mister Turnbull. She saw one parked two blocks away. The other was better hidden. She hadn't asked for the assistance, so she wondered briefly why they were really there. There were two possible conclusions and she knew both were true: they were support, and they were also control.

She turned on the engine, driving toward the water. The GPS announced she was within a half-mile of her destination. She stopped, switched off the GPS and turned it to the computer built into the system. She accessed the FBI's secure uplink. On the screen touchpad, she typed in the first name the Chair had given her: Admiral Hazard Groves.

She scrolled down, checking his information and nodded. Groves was retired and lived a half-mile away, alone. She accessed his address and then loaded it into the military satellite mapping system. Within seconds she had his house located, zooming in until she had an excellent picture of the building and the surrounding neighborhood. She kept the picture on the screen and began driving toward the house as she formulated her plan. It didn't take her long: he was an old man, living alone. It would be simple and direct.

* * *

From his upstairs window, Admiral Hazard Groves watched the moon come up over Chesapeake Bay, illuminating the water and the Naval Academy on his side of the bay. Based on the text message he'd received from General LaGrange and the lack of contact from Captain Kevin O'Callaghan, he was fairly certain this was the last night he would ever have. He was glad that he could see the Academy one last time. His hands trembled as he brought the old set of Naval binoculars up to his eyes. The exterior of the glasses was battered and scuffed from decades of shipboard duty. He scanned the Academy grounds, watching a few midshipmen hurrying across the campus in the late night cold. He remembered being young like them. He spotted a middie tucked into the shadows of a building, a cigarette in his hand. Groves's hand automatically reached out toward the phone to call the Office of the Day to report the midshipman, but he paused, as the reality of his own current situation washed over him, and a sense of priority interceded. He almost envied the young man his indiscretion, remembering some of the things he'd done during his years at the Academy.

Already tired, *too tired*, he thought, he lowered the binoculars to the blanket that covered his lap, helping to protect his frail body from the chill that penetrated even the well-insulated house. He placed his hands on the arms of his wheelchair, the large Naval Academy ring glittering on his ring finger, just outside the thin wedding band. His wife had died eight months ago, and ever since, his will to leave the house, to do anything, had diminished. He knew it was wrong, that he was failing in his duty, that it was a time for action, and he was caught between the pincers of guilt and sorrow, but his fatigue kept them from being very sharp.

He turned his wheelchair to the left and looked at a wall festooned with plaques, photos and certificates. A lifetime of service. He turned in the opposite direction and stared at a wall covered with photographs of his family. Wife. Two sons. A daughter. Eight grandchildren. And two great-grandchildren.

He smiled.

A low beeping sound came from down the hall. The motion detectors that surrounded the house. Normally they were routed to the NCIS detachment at the Academy, and a car would already be rolling out here to check. But Groves had gone on the computer and shut down the link earlier the previous evening.

Groves took a deep breath. He was decked out in his Dress Whites. The same set he'd bought as an ensign after graduation from the Academy. He liked to think he had maintained his trimness to be able to wear them, but he knew it was the cancer in his gut that had ripped forty pounds off his body in the last few months.

Nine rows of ribbons adorned his chest indicating service from the Korean War up to the Invasion of Iraq, when he had finally been shown the door by a Navy that didn't want his kind around any more. He was old school, a relic from a different Navy, where people mattered more than computers and missiles. Thinking about computers, he rolled his chair across the room to a laptop computer and hit the 'enter' key, sending the message he had prepared the previous evening. As soon as he received the acknowledgement that it had been sent, he accessed a wipe program and started it. A countdown appeared on the screen indicating the computer's hard drive would be completely clean in two minutes and that a message had been sent—to another Navy SEAL.

He pushed his chair to the far wall until he was underneath a flag encased in a glass frame. He parked below it, turning to face the hallway. Reaching into the bag hanging on the side of the wheelchair, he pulled out a silver-plated M1911 Colt Automatic with pearl handles. He'd been given it by the Marine contingent aboard an aircraft carrier he'd commanded many years ago. It took all his strength to pull back the charging handle, loading a round into the chamber. He laid the gun on his lap, covering it with the blanket, his right hand wrapped around the pistol grip.

Just in time, as a dark figure appeared in the doorway.

"Admiral Groves."

He was old enough to be surprised, and chagrined that it was a woman. She pulled back her hood, revealing her face. A short, beautiful blond.

"Who the hell are you?" Groves demanded.

"Just call me the Surgeon. Just as I might call you Philosopher."

"Why are you doing this?"

"Because I've been ordered to," she said, walking into the room as she drew a sword from underneath her robe. "You understand about orders, don't you?"

"I understand about serving my country and fulfilling the oath I swore to defend." He noted the large ring on her left hand. "Which Academy?"

"Air Force."

Groves laughed. "Leave it to a Zoomie to bring a sword to a gun fight." He pulled the trigger on the hidden gun. The sound of the .45 caliber pistol going off was deafening in the room, the round punching through the blanket and hitting the Surgeon in the chest, knocking her back a step. The recoil of the gun kicked Groves's hand up, snapping his fragile wrist with an audible crack.

The Surgeon's reactions were too quick for Groves to follow through his pain and shock. She dove forward, did a roll, and came to her feet just to his right, the blade flicking away the blanket. Even as the blanket flew up, the blade darted down, skewering the hand holding the gun, and compounding the broken bone in the wrist.

Groves gritted his teeth to keep from crying out in pain as the pistol clattered to the floor. The Surgeon pulled the sword out of his hand and took a step back, breathing slowly and deeply. With her free hand she felt in the cloak for the place the bullet had impacted. She pulled it out of the Liquid Armor and dropped it to the floor.

"You still have fight in you, old man. Commendable for a Squid. The other two went down much too easily."

Admiral Groves clenched his fist to try to stop the flow of blood. "If I were younger—"

"You wouldn't have gotten the advantage on me," Lily said. "My mistake. Where are your disks?"

"You'll burn in hell before you ever get my disks."

"Hell?" She seemed amused. "That's a story for children. There's only here and now. All that matters is if one is holding the sword or facing the point of the sword. Where are the disks?" She punctuated the question with a slice of the wakizashi, drawing blood from the old man's shoulder.

"Ruined the damn Academies letting women in," Groves said. "Women can never do the job that—"

The wakizashi sliced the other shoulder.

"—men can do." Groves acted as if he hadn't been cut. "I'd like to see a woman handle a tow line in a storm when the decks are slippery and the ship is heaving to and—"

"The disks," the Surgeon yelled over his diatribe.

"All you'd be good for," Groves said, "is serving me coffee. Had a female pilot when I commanded the *Truman* and she splashed a jet on a routine take-off. Put sixty millions dollars worth of aircraft into the ocean. Damn bitch."

"I earned—" the Surgeon began, but Groves cut her off.

"You've had different standards than the men since you entered the Academy. Yet you're supposed to do the same job. You *know* the standards were different. You've had men cover for you, thinking, maybe, just maybe, they might get a piece. Be honest about it. You think they were being altruistic? Bet your daddy never acknowledged you. You couldn't measure up if—"

The Surgeon took a quick step forward, the point of the wakizashi stabbing into the old man's stomach.

Groves gasped in pain, but he still managed a smile. "Women are too damn emotional. Took you long enough." With that, he wrapped his hands, blood pouring out of the one, around the blade, ignoring as it sliced into his fingers and ignoring the grinding of the broken bone in the one wrist. With his last surge of strength and all the discipline of over forty years in the service to his country, he shoved down on the heft of the blade, cutting through his gut, eviscerating himself.

* * *

Letting go of the handle, Lily took a step back. She stared at the dead man, breathing hard, trying to get under control. Then she nodded. "Commendable, Admiral," she whispered to the body. She knelt next to him

69

and leaned over. She kissed the old man on the lips, lingering a bit too long. She shivered and blinked, confused for a moment, then she straightened and saw the battle flag on the wall: a blue flag with white letters spelling out: *DON'T GIVE UP THE SHIP.*

Without thinking, she brought the wakizashi over her head in a two-handed grip and slashed down, slicing through the frame, breaking the glass and cutting the flag in two.

She slowed her breathing down to normal as she looked about. She picked up the .45 and tucked it in a pocket. She noted an officer's saber mounted on a plaque near the door and ripped it off the wall, tucking it under one arm. She pivoted, just as she had in Lucius's office, a military maneuver, and stared at the dead man, and then up at the sliced flag dangling off the wall above him, re-reading the words.

Lily smiled. "You almost fooled me, old man."

CHAPTER EIGHT

Kincannon was stretched out on the back seat, resting. Ducharme was driving, not liking the uncertainty that lay ahead in Baltimore. He glanced over at Evie. "The question would have been rude when you were a stranger, but since we're foxhole buddies, can I ask you something?"

Evie gave a cautious look. "Really, everything that's going on and that's all you've got? Why, don't you have a boyfriend, husband, lover?"

"I'm just trying to pass some time and it seems to be tied in with the long story you mentioned earlier," Ducharme lied.

Evie called him on it. "You're trying to figure me out. And rather bluntly, if I might say so. And you want to know who my powerful friend is."

Ducharme almost smiled. "Guilty." In the back seat, Kincannon rolled his eyes.

Evie played with a charm on one of her silver bracelets, and then finally turned to him with a sly grin. "Do you want the epic, the novel, the short story, or the theory?"

Fuck, Ducharme muttered in head. He glanced at the mileage marker, did a quick calculation, debated between short story and theory, thought a little bit more about how much she had said back in DC, and said: "Theory."

Her grin became a smile. "It's my 'Casablanca' theory of love. Now, don't interrupt me and I presume you've seen the movie?"

Before Ducharme could answer, Kincannon chimed in from the back seat: "'I remember every detail. The Germans wore gray, you wore blue'."

Evie relaxed back in her seat, which Ducharme took as a good sign, and he also felt his shoulders loosen slightly and the headache fade somewhat. He would deal with Baltimore when they got there. "Yeah, I saw it a long time ago. Vaguely remember it, although apparently not as well as Kincannon."

Evie spoke in a low voice. "You know how Bogart thinks of all the gin joints, she had to walk into mine? Well, my theory of love is that you really only need to have one great love affair—you know, to prove to yourself that you can do it. And it needs to end in some bizarre way out of your control so that you are both left with your love intact. You both are still in love and, but for circumstances beyond your control, you would still be together. Etcetera. Etcetera.

"Then you can get on with your life and never have to deal with that again. I mean, you can meet people and stuff, but you're never going to project that kind of expectation on another person again, so you're pretty safe. It's like you've been vaccinated. I think that poor Bogart almost had a heart attack when Ilsa traipsed back into his life. Because at any moment she could open her mouth and say just the stupidest thing and he'd realize she wasn't the great love of his life and then he'd have to start all over again. Really, why do you think he was so happy when that plane door slammed on her butt? Because he still loved her—that's why. That whole movie is just him sitting on a ticking time bomb. It's excruciating."

She sat up a little straighter. "If we live through this, play it again and watch his face whenever she starts to speak. Unbearable. Really."

"Nice pun." Kincannon started laughing.

"What?" Evie snapped.

Kincannon shook his head. "No offense. I'm just thinking of the visual at the end of the movie. I never thought of it that way. You are quite the skeptic."

"See, that's such a knee-jerk reaction. I have a theory of romantic love to cope in a culture built around an insane ideal. That makes me a realist. Which is part of what you wanted to know about me. Could have just administered a Myers-Briggs personality assessment."

Ducharme took both hands off the wheel for a moment and held them up defensively. "Ok. We're sorry. Sorry. So did you have an Ilsa—my mistake—a Rick?"

"Of course I did or it wouldn't be a theory. And technically, it's a male version of an Ilsa, because she, as we know, found one more great love after Rick."

Ducharme glanced in the rear-view mirror, then back at her. "Doesn't that prove your theory wrong?"

Evie shrugged. "It wouldn't be scientific if it couldn't be proved wrong."

Ducharme took the exit for Baltimore. "You know, you're a real piece of work, Evie Tolliver."

"I know," she whispered, more to herself.

"I want to hear all about your Ilsa/Rick guy as soon as someone's not trying to kill us."

"You'd be bored. And be a little more subtle in the future."

"We don't have time for subtle."

* * *

The blood from the cut on Lily's arm seeped through her black turtleneck sweater. The pain was exquisite, a bright red spike keeping her on edge and focused and providing her with a deep, dark pleasure.

She drove down a badly lit Baltimore street until the GPS prompted her to pull over. A brick wall surrounded an old, dark church. Leafless branches drooped over the cemetery surrounding the church, their limbs dusted with snow. Poe had written about places like this. Fitting that he was buried here.

Lily exited her van, walked to the front gate and found it locked. Pulling picks from the pocket of her cape, she made short work of that obstacle. She swung the gates open and walked through the light dusting of snow. A white monument to her right immediately caught her attention: an obelisk about five feet high.

She went over and wiped away the snow at the bottom of the monument: EDGAR ALLAN POE.

* * *

Ducharme checked the GPS. They were less than five miles from Westminster Church. This late at night there was hardly any traffic moving, especially given the storm. Fresh snow covered the area, making downtown Baltimore look deceptively clean.

He glanced over at Evie. "Are you going to tell me why the killer is going to make a mistake here? She seems to have been on target so far."

"She's going to what most people think is Poe's grave in front of the church, underneath the Poe Monument," Evie answered.

Ducharme pulled his MK23 out with one hand, noting that Kincannon already had his on his lap. "And he's not buried in his grave?"

"No," Evie said.

Ducharme made sure there was a round in the chamber. "So where is he buried, then?"

"Still in his first grave in the back of the churchyard," Evie said, and when he raised his eyebrows, explained: "In eighteen forty-nine, Poe was buried in back of the church in a plot to the right of his grandfather, General Poe. Edgar's grave had no marker, just the General's. However, in eighteen sixty-four, the General's marker was turned around from facing east, to

73

facing the west gate. In eighteen seventy-five, a bunch of school children donated money for a stone monument to honor Poe, and it was to be placed in the front of the church. Unfortunately, the gravediggers exhuming his body didn't know the General's marker had been reversed. So when they dug to the right, they uncovered the wrong coffin. Someone should have noted the mistake because they first hit Missus Poe, then another female relative, and then finally a mahogany coffin with a man's body in it. But Edgar Allan Poe had been buried in a walnut-stained poplar coffin."

Ducharme holstered the pistol. In the back, Kincannon was opening one of the cases and pulling out parts to a sniper rifle.

"No one really seemed to care at the time," Evie continued. "The wrong coffin was then buried under the Monument in the front of the church. So even in death, Poe continues to be a mystery. The Monument also has the wrong date of birth, January twentieth, rather than January nineteenth, which might suggest someone knew it wasn't really marking Poe's body.

"In nineteen thirteen a stone was placed in the rear, marking the real spot, saying it was Poe's original burial spot from eighteen forty-nine to eighteen seventy-five. It has a raven carved in it and 'Quoth the Raven, Nevermore' across the top. More importantly for us, the Poe Toaster leaves the roses and cognac at the old marker, not the newer monument. So, if McBride put something here, he put it where the roses and cognac would go."

"How do you know all this stuff?" Kincannon clicked the last piece of the rifle in place.

"I read books. I'm willing to bet the killer is working off the Internet. The thing about the Internet is that no one is verifying all the information posted there. Any fool with their own website or blog can post whatever they want. That doesn't mean it's factual." She paused. "The Poe stuff because McBride got me interested in it."

Ducharme made sure the cruise control was on. "All right, let's switch. You drive."

"What?"

"They've placed a tracking device in my gun and probably the truck. If we pull up to the graveyard, they'll know it. So we keep the truck moving and use it to our advantage." He grabbed her left hand and put it on the wheel. "Keep it steady and slide over me."

Evie gave him a look he couldn't quite decipher, then slithered over the central console, onto Ducharme's lap. Once she was in place, he hesitated a moment, feeling the warmth of her body, then he moved out from underneath her, climbing into the passenger seat. He noticed she gave him another strange look, before turning her attention back to the road.

"Cute," Kincannon said, but they both ignored him.

Ducharme took the bullet transmitter out of his coat and placed it in the little tray between the seats. Glancing at the GPS display he ordered: "Take the next exit."

Evie turned off the Interstate.

"You keep going on this road." He traced his finger on the GPS screen. "Do this loop until you see either of us. Steady speed. You ready?" he asked Kincannon.

His partner nodded, serious now, holding up the sniper rifle. Ducharme climbed between the seats to the rear and opened another one of the cases, pulling out a thermal scope. He grabbed the MP-5 with suppressor. He made sure there was a round in the chamber. Then he mounted the scope on top of the sub-machinegun. He slid the MP-5 inside his black coat and secured it there. "Slow down so we hit this light ahead," he ordered.

The light turned yellow, then red. Evie stopped the Blazer.

"See you soon," Ducharme said as he opened the door and stepped out as Kincannon exited the other side.

* * *

Lily stared at the stone base of Poe's monument, where she'd cleared away the snow. The worn brick covering the ground around it showed no sign of having been disturbed since it had originally been put down.

On one side of the monument was a metal plaque, inset into the stone. Lily ran her fingers across the metal, noting how it had been placed. There was chipping around the edge, as if someone had tried to remove it. Or perhaps someone *had* removed it, she thought. She abruptly turned and walked through the gate to her van, opening the rear and grabbing her backpack full of gear, including a crowbar.

* * *

In the passenger seat of the surveillance car, Burns took out his knife and an apple to ease his frustration.

"What are they doing?" Turnbull asked, watching the small red dot representing the bug, continue in a large circle for the second time. "Why don't they go to the cemetery?" He fiddled with the controls for the GPS tracker. The red changed to green. "Ducharme's still in the vehicle."

"The bullet transmitter is still in the vehicle," Burns corrected. "Don't confuse the two. I think we should go directly to the—"

"What you think isn't important," Turnbull snapped. "I have an operative at the cemetery already. And a quick reaction force in the area securing the perimeter."

Burns looked up. They were parked a half-mile from the cemetery, engine idling, the heater turned up. "Why is your operative already at the cemetery?"

"To check it out." Turnbull gave yet another vague answer.

"Who, exactly, is your operative?" Burns flicked open the switchblade.

"Classified."

"I'm a Special Agent with a lot of time in grade."

"Don't remind of things I already know."

"We are after the killer, right?" Burns asked. "And Ducharme and Evie have solid alibis. Do you think the killer—"

"The killer is looking for something," Turnbull said. "Ducharme and Evie are following the clues and we're following them. Sooner or later something will happen."

"Not much of a plan," Burns noted.

"Works for me and you work for me," Turnbull said.

Burns began to peel the apple. "You're the boss."

* * *

Ducharme paused a block away from Westminster Hall, sliding into the darker shadows of a storefront entrance, Kincannon at his side. Ducharme pulled the MP-5 out and turned on the thermal scope. He surveyed the area surrounding the church and cemetery. There were no hot vehicles parked in the area, so he began to scan the buildings overlooking the cemetery.

Within twenty seconds he spotted a watcher. A red form was kneeling among a cluster of stacked chairs at an outdoor café across the street from the cemetery. The red form had the darker outline of a sub-machinegun in its hands.

"Rooftops are clear," Kincannon reported, his eye to the thermal sight on the sniper rifle.

"I've got one watcher in front of that café," he replied. *So, Burns was on top of things*, Ducharme thought.

Kincannon shifted the rifle and looked. "I got him."

"I don't want to kill anyone," Ducharme said.

"Right," Kincannon said dryly. "The guns are just for show."

"They'll be wearing body armor," Ducharme pointed out. "If you have to shoot, do it center of mass. They'll hurt, but they won't be dead. They're on our side, after all."

"You sure about that?" Kincannon said.

Ducharme pointed up. "You take high. I'm going back and through that café."

"Roger that."

Ducharme paused, knowing Kincannon. "No killing."

Kincannon stared at him blankly for a second, then reluctantly nodded. "Roger that."

Knowing Kincannon, Ducharme reached out and put a hand on the Sergeant Major's shoulder. "Seriously."

Kincannon gave a lopsided grin. "No killing, Colonel. Except for *her*."

Ducharme went around the block and into an alley. He picked the lock in the rear of the café. He made his way to the front and peered through the glass. The man was still there, intently watching the cemetery and the street. He was dressed in body armor, a black SWAT jumpsuit and wore a black balaclava over his head, and night vision goggles. Not a single inch of flesh was exposed—he might as well have been a robot, Ducharme thought.

Ducharme quietly unlocked the front door. The man started to turn, and Ducharme smacked the barrel of the MP-5 against the man's temple. He dropped like a stone. Ducharme quickly ripped off the man's body armor. He paused when he saw a red trident patch velcroed on the man's jumpsuit, just above the breast pocket. TriOp-- *A fucking contractor, not FBI.* Ducharme ripped off the patch and stuck it in his pocket. He put the armor and balaclava on. He slid the night vision goggles over his eyes.

Ducharme pulled out two sets of flex cuffs and secured the unconscious man's wrists and ankles. Then he pulled the earpiece out of the man's ear and removed the radio. Ducharme pressed the earpiece into his right ear. He opened the man's sub-machinegun and took the bolt out, putting it in his own pocket. Then he dragged the body into the café and hid it behind the counter.

Low and fast, Ducharme ran across the road to the brick and iron grate fence that surrounded Westminster. He climbed the fence and dropped lightly to the snow-covered ground on the other side. Gravestones and leafless trees surrounded him. He took a step forward, but paused when he heard the sound of metal hitting stone echo through the cemetery. Evie had been right—the killer was on the other side of the church at the wrong grave.

The earpiece came alive with a crackle. "All units, check in."

"Sierra One. Wolf."

There was a moment of silence, then: "Sierra Two. Fox."

The silence lasted a bit longer, and then the first voice spoke again. "Sierra Three. Check in."

Silence. Ducharme knew he had Sierra Three's radio, but he didn't know what the man's code word was. These were not run of the mill contractors to be operating like this. Probably all former special operations. Opting for the bigger paycheck as a mercenary.

"Sierra Three. Check in."

Ducharme saw a stone with a rounded top to his right. He went to it. A raven was carved in the semi-circle below the top. And as Evie had said, etched into the stone arc were the words: *Quoth the Raven Nevermore.*

Ducharme knelt in the snow and read what was written below the arc and raven:

> *Original Burial Place of*
> *Edgar Allan Poe*
> *From October 9, 1849*
> *Until November 17, 1875*
> *Mrs. Maria Clemm, his mother-in-law,*
> *Lies upon his right and Virginia Poe,*
> *His wife, upon his left. Under the*
> *Monument erected to him in this cemetery.*

Ducharme wiped snow away from the ground in front of the marker, uncovering leaves and dirt. He stared at it carefully. He noted that where the front of the stone met the ground, last fall's leaves had been disturbed.

There was another clang of metal on stone.

"Sierra Seven, check on Three."

"This is Seven. Roger."

Ducharme drew his knife and dug into the semi-frozen ground. He hit something solid just a few inches down. He scraped away and uncovered an object wrapped in black plastic. He pulled it out and tucked it away in one of the pouches on the body armor. He heard the metal on stone once more echoing around the church from the front of the cemetery.

"This is Seven. Three is not in position."

"All units close in. Close in."

Ducharme ran toward the church, tucking the stock of the MP-5 into his shoulder. As he rounded the corner, he saw a short figure in a long black cape, head covered with a hood, and a pickaxe in her hands, chipping away at the front of the Poe Memorial.

Ducharme fired, double-tapping two head shots into the center of the hood, the only sound the soft explosion of gases through the baffles of the suppressor and the bolt moving back and forth inside the gun. She slammed into the Memorial and slid to the ground.

Ducharme rushed forward. He kicked the pick out of her hand and knelt on her chest, pushing her hard onto the bricks. She squirmed underneath him, unbelievably still alive. He shoved her hood back, expecting to see blood and brains. He blinked as he stared into her eyes, which were glaring back at him. "Who are you?" he demanded.

He noted a medallion on her cloak and he ripped it free, feeling the heaviness of the bulletproof fabric it was pinned to. He lined up the MP-5 right between those pits of darkness and his finger was sliding onto the trigger when he got slammed hard in the back, twice in succession, knocking his aim off.

The body armor took the impact as he dove forward. He continued with the momentum, rolling behind the Poe Monument, coming up to one knee, weapon at the ready, as more rounds hit the marker, sending stone splinters flying and causing him to duck for a moment. Ducharme fired center of mass at Two, hitting him in the body armor and knocking him to the ground, a gasp of pain echoing over the radio. He turned his eyes back to the monument and cursed when he saw the killer was gone, scurrying away into the darkness of the cemetery.

"Report?" The voice was calm, but Ducharme knew whoever was in charge of the containment team had lost track of what was going on. It was a window of opportunity, one that would shut quickly.

He staggered to his feet, every breath hurting, and ran back the way he had come, his mind swirling. Why hadn't the contractors moved on the killer in the front of the cemetery right away—they had to have seen her arrive? He climbed over the fence and saw an armed man dressed in black—Seven—standing in the street about twenty feet away, weapon at the ready. Ducharme pointed at his ear and then slashed his hand across his throat, indicating his radio was out of order.

Seven lowered his gun just as Kincannon, from his overlook position, fired twice into the man's body armor, taking the guard down.

It worked.

For the moment.

As Ducharme passed the guard, the man did a leg sweep from his prone position, knocking Ducharme to the ground. Ducharme rolled and sprang to his feet, just as the guard did. Instinct took over. Ducharme feinted a butt strike with the sub-machinegun, and as the guard reacted, lashed out with a sidekick to the front of the guard's right knee. The joint snapped back with an audible crunch, and the man screamed, collapsing to the ground in agony.

Ducharme sprinted away toward the rendezvous point.

* * *

"Report?" Turnbull had the radio handset in his hand.

"Doesn't sound too good," Burns calmly said, popping a piece of apple into his mouth, as a second voice cried out in pain over the radio. *Clusterfuck*, he thought. Sometimes it was nice not to be the boss.

"This is Five. Two and Seven have been hit. Three still missing. No sign of the intruder."

"Interesting," Turnbull said, not keying the radio.

"'Interesting'?" Burns looked over. "You've got two agents wounded and you lost the killer. You had her and you let her break your perimeter."

"The killer didn't shoot my men," Turnbull said. "If she did, they'd be dead."

"How do you know that?" Burns demanded. "Who did?"

Turnbull started the engine. "I told you Ducharme was a dangerous man. And resourceful. But he follows rules. That's his flaw."

* * *

Headlights led the way around the corner, and Ducharme ripped off the night vision goggles and removed the balaclava as the Blazer pulled up. He opened the passenger door and jumped inside as Kincannon piled in the back seat.

"Drive," Ducharme ordered.

"Which way?" Evie asked.

"Get back on I-ninety-five and head north." Ducharme pulled open the Velcro straps on the body armor and gingerly removed it. He tossed it onto the back seat and hunched his shoulders, feeling the bruises.

"What's wrong?" Evie asked.

"I got shot."

"*What?*" Evie was startled. Finally.

"I got shot in the back. Don't worry, the bullets didn't penetrate. Just going to be sore for a couple of days."

"Speaking from experience."

"Yes. And you were correct about the killer going to the wrong grave. She was at the Monument."

"What happened?" Evie asked.

"I hit her twice, head shots, but it didn't seem to have much effect," Ducharme said. "She was wearing a cloak with a hood. Had to be made from L.A.—Liquid Armor."

Kincannon whistled, finally impressed by something.

Evie looked confused. "Never heard of it."

"Something you don't know," Ducharme said. "They take a shear thickening fluid and soak thin layers of Kevlar with it, then stitch them together to make a thicker garment. It stays flexible until there's an impact, where it instantly becomes rigid. Cutting-edge technology. So cutting-edge, even the FBI and the Army—except Delta Force—don't have it yet. That, combined with my rounds being subsonic, saved her life."

"Lucky her," Evie said.

"She won't stay lucky," Ducharme said.

"Should have double-tapped her right between the eyes," Evie said.

"I was about to when I got shot," Ducharme said. "Sorry to let you down."

"Now, kids," Kincannon said from the back seat. "Play nice."

There was a short silence before Evie spoke. "Sorry."

"About?" Ducharme was stretching his back. "My bullets?"

"That you didn't get her. And that you were shot."

"I'll get her. We'll meet again."

Evie accelerated, glancing at the GPS display. "What did you find?"

"First thing is those guys weren't FBI." He pulled out the patch. "TriOps—an elite security contracting company."

"Fucking merks," Kincannon took the patch and crumpled it.

"And I'm not sure whether they were there to stop the killer or help her," Ducharme added. "They never made a move on her, even though they had the place surrounded."

"This is not good," Kincannon said. "Wheels within wheels."

"What about disks?" Evie asked.

Ducharme reached back to the vest and pulled out the packet. He cut open the plastic wrapping. "Six disks. Numbered two through seven."

Evie nodded. "That means McBride had seven all together. LaGrange probably had seven. That leaves twelve of the original twenty-six. Probably broken in half. Six each to two more people. Where would General LaGrange have put his other six?"

"How did you figure all that?" Ducharme asked.

"It's logical."

"It's an assumption."

"While you were running around, I've been thinking. If it were just McBride and LaGrange, there would have been twelve disks at Poe's grave. There were six. Project it. With a little bit of logic. Don't hurt yourself while doing so."

Ducharme considered it, trying to ignore the light sarcasm. "Then there're probably two more bodies somewhere and two more idiots like us running around blind with a single disk."

"They might not be dead yet," Evie argued, which earned a snort from Kincannon.

"If not, they will be soon," Ducharme said.

"Unless we save them," Evie argued.

"How?" Ducharme asked. "We don't know who they are. I think that's the reason the killer tortured McBride and LaGrange—besides trying to find out where the disks were. I also got this off the killer." Ducharme showed her the medallion. He saw a flash of recognition in her eyes, but she said nothing. It poked the beast inside of him, but he brought it under control. With difficulty.

They drove in silence for a while.

Evie turned onto the ramp for I-95. "Where are we going?"

"You figured out where McBride's disks were," Ducharme said. "I've got an idea where LaGrange's are."

"Where?"

"How many points?" Ducharme asked Kincannon.

"Depends if you're right or not," Kincannon warned. "If you are, it pretty much evens out the Poe grave thing."

"Smart asses," Evie said. "What about the owners of the other disks?"

"If you can figure out who they are," Ducharme said, "we'll give them a call and warn them. Otherwise, we go after what we can. The killer came after the disks first, so maybe they have a chance." *Not much of one,* Ducharme thought as he stretched his sore back out.

"So where are we going?" Evie asked.

"Another grave."

13 APRIL 1865

Abraham Lincoln was tired to his core, and had told his secretary he would not be seeing any more visitors today. He sat in his office, eyes closed, hoping the headache that had troubled him all day would go away. He should be rejoicing, partaking in the fruits of a bitterly won victory.

Just ten days previously, Richmond had fallen. Then four days ago, Lee had surrendered his Army of Northern Virginia. The whereabouts of Jeff Davis and the remnants of the Confederate government were unknown, but there was no doubt they were in full flight.

The Civil War was over.

At a cost Lincoln could hardly bear to contemplate. Ever since the rebels had fired on Fort Sumter, four years and one day ago, the telegraph wires had brought the grim numbers. Over a quarter million Union soldiers dead. No one knew how many Southerners, but given Grant and Sherman's ruthlessness the past year, Lincoln had no doubt the Confederate losses were about the same.

What scared him, kept him awake at nights and caused his current headache, was realizing that a larger job loomed—mending a broken country. One could win a war of arms, but it was the hearts and minds that concerned Lincoln. There was much bitterness and anger on both sides, and he knew he would have to walk a narrow and treacherous path to bring the country together.

He'd laid the groundwork years ago when he assembled his first cabinet: what some had dubbed 'the cabinet of rivals.' He'd tapped three men, opponents for the Republican nomination, and bitter enemies: William Seward, Salmon Chase and Edward Bates to fill positions in his administration as Secretary of State, Secretary of the Treasury and Attorney General, respectively. The move had shocked everyone in Washington, including the three men. They'd demurred initially, and Lincoln recognized in them the same disdain others in the Capitol had for his rustic background and lack of political experience, especially since he'd been sent packing from Washington after only one term in Congress.

Lincoln knew, though, that bringing the country together after four years of war was going to take much more than bringing respect and cooperation from three such strong egos. He also knew a few of the men were Cincinnatians, a price he had been willing to pay to keep the country together.

Lincoln heard the private door to the Oval Office open. There were only five people who were allowed to come through that door. He hoped it was Mary, but the heavy clump of boots informed him the hope was in vain. More problems.

He opened his eyes and relaxed slightly. The mighty Ulysses. Still glowing from the surrender at Appomattox. As always, Grant held out a cigar as he settled into the seat across the desk from Lincoln.

"No, thank you, General," Lincoln said, as always.

"The city is alive, President," Grant said. "You should go out and pick up some of the energy. Bask in the glow of victory."

Lincoln grimaced. "Basking is not my forte." Grant had two modes: in battle and energized, or morose and drunk. The drinking had been a large issue, but Lincoln took results wherever he could find them. However, it was hard to tell which mode the General was in this evening. Lincoln could smell the alcohol, but Grant appeared strangely animated. Victory could do that, Lincoln supposed.

Grant fiddled with his cigar, seemingly uncertain, something Lincoln had never seen in the man. His decisiveness had been his greatest attribute. "Is there something amiss?" Lincoln asked.

"Sir—" Grant began, but halted.

"Go on," Lincoln said, feeling his heart sink, knowing this was to be another burden of some sort.

"There was a meeting earlier today," Grant said. "I met with the Chair and the Philosophers."

Lincoln stiffened. "And?"

"They are very concerned." Grant had his eyes downcast. "The war is over. Of that there is no doubt." Grant lifted his dark gaze, meeting Lincoln's eyes. "I told them to wait. To let things settle down. But they wanted me to talk to you."

Lincoln knew what Grant was talking about, but he still felt a surge of anger. So soon. He had not expected this so soon. "I did not seek power for glory or riches. You know that better than most. I took the steps I did for the Union. And I didn't hide them."

Lincoln knew he had done many things in violation of his oath of office and the Constitution. He'd unilaterally expanded the military; suspended habeus corpus; proclaimed martial law; had citizens arrested; seized property; censored newspapers; and, perhaps most galling to many, issued the Emancipation Proclamation. All without consulting Congress. He imagined old Polk would be laughing heartily if he could have seen the events of the last four years.

"I understand that, Mister President," Grant said. "That's why I have gotten the Chair to keep the Allegiance in hiding. I told him it would not be needed. Not now, nor *in the future. Once peace has taken hold, I am sure we will be back to where we were before the war.*"

It will never be the same, Lincoln thought, but did not say. He pressed a long finger against his temple, trying to calm the pounding in his head. "*You are quite correct. The Allegiance will not be needed. I will relinquish all those extra powers I have assumed in the name of the emergency as soon as the country returns to normalcy.*"

"*And the Cincinnatians?*"

"*They too will be in check. I needed their support for the war, but not any longer.*"

Grant heaved a sigh of relief. "*Very good, sir. I will tell the Chair.*" Grant stood to depart.

"*General.*"

Grant turned. "*Yes, sir?*"

"*Remember this meeting. I once walked into this room with the Allegiance years ago. You just walked in with the threat of the Allegiance. Some day if you sit in this room, remember what happened, and remember the dangers of the power of this office and of the Cincinnatians.*"

Grant removed the cigar from his mouth and nodded. "*I will, Mister President.*"

"*Very good.*" Lincoln remembered something. "*Mary wants to go to the theater tomorrow night. Would you and Missus Grant like to join us?*"

"*I will consult with her, but I see no reason why we would not.*" Grant turned for the door.

"*Very good,*" Lincoln said.

Grant paused as he opened the door. "*What theater, sir?*"

"*The Ford Theater.*"

CHAPTER NINE

Burns stared at the Poe Monument. Someone had chipped away at the front of the Monument trying to remove the metal plaque of the poet's image. He could sense Turnbull behind him and, every once in a while, hear the senior agent whisper something into his phone. The two wounded personnel had given brief statements and then been carted away in un-marked ambulances that never turned on their lights or sirens. The cemetery had been quickly swept, and it was clear. One thing was clear to Burns—the men surrounding the cemetery were not FBI. He'd worn the badge long enough to tell his own.

"Well?" Turnbull said, putting away his satphone. "What have you got, Mister Profiler?"

"Not much to profile on," Burns said, "but I've been on the job long enough to read a crime scene."

"And?" Turnbull glanced at his watch.

"The killer was here, trying to get this plaque off. Ducharme came from around the back, after incapacitating your number Three. By the way, we can assume he found the bullet-transmitter and left it in the Blazer. He and the killer got in a gun battle. Ducharme shot your number Two in the body armor—he meant to disable, not kill. Then he escaped the same way he came in. He ran into your number Seven. His back-up—I'm assuming that would be Sergeant Major Kincannon—hit Seven twice in the back with non-fatal shots. That didn't incapacitate Seven, so Ducharme took out his knee. Pretty effective. Pretty brutal. But non-lethal."

"And?"

Burns walked toward the rear of the cemetery rather than answer, Turnbull reluctantly following. "Whatever they were looking for, I think Ducharme found it back here." He pointed at the disturbed dirt in front of the Poe marker. "While you were getting the area cleared, I called the curator of the Poe

Museum. Woke him out of his deep slumber. Curiously enough, he says there's a slight possibility Poe is actually buried here, not under the monument out front. I could tell by the way he said it, that 'slight' actually meant 'strong' possibility, and he was covering the Museum's ass."

"So how did Ducharme know that?" Turnbull mused.

Burns was surprised Turnbull even asked the obvious. "Evie Tolliver." He kicked the dug up dirt with the tip of his shoe. "Don't suppose you want to tell me what he dug up?"

"No."

"You don't give a shit about catching this killer." Burns said it as a statement, not a question.

"The killer is your responsibility," Turnbull replied. "I have others."

Burns spread his hands. "How can I catch her if you keep me sitting in a truck while she—"

Turnbull cut him off. "You can have her when the time is right."

"She's your operative, isn't she?"

"Then I would be part of a murder conspiracy," Turnbull said.

"You didn't answer."

"Of course she's not my operative," Turnbull said.

Burns detected not the slightest bit of sincerity. "How many people have to die before—"

Turnbull cut him off again. "There are much higher priorities right now than a few bodies." Turnbull stepped closer, getting inside Burns's personal space. "Do you believe in defending your country, Agent Burns? Do you believe in defending it by any means necessary?"

"I believe in the law."

"The law only goes so far. Even the Founding Fathers knew that."

"What do you mean?"

"Forget it," Turnbull said.

"I don't know about the killer," Burns said, realizing what he was up against and getting back on task, "but this tells me something about Ducharme."

"And that is?"

"He—and his sidekick, Kincannon—deliberately shot your men—"

"Our men," Turnbull cut in.

"—your men in their vests, even though all their Special Operations training focuses on killing with two headshots. Double-tapping. He doesn't want to kill."

"That means he's weak."

Burns shook his head. "You're underestimating him. Both of them—Tolliver and Ducharme. He's more than capable of killing when he has to. He took out that man's knee because he was acting on instinct, not thinking. The issue is whether he wants to kill. Before, it's always been under the auspices of being a soldier. He's operating outside the normal parameters of what he's used to. He stays out there long enough, he'll adapt. It's what people do."

"It'll be too late," Turnbull said, walking away and punching a number into his satphone.

"Will it?" Burns whispered to himself. "For who?"

* * *

Lily felt her satphone buzz, and checked the screen.

YOU FAILED

She went rigid at the words. She stopped checking where the rounds had hit the hood of her Liquid Armor cloak. She quickly texted her reply.

>>>I STOPPED THEM FROM GETTING THE DISKS<<<

THEY GOT THE DISKS. YOU WERE AT THE WRONG MONUMENT

She shifted in the van's seat. >>>I WAS AT POE'S GRAVE<<<

HE IS BURIED IN THE BACK. DUCHARME IS MOVING NORTH ON I95 WHY?

>>>NO IDEA<<<

She rubbed the side of her skull. The skin was tender and there would be bruises where the bullets had hit the hood. But the bone was intact and there was no blood. She had a bit of headache, but she could deal with that.

DO YOU HAVE LOCATION LAST PHILOSOPHER?

>>>YES<<<

WHERE?

>>>PHILOSOPHICAL HALL PHILADELPHIA<<<

THEIR INNER SANCTUM

Lily was pissed about the lack of intelligence support. If Turnbull knew about Poe's grave, why hadn't he told her? Most likely he hadn't known either until after the fact. Fucking desk jockey.

>>>YES<<<

FIRST. MAKE MEET BWI LONG TERM PARKING SPACE DELTA 42

Lily frowned.

>>>MEET WHO?<<<

CONTRACTORS. PAY THEM

>>>PAY THEM WHAT?<<<

WHAT YOU VALUE. DO IT. DUCHARME IS MINE

The screen went blank.

She pulled up her left sleeve. There were three cuts there, all as badly healed as the ones on her left arm, but longer, almost encircling the entire arm like a bad tattoo. She drew her sword.

The wakishashi was a weapon her grandfather had brought home from World War II as a prize. He'd received a samurai sword and the shorter wakishashi blade as a token of surrender from the Japanese Army General who was part of the delegation that flew to Manila to negotiate the original surrender with MacArthur, which actually ended World War II, two weeks before the more formal ceremony on board the USS *Missouri* in Tokyo Bay.

Naturally, the samurai sword had gone to Lily's younger brother, even though he had shown little interest in things military. Her father had dealt her the wakishashi very reluctantly as an heirloom upon her graduation from the Air Force Academy. She imagined the samurai sword was gathering dust somewhere in her banker brother's attic. She planned on visiting her brother soon and claiming the sword. As soon as this mission was over. It would be an enjoyable visit. For her. Not him.

She pressed the blade against her skin, just below the last cut, slicing in. She rotated the blade as far as she could around the arm. Blood flowed, but she ignored it. She lowered the sleeve and went to the computer set on the bench against one wall, taking the seat bolted to the floor in front of it.

"Blood for blood," she whispered.

* * *

"They're still tracking us," Evie said.

Ducharme glanced over from the driver's seat as they rolled up I-95. "Are you asking or telling me something I already know?"

"What's your problem?" Evie asked.

"My problem," he told her, "is I'm fumbling around in the dark, here."

Evie stared at him. "Your uncle was murdered. My friend was murdered."

"And we're off on a half-ass wild goose chase after wooden disks two hundred years old," Ducharme said. His head was pounding, his mind sliding into the dark pool, the beast snarling and grumbling.

"Your logic is backward."

Ducharme tightened his jaw for a second. "What the hell do you mean?"

"Easy, Duke," Kincannon said in a low voice.

Evie spoke. "If someone is willing to kill to get them, then it's not a wild goose chase as you put it. The disks are obviously important just from that simple fact, *and* because your Uncle and my friend died to protect their whereabouts. We'll know why when we read the message encoded onto the Jefferson Cipher."

"What if it just says 'congratulations?'" Kincannon asked.

"It will be twenty-six letters long," Evie said. "You want my best guess what this is about?"

"I want something." Ducharme hit the wheel with his fist. "I want to know why my uncle died. Why didn't those contractors move in on the killer even though they had that graveyard under surveillance?"

"Wheels within wheels, as the Sergeant Major noted," Evie said.

Kincannon cleared his throat. "Perhaps the government itself is doing it."

"You guys are the government," Evie said.

"Not *that* government," Kincannon said. "The government is not this monolithic organization that most people think it is."

"Watch the big words," Evie said.

"Funny woman," Kincannon threw back.

"I understand compartmentalization in the government," Evie said. "Hell, half the time people at Langley didn't know what the person in the next cubicle was up to. But that's information, not power. There's a *they* out there. People in the shadows. Pulling strings."

"What exactly are *they* behind?" Ducharme demanded, as he glanced in the rearview mirror to see if they were being followed. "And who are *they*? My first team sergeant had a saying: 'There's no *we* and *they*, until *they* fuck up.'"

"Sounds like a smart man," Evie said.

Ducharme nodded, feeling the beast settle down. "He also said there were two types of soldiers."

Evie bit. "And they are?"

"The steely-eyed killer and the beady-eyed minion. And it's hard at first glance to tell them apart."

"Now me," Kincannon threw in, "I'm neither. I'm a free spirit. I've been everywhere but the electric chair, seen everything but the wind."

Evie rolled her eyes. "Are you two done?" She held out her hand. "Let me see that medallion."

Ducharme fished it out of his pocket and gave it to her. The medallion was shaped like an eagle with an image engraved in the center of two men.

"This is *they*," Evie said.

"What?" Ducharme asked as Kincannon said: "Who?"

"Ever hear of the Society of the Cincinnati?" Evie said.

"No," Ducharme said. "Should I have? Did I miss something important in college?"

"You didn't go to a real college," Kincannon chided. "Hudson High, remember?"

"Thanks for the reminder," Ducharme said. "The Society of the Cincinnati?"

"Named after the town?" Kincannon suggested.

"The town was named after it." Evie paused. "'*Omnia relinquit servare remplublican*: Roughly translated as: *He abandons everything to serve the Republic.*' Though they really should have used the imperfect subjunctive for the verb."

"Of course," Kincannon muttered. "Everyone knows that."

"What the hell are you talking about?" Ducharme demanded.

"That's the motto of the Society of the Cincinnati. Its abbreviated version is engraved here on the medallion." Evie pointed. "The Society was named after Lucius Quinctius Cincinnattus, a Roman consul who twice became dictator in order to save Rome from its enemies. He was called forth in times of crisis to defend Rome, and when the crisis was over, he went back to his farm. Supposedly," she added. "That's his image in the center being given his sword by the Roman Senators and on the other side—" she turned it—"is an image of him at his plow being crowned by 'fame.' Subtle, don't you think?

"And yes, you should have learned about it. Most especially going to Hudson High as you put it, because military men invented the Society. The Society of the Cincinnati is the oldest and most powerful organization in the country, although few have ever heard of it. Its founding pre-dates the Constitution. In seventeen eighty-three, General Henry Knox, the head of Washington's artillery, organized the first meeting of the Society at the Verplanck House near Newburgh, New York, not far from your West Point. George Washington was voted in as the first President of the Society. Membership was limited to those officers who had served in the Continental Army or the Navy, no less than three years, or who had been killed in the line of duty."

"Fat lot of good it did for the dead guys," Kincannon said. "What did they do—prop them up in their chairs?"

"It was good for their heirs," Evie said. "Subsequent membership requires an ancestor who meets those requirements."

"A good old boys' club," Ducharme said.

"An elitist club maintained through primogeniture," Evie said.

In the rearview mirror, Kincannon rolled his eyes.

"Through what?" Ducharme rubbed the back of his skull, which was starting to pound. "Pretend I'm a simple soldier and keep the language easy."

"I think you're anything but simple," Evie said.

"You don't know me."

"True," Evie said, staring at him. "I don't. And you don't know me even though you tried."

"No shit," Ducharme said. "Except I do know you have a theory about love."

"Primo-whatever-the-fuck?" Kincannon demanded from the back seat.

"Primogeniture is inheritance," Evie said. "Simply being born to the right people—aka those killed in combat during the Revolution—thus requiring no effort, skill or qualities of the individual. Benjamin Franklin and Thomas Jefferson vehemently opposed this. They felt it was establishing a 'noble order' in a country that had just revolted against such a thing."

"So if this group is so powerful, how come I've never heard of this Society of Cincinnati?" Ducharme asked.

"That's the way they like it, although with a little effort anyone can look them up. You can find out about them on Wikipedia. The entry there makes the group sound pretty tame. However, the inner sanctum of the Society has been working from behind the scenes, out of the face of public scrutiny, since its founding. Although Knox organized the first meeting, Alexander Hamilton chaired it and in essence was the force behind it."

"What does the Jefferson Cipher have to do with this Cincinnati group?" Ducharme asked.

"Bear with me," Evie said. "What do you know of the founding of our country?"

"What I was taught in history courses." Ducharme checked the road ahead and then the rearview mirror once more, knowing that the tail was probably just out of sight, tracking them from a transmitter secreted somewhere on the vehicle and the false bullet. The issue of the tracking devices was something he still hadn't made a decision about. "I doubt my memory equals yours."

Evie ignored the comment. "Our two party system came out of the early conflicts between those who were known as the Federalists—led by Alexander Hamilton—and the anti-Federalists, led by Jefferson.

"The Federalists wanted power consolidated with the national government and the ruling class to hold most of it. They believed the first federal government we had, formed under the Articles of Confederation, was much too weak. Their main goals were to move power to the Federal level, increase protectionist barriers, collect taxes and build up the military."

"Sounds familiar," Kincannon dryly remarked.

Evie nodded. "The Federalists also wanted to limit protest, both among the press and civilians, against a society with a very unequal distribution of wealth and property."

"You sure you're not talking about the present?" Kincannon asked.

"That's my point," Evie said. "Most people haven't learned from history even though it repeats itself over and over again. The battle between the ideologies of the Federalists and the anti-Federalists continues unabated. The details change, but the essence is the same—the handful of rich and powerful against the rest of the people. The desire of the wealthy for even more wealth, no matter what it costs everyone else. Besides being unfair, it's a doomed philosophy because the mass of people makes the country function, not just the chosen few. When the gap between the ordinary person and the rich gets too wide, a country is doomed. The Romans learned that the hard way."

Ducharme was driving them across the high bridges that arched over the Susquehanna River. Delaware was not far ahead.

Evie's voice became low and steady, almost matching the rhythm of the tires on the highway. "Back then, the Federalists were greatly helped by the spin they put on the response to Shays' Rebellion in seventeen eighty-six."

"Never heard of it," Kincannon said.

"History." Evie shook her head. "Shays' Rebellion was an armed insurrection by farmers in western Massachusetts who were getting crushed by mounting debt as the lingering cost of the Revolutionary War was being passed down to them."

Kincannon snorted. "Sounds a bit like the real estate crash and the mortgage emergency and the growing national debt from the War on Terror. I know people, good people, military people, who've lost their savings and their houses."

"It was just as nasty back then," Evie said. "The farmers in Western Massachusetts had a barter system and didn't use cash. The tax collectors— political appointees—knowing that, demanded cash. So speculators from Boston went to the western part of the state and bought land at pennies on the dollar. A nice scam. A conspiracy between the speculators and the tax collectors, who received lucrative kickbacks. Some of the farmers revolted. The federal government, with practically no standing army, couldn't deal with the revolt, and Massachusetts was forced to hire mercenaries to put it down."

Ducharme thought of all the former soldiers he knew who were now doing 'contract' work for the government in Iraq, Afghanistan and other places: in essence, mercenaries, although no one uttered the word publicly. 'Security contractors' was the politically correct phrase, like the TriOp personnel they had just encountered. A chilling thought: *Where was the loyalty?*

"What's interesting," Evie said, "is Jefferson's response to the rebellion. He thought it was a *good* thing. The saying on my cigarette case is part of his response. He prefaced it with: 'God forbid we should ever be twenty years without such a rebellion.' Jefferson felt the government needed to fix the problems that caused the rebellion.

"Of course, the Federalists didn't feel that way. They seized on the failure of the national government to crush the rebellion—rather than focus on the causes of the revolt—to push to replace the weak Articles of Confederation with a stronger Federal government.

"The Federalists succeeded in defeating the rebellion and consolidating power at the Federal level, of course, but the anti-Federalists, who wanted powers devolved to the states, and people to be relatively equal, pushed back to get a Bill of Rights. Thus the two building blocks of our government, the Constitution and the Bill of Rights, were a compromise between these two parties. The Constitution was ratified in seventeen eighty-seven, and the Bill of Rights in seventeen ninety-one."

"Thanks for the history lesson." Ducharme's head was pounding. "What does that have to do with things today?"

"When I say Federalists, think the Society of the Cincinnati," Evie said. "Our current enemy. And it's still around. Even has its headquarters in Central DC with a plaque right outside that anybody walking by can read. Hell, you can take a tour of part of their building, which I've done. A bunch of Presidents were awarded honorary memberships—those whose policies the Society approved of." She dangled the medallion. "George Washington was given one of these encrusted in diamonds as the first President General of the Society. Each succeeding President General wears it. The Society wasn't so un-noticed when it was first established. In fact, it was seen by Jefferson and Franklin as a major threat to the fledgling Republic of the United States."

"So you think this Society of Cincinnati is behind the killings?"

"Obviously, since you took the medallion off the killer. This is bronze, which means she's an apprentice to the Society. Probably earning her way in to full membership through blood, although as far as I know, there has never been a full female member of the Society of Cincinnati."

"If this Society is out in the open," Ducharme said, "there must be a secret inner core that's really running things."

Evie nodded. "I've heard that whoever currently wears the diamond medallion calls himself Lucius. And that the American chapter has made connections with foreign organizations like it. Sort of a secret society Mafia, except they control most of the world's wealth."

"So this Lucius fellow is behind the killings?" Kincannon asked.

"I would imagine," Evie said. "But it's all so shrouded in secrecy—even when I was with the Agency, I knew there was a whole other playing field out there. And if you study history, you realize there are always people in the shadows who have the real power."

"How do you know all this arcane stuff?" Ducharme asked.

"I read. A lot," Evie said. "And I remember what I read."

"Everything?" Ducharme said. "Like a photographic memory?"

Evie shook her head. "Not photographic. It's called Eidetic Memory. Eidetic comes from the Greek word eidos, which means form or image. The written language has a form to it. Words are placed in sentences in a certain way. Because of the patterns, I can remember what I read."

"I don't understand," Ducharme said.

Evie thought for a second. "OK. Scientists have found that chess masters who have eidetic memory can recall thousands upon thousands of board layouts. However, if the pieces are put on the board in a nonsensical or impossible layout, for example a friendly pawn in the first row, they can't remember the layout. So it's the form they remember first, not the location of the individual pieces, even though once they remember the form, they can remember the location of every single piece. I remember the substance of everything I read and its context in terms of the larger tapestry of history, not every individual word unless I choose to focus on it, such as sayings and quotes that I consider of significance. I put all the substance into patterns. Many of these patterns have connections in one way or another. For me, the greatest pattern is history through reading. Everything is connected in some way in history and thus in my brain."

"And you have a great memory, right?" Kincannon asked with a grin.

Evie nodded. Ducharme could almost swear she was blushing. "I do have a pretty good memory."

"Any other special skills we should know of?" Kincannon asked.

"I have a black belt in hapkido."

"Can you cook?" Kincannon asked.

"I can boil water."

Kincannon laughed. "Damn. If you could cook, I'd propose right now."

Ducharme sighed. "Great. 'Of all the gin joints in the world—'"

"It wasn't coincidence," Evie said.

"No. It wasn't." Ducharme moved his hand from the back of his head to where the bullets had hit his back. "We'll get her."

"What about those who are pulling her strings?" Evie asked.

They drove on in silence.

CHAPTER TEN

Lily walked through the long-term parking at Baltimore-Washington International, the only sound the click of her boot heels on the pavement. This time of the morning, there wasn't even the roar of aircraft taking off or landing. A dead zone.

She smiled and pulled back the hood on her cloak, revealing her golden hair to the sputtering arc lights illuminating the lot. She had a metal briefcase in her left hand. She paused when she heard whistling coming from somewhere ahead.

"Hello?" she called out in what she hoped was a frightened voice. It was a stretch for her.

The whistling was circling to her right. She took a step back and clutched the briefcase to her chest. "Hello? Mister Turnbull sent me."

There was silence. Then a voice with an Irish brogue spoke from behind her: "Evening, lass."

Lily turned, stumbling on her heels as she did so. "You startled me!" She held the briefcase out. "Here. This is yours."

The man walked closer. He was short and wiry, barely taller than her.

"Now why would our Mister Turnbull send such a pretty thing to make delivery on such an ugly thing?"

"I just do what he tells me," Lily said. He was about five meters away, his right hand in the pocket of his jacket, a lit cigarette in his left. He took a few steps closer, then paused, taking a drag.

"You do everything he tells you, lass?"

Lily considered the question, torn between telling the truth and lying to complete the mission. There had been an honor code at the Academy. Admiral Groves was still on her mind. She chose neither. "I have your payment." She put the briefcase on the ground and took two steps back from it.

"Payment for what?" the man asked, taking two steps forward.

"I have no idea, nor do I wish to know," Lily said. "Good evening, sir." She turned around and began walking away.

"Now hold on there, lass."

Lily paused. She smiled, then wiped it away as she turned. The man was next to the case, but had yet to pick it up.

"No need for you to rush away, is there?"

"I just do what I'm told," Lily said.

The man laughed. "Do you now? Do you indeed?"

Lily heard movement to her right, where a large black van was parked. "You've been paid."

"But why are they paying us when we didn't complete the job?" the man asked.

"Perhaps your services were no longer needed."

The man laughed. "Now, lass. I'm not stupid. I've been in this business a long time. I'd be willing to bet the pot at the end of the rainbow that what is supposedly in this briefcase is not gold, but either explosives or a tracking transmitter."

Lily shrugged, feeling the weight of the armor cloak on her shoulders. "I have no idea. I just do what I'm told."

"You keep saying that." The man took something out of his pocket, put it next to the briefcase and began backing up. "So why don't you do what I tell you and come over here and open the case. Then, if you're still able, run that detector over it."

Lily walked forward, knelt next to the case, flipped the latches and opened it. Bundles of money were packed tightly inside. She took the detector, turned it on, and ran it over the money. The bright light remained green. She placed it on top of the money and stood.

"Satisfied?"

The man came walking forward, smiling. "Somewhat."

She heard a van door slide open behind her and footsteps approaching. "I'll be on my way."

"No so fast," a voice from behind said.

Lily slowly turned. A man in Army greens was approaching, a gun held in his hands. Lily recognized a Glock 10mm, semi-automatic. A good gun, but not Army issue. He had gold oak leaves on his shoulders, the same rank Lily had held before her ouster. He stopped four feet from her. Proper training. Out of arms reach, maintaining the advantage the gun gave him.

Lily heard the slight squeak as the briefcase was closed. The major's eyes shifted ever so slightly, looking behind her to his partner, and she sprang into action. As there was the click of the briefcase closing, she had the wakizashi out and slicing. The major's eyes shifted back to her just as the blade slashed through the extra foot of buffer he'd thought he had, and severed gun hand from arm.

She followed the momentum, spinning. The other man was scrambling for the gun in his pocket and she slammed the blade into his upper arm, slicing through so hard, it buried itself inches deep in the side of his chest.

"Jesus, Mary and Joseph!" the man exclaimed in shock.

The Surgeon spun about, cutting the opposite way, taking off his left arm at the same point.

Blood was spurting from both severed limbs.

She didn't pause to admire the view, swirling back to the major. He was on his knees, trying to pry the gun from his dead hand. She ended his efforts by taking his head off with one clean blow.

Lily stepped back, finally appreciating her work as arterial blood spurted from the neck for several moments before the body toppled over. She faced the armless Irishman and imitated his brogue. "Kind of sucks, don't it, lad?" She laughed, feeling the freedom of the kill. She stretched her arms over her head, blood dripping from the blade.

"Ah, fuck, fuck, fuck me," he muttered, staggering, blood pouring.

Lily knew he wouldn't last much longer. She wanted to try something.

She spun into a 360, going down to her knees, putting her shoulders and arms and body into the blade. It went through the first ankle cleanly. She could feel the tug as the steel cut the second, but it was through.

He was down, more blood pouring out of both severed ankles. She stood over him and showed him the blade. "Top quality steel. Not that cheap shit your people put on the *Titanic* that ripped apart when it hit the iceberg. Top of the evening to you, lad."

His face was a mixture of shock and confusion. Lily laughed. She sheathed the sword, picked up the Glock and briefcase, and walked away.

She began whistling.

* * *

Ducharme glanced over at Evie. "Why did Burns kowtow to you? I doubt because you're the Curator of Monticello. Was it because you were in the CIA?"

Her face tightened. "It's because of my ex-husband."

"Who is?" Ducharme pressed.

"He's still in the Agency and has some clout."

"Was he your Rick?" Kincannon asked.

"Yes."

"What happened? Why'd you split? Leave the Agency?"

"Both for the same reason," Evie said. "My father—" she paused, and then continued. "My father was Army. Old school. Went to Vietnam when he was eighteen as a private and never looked back. Got a battlefield commission on his second tour there. Rose through the ranks. Retired thirty-three years later as a three star general, after commanding V-I-I Corps in Germany just before Desert Storm. Actually, he was forced to retire after disagreeing with the plan to invade Iraq."

"Damn," Kincannon said. "That's where I recognized the name. Served under your father a long time ago."

Evie continued. "While he was in, he was gone most of the time. My mother died when I was twelve. Drank herself to death. My father put me in boarding schools near wherever he was stationed." She fell silent after that brief, grim summary.

Ducharme winced as Kincannon pushed. At times the Sergeant Major was a blunt instrument where something more delicate was called for. "And? I don't get the connection with your father and your divorce and leaving the Agency."

"I didn't leave the Agency," Evie said. "They gave me the boot. And when they did, so did Donald." She looked over her shoulder at Kincannon. "My father said the worst moment of his life—and this was a man wounded four times in combat—was the day after he retired and flew back to the States. He got off the plane and there was no one there. Not a soul. You know how the Army fawns over generals. Especially three stars, a Corps Commander in charge of a hundred thousand troops. He got off that plane and he was suddenly a nobody."

She shifted her gaze to Ducharme. "Can you imagine how devastating it was? To be out of something you'd given thirty years to, bled for? And now to realize it all meant nothing in the end. Without the uniform, he didn't exist."

"Happens to everyone," Kincannon observed. Sympathy wasn't his long suit, but Kincannon wasn't one who dwelled on future possibilities, even though he faced the same fate.

"My father lost it. Completely. He turned against everything he'd been committed to. He made speeches against the war—and you have to remember that first one was kind of popular. It just got worse. He ranted. He went crazy. He gave himself a heart attack. He died. Synopsis version," she added, with a glance at Ducharme.

"So what the fuck?" Kincannon said. "What's that have to do with the Agency?"

"My father had enemies—people he'd pissed off—and even with him dead, they went after him. They pulled my top secret Q-clearance. No clearance, I was done at the Agency. I was done at the Agency; Donald was done with me. I was an embarrassment.

"So I went back to college. Got my PhD. Got the job at Monticello, a nice out of the way place for me to work, still a Federal employee, got my health insurance, got a retirement down the line. And that's my story. Satisfied?"

"Not really," Ducharme said.

"Now, now," Kincannon said in his gentlest voice. "And McBride?"

Evie shrugged, but it was a weak attempt to hide her emotions, Ducharme could see. "My mentor. My friend."

"*Do* you know where the thumb drive is that decrypts McBride's computer?" Kincannon asked.

"No," Evie said. "There are a lot of loose ends. I don't quite understand the time delay on that message from LaGrange. You mentioned that it was a quote from Custer's last order."

"Custer's last written order," Ducharme said. "Who knows what the hell he was ordering when they got over-run. Probably *'retreat'* when he crashed on the harsh rocks of reality. He was a lousy officer. Did you know he *twice* shot his own horse in the head while hunting mounted? I mean, what the hell? And while he executed some of his own Seventh Cavalry soldiers for going AWOL, he himself went AWOL when he wanted to see his wife."

"The order," Evie prompted.

So she was the only one who got to go off task and play 'did you know.' "It was an order given by someone who was going to die. I think my uncle knew there was a good chance he was doomed. I'm not sure his will to live was very strong after his son's death." Ducharme took a deep breath, collecting himself. "And he didn't want me there when he was killed. Perhaps he feared for my safety. But he wanted me to know what happened. Or if he hadn't been killed, to meet with me after he rendezvoused with your Mister McBride."

"And now where are we headed?" Evie asked. "Something to do with that order?"

Ducharme nodded. "West Point. To another grave. Of a man who gave an order, not yet knowing he was about to die."

4 MARCH 1905

President Theodore Roosevelt listened to the sounds of revelry from the ballroom with deep satisfaction. He had the people's mandate now. Even though he'd been President for three years, ever since McKinley was struck-down by an assassin in Buffalo in 1901, he'd felt a degree of lame-duck status. He'd held power because of a single bullet, not the will of the people. At least that's what some had whispered. Not swearing his oath of office on a Bible after McKinley expired had also caused great controversy, an oversight he had not repeated earlier today.

"Father."

Roosevelt's shoulders slumped as he heard the familiar voice. He didn't bother to turn. "Yes, Baby Lee?"

"I come bearing greetings," Alice Roosevelt said.

Roosevelt finally turned and faced his daughter. She was his first born, but he had spent little time with her over her twenty years of life. He supposed that had contributed to her independent spirit, to the point where many considered her out of control. Sometimes he regretted abandoning her to relatives after her mother, his wife Alice, died two days after her birth. But on the same day, his own mother had died, and the dual blows had been too much to take. He'd headed west, losing himself on the frontier for several years with his grief.

"From whom?" Roosevelt asked. Sometimes he missed those days, riding with Sheriff Bullock of Deadwood, hunting, ranching and just being out in nature. Almost as much as he missed his first wife. He never used her name and thus he never used his daughter's given name, something he knew irritated her, but he could not bear the pain.

Alice was draped in a silk dress, risqué to say the least. Roosevelt knew better than to say anything to her about it. He'd been asked once by a visitor, after Alice interrupted a meeting in the Oval Office for the third time, whether he could control her. He'd answered truthfully: 'I can either run the country or I can attend to Alice, but I cannot possibly do both.'

"From the American Philosophical Society."

Roosevelt stiffened, focusing on his daughter. "What do those old fools want?"

Alice almost twirled, the silk catching the light. She'd bought enough of it on the recent junket to Japan and China to make a thousand dresses. He did have to admit, though, that she had done well diplomatically, enchanting the Emperor of Japan and the Empress Dowager of China. Of course, she'd also jumped into the ocean liner's swimming pool fully clothed along with some fool congressman. Wherever she went, scandal followed.

"They are not all old fools," Alice said.

"Just tell me what they want so I can get back to the celebrations," Roosevelt said, looking past her to the door leading to the election party.

"Ah, father," Alice said, coming close and looking up at him with soulful eyes. She had inherited her mother's beauty, and sometimes he wondered if that's why he kept his distance from her—the memory was too sharp, the pain too deep. He averted his gaze.

"Yes?"

"I know this is your party, Father," she said. "But really, you'd want to be the bride at every wedding, the corpse at every funeral, and the baby at every christening. You like the attention."

"The old Philosophers," he prodded, trying to get her back on task. Her tongue was as sharp as her wit, and he bore many a scar from both.

"As I said, and you did not hear, being occupied with your own thoughts as always, they are all not so old anymore. In fact, one is quite young. The youngest ever elected Chair."

"What fool did they pick?"

"And not just the youngest," Alice said, with a smile that lit up the room, "but also the first woman."

Roosevelt felt an icy feeling grow in his gut, much as he had felt in Yellowstone the first time he faced a grizzly. "They didn't."

"They did."

Roosevelt closed his eyes and sighed. This was the last thing he would have expected. Which is why, he knew, the guardians of the Allegiance had done it. "What do they— you-- want?" he demanded through gritted teeth.

Alice hopped up and sat on the lid of a grand piano, her legs dangling, exposing too much ankle. "We know you inherited the Spanish-American War after McKinley's untimely departure from this mortal coil. We were not pleased with the 'causus belli' for that war. 'Remember the Maine,' indeed." She peered at her father. "You were under-secretary of the Navy at the time. Perhaps you know something about that event you have not shared with your own daughter?"

"It was a Spanish mine," Roosevelt snapped. "There is nothing more to it."

"A most convenient mine," Alice said. "We sense the long reach of the Cincinnatians." She waved a hand, dismissing that topic. "The Allegiance has only been invoked once and even then, didn't have to be used. Another President was warned. We see a dangerous trend, though. Jefferson, Polk and Lincoln all superseded their authority. Johnson did too, but he got impeached, simpleton that he was. The Cincinnatians have

pushed this country into illegal and unjust war more than once in their desire for an American Empire. Much like the Romans did so long ago."

Alice continued. "But you have to allow those three earlier Presidents their motives. Both Jefferson and Polk saw a threat to our country's commerce: Jefferson not wanting to lose access to New Orleans, and ending up with much more than he could have ever dreamed of in territory; Polk wanting access to San Francisco, and also ending up with much than he too could have ever dreamed of. Lincoln's motivation was to preserve the Union at any cost, although one might see an inherent paradox from the Founding Fathers in that. The Confederacy was, after all, exercising its states' rights to separate from the Union. Something Jefferson would most likely have applauded."

Roosevelt knew this was revenge. For all those years he'd shuttled her from relative to relative. He'd once tried to send her to a very proper school for girls in New York City, and she had sent back a letter promising: 'If you send me, I will humiliate you. I will do something that that will shame you. I tell you I will.'

And now she had done something far, far worse.

"You've won four more years, Father," Alice said. "Congratulations. But we know what you have done and what you want to do. The Philippines. Colombia. Honduras. The Dominican Republic. Cuba. The Canal you want to have built." She laughed, a most pleasant sound, contrasting the words that came from her mouth. "'Speak softly and carry a big stick. You will go far'?"

"What do you want?" Roosevelt finally gave in, facing her directly.

"Jefferson wrote 'Conquest is not in our principles. It is inconsistent with our government.' You seem to take the opposite point of view, Father."

"What do you want?"

"We know you are popular. We know confronting you with the Allegiance would be dangerous for the country. So we offer a compromise. You get four more years. But we want you to publicly promise tonight, this very evening, that you will not run for re-election in nineteen-oh-eight."

Roosevelt took a step back, as if he'd been hit by a bullet. "You joke."

"I'm afraid not, Father. We will confront you if you don't make the promise. It will be a bloody mess, for both you and the country, if the military has to act after you are confronted. You can spend the next four years enjoying your Presidency or defending it."

"A lot can happen in four years," Roosevelt said.

Alice nodded and hopped off the piano. "I know, Father. But I also know you. I told the other Philosophers that if you gave your word, you would keep your word."

A muscle rippled along the side of Roosevelt's jaw.

Alice hooked her arm through his and propelled him toward the door. "Come. Let's have you make the announcement, then join the party." She paused just before the door and looked up at him. "After all, Father, four more years; certainly enough time for you to enjoy the Presidency. And then you can go back to civilian life and enjoy your family. Correct?"

With those last bitter words she shoved open the doors to the waiting crowd, that cheered upon seeing the newly elected President.

CHAPTER ELEVEN

Lieutenant General Atticus Parker (US Air Force, retired) checked his watch once more and drummed his fingers on the arm of his chair. He glanced at the door to his office, then turned his head and looked out the window, where he could see the rear of Independence Hall, a view he found appropriate in the gray of early dawn. "Covering its six," as they used to say when he flew fighters. He was seated in a room in Philosophical Hall on Fifth Street, on the same block as the more famous hall where the Declaration of Independence, the Articles of Confederation and the United States Constitution were all signed. A pretty powerful trifecta of documents. In Parker's opinion, the greatest political writing in the world, albeit a considerable amount of it borrowed by the Founding Fathers from other earlier writers, truth be known.

Philosophical Hall was mostly ignored by tourists, even though it was the only other building besides Independence Hall on Independence Square. Most tourists saw the sign outside and thought it was some sort of place for old men to sit around and chat about esoteric subjects. It was so far off the radar, that for almost a century, the building had been closed to visitors, and no one had registered a complaint. A part of the building had only recently been opened to the public where they could view such wonders as the chair Thomas Jefferson sat in when he wrote the Declaration of Independence, Benjamin Franklin's clock and library chair, and an eclectic gathering of small exhibitions from the collection of the American Philosophical Society, for which the building had been the headquarters for over two centuries. Most tourists preferred to see a cracked bell further down the street.

Philosophical Hall was the only privately owned building on Independence Square, a little known fact that the Society preferred not be publicized, because it might raise questions that they would also prefer not to answer, as people would wonder where the money came from. Hiding in plain sight was a tactic the Society had adopted from the very beginning, putting its scientific and exploration exploits in the foreground and cloaking its true power in secrecy.

Parker sighed deeply and switched his gaze from the outside, to his watch, then to the visages staring down on him from the paintings that cluttered the walls of the office: Benjamin Franklin, of course, the founder of the APS in 1745; George Washington, a man who could straddle every fence; John Adams; Thomas Paine; James Madison; the Marquis de Lafayette; Charles Darwin; Robert Frost; Baron Von Steuben; Tadeusz Kosciousko; Thomas Edison; Louis Pasteur; Margaret Mead, Meriwether Lewis and William Clark, and others whose names reverberated through the annals of science and exploration. Two paintings were centered right next to each other as if paired for some special reason: Thomas Jefferson and Alexander Hamilton.

The Jefferson painting had historical significance. It was one of only two copies that Thomas Sully, who had done the original, had painted based off that work. The original was at West Point, which had commissioned the full body portrait of the Founder of the Academy. The two copies were half that size, from the waist up. The twin to this one was in the Rotunda at the University of Virginia.

The portrait of Hamilton was not so well rendered. From the Society's records, Parker knew that Hamilton had been extended an honorary membership by Thomas Jefferson as part of an attempt at conciliation. Hamilton had accepted, but since he was best known for initiating the National Debt, starting the National Bank, and founding the Federalist Party, his contributions to the Philosophical Society were negligible.

At least that's what the records said.

Parker knew better. It was in this building, in this room, on opposite sides of this very desk, that President Jefferson and Hamilton had negotiated with each other to try to determine the direction the fledgling United States would continue to go in. Hamilton wanted a form that might almost be considered a monarchy without the hereditary king: he proposed that the President and Senators all be elected for life and that state governments be abolished. And he was the point man of the Society of Cincinnati, trying to gain power for that organization.

Jefferson believed in the people and wanted limits on the Federal government. He thought the government served the people, not the reverse.

The arguments must have been fierce and loud, Parker imagined. And resulted in a bitter compromise that only a handful of people throughout history had ever been aware of: The Jefferson Allegiance.

Above the two portraits was a pair of sayings:

Nullo Discrimine. The motto of the APS, which meant: "We are open to all."

Not exactly, thought Parker.

And next to it, the motto of the defunct Military Philosophical Society: *Scientia in Bello Pax.* "Science in War is the Guarantee of Peace."

It helps, he thought.

Parker figured the two sayings said a lot about the schizophrenic nature of the secret inner circle of the Society.

Parker leaned back in the chair, the worn wood creaking. He felt as old as the chair, but he also felt vibrant and alive for the first time in a long while. The possibility of impending death had a tendency to do that, as he knew from his experiences in aerial combat. Once more he made a time check. She was late, which was most unusual.

McBride was dead. A successor had been activated.

General LaGrange was dead. As was his son, who had been the first successor. A new successor had picked up the mantle.

The report on Admiral Groves had just come in. Dead also. He'd written that his successor had also been killed, but that a replacement had been alerted.

And Parker's own successor was late.

He looked at the flat-screen computer monitor on top of the old wooden desk that had been in this room since the founding of the Society. The email from Admiral Groves consisted of only five words: DON'T GIVE UP THE SHIP. Parker had spent no time in ships, but rather over thirty-five years in the cockpits of planes, becoming rated on more types of aircraft than anyone else in the Air Force, making him a mini-legend inside a closed circle of people who knew what such a feat meant.

"Damn Navy," Parker groused as he stared at the words. Who the hell wanted to confine themselves to the two dimensions of the ocean surface when you could roam free in the three dimensions of the sky? Now submariners, Parker would allow, could move three ways, but so slowly, what was the point? And the very element they moved in could kill them. The air didn't kill pilots. Other pilots or the ground did.

Slowly, Parker typed the saying on the keyboard. He accessed the first link that came up, having little patience with computers. June 1813. Captain James Lawrence, commander of the *USS Chesapeake* fought a British Frigate outside of Boston Harbor. And lost, Parker noted. "Goddamn Squids," he muttered as he scrolled down. Apparently Lawrence was mortally wounded, and as he lay dying he gave his last command: *'Tell the men to fire faster. Fight 'til she sinks, boys. Don't give up the ship.'*

Of course, they gave up the ship. Another defeat trumpeted through history as magnificent to the point where it was considered a victory. There were too many of them throughout history in Parker's opinion. Where the loser got the glory. He saw that the last part of Lawrence's dying words were appropriated by Commodore Oliver Hazard Perry—Admiral Groves's namesake—and sewn onto his battle flag.

At least Perry won a few battles, Parker noted. And did his own famous quote: *'We have met the enemy and they are ours.'* This, after defeating a British fleet on Lake Erie during the War of 1812. *Not exactly a 'real' war*, Parker thought. Especially considering the battle most Americans remembered it for, New Orleans, under General Andrew Jackson, occurred *after* the peace treaty had already been signed. Many good men dying for nothing.

Where the hell was she? Parker wondered.

Parker rubbed his forehead. He was getting old and cynical and needed to focus. "Connections," he said to himself and smiled, sadly remembering the ribbing his grandkids gave him for speaking to himself. He began clicking links, reading, trying to weave the threads together that Groves had left with that five-word message. He knew the ultimate goal was a grave, but the question was: Whose grave?

Perry's?

Newport Island Cemetery in Rhode Island.

Parker shook his head. Not enough connections.

Lawrence's?

Parker stiffened when he saw the result. Originally buried in Halifax, Nova Scotia, but re-interred in Trinity Church cemetery in New York City. Parker took a deep breath and looked up at the two portraits facing him. He knew Alexander Hamilton was also buried in Trinity Church cemetery. Entombed there after being mortally wounded during his famous duel with Aaron Burr in 1804.

He checked his watch. It was time. He couldn't wait on his own successor any longer.

Parker got up, his old joints protesting, and walked to the Sully painting. He carefully lifted the image of Thomas Jefferson off the wall, revealing the face of a safe. Parker placed his thumb on an indent and pressed his eye up to a rubber oval. The safe's locking mechanism read the fingerprint and the retina. There was a soft click. Parker twisted the handle and opened the door.

Instead of money or treasure, there was only a yellow Post-it note inside. He removed the note, shut the safe, and replaced the picture.

Parker placed the note next to the keyboard for the computer. It had eight phone numbers, arranged in two columns of four. One in the first column was worthless and he crossed that one out. Parker pulled out his satphone and linked it to the computer via Bluetooth. He entered three of the numbers in the first, and the backup in the second. Then he sent the results of his search to all four via text message.

He was getting ready to shred the Post-it when the door burst open and a beautiful woman wearing a black cloak strode into the room, a pistol in one hand, pointing right at him, a sword, of all things, in her other.

"Do not move, General," she said.

"Who the hell are you?" Parker demanded, crumpling the Post-it, hoping she hadn't seen it.

"Where are your cipher disks?"

Parker was looking at the hand that held the sword. "You're an Academy grad? Which one?"

She seemed taken aback. "Air Force Academy."

Parker snorted. "What class? And what's your name?"

"Ninety-eight. They call me the Surgeon. You don't need my name. But I know all about you, General. All your ratings, all your medals. Because of that, if you tell me where your disks are, I'll let you live."

"Do you remember the Academy honor code?" Parker asked. *Class of '98*, he thought. *Unbelievable.* He glanced past the Surgeon's shoulder toward the door, then back at her.

"I'm not a cadet anymore." But the Surgeon's face flushed.

"You're an Academy graduate," Parker snapped. "That's life-long."

"I *will* let you live if you give me your disks," the Surgeon said.

"A liar *and* stupid," Parker said. "Don't put me in the same cesspool as you."

The Surgeon took a step closer, the hand with the sword rising. Parker glanced at the information on the computer screen and grimaced. He went to tap the delete key and a bullet hit him in the shoulder, knocking him away from the computer, and spinning him halfway around in his chair. He groped for the desk, trying to turn back. He reached again for the keyboard when the woman brought the sword down point first, pinning his forearm to the arm of the wooden chair. His hand spasmed, and the Post-it fell from his useless fingers.

The woman jammed the muzzle of the gun under his jaw. "The last of the Philosophers. Tired old men who have failed. Utterly and completely. By my hand. A woman's hand. I actually thought you would be more of a challenge. Where are your disks?"

Parker was surprised there wasn't much pain from his right arm. He'd never been wounded in all the aerial encounters he'd fought, but he'd often wondered what it would feel like. *Not too bad*, he thought as he reached for the keyboard with his left hand.

She fired the gun, the bullet punching through the center of his hand. Parker sat back in the chair, staring at the sword in his right arm and the hole in his left hand. Blood was seeping out of both wounds.

"Your cipher disks?"

Parker shook his head. "Never. You are so wrong."

She paused, her eyes searching his face. "Wrong about what? You just spoke a truth. What am I wrong about?"

"You're being used," Parker said.

"Of course," she said. "I allow it because it gives me what I want."

She twisted the blade that had gone through his forearm, the steel grating against bone, and he bit back a scream. Not-so-bad had turned into excruciating. The woman holstered the pistol and reached inside her black cloak and pulled out a long, thin cylinder. Parker blinked through his shock, trying to see what it was. With a quick jerk, she pulled the sword out of his forearm. He gaped in pain and relief, a bizarre mixture of feelings. There was a clicking noise and then a hiss. Parker's eyes widened as he saw the bright blue flame from the small blowtorch in her hand.

He screamed as she ran the flame over his left hand, cauterizing the wound and stopping the bleeding. She slammed the sword back down into his other forearm, pinning him to the chair once more.

"Your disks, old man," she said as she pulled the blowtorch away. "We can go for a long time now. The blade, then the flame."

The stink of burned flesh filled the room. Pain without relief overwhelmed Parker's mind; blinding, searing agony, unlike anything he'd ever felt. He blinked the sweat out of his eyes, and saw that the Surgeon was looking at the computer screen. "Alexander Hamilton's grave?" she said. "What does that have to do with anything?"

She reached down and moved the cursor to the 'history' button. Clicking on it, she could see his most recent pattern of searches. "So you're aware of Groves's flag? I knew that was important."

Parker could only groan in pain and frustration. The Surgeon bent closer to the screen to read. "It's all about graves, isn't it? You Philosophers have hidden your disks in graves. First Poe's, now Hamilton's. Who else? Whose grave did you put *your* disks in, General?"

"No one's and everyone's."

The Surgeon paused, staring at him. "You just said a truth. But it makes no sense. You put your disks in 'no one's and everyone's' grave?"

"You're a fool," Parker managed.

The Surgeon shook her head and turned back to the computer.

Parker took a deep breath, knowing he had the barest window of opportunity, as she wasn't watching her six. He reached with his crippled left hand and jerked the sword out of his right forearm, then jumped to his feet and dashed toward the window he'd just been gazing out of. He dove for it, the hands of the Surgeon just missing him as he smashed through the old, leaded glass.

He felt a moment of freedom. He was flying.

* * *

Lily bit back a curse at losing her prey. She was unfulfilled. She strode over to the paintings and slashed the one of Jefferson to shreds, venting her frustration, feeling a pounding on the side of her head. She drew a deep breath; slowly getting her anger under control, then sheathed the wakizashi and removed Hamilton's painting.

She retraced her steps and exited the office. And bumped right into a woman rushing through the door.

Lily stared in disbelief. "Elizabeth!"

The other woman was even more surprised. "Lily?" Elizabeth's eyes shifted from Lily's face to the painting and then past her, into the office and the shattered window.

Lily dropped the painting and whipped out the sword. Elizabeth's right hand was scrambling underneath her leather flight jacket as Lily slashed the blade across her throat.

Blood spurted out in an achingly beautiful crimson arc, splattering Lily.

Elizabeth didn't give up, pulling a pistol from underneath the coat, even as she bled out. Lily automatically whipped the blade down, flat-edged, slapping down the gun.

Elizabeth dropped to her knees, eyes blinking, mouth moving, trying to say something that she didn't have the air to make audible. Then collapsed forward.

Lily stood still—blood, Elizabeth's blood—dripping from her clothes, her earlier frustration gone. She took in the moment, relishing it, but the sound of approaching sirens cut into her reverie. Lily knelt next to the dead woman, rolling her over. She quickly searched for disks or a further clue where they were. She found a single disk with the number "14" on the side. She slid it into a pocket. Lily reached for the left hand and held it up. An Air Force Academy ring graced one finger. It was her year: 1998.

She remembered seeing Elizabeth outside the chapel one fine Colorado morning. Lily pressed a hand against the side of her head, increasing the pain from the bruises, trying to regain control.

Lily pulled off the ring and started to put it in the pocket of her liquid armor cloak, then paused. Shaking her head, she placed the ring over Elizabeth's heart.

Then Lily picked up the painting and ran down the stairs.

She safely made it to her van as the first police cars were pulling up to Independence Square.

* * *

Driving up the Palisades Parkway on the west side of the Hudson River toward West Point automatically generated a strong sense of dread in Ducharme, starting deep in his stomach and reaching up to wrap tendrils around his heart. He was conditioned to it, like Pavlov's dog. West Pointers developed it from that first trip reporting for R-Day (Reception Day), through all the times they returned to their 'Rockbound Highland Home,' as the school's alma mater ominously described the Academy.

It was January, the 'Gloom Period' when everything at West Point would be gray: the weather, the uniforms, the buildings and the attitude.

Six bells and all is well
Another weekend shot to hell
Another week in my little gray cell
Another week in which to excel.
Oh hell.

"What's wrong?" Evie asked.

"Nothing." He erased the grimace that had stolen onto his face remembering the ditty all cadets memorized and chanted on Sunday evenings.

"Going back to Hudson High," Kincannon chimed in. "Never fun. Unless you're General Macarthur coming back to make a speech. It's an interesting place to visit, but you wouldn't want to live there."

"It's—" Ducharme began, but his satphone buzzed. He pulled it out, keeping one hand on the wheel. He didn't recognize the incoming number for the text message or the area code: 215. The caller ID was three letters: APS. A low tone sounded to his right and he glanced at Evie. She retrieved her iPhone.

"I've got a text message," Evie said.

"What number?" Ducharme asked.

"215-555-2376."

"I think I just got the same message," Ducharme said. "Do you recognize it? Someone you know?"

"No. And no one I know, knows you."

"Excuse me," Kincannon said.

"Present company excepted," Evie allowed.

"What's the message?" Kincannon asked. Ducharme handed his phone over his shoulder to Kincannon as Evie began scrolling on her phone.

"It's the history of a computer search," Evie said. "Starts with the saying *'Don't give up the ship.'*"

"Got the same thing here," Kincannon confirmed.

"Who said that?" Ducharme asked.

"Some Navy person," Evie replied.

"*Now* you get vague," Ducharme chided. "Wasn't it a battle on the Great Lakes?"

"Hold on," Evie said as she scrolled down on her iPhone. "Not the Great Lakes. June eighteen thirteen. Captain James Lawrence, commander of the *U.S.S. Chesapeake.* A battle near Boston Harbor. Lawrence was mortally wounded. His last command was: *Tell the men to fire faster. Fight 'til she sinks, boys. Don't give up the ship.'"*

"Firing faster isn't always best," Kincannon noted. "It's better to fire accurately. I've seen guys fire on automatic in combat when an accurate single shot would have--"

Evie moved on. "Apparently you're right. It didn't work." She scrolled further down on her iPhone. "The Americans surrendered. Let's see. OK, here's what you were thinking of. Commodore Oliver Hazard Perry had the phrase sewn onto his battle flag and he won a victory in the War of eighteen twelve, defeating a British fleet on Lake Erie."

"Who the hell sent us this?" Ducharme asked. "And what does it mean?"

"Whoever sent it had both our numbers," Evie said, "so I'd assume it's one of the other—" she paused. "Hold on a second." Her fingers were flying over the face of her iPhone. "OK. Two-one-five area code is downtown Philadelphia. Then I would assume APS stands for American Philosophical Society. McBride was a member of it." She was nodding. "That makes sense. Yes. It makes a lot of sense. The APS was founded by Benjamin Franklin even before the Society of Cincinnati. Thomas Jefferson was President of it for a long time."

"So the call came from one of the other guardians of the Cipher?" Ducharme was trying to put the pieces together and wondering about the quick leaps in logic she was making.

"Most likely." She looked back down at her iPhone. "Perry was known for the saying: *We have met the enemy and they are ours.*"

"So why is this unknown person sending us *this* history lesson?" Ducharme rubbed the back of his skull.

"Must be the clues to more disks," Evie said. She scrolled further. "Yes. Whoever it was, was looking for more graves. He—or she—checked where Perry was buried. Rhode Island. Then Carpenter. Buried in Halifax. Wait. He was re-interred in Trinity Church Cemetery in New York. Damn."

"What?" Kincannon asked from the back seat.

"Trinity Cemetery in New York. You know who else is in that cemetery?" She didn't wait for an answer. "Alexander Hamilton is buried there."

Ducharme glanced over at her. "Someone put their disks in the grave of the leader of their mortal enemy?"

"Maybe. It would be good misdirection." Evie had the thousand-yard stare again, and Ducharme figured she was off in whatever lala land she went to when deep in thought.

"Kincannon," Ducharme said.

"Yeah?"

"Call that number back. Find out who sent us this."

"Roger that." Kincannon hit callback on the cell phone. There were a few seconds of silence. "Who is this?" A pause. "Hey, *you* texted *me*."

Another pause. "Fuck you." Kincannon clicked the 'off' button. He met Ducharme's eyes in the rear-view mirror. "That was an FBI agent at a homicide site—which is indeed the American Philosophical Society headquarters. I think whoever sent the message isn't with the living anymore, and like your Uncle's message, it was sent on a time delay."

"Damn bitch," Ducharme said. "Third one down from the originals,"

"You know," Kincannon said, "if the two of you got this message, then there's probably two others who go the same message."

"What do you mean?" Ducharme asked.

"Each of you got a disk from people you considered mentors," Kincannon said. "That wasn't by chance. You're their replacements. And since there were two other Philosophers, that means there are two other replacements out there."

"The next generation like us," Evie said.

"Lucky us," Ducharme muttered.

"It's a great honor," Evie said.

"Isn't it primogeniture, or whatever you call it?" Kincannon corrected. "Inheritance?"

Evie shook her head. "No. We were chosen because of who we are, not who we were born to. For some reason Mister McBride saw something in me and General LaGrange saw something in you. They're trusting us with the fate of the country."

She sounded so excited, Ducharme almost expected her to burst out in song, release some balloons and do a cartwheel. "There might have been more deaths in this." He looked over his shoulder briefly at the Sergeant Major. "Charlie LaGrange. I think he was the General's first choice. I was back up."

Kincannon's face got hard, eyes flat. "Somebody needs dying."

"Someone does." Ducharme shook his head. "Not her style, though. She's always uses the blade."

Kincannon wasn't fazed. "Then someone else needs dying."

Ducharme was groping around in the dark, searching for a truth he didn't understand. He knew Evie was withholding something from them. Maybe a lot of somethings.

He focused back on the road. If what Kincannon said was true, there was a high possibility one of their 'comrades,' for lack of a better term, would be en route to Hamilton's grave.

"Fuck," Ducharme exclaimed, another piece tumbling into place.

"What?" Evie was startled.

"If whoever sent that message is dead, there's a good chance our killer got the same information off the phone that sent it. She'll be heading for Hamilton's grave too."

"Let's go kill her," Kincannon had his pistol out, checking it, as if New York were a block away.

"One thing at a time," Evie counseled from the front seat. "Plus, we're probably closer than either of them, even continuing to West Point and then back to the city. And something's not right about this."

"There's a lot not right about this," Ducharme said.

She held up her iPhone. "Whoever sent this message was searching for disks. But they sent the information to both of us. Which means they know who we are. But we don't know who the other new Philosophers are."

He didn't quite follow. "So?"

"And the message was sent from APS headquarters in Philadelphia."

"And?" Ducharme ran a finger across the scar under his eye. "We know that."

"It's not adding up the way we just added it up," Evie said.

"You going to tell me what the hell you're talking about?" Ducharme demanded, out of patience.

"We need to find out who died in Philadelphia."

Kincannon had his secure cell phone out. "Wait one. We can tap into classified FBI commo traffic on the terror alert net. The military does at least coordinate that with them." He typed. "OK. FBI has a possible homicide of one General Atticus Parker, US Air Force retired at Philosophical Hall in Philly. Seems he took a header out a window."

"Could be suicide," Evie said without much conviction.

"He was tortured before falling. Blade. Flame. Probably not a suicide," Kincannon dryly noted.

"That's definitely our friend from Baltimore," Ducharme said.

Kincannon continued. "There's a second body at the site: a Major Elizabeth Peters, US Air Force. Killed with a blade."

"Parker's replacement?" Ducharme asked.

"Most logically," Evie said.

"So we're down to three," Ducharme said.

"*And,*" Kincannon added, "We got us another killing outside of Annapolis. Admiral Hazard Groves, US Navy, retired. Tortured. Also killed with a blade. He was gutted, hari-kari or whatever the fuck style that is the Japanese do. Since the blade wasn't still in his gut or at the scene I'd say he didn't kill himself either."

"Damn," Ducharme said. "She had a busy night."

"Is that what you call it when five people are murdered?" Evie demanded. "'A busy night?'"

"You were thrilled with our great honor just a minute ago," Ducharme said.

"Easy." Kincannon leaned forward between the seats. "Fighting among ourselves ain't gonna help none."

Ducharme slumped back in his seat and focused back on the road. "So all the old guards are all dead," he said. "LaGrange, McBride, Groves and Parker. And two of the new ones. Peters and Charlie LaGrange."

Evie held up her iPhone, pointing at the screen. "Groves's disks are the ones these clues are for. Which is strange. Why would Parker send us Groves's clues and not his own?"

"Most likely because he thought Peters would get them or already had them," Ducharme said.

They continued up the Palisades Parkway in silence. As they crossed the New Jersey/New York border, the Parkway veered away from the river and passed underneath the New York Thruway. The land became hillier, the terrain more forested and strewn with boulders left behind by retreating glaciers ages ago. They reached the traffic circle for the Bear Mountain Bridge. Ducharme turned off the circle onto 9W, images of other times he'd made that turn and under what circumstances randomly passing through his brain like a slideshow. Charlie LaGrange was in many of them, and Ducharme forced himself to think about other things, facts, anything to avoid the pain and to avoid riling up the beast.

They drove past the Revolutionary war sites of Fort Clinton and Fort Montgomery, which had guarded the southern approaches to West Point. Geography dictated the original placement of a major fort at West Point. It was located on the west bank of the Hudson, where the river narrowed and made a sharp turn. During the Revolution, control of travel on the river had been considered essential to both sides. If the British gained control of it from their base in New York City, they could cut off the troublesome New England colonists from the rest of the country, and effectively end the Revolution. To prevent that, the Colonists occupied West Point and built a massive chain, which they floated on wooden rafts across the Hudson. They covered the chain with artillery fire to prevent passage of British warships.

Armed military police were stationed at the Highland Falls entrance to the Academy. Ducharme pulled up to the soldier manning the gate and powered the window down, showing the guard his identification card. The MP saluted and waved them through.

"Welcome home," Kincannon said.

* * *

The MP waited until the Blazer was out of sight, then went into the guard shack and typed the Blazer's license plate into his computer. The result that came back wasn't good. He reluctantly punched a number into the phone. "Sir, as per the terror alert, we've got three people in a vehicle just entering post. Two males, one female. Government plate on the truck, no trace on the plate."

"Roger that. We'll take it from here."
The phone went dead and the MP gave it the finger.

CHAPTER TWELVE

Lily was in the back of an un-marked, black, FBI Bell Jet Ranger helicopter, racing from the FBI Field Office in Philadelphia toward New York City. She was looking at the yellow Post-it she'd recovered from the floor of the Philosopher's office in Independence Hall. There was a red stain on one edge.

She pulled out her satphone and dialed the top number. It rang twice, then was answered by a woman: "Hello?"

"To whom am I speaking?" Lily asked.

"Who did you hope to be speaking to?" the woman demanded.

Lily smiled coldly. "Someone I'm going to kill."

"Oh."

There was a long silence. Then a man's voice came on, low, with a slight New Orleans drawl. "Next time you won't be so lucky."

Lily gripped the phone tighter, blood oozing out of the cuts on her arm. "My friend from the cemetery. Luck had nothing to do with it. You did a sloppy job."

"I got what I went there for. Did you?"

She automatically put her hand to the side of her head, massaging it where the bullets had impacted.

"You got a name, missy?"

"Don't call me that. Call me 'the Surgeon.'"

"And I'm Captain America." The smart-ass was silent for a moment. "I saw what you did in Washington, missy. That's what a butcher would do, not a surgeon. I'm going to stop you from—"

"And your name, or should I call you Captain?"

"Colonel Paul Ducharme. US Army. You had a busy night."

"You're going to fail, Colonel Ducharme."

"You already did." The connection went dead.

Lily crumpled the Post-it and shoved it into the pocket of her Liquid Armor cloak. Then she opened the large plastic case on the floor of the helicopter in front of her and began selecting what she'd need.

* * *

"That was interesting." Ducharme handed Evie back her iPhone.

"Feel better?" Evie slid the phone into a pocket. "Yours bigger than hers?"

He didn't take the bait.

"Why did you tell her your real name?" Evie asked.

Ducharme shrugged. "We already know this person—who calls herself the Surgeon—has connections to the government. She called you. She can find our names."

To that, Evie had no reply. They drove past the Thayer Hotel on the right and Buffalo Soldier Field on the left, where Ducharme had spilled blood playing intramural football and soccer as a cadet.

They drove onward, passing a low stonewall that flanked the sidewalk to the right. Officer's quarters were perched on the hillside above them to the left. A couple of cadets, bundled up against the cold in bulky sweats, jogged by, their breath smoky in the cold air. A cloudy, grey sky seemed to be reaching down to blanket the ground. The 'Gloom Period' in all its dreariness.

Large foreboding buildings covered in grey stone appeared ahead: the main campus of West Point, although Ducharme couldn't recall ever hearing anyone call it a campus. It was the Academy, pure and simple. Not your average college. A rockbound, highland home to the sentimental; Hudson High those who were not.

Mahan Hall went by on the right and New South Barracks on the left, where Ducharme had spent four years as a member of company G-1. Then Bartlett Hall, home to the hard sciences on the right and old Pershing Barracks, still standing from the days of MacArthur, on the left. Ducharme glanced up at the clock tower where, according to legend, MacArthur and several other cadets had hauled the reveille cannon to the top as part of a cadet prank in one night. It took two weeks to remove it.

"Someone liked stone and grey," Evie noted.

"Keen powers of observation." Ducharme slowed down as the Plain appeared directly ahead. West Point was centered on a parade field with a large statue of George Washington mounted on a steed overseeing it.

Ducharme had spent untold hours out there drilling and marching. A memory popped to mind and he felt a momentary thrill, remembering Passing in Review as a Firstie—a senior cadet—in command of his company, barking orders. Which was immediately followed by an earlier memory of the feeling of disorientation from his first day at the Academy, R-Day, Reception Day, when he'd marched out there, head shaven, having been screamed at all day, and raised his right hand and sworn an oath, the words of which had never left his mind:

I, Paul Ducharme, do solemnly swear that I will support and defend the Constitution of the United States against all enemies, foreign and domestic; that I will bear true faith and allegiance to the same; and that I will obey the orders of the President of the United States and the orders of the officers appointed over me, according to the regulations and the Uniform Code of Military Justice. So help me God.

"Having a moment?" Evie asked.

Ducharme blinked. He had stopped the Blazer and was staring through the windshield at the Plain. He didn't remember stopping, and that scared him. Traces of snow streaked the withered crew-cut grass, the blast of winter's fury coming down the Hudson River having left its mark. Looking up, he could see that Storm King Mountain's top was masked by low clouds.

"I'm all right," he said. "Was just thinking about taking my oath of office out there, years ago."

Evie nodded. "Did you—" she pause, gave a sheepish smile, then continued—"know that the oath of office was the very first Federal law ever enacted? June first, seventeen eighty-nine, First Congress, First Session, Chapter One, Statute One. Apparently, the Founding Fathers took the matter very seriously as it was the absolute first thing Congress concerned itself with. They didn't want the military swearing allegiance to any person. They wanted the allegiance to be to the Constitution, which is the core of the country."

"The President is in there," Kincannon said from the back seat. "You know POTUS? The big cheese? The commander-in-chief?"

"Only that you'll obey the President's legitimate orders," Evie said. "The Oath is to the Constitution with no qualifiers. Pre-empts all else, including the President. Also, there's the part about all enemies, foreign *and* domestic."

Ducharme opened his mouth to say something, but pain stabbed through his mind like a spike of molten metal. He struggled to focus, pressing his foot on the brake. It passed less than a second later, and he blinked hard.

"What's wrong with you?" Evie asked, putting a hand on his right forearm to lessen the thrust of the question.

Ducharme looked in the rearview mirror. Kincannon nodded slightly. Ducharme leaned back in the seat, closing his eyes. "I was in Afghanistan running an MTT—Mobile Training Team—with the Afghan army, teaching counter-insurgency. We were driving down a road and some kid came out with a can of Coke, trying to sell it to us. Except it was a bomb. I sensed it, tried to knock it away, but it went off." He reached up and touched the scar under his eye. "Piece of metal went in. No big deal. But it was the trigger for a larger ambush. Because then a buried IED went off. Threw our Humvee ten feet and buckled it. The kid was pretty much vaporized. Apparently he wasn't in the know on the bigger plan for the ambush. Or maybe he was and just didn't give a shit about living anymore."

He fell silent, remembering.

"And?" Evie persisted.

"The Humvee was Up-Armor, so we had some protection," Ducharme said. "The blast-proof glass wasn't perfect in this case. Ever since, I've had some pain episodes. They're very short. A second at the most. According to the Army I've been fixed and am serviceable once more."

"I'm sorry," Evie said.

Ducharme wasn't sure what to say. He realized no one had ever said they were sorry. Not the Army, not the Administration, not the General who pinned the Purple Heart on him and quickly moved down the line in the hospital ward. There had been a lot of wounded to pin and forget.

"It hasn't been a problem," he lied. "A lot of people in the War on Terror have sustained brain injuries from IEDs. But since you can't directly see the damage, it's been largely ignored. Some are even saying it's PTSD, not a real injury, which I can tell you is bullshit."

"A lot of things have been ignored," Evie added, touching his arm.

Ducharme was flustered. He noted in the rearview mirror that Kincannon was pointedly staring out the window. "Yeah." He took his foot off the brake and continued down the road.

Ducharme looked about and had his first surprise. He hadn't been back to the Academy since graduating. Where tennis courts had once graced the landscape behind a scowling statue of General Patton holding a pair of binoculars, was a large building, albeit one bearing the same gray stone granite façade. Had he simply forgotten about the building?

"That's new," Kincannon muttered, which was a relief.

"Well, it's appropriate," Evie said as they rolled past and saw the sign in front of the building: *Thomas Jefferson Hall Library*. "Looks like someone finally remembered who founded this place. And picked the most appropriate building to put his name on. Probably a statue of him inside."

"Funny." Ducharme was at the stop sign, getting ready to make a left and continue on around the parade field when Evie spoke again. "I want to go into the library."

Ducharme looked at her. "We're not here to sightsee." He tapped the watch on his wrist. "We're on the clock. Good chance someone's going to be dying in New York City today."

"There's something I want to check on, something that seeing that library reminded me of. Something that could be important."

Ducharme sighed. She had that info-bot look again. "Going to tell me what that is?"

"I'm going to show you," Evie said.

Ducharme pulled into a spot clearly marked 'No Parking.'

"Breaking a rule?" Evie asked.

"Fuck the MPs," Ducharme snapped. "They wouldn't dare mess with this vehicle."

"That's the spirit," Kincannon said.

"Is it special? Covert?" Evie asked. "Will they not be able to see it?"

"Real funny, woman." Ducharme got out, meeting Evie and Kincannon on the sidewalk outside the façade of the new library. They walked in the front doors of the library, a blast of warmth greeting them. Along with a portrait of Thomas Jefferson hanging on the wall to the right.

Evie stopped to admire it. "This is Sully's original portrait of Jefferson. A classic."

Ducharme had vague memories of seeing the painting in the old library somewhere. He hadn't exactly lived among the stacks as a cadet. "This is what you wanted to see?"

"Partly," Evie said. "A copy of this hangs at the University of Virginia. The other copy done by Sully hangs in Philosophical Hall in Philly. But there's also something we need to check." She led the way to a computer and sat down in front of it.

A cadet wearing the diagonal white belt, polished breastplate and saber of a cadet on duty came walking up to them. "Excuse me, sir, these computers are for official use only and the library is only for—"

Ducharme pulled out his identification card and put it in front of the cadet's face.

The cadet snapped to attention. "I'm sorry, sir." He spun on his heel and quickly walked away.

"Now that's discipline," Ducharme told Kincannon.

Who, of course, laughed. "Don't get too used to it."

Evie ignored both of them, immersed in her work. She wrote down something on a slip of paper and then headed toward the stacks.

"Should we follow?" Kincannon asked.

"I think she can survive the stacks on her own," Ducharme said. He looked at the cadets hard at work, studying, researching. The atmosphere was different than Ducharme remembered: this was now a military academy during wartime. Ducharme had graduated before 9-11. Every cadet here now had made the decision to come to the Academy knowing that the country was already at war. War was all they knew for years. *How had everything gone so wrong?* The question reverberated through his brain.

"We might need some reinforcements," Kincannon said. "I'm gonna make a call or two."

Ducharme glanced at the Sergeant Major. He had his satphone out and was scrolling through his long list of contacts. Having been on active duty for twenty-five years, Ducharme knew the Sergeant Major had a very long list. Apparently he found someone to his liking, because he took a few steps away and made a call.

"Anyone I know?" Ducharme asked when Kincannon was done on the satphone.

"Chopper pilot whose ass I saved in Iraq. Stationed up at Stewart Airfield in the National Guard."

"He going to help?"

"Of course." Kincannon looked insulted. "I rescued her after her bird was shot down."

"Her. Right. That all you did?"

"She was grateful," Kincannon said with a warm grin. "Nice lady. Very nice lady. And a damn good pilot. I fear she took advantage of me."

"Poor her," Ducharme said.

Evie was coming back to them, a book in her hands. "Let's go."

"Aren't you going to check it out?" Ducharme asked.

"You are a rule follower," Evie rolled her eyes. "We've got people getting killed and you're worried about checking out a book?" She walked out the door. She tapped her wrist, which, of course had no watch strapped to it. "We're on the clock."

"I guess we're going," Ducharme told Kincannon.

Kincannon snapped to attention. "Yes, sir."

"I'm surrounded by funny people," Ducharme muttered.

"Better than the alternative," Kincannon said as they went out the doors back into the winter cold. "Sometimes all you can do is laugh at the absurdities."

Ducharme glanced at the painting of Jefferson on the way out. "Sometimes you can do more."

* * *

The Blackhawk helicopter flew up the Hudson River, Manhattan to the right, and the Palisades to the left. The pilots had it low, fifty feet above the surface of the dark water. In the back, Burns stared at Turnbull who was talking on the satellite link. Turnbull had been on the link since they left the FBI field station in Baltimore after catching a few hours of sleep on cots.

Burns was waiting. He was good at waiting. He'd watched Turnbull texting at certain times. He knew about the secure burst text mode the top levels of the FBI were now using; in fact, he'd been part of the FBI Task Force assigned to test the program.

Turnbull pushed the off button and began to make another call. Burns reached over and grabbed the man's wrist. "Evie Tolliver's file?"

Turnbull gave him an irritated look. "Tolliver isn't a suspect."

"She's part of this, like Ducharme. I need to know about her."

Turnbull stared at him for a few seconds, his face unreadable. "Fine. I'll Bluetooth it to your satphone."

As Turnbull worked the keys on his phone, Burns pushed a button on the back of his. There was a beep as the information was downloaded. And that wasn't all that was being transmitted—Turnbull might have the latest technology, but that didn't mean he knew all its possible uses. Not only was Burns's phone getting the data, it was sending a virus to Turnbull's phone.

The download finished, Turnbull turned away and went back to talking on his phone.

Burns checked his satphone. It had copied not only the file, but also the text-burst encryption on Turnbull's satphone perfectly. With the virus he'd sent, any text message that went to Turnbull's satphone, would now also go to Burns's.

Burns put the satphone to his ear. He checked in with his office, then, using keywords, scanned the terrorist alert network summary the FBI put out every morning. High profile, new cases were listed first. He scrolled through the list, pausing when he read about the death of Admiral Groves in Annapolis. A blade had been used. The man had been cut, his office ransacked. Burns called the FBI officer in charge and asked if anything was missing: a flag.

The murderer had struck again. He looked at Turnbull, who seemed most unconcerned.

He went back to his phone. The FBI officer told him they had two, more recent, deaths in Philadelphia that had already been linked by the FBI as probably having been committed by the same person: the first might have been listed as a suicide except for the blade wounds—and a new wrinkle, a burn—on a retired General Parker of the American Philosophical Society. And the throat cut on another Air Force officer, Major Elizabeth Peters.

Burns sighed. Another trophy for the murderer: this time a painting was missing from the office Parker worked in as the executive secretary for the APS. A painting of Alexander Hamilton. And a rare, valuable painting of Thomas Jefferson had been slashed to ribbons. *A sign of rage*, Burns thought. The killer was getting frustrated. *Not the only one.*

Burns thanked the officer and disconnected, telling him nothing about the killings in Washington or the confrontation in Baltimore. This was indeed, deep shit. The fewer involved, the less would go down. Plus, there was no doubt in his mind this was much, much bigger than a multiple homicide investigation.

Burns finally accessed Evie's file. He scrolled through it as the Tappan Zee Bridge appeared ahead, a ribbon of steel slicing across the sky above the river.

He paused as he noted that her ex-husband, Donald Freemont, was still in the CIA. He read about her father, and understood why she had been run out of the CIA, and the cause of her divorce. *Deep shit indeed.* Her CIA training explained a lot of what he'd seen in the interrogation room. Compartmentalization and detachment.

They flew underneath the Tappan Zee Bridge and Burns sat back, trying to pull the pieces together. Five deaths. The trophies. The killer. Ducharme. Evie. And most of all, Mister Turnbull.

Movement to the right caught Burns's attention. He looked out and saw an Apache gunship and another Blackhawk helicopter flanking them. Inside the cargo bay of the Blackhawk were ten heavily armed personnel.

"That's not HRT," Burns said, referring to the FBI's Hostage Rescue Team. "And the FBI doesn't have any Apache gunships."

"That's not your concern," Turnbull said.

"What are they looking for?" he asked Turnbull. Seeing the confusion on Turnbull's face, Burns clarified. "Ducharme and Evie. What are they looking for? It's more than just the killer." He knew he wouldn't get an answer, but he wanted to see the reaction.

Turnbull stared back at him silently. He held up a finger as he listened to something on his satphone. Then he glanced over at the GPS display and nodded. "They're at West Point. Just went through the gate."

"Why?"

Turnbull moved the finger to his lips. "Hush-hush, Agent Burns."

Burns bit back a reply. He pulled out his notepad and turned back to the beginning of this case. Head-Heart. He accessed the Internet on his satphone, and looked up the letter that Jefferson had written so many years ago and began reading.

18 FEBRUARY 1945

President Roosevelt sat at his friend's deathbed, aware that soon someone would be sitting by his. He felt the slightest movement through the wheels of his chair. The USS Quincy, *named after the birthplace of two Presidents, was one of the new Baltimore Class cruisers churned out by the United States since the start of World War II. The sea off the coast of Algiers had minimal effect against its heavy metal sides.*

The man in the bed, Major General Watson, had been by Roosevelt's side through the entire war. To lose him now, with the end in sight, deeply saddened Roosevelt, sapping the satisfaction from the accomplishments of the past three weeks. Via the Quincy *he'd met Churchill in Malta on the 2nd of February, Stalin and Churchill at Yalta after that, then King Farouk, Emperor Haile Selassie and Saudi Arabian King Ibn Saud on the Great Bitter Lake a few days ago.*

Watson had collapsed after they passed through the Suez Canal and not regained consciousness, nor was he likely to according to Roosevelt's personal doctor. Roosevelt's hope was that his friend would last until they got back to the States so that he could accompany him back to his home, adjacent to Monticello in Virginia. Roosevelt had stayed at Watson's Retreat at Kenwood numerous times during his presidency, often making the quarter mile journey next door to Jefferson's house in the company of Ed Watson and his wife.

The hatch to the cabin swung open and General Marshall came inside, securing the heavy metal door behind him.

"George," Roosevelt acknowledged.

"Mister President." Marshall came over and looked down at Watson. "No change?"

"I am afraid not."

"The Ambassadors will be on board shortly," Marshall said. "Your briefing for them is prepared."

The last thing Roosevelt felt like was another meeting. But briefing his ambassadors to the United Kingdom, France and Italy, on the agreement at Yalta was imperative. "I'll be ready." His hands were gripping the arms of his wheelchair. "I've known Ed a long time."

Marshall took a chair from the tiny desk in the cabin and settled his bulk into it. "He was in Washington on and off for decades. Wasn't he an aide to President Wilson?"

Roosevelt felt uncomfortable discussing Ed as if he were not here. "He's been with me since thirty-three," Roosevelt murmured. "Longer than anyone else except Eleanor."

"I was talking with General Watson last week about something interesting," Marshall said.

Something in the General of the Army's tone roused Roosevelt out of his melancholy. "And that was?"

Marshall leaned back in the metal chair and waited as ship's orders were broadcast throughout the cruiser, and then relative silence fell once more. "In ancient Rome when a general or emperor won a great victory, there would be a Triumph in Rome when they returned. A great procession into the city to celebrate the victory."

Marshall paused, then continued. "General Watson reminded me of something. He said that the victorious leader, riding in a chariot, had a slave standing behind him. The slave held a wreath over his head and whispered in his ear: 'Respice post te! Hominen te esse memento.'"

"My Latin is rusty," Roosevelt said dryly.

"It means: Look behind you! Remember that you are but a man.'"

"A warning," Roosevelt said, arching an eyebrow.

"A reminder," Marshall said mildly. "Your cousin, Teddy, made a promise in nineteen-oh-four, not to run again in oh-eight. He kept that promise. But he did run in nineteen twelve under his own Bull Moose platform. He won all but two of the Republican Primaries, but still lost the nomination at the convention. Have you ever wondered why he lost that nomination?"

"My cousin and I were never on such an intimate level of discourse."

Marshall nodded toward the figure in the bed. "You know General Watson is one of the Philosophers, of course?"

Roosevelt put a hand on the left wheel of his chair and pulled back, turning to face the head of the Armed Forces. "Yes."

"He told me that your cousin lost the nomination because the Philosophical Society opposed him."

"But Teddy still ran on his own ticket," Roosevelt pointed out. "Damn near won it all because he was supported by the Cincinnatians. Most votes anyone outside of the two parties has ever received. Beat out the Republican candidate who'd been nominated."

"But he didn't win. Wilson did."

Roosevelt glanced at the man in the bed, then back at the man in the chair. "True."

"You've been elected four times," Marshall said. "Twice as much as any other President. You got us through the Depression and through the war. The end is in sight."

"It is," Roosevelt agreed, waiting for the bottom line, knowing that Marshall was maneuvering the way a politician would, not a general. Roosevelt also knew that the five

star general was telling him what Watson would have, if he could. Those trips to Monticello had not been without their lessons.

Marshall continued. "In thirty-nine, despite the country's neutrality, you declared a state of limited national emergency. There is no such term in the Constitution or even in subsequent laws passed by Congress. In March of nineteen forty-one, you got Congress to pass the Lend-Lease program."

Roosevelt pulled out his cigarette holder and loaded it. "Are you telling me my accomplishments or my crimes?"

"Both."

Roosevelt chuckled. "Do you know how I got Lend-Lease through Congress?" He didn't wait for an answer. "I had my people push it through while sixty-five House Democrats were at a luncheon."

Marshall didn't seem to appreciate the humor. He continued. "In May of forty-one, when we still weren't at war, you dropped the 'limited' from the state of emergency and declared a state of unlimited national emergency. Under this, you could, and did, organize and control the means of production, seized commodities, deployed military forces abroad, imposed martial law, seized property, controlled all transportation and communication, regulated the operation of private enterprise, and restricted travel."

Roosevelt spread his hands as an innocent man would. "Would you have preferred I had not done those things?"

Marshall pulled a lighter out and lit the President's cigarette as he brought it to his lips. "No, sir. They were necessary to win the war."

"And I told Ed that I'd restore all our liberties as soon as the war is over."

"Yes, sir," Marshall agreed. "And that is why the Philosophers have not taken action despite the unconstitutionality of many of your actions. The Jefferson Allegiance remains in check."

"So what is the problem?" Roosevelt asked, more sharply than he intended.

Marshall went over and swung open one of the small portholes to let fresh air in. "The recent conferences, sir."

"I thought they went quite well."

Marshall blinked. "Sir. Stalin is a thug. A despot. You and Churchill handed him Eastern Europe on a platter."

"He promised to hold elections," Roosevelt said. "More importantly, even you agreed that we need the Russians for the final invasion of Japan."

"I do agree with you on that," Marshall allowed. "But it went too far. You gave up Poland. You agreed that citizens of Poland and Russia would be repatriated whether they wanted to or not. You gave Stalin practically everything he wanted."

"Stalin agreed to join the United Nations once we form it," Roosevelt countered.

Marshall appeared not to hear. "And the meeting with King Ibn Saud. Sir, there are great strategic implications in the Middle East for the future. Both in terms of the displaced Jews, but more importantly, the oil. Japan went to war with us when we embargoed their oil. The Germans went into Russia for the oilfields. Oil is the key. I fear we're setting up problems that are going to take generations to untangle."

"You say 'we,'" Roosevelt noted, *"but you mean me."*

"Yes, sir."

Roosevelt nodded ruefully. *"Do you think I don't know that?"* He nodded toward the comatose General in the bed. *"I hope I go quickly."*

"Sir, Stalin took too much away from Yalta. And Ibn Saud too much from the Great Bitter Lake conference."

"We need the Russians for Japan—" Roosevelt began, but Marshall leaned forward and whispered.

"Sir. We have the Manhattan Project."

"If it works," Roosevelt replied. *"That's a mighty big 'if' to roll the dice on the lives of millions of American servicemen. Frankly, I'd rather it be Russian blood spilled in Japan than American."*

"Sir, we must look beyond the end of the war and—"

"Please," Roosevelt said in a low voice. He pulled the remnants of his cigarette out of the holder and slid another in, then extended it to Marshall who dutifully lit it. *"I can't see beyond the end of war, George. It's been thirteen years. I'm tired. I'm sick. My friend is lying here dying. I'll be gone soon enough. Enact your Allegiance if you want, but by the time you do, I doubt there will be a need."*

Roosevelt leaned his head back against the rear of his wheelchair. *"I am looking behind me. And I am but a man."*

CHAPTER THIRTEEN

They drove around the West Point Plain. Cullum Hall on the right. Followed by a statue of a Revolutionary era soldier on a pedestal overlooking the Hudson.

"Is that Kosciuszko?" Evie asked, looking up from the book.

"Yeah," Ducharme waved a hand, his thoughts elsewhere, muddled, confused and with a growing sense of the beast rebelling in his chest.

"Can we stop?" Evie asked.

"This isn't a damn sightseeing tour," Ducharme snapped. Still, he halted the Blazer and Evie hopped out.

Ducharme looked at Kincannon. "She's holding something back."

"No shit."

"Why?"

Kincannon shrugged. "Probably doesn't trust us. I get the feeling the only person she trusted was that McBride fella."

"Great."

"You trust her?" Kincannon asked.

"No."

"There you go." Kincannon had his commando knife out, spinning it around on his palm absent-mindedly. "I think she's okay, though. It's not about us—it's the way she views the world."

Ducharme blinked. "Why do you think she's okay?"

"Ain't like we got a whole lot of people on our side right now. Plus, I remember her father as a division commander at Fort Hood. A good man. Came up through the ranks through a battlefield commission. Gave a shit about the troops. Rare in a general. Some of that stuff gets passed down."

Ducharme got out of the Blazer. Evie was staring up at the statue of Kosciuszko like a groupie at a rock star.

"Yeah, yeah," Ducharme said. "Polish guy. Helped design the fortifications here. Can we go?"

"Thomas Jefferson considered Kosciuszko the purest son of liberty." She shifted her gaze from the statue to him. "He truly understood the concept of democracy. After the Revolution, he went back to Poland and led a revolt against Russia. He might have won if the politicians hadn't screwed up. He was imprisoned by Catherine the Great, but was finally released when the Emperor Paul took the throne. Gave him a nice sable coat and even offered him his own sword out of respect. Kosciuszko declined. You know what he said?"

"No, but you're going to tell me."

"Kosciuszko said: 'I no longer need a sword—I no longer have a country.'"

Ducharme squinted up at the statue, impressed.

Evie continued. "I'm telling you this because I'm not sure you really understand the implications of what we're doing. Our country—the United States as we know it—is on the brink of being gone. We've been sliding for so long, people don't realize there's a point of no return if the Cincinnatians achieve complete, unfettered, power. And what's going to replace it—well, I don't think you're going to be *allowed* your sword to protect the Constitution, never mind not need it."

With that she turned and walked back to the Blazer. She slammed the door after she got in.

Ducharme clenched his fists, took a couple of deep breaths. Then he got back in the driver's seat and continued around the Plain. Next on the right were Trophy Point and Battle Monument. He pulled to the side, jumped the curb near the monument and slammed on the brakes. He twisted toward Evie who was reading the book she'd stolen. "What the fuck aren't you telling us?"

Evie looked up, startled by his voice, the sudden braking having passed un-noticed. "What?"

Ducharme spoke slowly, each word hard-edged. "What-the-fuck-haven't-you-told-us?"

"I've told you what I know and what I can deduce—" she began, but Kincannon's drawl cut through from the back seat, low but commanding, the edge there, quivering on the brink of darkness.

"Evie. Listen up. *We* know *you* know more than you're telling us. Maybe you aren't sure of something and worry we'll misinterpret. Maybe you don't trust us. Maybe you were so used to keeping secrets in the CIA. I damn sure ain't certain what it is. But you're holding something back, and that for damn certain could get us all killed. We've crossed into bandit country now and it's us against everyone. We're either a team or we ain't. And if we ain't, we're fucked."

Ducharme's harsh breathing echoed inside the Blazer, and the cold wind howling off the Hudson and Storm King Mountain battered against the outside of the Blazer.

Evie reached into her pocket and unfolded a piece of paper. "This."

Ducharme and Kincannon read:

FIND THE CIPHER, FIND THE ALLEGIANCE
ONE PHILOSOPER CHAIR, THREE PHILOSOPHERS
YOU ARE NOW THE CHAIR
A PHILOSOPHER WILL MEET YOU HERE

They both looked at her and waited.

"That's McBride's handwriting," she said. "He left that note for me in his briefcase along with his first cipher disk. It confirms that there were four: a Chair from the American Philosophical Society and three Philosophers."

Kincannon nodded. "So a lot of these theories you've been laying on us—you already knew they were real?"

"Yes."

"Fuck," Ducharme slammed a fist into the steering wheel.

"And this Allegiance?" Kincannon asked.

"We're looking for the Jefferson Cipher in order to find something called the Jefferson Allegiance." She glanced at Ducharme. "I'm sorry."

Ducharme said nothing for several long moments, and then he gave a slight nod. "All right."

"And this Allegiance is?" Kincannon asked.

"I don't know." She held up a hand as Ducharme started to say something. "I really don't know for sure. Some say when Jefferson was President he brokered a secret agreement with Alexander Hamilton."

Kincannon nodded. "What kind of agreement?"

Ducharme was now rubbing the back of his head, trying to forestall the pounding.

"I've found nothing solid in my research," Evie said. "But I think it's something so powerful it's kept the government from sliding into an Imperial Presidency for over two hundred years; *and* kept wealthy groups like the Cincinnatians from becoming overt in their push for power. Pretty remarkable that it hasn't happened, so, as I told Agent Burns, when something is obvious, accept the obvious. Before all this, from all I'd read, I believed there was a good chance the Jefferson Allegiance existed but there was nothing conclusive." She tapped the page. "With this, I know for certain it does."

"So it's a document of some sort?" Kincannon clarified.

"I would say so," Evie replied.

Kincannon shook his head. "I can't imagine a document that powerful."

"Wouldn't you say the Declaration of Independence was pretty powerful?" Evie asked.

Kincannon nodded. "Yes, but everyone knows about it. You're talking about something that's secret."

"We'll learn how powerful it is when we find it," Evie said.

Ducharme took a deep breath and let it out. "So this killer is ultimately after the Jefferson Allegiance?"

"Yes."

"Through the Jefferson Cipher."

It wasn't a question, but Evie answered anyway. "Correct."

"To use it or destroy it?" Ducharme asked.

"Good question," Evie said. "I'd say primarily to keep us from getting it. So if push came to shove, I'd say the killer might destroy it."

Ducharme mulled that over. "But she wouldn't want to destroy the Cipher. Because that means the wild card of the Allegiance would still be out there, and there's no guarantee the Cipher is the only way to find it. She's got to get her hands on the Allegiance."

"That's logical."

"Now that we're truth telling, do you have the encryption thumb drive for the computer?"

"No."

Ducharme took a deep breath and exhaled it slowly. He turned and looked at Kincannon. The Sergeant Major nodded. Ducharme looked at Evie. "All right. We're in. But no more keeping things back from us anymore. Got it?"

"Got it."

They pulled back out into the road. They left the Plain behind and passed the Superintendent's house on the left. Another stonewall to the right. Old houses went by on the left: the quarters for the heads of the various academic departments at the Academy. The cemetery came up on the right, across the street from the firehouse.

"Where are you going?" Evie asked as Ducharme drove past the entrance.

"Never take the direct route," Ducharme said. "One of Rogers's Rules of Rangering."

"Right," Evie said, looking back down at the book she was thumbing through. "You're big on rules. Rogers who?"

"Major Robert Rogers," Ducharme said. "Led Rogers's Rangers during the French and Indian War. His first rule was: 'All Rangers are to be subject to the rules and articles of war; to appear at roll call every evening on their own parade, equipped each with a firelock, sixty rounds of powder and ball, and a hatchet.'"

"Where's your hatchet?" Evie asked.

"I've got a knife," Ducharme said

He turned right, into the old Post Exchange parking lot, which bordered the cemetery. He parked at the edge of the lot. The cemetery was on the same level as the Plain, a hundred feet above the Hudson. Along the river side of the cemetery was a low stone wall, then a precipitous, wooded drop to Target Hill Field on the edge of the river. The Academy's sewage treatment plant was also down there—right where the two mile run course for the cadets' annual physical fitness test began and ended. He checked his MP-5. "Let's go."

Evie marked a page and put the book in McBride's briefcase. She exited along with Kincannon. She carried the briefcase with her.

"Wait one," Ducharme said. He opened the tailgate and pulled out a small electronic device that looked like a TV remote. He ran it around the Blazer. He stopped when a light blinked red near the front right quarter-panel. Reaching into the wheel well, he felt around. He pulled out a cockroach-sized transmitter and put it in the same pocket the bullet-transmitter was in. He completed his circle of the Blazer without another alert. While he was doing that, Kincannon was on his satphone.

Ducharme stowed the electronic device. "OK. It's clean now." He tossed the bugs underneath the truck since they already had transmitted this location. He looked at Kincannon. "Let's gear up."

They grabbed bulletproof vests and put them on. Ducharme crooked a finger at Evie and handed her a vest. She donned it and quickly covered it with her coat. Ducharme and Kincannon put on black jackets over their vests to maintain a modicum of covert activity. Ducharme handed Kincannon an MP-5 and grabbed his own. They slung them on Velcro straps underneath the jackets. He studied the weapons locker, then grabbed a small caliber gun with a long suppressor on the end and offered it to Evie.

She took it, slipped it in a pocket, and then asked: "Got anything bigger?"

"Does size matter?" Kincannon asked.

"Funny guys," Evie said.

Ducharme waved his hand over the locker. "Your choice."

Evie grabbed an MP-5 sub-machinegun with a suppressor. She slammed a magazine of nine-millimeter rounds in, pulled back the charging handle, checking the chamber.

"My kind of gal," Kincannon said. "Don't suppose you can ride horses?"

"I could learn with the proper motivation," Evie said.

"And what motivation would that be?" Kincannon asked.

"Would you two stop it," Ducharme said.

Kincannon ignored him and reached into his pocket and pulled something out. "Here." He flipped a large coin to her.

Evie caught it, then turned it over. On one side on a scroll on top was inscribed: *Quiet Professionals*. Below it was a dagger with crossed arrows and a scroll around the base that read: *De Oppresso Liber.* "To free the oppressed," she translated.

"Special Forces motto," Ducharme informed her.

"Interesting." She turned it over. An eagle was above a space where something could be inscribed.

"Always carry a blank one?" she asked.

Kincannon nodded. "Never know when you have to build a team."

"Or impress a woman," Ducharme added.

"I can't—" she began, but Kincannon cut her off.

"We're a team. We count on each other."

Evie swallowed hard. Ducharme shifted his feet, checked the gun once more. She finally nodded, sliding the coin into her pocket.

"Hold on a second," Ducharme said. "Do you know how to use the silenced pistol if you have to?"

"I told you tradecraft was more our thing than violence," Evie said. "I assume, aim and pull the trigger."

"Not quite," he told her, reaching in her pocket and pulling it out. "This is a High Standard HDM. Twenty-two caliber, long rifle cartridge. Small bullet, not very powerful. Which means you aren't going to be able to shoot far and your round isn't going to knock anyone off of their feet, as you probably know. But it's suppressed, it's quiet, there's no kick and you've got ten rounds. This is a weapon of last resort, when someone's so close you can feel their breath. Then you shoot them. The eye is best, easy entry into the brain."

Evie was staring at him.

"What?

"We had a moment there with the coin," she said. "But—" she shook her head, and took the gun. She slid it into a pocket on her long coat. "Let's go visit some graves."

"Wait one." Ducharme grabbed some more ordnance, stuffing the pockets on his vest. Kincannon did the same.

"All right," Ducharme said. They walked past some trees into the cemetery.

A concrete pyramid about 20 feet high was directly in front of them. Walking toward it, Ducharme noted a fresh grave. The marker indicated it was for a member of the class of 2010, killed in Chile. The Long Gray Line was giving more bodies to the country.

The pyramid was a mausoleum. Beyond it was an elaborate marker consisting of several clusters of columns holding up an intricately carved, arched roof, upon which was perched a stone eagle.

"Somebody liked themselves," Evie muttered, diverting to take a closer look.

Ducharme and Kincannon followed. The marker indicated it was the burial place of Major General Daniel Butterfield. The name triggered something in Ducharme's mind, reminding him of Arlington for some reason. He struggled to connect the dots, and then it came to him in the form of a remembered sound. "Did you know," he began, earning a roll of the eyes from Kincannon, "that General Butterfield wrote Taps? And that he was awarded the Medal of Honor."

"Exciting," Evie said. "Did he get the Medal for writing the bugle call?"

"No," Ducharme said with exaggerated patience. "For grabbing the regimental colors and rallying his troops during a battle in the Civil War."

Evie turned to him with challenge in her eyes. "Did you know, if he's the Butterfield I think he is, that his father started American Express?"

"A point each," Kincannon said.

Evie wasn't finished. "And that Butterfield himself was heavily involved in Black Friday in eighteen sixty-nine when, as Assistant Treasurer to the United States under President Grant, he tried to sell insider information about government gold selling? Nothing much ever changes. It's always about money and the people who have it wanting more."

"She's ahead again, Duke."

"You do know your history." Ducharme moved forward toward his destination. "By the way, Butterfield *wasn't* a West Point graduate."

"Then what's he doing in here?" Evie asked, hurrying to keep up.

"Probably gave someone some gold," Kincannon said.

The markers were getting older as he went further into the cemetery. A large tree hung over an obelisk at the next row of graves. A small placard was nailed on the trunk of the tree identifying it: *Fagus, Sylvatica, Pendula, A Weeping Beech.*

Ducharme walked around the tree and looked down, to see who or what the tree wept over. The bronze plaque on the base of the obelisk told him he had reached his destination:

GEORGE A. CUSTER
LT. COL 7th CAVALRY
BVT. MAJ GENL., U.S. ARMY
BORN
DECEMBER 15th 1839 HARRISON CO. OHIO
KILLED
WITH HIS ENTIRE COMMAND
IN THE
BATTLE
OF
LITTLE BIG HORN
JUNE 25TH 1873

CHAPTER FOURTEEN

"The man himself," Kincannon said.

"It's not true." Ducharme was walking around the obelisk.

"What isn't?" Kincannon asked.

"His entire command wasn't wiped out. Just the part that rode with him. Troops C—commanded by Custer's brother Tom, L—commanded by his brother-in-law, Lieutenant Calhoun and E, F, I. The rest of the Seventh Cavalry survived."

His therapist would be proud that he could recall all that. He could remember distant facts, but anything that was close, that had emotion attached to it, was another matter. His mind skipped a track, and he remembered Evie talking about Jefferson's Head-Heart letter. He was beginning to understand there was a strong line connecting the two. Unfortunately for him, the line was twisted in a Gordian knot he couldn't comprehend and was afraid to cut through.

"Right," Evie said, looking around, distracted.

"It was important to those who lived," Kincannon noted sagely.

"Robert Anderson." Evie was a few markers down.

"Yeah." Ducharme searched for any sign that the area had been recently disturbed. "Commander of Fort Sumter when his former student, General Beauregard, fired on him from the Battery in Charleston." He was feeling better about his brain that it could bring up this old information so easily.

"This is like a who's who of history," Evie said, beginning to drift further away, looking at other markers.

Ducharme rubbed the back of his head, another thought trying to bubble up. He looked over at Kincannon. "Some say Custer isn't actually buried here. It wasn't like they recovered the bodies right away after the Battle of the Little Big Horn. The relief column buried the dead where they lay, a tad worried that the force that wiped out Custer was still in the area. And I'm sure they didn't bury them deep as they were kind of in a hurry. More like throwing some bushes and a handful of dirt over the maimed bodies. No one was exhumed until the following summer, when they think they recovered Custer's body and brought it back east. Could have been damn near anyone's corpse after a year in a shallow grave in the Black Hills."

"Poe wasn't in his grave," Kincannon said. "But there ain't no other monument to Custer around here like there was for Poe in Baltimore."

Ducharme's eyes narrowed as he noticed that the earth seemed to have been disturbed at the rear of the marker next to Custer's:

ELIZABETH BACON
WIFE OF GEORGE A. CUSTER, MAJOR GENERAL U.S.A
APRIL 8, 1842: APRIL 4, 1933

Ducharme knelt and began to dig in the almost frozen ground with his knife.

* * *

Back at the parking lot, an unmarked CID—Criminal Investigation Division—car rolled up next to the Blazer. The junior man in the car pulled out his satphone and made a call. He reported the Blazer, and listened for a moment. He received his instructions, a look of displeasure on his face.

He switched off the phone and looked at his partner. "The FBI wants us to hold here and await reinforcements."

"Bull," his partner said. "This is our turf."

"Orders."

"It's our turf," his partner said once more. "Fucking FBI. This is *military* jurisdiction. We protect our own."

The younger man frowned in thought, and then nodded. "You're right. Let's take these terrorists down."

* * *

The Bell Jet Ranger landed on the East 34th Street heliport and Lily exited, carrying a large plastic case in one hand and her carry-all in her left. A black government Suburban was waiting for her, keys in the ignition. She got in and started it. She accessed the GPS unit and typed in the address for Trinity Church cemetery: 74 Trinity Place. She saw it was located where Wall Street and Broadway came together in the southern tip of Manhattan.

Anticipation filled her. She reached down and loosened the wakizashi in its scabbard, breaking the bond her classmate's dried blood had made between metal and leather.

* * *

Ducharme kept digging with his knife. He pushed deeper, cleared more dirt away, and was rewarded as the tips of his fingers numbly registered something plastic. He dug further and pulled out a shoebox-sized container, wrapped inside black plastic.

"Inbound," Kincannon warned a second before Ducharme heard the sound of helicopter blades.

Could be just a normal flight. Ducharme quickly dismissed the hopeful imagining. "Your friend?"

Kincannon cocked his head, listening. "Nope. Apache and Blackhawk from the sound."

"What the hell is she flying?" Ducharme muttered. "A duck?"

"Huey," Kincannon said.

"Close enough." Ducharme stuck the package in the butt pack on the back of the vest and looked for Evie. She was about fifty meters away, near the stone wall, looking at another grave.

"Ground company," Kincannon said, drawing his MK-23.

Ducharme looked back the way they had come. Two men in civilian clothes, pistols drawn were coming through the cemetery. They were close together, and the way they held the guns told Ducharme they weren't well trained. Run of the mill Military Police.

"Easy, Jeremiah," he muttered. "Let's take them out as peaceful as we can."

"'Peaceful'," Kincannon said. "Right. Peace is my middle name." He slid the MK-23 back into its holster.

Ducharme drew out his identification card. "Colonel Ducharme," he yelled as he headed toward the two men, holding the card up. Kincannon was at his side.

The two men had their pistols half at the ready, unsure. Ducharme walked toward them, not breaking stride. His confidence fed into their uncertainty. They lowered their weapons just as Ducharme and Kincannon arrived. Without breaking stride, Ducharme slammed the one closest to him in the solar plexus with a cat's paw strike, knocking the wind out of him. Kincannon was more direct and violent, drawing his pistol and rapping the man in front of him on the side of the head. He dropped like a stone.

Ducharme knelt next to the gasping man, going through his pockets. He looked up at Kincannon: "CID." He looked down at the man. "What were you told?"

The man tried to speak, gasped, then managed to get out: "Terror suspects. FBI alert. They're on their way."

Ducharme hit him with a sharp blow on the temple and it was lights out. "Let's go," he ordered.

They ran for the Blazer, but halted as a flight of helicopters roared overhead, two Blackhawks and an Apache. *Bringing out the big guns*, Ducharme thought. One of the Blackhawks came to a hover right in the PX parking lot, the side doors sliding open.

Two thick ropes tumbled out.

"Back to the cemetery," he ordered and they reversed course.

Looking over his shoulder he could see a line of men fast-roping down to the ground, dressed in black and with automatic weapons slung over their shoulders. Not good odds, he thought as they sprinted past grave markers toward the stone wall at the rear of the cemetery.

"Over?" Kincannon yelled.

"Yes," Ducharme replied. "Target Hill Field. Tell your friend."

Kincannon vaulted the wall, then turned to help Evie but she hurdled it easily, MP-5 in one hand, briefcase in the other. Ducharme looked over his shoulder—ten men spread out in tactical formation coming toward them at a dead run. Then he was over the wall and scrambling downhill. Despite the steep incline, Kincannon was on his satphone. They tumbled downslope, narrowly avoiding impacting on trees.

They reached flat ground and the edge of the trees. A large soccer field was in front of them. Beyond it a road, and then the Hudson River. To the right, the sewage treatment plant. And the wind was blowing the wrong way, which was the least of their problems. He could hear the FBI personnel making their way down the slope behind them.

"Kincannon?" he yelled as they sprinted across the frozen soccer field.

"She's inbound," the Sergeant Major yelled back. "Two minutes."

"I don't think we've got two minutes." Ducharme drew the MP-5 out from underneath the coat as he ran and glanced over his shoulder. No one yet.

They reached the fence next to the road where Ducharme used to be tested as a cadet on his two-mile run and max out his score. He was breathing hard. It'd been many a year and many a war since he'd been in that kind of shape.

"Not much cover," Kincannon noted as they went through a gap in the fence and stood on the road facing back the way they'd come. Dead end to the right, sewage plant to the left, Hudson River behind them. Bad guys coming from the front.

"No shit." Ducharme pulled out the telescoping stock of the MP-5 and tucked it into his shoulder, looking toward the tree line at the base of the cemetery hill. "No killing," he reminded Kincannon and Evie, who had the MP-5 to her shoulder.

"Right," Kincannon said. "Almost forgot. What do we do when they try to kill *us*?"

Ducharme fired a controlled three-round burst at the first dark clad figure that came out of the tree line. He hit center of mass in the body armor and the merk was punched back into the trees by the impacts.

Ducharme could hear blades now, a different pitch than that of the Apache or the Blackhawk. He glanced to the right and saw an aging Huey helicopter coming in low over the Hudson River, under the thick clouds.

"One minute," Kincannon said.

Three black clad forms broke from the tree line. Ducharme, Kincannon and Evie fired in concert, efficiently, accurately, and all three went down with shots to their body armor.

"I think they're gonna get pissed soon enough and shoot back for real," Kincannon said in a level voice, as if he was commenting on the weather.

"Likely," Ducharme agreed.

A voice yelled out of the woods. "You've got no way out. Lay down your weapons or we will use deadly force."

"We're going STABO," Kincannon said to Ducharme and Evie, ignoring the voice.

Ducharme reached over and grabbed her, no time for niceties. He ripped off her coat, turned her around, and peeled back the Velcro enclosure on the rear of her combat vest. A nylon strap with a snap hook on the end of it was exposed. "You're first. Kincannon second. I'll be last."

"What about this?" she asked, holding up the briefcase. Ducharme hooked the two handles through the snap link.

Kincannon had thrown his coat to the ground and retrieved his rig. He hooked it into a loop on the bottom front of Evie's vest. Ducharme hooked his strap into the loop on the front of Kincannon's vest.

"We're only gonna get one pass," Kincannon said, eyeing the chopper that was banking hard toward them. A rope dangled below it, barely above the frigid waters of the Hudson.

Ducharme was totally focused on the rope as it came racing toward him. There was a loop on the end, and the wind and downdraft from the blades and the forward momentum of the aircraft had it flying all over the place.

The pilot was good. The Huey flared as it came over land toward them, slowing down abruptly. Ducharme ran forward ten feet and slammed down the snap link on the rope, getting a solid connection. He gave a thumbs up even though he knew the pilot couldn't see him, and the chopper was moving again. With or without them, the pilot was getting the hell out of here as half a dozen streams of tracers arced out of the woods toward it.

Evie yelled something as she was lifted off the ground. Then she gasped as Kincannon was lifted off below her, jerking her vest taut around her. Ducharme fired blindly and high toward the woods, trying to give some semblance of covering fire.

He was lifted off his feet.

Like vertical dominos, the three of them dangled below the Huey as it banked around and then started gaining altitude. Ducharme saw a string of red tracers go by, less than five feet away, hearing the crack of the bullets.

The pilot was heading toward Storm King Mountain. The turbine engine whined, straining for power as the blades clawed for altitude. The chopper bankd once more, averting the direct route to Storm King and staying below the clouds. Ducharme's sigh of relief was brief as he saw something moving behind them. An Apache helicopter was lifting above the tree line at the PX, a Blackhawk beside it.

* * *

"They've got friends," Burns noted. The three people dangling below the helicopter were like little beads on a string.

"Friends aren't going to help them," Turnbull said.

"They're doing pretty good so far."

"So far is over."

* * *

They passed over Washington Gate and Route 293 was below as the Huey descended. The pavement was coming up, and Ducharme bent his knees as his boots hit and he stumbled, his knees scraping on the road, then he was on his feet. Kincannon hit the ground running, unhooking himself, then grabbed Evie, unhooking her and the briefcase. The Huey settled down in the middle of the road, blades racing.

"On the chopper!" Ducharme yelled.

They ran to the chopper and piled on board. As soon as they were in, the Huey was airborne again.

* * *

"There it is," Turnbull said.

The Huey had disappeared below the trees for a few seconds, but now it was ahead of them, about a mile away.

"They're on board," Burns calmly noted. "Why are we chasing them? They're not suspects in the murders."

"You're not that stupid, are you?" Turnbull asked.

Burns pulled an apple out of a pocket and flicked open his switchblade, meeting Turnbull's eyes. "Nope. I'm not."

Turnbull nodded. "Good."

* * **

The chopper shuddered hard, banking at the limits of its design structure. There was one pilot; all Ducharme could see was her helmet and strands of red hair poking out from underneath the back of it in haphazard directions. She looked over her shoulder, face hidden by a dark visor.

"We got company," she yelled. "You have a plan?"

Ducharme looked out of the cargo bay. The Apache and Blackhawk were closing fast. Evie was against the rear bulkhead, clutching the briefcase, which held the disks they'd found so far, the library book and McBride's computer. Ducharme connected his strap to a bolt in the ceiling, while Kincannon hooked in to one on the floor of the chopper. Ducharme slipped on a headset.

"Paul Ducharme," he said as he went to the left edge of the cargo bay and cinched the strap so that it was at the limit of its play as he leaned outward. Then he tucked the stock of the MP-5 into his shoulder.

"Jessie Pollack. You *are not* going to take on an Apache with a sub-machinegun." A short pause. "Are you?"

"You got something better to get them off our tail?" Ducharme made a quick estimate. "'Cause they're going to be on top of us in thirty seconds."

"Hang on," Pollack said.

Ducharme saw Long Pond flash by on the left and knew they were getting close to Camp Buckner where he had spent his 'yearling' summer at the Academy. His stomach did a lurch as the Huey abruptly dropped altitude, now skimming just above Route 293. The chopper flared, and then turned hard right into Camp Buckner, below treetop level, right above a road.

The Apache and Blackhawk screamed by, missing the turn. The Apache looped, doing a roll, coming after them. The Blackhawk was forced to do a more conventional turn.

They'd gained probably ten seconds with the maneuver. Lake Popolopen appeared ahead and Pollack skimmed it. A gash in the ridgeline ahead beckoned where a creek ran into the lake and Pollack flew into it, trees at eye level on either side, dangerously close. Ducharme glanced at Evie. She was staring back at him.

"Having fun?" Ducharme yelled back at her.

"No."

So much for small talk, Ducharme thought. The Apache was in the gash about a quarter mile behind them. The large snout of the 30mm chain gun poked out below the cockpit. It moved ever so slightly, 'slaved' to the gunner's helmet. Hellfire missiles dangling on the stubby wings on either side. If the pilots wanted, they could have splashed the Huey a long time ago with either weapon. Which meant they wanted to force them down.

The radio crackled. "Huey helicopter, this is Agent Turnbull of the FBI. You are ordered to set down or you will be fired upon. Over."

They cleared the top of the ridge, and Pollack pushed them down. "You gonna reply?" She asked on the intercom.

"Fuck the FBI," Ducharme said.

"That's the spirit," Pollack said. "Except when the Blackhawk catches up, they'll box me in."

The radio came alive once more. "Colonel Ducharme. This is Agent Turnbull. This is way beyond your pay grade. Land immediately, give us what you've got and you're free to go."

Ducharme saw the Blackhawk appear above and behind them. The Apache was directly behind; inching so close he could see the two pilots clearly.

Pollack spoke up on the intercom. "The Sergeant Major said this was important. He's a lot of fun, but he's definitely a no bullshit kind of guy when it comes to business."

"That he is."

"Screw it," Pollack said. "Country's going down the crapper anyway."

The Blackhawk went by, about a hundred feet higher in altitude. It picked up speed, easily outpacing the older, Vietnam era chopper.

"What's he going to do?" Ducharme asked.

"Try to stop me," Pollack said. "Thruway's ahead."

Ducharme saw the wide lines of the NY State Thruway about a mile ahead. The Blackhawk suddenly turned and faced them, diving down toward the ground. It flared, directly in their path, hovering. A thousand feet ahead. Nine hundred.

"Ducharme?" Turnbull's voice was flat, calm. Eight hundred. "Don't make this any harder than it needs to be."

Ducharme keyed the radio. "It needs to be hard." Seven hundred. Ducharme leaned out of the Huey, trusting the harness to hold him. Six hundred. He put the MP-5 to his shoulder, aiming forward.

"Don't do anything stupid," Turnbull warned. Five hundred.

It would be ineffectual at this range, but Ducharme fired a sustained burst anyway, emptying half the magazine. Every third round was a tracer, arcing out in a red blaze toward the Blackhawk. Four hundred feet.

On the other side of the cargo bay, Kincannon joined in, firing his sub-machinegun.

"I will fucking shoot you down," Turnbull yelled, finally some emotion into his voice.

"No, you won't." Ducharme aimed. Three hundred feet. "Wood disks burn pretty easily." Two hundred. He fired, emptying the magazine, seeing sparks as rounds hit the armored front of the Blackhawk. One hundred feet.

Hanging further outward on the harness, Ducharme dropped the magazine out of the well and slammed another one home. Then he dropped it to the end of its sling. He reached into a pocket on the combat vest. The Blackhawk was right in front of them. Ducharme's stomach lurched once more as Pollock dropped them hard. He didn't think there was enough room between the bottom of the Blackhawk and the top of the trees.

And there wasn't, as a branch slapped Ducharme in the side. The Huey stuttered as its nose smashed through treetops. Its blades were scant inches from the Blackhawk's wheels. Then they were through. Ducharme twisted, and with all his might threw a handful of mini-grenades up and to the rear, barely missing the Huey's own blades.

They went off, puffs of explosions right below the Blackhawk. Then he lost sight of it as the Huey banked hard, right on top of a railroad track.

"I got an idea," Pollack yelled into the intercom. "I know this area."

Ducharme regained his balance and looked back. There was no sign of the Blackhawk, but no sign of a crash either. The Apache was coming, having backed off during the game of chicken.

"I'm ordering the Apache to shoot you down." Turnbull did not sound pleased.

"I don't think so," Ducharme said.

A string of big-ass 30mm tracers sliced across the front of the Huey as the Apache swung wide to get a firing angle.

"You've been warned," Turnbull said.

The Huey rolled right. Ducharme braced for a crash as they went below the rail tracks. Then he realized the tracks were on a long trestle, arcing across a valley. The Huey slowed as Pollock flared it. The Apache flashed by overhead, turning hard away from the tracks.

Pollock turned them toward the long trestle. Massive iron girders reached up from the valley floor to support it. Pollack flew right between two of the supports, blades barely clearing on either side, then swung around to face back the way they'd come. She put one of the sets of girders between them and the approaching Apache. Not the best cover in the world, Ducharme thought, but better than nothing at this point.

"Come on, come on," Pollack was whispering into the intercom.

Ducharme leaned out and fired the entire magazine at the approaching attack helicopter. Several of his rounds richocheted off the iron girders.

The Apache reached the gap they had just flown, and the pilot must have realized his mistake at the last second, trying to stop. The tips of the blades clipped the iron girders. Sparks flew for several long seconds, then the

Apache backed off, losing altitude quickly. Ducharme watched it land hard in the field below.

22 MARCH 1962

President John F. Kennedy, as was the custom for his lunches with J. Edgar Hoover, had the Oval Office emptied of everyone, even his brother Robert. To Kennedy, today was looking to be a particularly odious session, as Hoover was carrying a particularly thick file.

Kennedy had been advised by Eisenhower to continue a tradition begun by FDR: inviting the head of the FBI to lunch at the White House every month. It was under the principle of keep your friends close, but your enemies closer. Since taking office, Kennedy had stretched the interval out to every two months, and he was hoping he could eventually go without seeing the grotesque man at all. Bobbie wasn't happy about the luncheons either, because technically Hoover worked for the Attorney General, although the man never acted like he answered to Bobbie. Or even the President, Kennedy reflected as he sat on the couch across from Hoover, a low, ornate, coffee table between them; Jackie's choice.

Hoover dropped the thick file onto the coffee table with great relish. Kennedy didn't rise to the bait. Instead he waited as his secretary refilled his coffee cup, offered some to Hoover, and then departed. Kennedy took a sip of coffee and waited some more, refusing to descend into Hoover's gutter.

"Interesting wiretaps," Hoover finally said. "Should I set the stage for them?"

Kennedy shrugged, knowing the old man would say what he wanted, regardless. His back was aching and he shifted, trying to adjust the brace strapped around his body. He glanced at his watch, thinking ahead to his schedule for the afternoon.

His thoughts came to an abrupt halt at Hoover's next two words: "Judith Campbell."

Kennedy tried to stay relaxed. "Who?"

Hoover gave that sickening smile of his. "Las Vegas. Nineteen sixty. The filming of Oceans Eleven. *Your 'buddy' Frank Sinatra. He introduced you to her. Don't you remember?"*

"I can't recall. I don't even remember being in Vegas."

The smile grew wider. "I can assure you that you were," Hoover said. He opened the folder and on top was the picture of a woman. He slid it across to Kennedy, who didn't pick it up.

"She's quite beautiful," Hoover said. "Interesting timing. You were seeking the democratic nomination at the time. Apparently you were seeking more than that, as you became involved with Miss Campbell."

"I'm afraid your information is—"

"Incorrect?" Hoover completed for him. "Do you know how many times I've heard that? I never share information unless I am certain *it is correct." He grabbed the next picture in the folder and tossed it on top of Campbell's. Kennedy's stomach tightened.*

"Perhaps unknown to you at the time, but certainly known afterwards, was that Sinatra also introduced Miss Campbell to this man." He leaned forward and tapped the picture. "Sam Giancana. A criminal. Head of what is called 'the Outfit' in Chicago. Since there is no organized crime in this country, the Outfit is a bunch of thieves and murderers." The sarcasm was dripping from Hoover's words.

"It wouldn't surprise you, of course, to know that Miss Campbell is also Mister Giancana's mistress?"

Kennedy couldn't tell if it was a question or not, so he remained silent.

"Of course not." Hoover answered his own question. "Since Miss Campbell calls you here at the White House using the phone in Mister Giancana's apartment in Chicago." Hoover picked up a third picture and threw it down. "Your father. Joseph Kennedy. He had dealings with men like Giancana, especially during Prohibition. I believe the Sinatra introduction was at his behest."

Kennedy had not thought of that, but he knew as soon as Hoover said it, that it was true. Chicago. Of course. His father pulling strings.

Hoover pursed his lips as if in thought. "Now this part is not validated, but comes from credible sources. It seems someone from your campaign gave a bag of cash to Giancana back when you were seeking the Democratic nomination. You did win Illinois, mainly because of a huge push in Chicago. Some would say a statistically impossible push. A lot of votes from the grave."

"What do you want?" Kennedy had had enough.

Hoover picked up the next item in the folder. A thick sheaf of papers. "Come now, Mister President, are you really trying to hire this Giancana fellow and his 'Outfit' to assassinate Castro?"

"What the hell are you talking about?"

Hoover blinked. "You really *don't know about that? Curious. Your precious CIA is keeping secrets from you, too. But, like me, they know* your *secrets."*

"What do you want?"

Hoover reached over and grabbed the sheaf of papers and the photos, making a large show of putting them back into the folder and shutting it. Kennedy didn't miss that there was a lot in that folder that Hoover had not brought out.

"It isn't what I want. It's what we *want." Hoover lifted the lapel on the right side of his suit jacket, revealing a medallion. "The Society of the Cincinnati, Mister President."*

With his other hand he tapped the thick folder. "We have you—and your brother—by the balls, to use a crude but appropriate metaphor. If I ask for something, we want it. Do you understand?"

Kennedy just stared back at the old man.

Hoover stood, tucking the folder under one arm. "Right now, all we want it is for your brother to change his mind and sign off on the paperwork on his desk to wiretap Martin Luther King."

"I don't—" Kennedy began, but stopped as Hoover waved the folder, as if fanning himself. "All right."

5 AUGUST 1963

"I love you, too," President Kennedy said, and then hung up the phone, severing the line to his wife in Hyannis Port.

"How is Jackie?" the only other occupant of his private dining room on the second floor of the White House asked.

Kennedy grimaced, both from the pain in his back and the recent conversation. "Not good. The heat is bad, she feels ill and she's scared."

"Of course she's scared. She already lost one child. I know how she feels."

Kennedy watched as Mary Meyer took a sip of her drink. He enjoyed her company— one of the few people he felt comfortable being alone with and simply talking, but to be honest, he still missed their affair.

"Graham shot himself," he said, referring to the Washington Post *publisher who had killed himself with a shotgun just two days previously. And who, back in January, had pushed his way to the podium at a conference of newspaper editors in Phoenix—even though he wasn't supposed to speak—and drunkenly delivered a tirade that included references to the President's 'new favorite,' Mary Meyer. He had been wrong about the 'new' part, Kennedy mused. He'd known Mary since college, and she'd long been a staple of White House life.*

"I heard," Mary said. "I feel for his wife. He'd just gotten out of the hospital. They thought he was better."

"He was out of control," Kennedy said. He had been intimate many times with Mary, and even though that part of their relationship had ended with the dual pressures of Graham's publicity and Jackie's pregnancy, he still felt a tight bond. He'd once smoked marijuana with her, even tried LSD—not his thing—and she'd been there with him through the Cuban Missile Crisis, Bay of Pigs, and many other significant events of his Presidency. Always someone he could confide in and count on for solid advice. "What's wrong, Mary? Is it Jackie? She's fine with your being here."

149

Mary Meyer shook her head. "I was approached by some men. They wanted me to give you a message and they showed me something."

"What men?"

She shook her head. "I can't tell you, except that they're for real. Three high-ranking generals and someone—let's say he's on a level with Graham."

Kennedy frowned. "What did they show you?"

"A document." Mary got up from her end of the table and sat caddy-corner to the President and took his hand.

Kennedy was surprised at the move and the look on her face. "What is it? What's wrong?"

"Have you ever heard of the Jefferson Allegiance?"

Kennedy gripped her hand tighter. "A rumor of it. No one has ever confirmed its existence though."

"It exists. They showed it to me."

Kennedy could feel his back tighten, the old injury from PT-109 coming back to haunt him as it always did when he was under stress. "Why did they show it to you?"

"They wanted me to give you a message. And they knew you trusted me."

"Go on," Kennedy prompted.

Mary's tongue snaked over her lips, a sign of how nervous she was. "They said that they respected what you did during the Missile Crisis. That it was important that one man be in charge and handle things. That it was one of those unique moments with high stakes where the responsibility and decision-making had to rest on the President's shoulders."

"But?" Kennedy prompted.

"The Bay of Pigs. The Wall being built in Berlin. Your recent speech there worried people. They felt you were continuing to challenge Khrushchev. That it had become personal. And the involvement in Vietnam greatly concerns the military men."

Kennedy scoffed. "There are only eleven thousand men in Vietnam—all advisers. And the Pentagon has promised they can be withdrawn by the end of the year after they crush the Vietcong rebels. Vietnam is not an issue."

"That is not the way the Philosophers see it."

"The 'Philosophers'? So it's true that they guard the Allegiance." He stared at her. "Is it as powerful as rumored?"

Mary nodded. "If they invoke it, they would remove you from office. And that's just the beginning."

The silence in the dining room lasted a long time before Kennedy spoke again. "What do they want?"

"For you to use the National Security Council for advice more often. To back off Vietnam. Back off of pressing Khrushchev."

"Do they want an answer?"

"They told me they would get their answer from your actions."

"I don't like being threatened," Kennedy snapped. "I get it from both sides. The damn Cincinnatians and Hoover. Now the Philosophers. I'm sick of it."

"There's something else," Mary said.

"What?" Kennedy knew he was being short, but the pain in his back and this information along with Jackie being miserable in Hyannis Port was ruining what he had hoped would be a pleasant evening.

"Did you know the CIA is trying to use the mob to kill Castro?"

Kennedy leaned back in his chair, trying to ease the pain in his back, pulling his hand out of hers. *"Hoover said something to me about that. I thought he was bluffing."*

"I asked Cord," Mary said, referring to her ex-husband, who was high in the ranks of the Agency. *"He said 'of course not,' which means of course they are."*

"Goddamnit," Kennedy slammed a fist onto the tabletop, causing the crystal to bounce.

"The Philosophers want you to get on top of that. After the Bay of Pigs, there can't be another Cuban fiasco. They say it's very complicated and dangerous and that the Cincinnatians are involved."

"Who the hell runs this country?" Kennedy demanded.

Mary got up and walked behind his chair. She leaned over and wrapped her arms around his chest. *"I'm worried, Jack. Very worried for you. Cord didn't just lie to me. There's something going on. Something very dangerous. Promise me you'll be careful?"*

Kennedy was hardly comforted by her touch or her words, but he nodded anyway. *"I promise."*

CHAPTER FIFTEEN

Burns watched as the pilots inspected the damage to the underside of the Blackhawk. The landing had been hard, but without injury to anyone on board. The Apache had called in shortly afterward that it too was down.

"They took out two advanced helicopters with a Vietnam era chopper," Burns noted.

"I've told you I don't like it when you tell me something I already know," Turnbull snapped. He'd already been on his satphone, calling in the second Blackhawk, which had stopped to pick up the quick reaction force from Target Hill Field. And alerting all airfields within range to report if a Huey landed. The calls from various agencies and the military were piling up and keeping this under wraps much longer was going to be impossible.

"Wood disks?" Burns calmly asked, putting on his fedora.

"Nothing to concern yourself with."

"I assume he was referring to the disks that Tolliver and Ducharme had." Burns checked his Fedora in the plexiglass window of the chopper. "The Head and Heart."

Turnbull paused. "What?"

"The Head-Heart letter that Tolliver referenced in the interview. Curious the killer would signal that in the first murders."

"Not curious," Turnbull said.

"How so?"

"Jefferson argued with himself in that letter. It meant he was uncertain."

"I just read it," Burns said. "He seemed pretty certain at the end."

Turnbull gave a cold smile. "But look at the bigger picture. The Heart seems to win the argument in the letter, but in reality, Jefferson never saw Missus Cosway again. So while he felt what he thought was the right thing, he did the wrong thing."

152

"Perhaps he was balanced," Burns said. "Are we going after the killer at all? Or are we going to keep chasing Ducharme and Evie?"

"We'll get the killer, don't worry."

"But not yet," Burns said.

"Not yet."

"Because there's something you need her to do. In fact, it seems like we're trying to stop Ducharme and Evie from stopping her."

Turnbull turned his back and went back to issuing orders on his satphone.

"Wood disks," Burns muttered to himself. He pulled out his satphone and checked to see what text messages Burns had received or sent.

One received.

He pulled it up.

>>>PARKER SAID HIS DISKS WERE IN A GRAVE<<<

Burns waited as a second line of text was decrypted.

>>>NO ONES AND EVERYONES<<<

Burns frowned. What the hell?

>>>WHAT DOES IT MEAN?<<<

Burns almost laughed out loud, realizing whoever was texting also had no clue.

* * *

People were grabbing lunch from vendors along the edge of the cemetery. Fat-cat Wall Street financiers, secretaries, Con Edison hardhats. The men and women in business suits particularly irked Lily for some reason she couldn't quite identify.

The first church on the site, according to the brochure she'd picked up entering the cemetery, had been built in 1698. Skyscrapers surrounded her, dwarfing the latest iteration of the church built in 1846, which had once been the most prominent feature on the southern Manhattan skyline.

She finished texting what she'd learned from Parker to Turnbull, hoping he had some idea what the old General had meant. She sat on a crypt just in front of Hamilton's grave, her L.A. cloak wrapped tight around her body. It was a cold blustery day, not conducive to sightseeing.

She squinted at the brochure that listed notables buried in this small slice of dirt amongst the steel and concrete of the city. Alexander Hamilton was listed first. Then Robert Fulton, credited with making the first practical steamship.   Also listed: Captain Lawrence, as she already knew, the connection to the saying on the wall of Admiral Groves's office.

She looked up, scanning the cemetery. A couple hustled through, pausing long enough to stop at each important grave and snap a photo, then hustle on. Touring by checklist.

Her satphone vibrated. She pulled it out.

LOCATION?

Her fingers flew over the keys in response to Mister Turnbull's query.

>>>NEW YORK CITY<<<

WHY?

>>>BELIEVE GROVE'S DISK IS HERE<<<

WHERE EXACTLY?

>>>HAMILTON'S GRAVE<<<

Lily took a deep breath and scanned the cemetery before looking down for the next incoming text.

INTERESTING

She listed out the numbers from the Post-it and sent them to Turnbull along with how she found them.

>>>ONE WILL COME HERE FOR DISKS<<< She added.

AND?

She looked about once more, and then her fingers flew over the pads, typing out her reply.

>>>KILLING 2D GENERATION WILL BE SAME AS GAINING CIPHER<<<

NO. WE MUST GET CIPHER
>>>I KILLED PARKER'S REPLACEMENT. GOT HER SINGLE DISK<<<

There was nothing for a few moments.

WHERE ARE REST OF PARKER'S DISKS?

>>> I SENT YOU THE RIDDLE HE TOLD ME<<<

ANY IDEA WHAT IT MEANS?

>>>NEGATIVE<<<

The screen went blank.

Lily surveyed the monument. There was no sign it had been tampered with. She went to the front and knelt as if in prayer. She slid out her sword and probed the ground front. The blade slid into the dirt freely. She continued, glancing over her shoulder every once in a while, but there was nothing. She went to the back of the monument and did the same.

Nothing.

Lily slowly got to her feet, putting her sword away. *Wrong twice?* She blinked, feeling a shooting pain in her head for the briefest of moments. It passed as quickly as it had come, and she forgot about it as she considered the situation. She sat back down on the crypt in front of Hamilton's grave, mentally backtracking through what she'd seen on the computer in Philadelphia.

She saw a man enter the cemetery from the Wall Street side. He was moving slowly and looking about a little too much. Her fingers slithered around the grip of her wakizashi underneath her cloak.

* * *

Instead of flying them back to Stewart International Airfield, where there would no doubt be a reception committee, Pollock choppered to a local medical clinic, landing on the helipad in back of it. Pollock shut down the chopper as Ducharme stood off to the side with Evie and Kincannon.

Pollock took off her flight helmet, revealing mussed red hair tinged with gray, her sweat-soaked face covered in freckles and a deep frown. "What's going on? We made two helicopters go down. I haven't heard anything on the emergency net, so I think everyone on them is OK, but still . . ."

Kincannon held up his hand. "Honestly, the less you know, the better for you."

Pollock seemed to consider that, then nodded. "OK. I'm going to check on what the latest news is." She walked toward the clinic.

"You have good friends," Evie said to Kincannon.

"Blood bonds," Kincannon said. "People who haven't been in combat don't understand it."

She tilted her head toward him. "Have we seen the elephant?"

Kincannon appeared startled, but then slowly nodded. "Yeah. We have."

Evie nodded. "You know what Thomas wrote in the Head-Heart letter about friendship? *Friendship is but another name for an alliance with follies and misfortunes of others.*"

Ducharme laughed. "Cynical, but sounds like what we've been doing." He checked his watch. "We probably need to head to New York City as soon as possible."

She shook her head. "I don't think Admiral Groves's disks are at Hamilton's grave."

"You don't?" Kincannon asked. "Why not?"

She held up the book that she had stolen from the library. "Oliver Hazard Perry. Since Groves was his namesake, I think Perry is key, not Captain Lawrence. Plus, it was the flag—which was Perry's—that hung in Groves's office. So the line of deduction is that the saying, as appropriated by Perry, and put on a flag, is the key. Not just the saying."

Ducharme moved closer. "OK. And?"

"Follow the logic thread of history," Evie said. "The saying from Lawrence. The flag with the saying on it. And the ships Perry commanded that flew the flag."

Ducharme nodded. "Following so far."

"OK. Brief history summary if you will bear with me." Her eyes got that distant look. "Perry's flagship in the Battle of Lake Erie was the *Lawrence*, named after our man, Captain Lawrence. It got blown to bits during the battle and over eighty percent of his crew was killed or wounded. I don't see Lawrence's grave being important either in terms of the saying or the ship named after him. Perry transferred his flag—with the famous words on it—to the *Niagara*. He forced the surrender of the British and uttered his own famous phrase: 'We have met the enemy and they are ours.'"

Ducharme waved his hand, indicating she should fast forward.

"And?" Kincannon asked. "The disks are at Niagara Falls?"

"No. We have to remember we're dealing with history and graves." She tapped the book. "OK. Perry was a big hero now. After the war, in eighteen nineteen, he was selected by the Secretary of the Navy to lead a diplomatic mission to Venezuela."

"All right," Ducharme said, with barely concealed irritation. He wanted the answer, with little patience for the reason for the answer.

"OK. What's important here is the name of his new—and final—command. The *USS John Adams*. Named after the country's first Vice President and second President. Now, Adams is appropriate. Very appropriate to our current situation and Thomas Jefferson."

She opened her mouth and paused, realizing she was about to utter her familiar phrase, then decided the hell with it. "Did you know that John Adams and Thomas Jefferson died on the exact same day?"

"Nope." Ducharme didn't seem too impressed.

"Do you know what day it was?"

"No, but I'm sure you're going to tell me."

"The Fourth of July, eighteen twenty-six. They both died exactly fifty years to the day after the signing of the Declaration of Independence."

"You're shitting me."

Evie experienced a small thrill at finally getting through to him. "Adams's last words were: 'Thomas Jefferson survives.' Except he didn't know that Jefferson, who had been very sick for a while, had indeed managed to hold on until the Fourth, but succumbed earlier in the day."

"That's fucking bizarre," Kincannon said.

Ducharme shivered for a moment, that dull look coming into his eyes. Evie waited, wishing there was something she could do to help, but it passed quickly.

"So," Ducharme finally said. "The disks. Where are they?"

"John Adams."

"What about him?"

"Perry contracted Yellow Fever and died during the trip to Venezuela on board the *John Adams*. It was the last ship over which that flag flew. Johns Adams was the second president.

"The disks," Ducharme said, always one to focus on the current problem instead of the reasons for it. Which could be a dangerous flaw, and something Evie recognized. Because as she kept trying to point out to him, current problems were always tied to past problems.

She touched his arm. "If I were going to hide a piece of the Jefferson Cipher, I'd put it in Adams's grave, not Hamilton's. Although Jefferson and Adams sparred over a lot of things during their long careers, by their twilight years, they were in constant correspondence and very much in agreement on many critical issues."

"But you're not certain," Ducharme said.

"No."

"And the Surgeon is probably at Hamilton's grave as we speak. Along with Groves's replacement."

"Most likely." A tremor moved through her chest, as she understood what Ducharme was saying. "The Cipher is the most important thing."

"Not the person?" Ducharme held up a hand. "I'm sorry. That was cheap."

"It was," Evie said, "but not any different than what I said to you earlier." She took a deep breath, getting her mind back on task. "Do you have the disks from Custer's grave?" Evie asked.

"Yeah." Ducharme pulled the box wrapped in plastic out of the butt pack and used his knife to cut away the plastic, revealing a wooden cigar box. He opened it, Evie and Kincannon watching over his shoulder. There was a long, thin object wrapped in the same plastic and underneath a round, thin object wrapped in the same. Evie reached over his shoulder, pressing her body armor against his, thinking: *well this is just plain weird.* She grabbed the round object and then reached out. "Your knife, please?"

Ducharme handed it to her. "Careful."

"I know which end is sharp."

He laughed, a surprisingly light sound for someone so grim, and his face changed once more, from stone to something more open. "No offense. I've just always cut myself on every knife I've owned. It's as if the blade doesn't take some of my blood, then it's not mine."

"Maybe you're just awkward with knives?"

"Maybe."

She cut open the plastic and frowned. "Not disks." She held up a 8mm film tape inside a hard plastic container. "This is old, very old."

"When did they stop using that kind of film?" Ducharme asked.

"No idea." Evie looked at Kincannon.

"What?" Kincannon said in mock horror. "You think I'm that old?"

Ducharme unpeeled the plastic from the long object, revealing a metal cigar tube. He unscrewed the end and slid out a piece of paper. "My uncle wasn't going to make it easy."

"What's it say?" Evie asked as Ducharme unrolled the paper.

Ducharme handed it to her:

FRP: EXCALIBUR
A/D: 270 DEGREES, ONE HUNDRED AND SIX METERS
IRP: BASE OAK
MODE: 6 INCHES, DIRT
Watch and learn.

"What is this?" Evie handed it back.

"It's a cache report. A format that gives directions to where something is hidden. In this case, it must be the disks. You've got your Far Reference Point, then directions from it to the Immediate Reference Point and how the item is hidden. Didn't they teach you that at the Farm?"

"It seems a little outdated," Evie said.

"A wooden cipher wheel seems a little outdated," Ducharme noted.

"A point for the man," Kincannon said.

Evie laughed. "OK. So we have to find a mythical sword first?" She sat on the edge of the cargo bay of the helicopter. "Why couldn't LaGrange leave the disks at the grave?"

Kincannon spoke up. "Why couldn't McBride leave all his in the briefcase?"

Evie nodded with a smile. "Point taken and earned."

Ducharme tapped the report. "LaGrange is making it difficult to track and he's making sure only someone who'd been a cadet could understand."

"OK. Where's Excalibur?" She eyed him. "Do you have to draw it out of a stone somewhere?"

Ducharme shook his head. "No. It *is* stone. An engraving above the entrance to the Cadet Chapel. So we go two hundred and seventy degrees, due west, one hundred and six meters, from the chapel door, to an oak tree. The disks are buried six inches down from the base."

"So we have to go *back* to West Point?"

"I do," Ducharme said. "The 'watch and learn' must be about the tape."

Evie hefted the battered leather case. "I wish we could read his journal. I think it would give us a lot of the answers we need."

"Well," Kincannon said, rubbing the stubble of beard on his chin. "Seems to me these folks went out of their way with the tradecraft to keep their secrets, *but* at the same time they always left a way to find what you're looking for. So there's got to be a way to find that decrypter for the computer. He left the computer with *you*. He knew you'd figure it out."

Evie closed her eyes in thought, and then opened them. "It has to be something simple and direct. Simpler than finding the disks. Because McBride probably thought it would be the first thing I'd do—try to figure out how to read his computer, maybe find out what exactly is going on. I don't think he expected so much killing, so fast."

"All right then," Kincannon said. "Put yourself back to where and when he gave you the briefcase."

"I was at work," Evie said. "Monticello. And—" she paused, her face lighting up. "It makes perfect sense."

"A grave," Ducharme said. "Jefferson's."

Evie nodded. "And like Poe's, one where the marker isn't right. Jefferson's original marker was degraded by souvenir seekers chipping off pieces. It was donated to the University of Missouri on the fourth of July in eighteen eighty-five."

"The University of Missouri?" Kincannon wasn't following.

"The first state university that came into being in the territory Jefferson bought with the Louisiana Purchase."

"So it's there?" Ducharme asked.

Evie shook her head. "No. McBride would have kept it close. They put a new marker over Jefferson's tomb at Monticello. A larger replica of the original surrounded by an iron fence. I think this time, what we're looking for stayed with the body, just like it stayed with Poe's body, even though they moved the original marker."

"The disks are the priority," Ducharme said. "They lead to the Allegiance."

"But we might need to know what McBride's written in his journal to understand the Allegiance," Evie argued. "He wouldn't have given it to me for no reason."

Ducharme summed the situation up. "We've got Adams's grave possibly with disks, and Jefferson's grave with possibly a decoder. And then, we might have one of our fellow—what do you call it—Philosophers—heading toward Hamilton's grave."

He seemed about to say something else, when Pollock came walking out, helmet under her arm.

"What now?" the pilot asked. "My motto is 'you call, I haul.' I shut off my transponder and if I do nap of the earth, I can stay off radar."

Evie looked at Ducharme. "We have to split up."

"Not a sound military tactic," Ducharme said. "Didn't work well for Custer."

"You feel like Custer?" Evie asked.

"No," Ducharme said. "But-" he paused. He rubbed a hand across his face, pausing as his fingers touched the scar underneath his right eye. He glanced at Kincannon and the Sergeant Major nodded.

"A lot of ground to cover and we need to do it quick to stay ahead of these people," Kincannon said.

"If we're ahead of them," Ducharme hedged.

"What you gonna do, Ranger?" Kincannon chided.

"All right," Ducharme said. He turned to Pollock. "Jessie, you got a ride Evie and I can use? Just to get to West Point?"

She nodded. "That old pickup over there is my friend's who works here. He'll let you use it."

Ducharme snapped out commands, his mind made up. "Evie and I take the pick-up, go to just outside Stony Lonesome gate. I'll infiltrate West Point on foot, recover the cache." He hit some buttons on his satphone. "Lojack says our Blazer is there—in the military police impound lot. I doubt the Feds—or whoever the hell these people are—left anyone there with it—they were all chasing us and they already went over the vehicle in DC. Evie, while I do that, you try to find something that will play that film." He turned to the Sergeant Major. "Jeremiah, you go with Jessie. Fly to Monticello and see if anything's buried at Jefferson's grave. Then we'll all link up at Adams's grave."

* * *

The man had passed through without stopping, putting Lily even more on edge. Maybe she was wrong about the grave. Too many mistakes.

"A history buff, perchance, good lady?"

She spun about, almost unsheathing the sword. A man dressed in Colonial America regalia, from large buckle shoes to tricorner hat, was standing on the path, a cane under his arm. He had a big, bushy beard and small, old-fashioned glasses perched on his bulbous red nose. Ben Franklin come to life. If he started miming, she was going to cut him down where he stood. Perhaps with a few painful slices before a fatal one.

He stepped forward. "Ah. Alexander Hamilton. Quite the controversial figure. And the duel, good lady, the duel that caused his poor soul to end up here, it happened not far that way."

He pointed vaguely to the southwest. If this guy ever had to navigate his way in enemy territory he'd be dead before nightfall.

He continued annoying her. "Many sources say Hamilton deliberately missed. That he thought he had a gentleman's agreement with Burr that both would miss, honor would be assuaged, and they could go on with their lives. But Burr was no gentleman. Any who knew the cur would have been sure of that. After all, Burr lost the eighteen hundred Presidential Election to Jefferson by one vote, and, having to choose between what Hamilton viewed as two evils: Jefferson and Burr—Hamilton threw his support behind Jefferson and had one of his Federalist congressman swing the election to Jefferson."

She tensed when the re-enactor stepped closer and reached under his frock. She was ready to strike as he withdrew an antique pistol. "The pistols used in the Burr-Hamilton duel—looking very much like this one—had been used previously, in a duel whence Hamilton's own son, Philip, was slain."

"Don't you have a job?" She looked past him and saw another man enter the cemetery and knew right away that if she was wrong about the location, so was the latest generation of Philosophers. The newcomer had that attitude that only came from being one of the elite—Special Operations. They could dress in civilian clothes, grow beards, slouch, but they couldn't lose that aura. He wore a long black leather coat—too much watching of "The Matrix"— and a baseball cap pulled down low over his eyes. He moved as if he owned the cemetery and feared nothing.

She tightened her grip on the sword.

"This *is* my job." The re-enactor sounded insulted. "Well, I do have a role off-Broadway in a production of—"

"Shut up," Lily hissed. She accepted that some people truly were idiots as the man continued.

"They say Hamilton was carried to his home in upper Manhattan where he lingered for a night after being rowed back from New Jersey, and then perished. But that is not true. He was taken to a friend's home near the landing site. You can even walk down Jane Street in Greenwich Village and see a small plaque on the front of a brownstone proclaiming it to be the location of the house where Mister Hamilton expired.

"Burr, of course—"

"Leave!" Lily put all the command she had learned at the Academy and in the Air Force into her voice, and finally got through to the idiot. The re-enactor grumpily slouched away, in search of better listening and perhaps someone who would buy him a drink.

The newcomer looked down at a piece of paper in his hand, and then around. The re-enactor went up to him, they had a brief discussion, and then the re-enactor continued in search of other victims. The man's eyes locked on Hamilton's grave. He glanced at her, checking her out as men always did, but didn't see a threat. A subjective dismissal she was too familiar with.

She pulled out her satphone and dialed the third number on the Post-it. It rang several times. On the fourth ring she saw the man pull out his own satphone.

"Hello?"

Lily pressed the off button and slid the phone back into her pocket. The man looked confused for a moment, then shrugged, putting the phone away. He walked over to Hamilton's grave, staring at the monument, less than ten feet from her. The monument was a stone obelisk placed on top of a pedestal that had four urns at each corner. On the front was written:

The corporation of TRINITY CHURCH *has erected this*
In Testimony of the Respect
FOR
The PATRIOT *of incorruptible* INTEGRITY
The SOLDIER *of approve* VALOR
The STATESMAN *of consummate* WISDOM
Whose TALENTS *and* VIRTUES *will be admired*
Long after this MARBLE *shall have mouldered into*
DUST
He died July 12th 1804 Aged 47

The man laughed. "He sure thought a lot of himself."

Lily raised an eyebrow. "That's his eulogy, written by someone after he was dead."

The man shook his head. "It's bullshit. Take his incorruptible integrity for example. Hamilton had so many affairs people started naming their Tomcats after him. Martha Washington was one of the first to do it."

The man was young, fit. Tanned skin despite the winter.

"I'm Lily. And you are?"

He looked at her squarely, a bit taken aback at her directness. She'd never understand the social 'dance' between the sexes, but she found it most useful at times in getting what she truly desired. "Vince."

She had learned early on at the Academy that a man could be easily distracted by a woman. "You're military aren't you, Vince?"

He smiled once more, full of confidence. "Yes. Navy SEALS."

"I thought so." She nodded at the monument. "You don't seem to like him."

"Hamilton?" Vince shook his head. "Got to give him credit for what he achieved, but he sure had a twisted brain."

"'Twisted?'"

"He was big into money and being born to the right people, yet he came out of squalor. Kind of weird."

Lily found comfort in running her hand over the top of her sword grip underneath her heavy cloak. "How so?"

"He was born in the Caribbean on a small island, poor and illegitimate," Vince said. "Mother died when he was young; he had nothing. Got to give him credit that he worked his way up. Made his own way in the world."

"You know a lot about Hamilton?" Lily asked.

"I did some research on my way here," Vince said vaguely. "You a fan?"

She got off the crypt and stood close to the Navy SEAL, her hand curling around the handle of the wakizashi, sliding it up a few inches in its sheath. "I think he was a brilliant man. A true patriot."

He shrugged. "Should have been faster on the draw with Burr, though."

"Hamilton was a gentleman and had pride," Lily said. "He deliberately missed Burr, and then the coward shot him."

Vince shrugged again. "Then he was stupid as well as arrogant." He was dismissing her; she felt it. It was the way she'd been treated by men in the military. Somehow they could sense when she was near that she would not give them what they really wanted from her.

She stepped closer, inside the area that people considered their space. He seemed startled and really looked at her now. She could tell he liked what he saw. They always did until it was too late.

"Lily," he said. "That's a nice name."

"Do you read Keats?"

"Who?"

She gave an alluring smile. "*La Belle Dame sans Merci.* It's a poem he wrote. My father gave me my name from it."

"What does it mean?" Vince asked, his eyes locked into hers. She was very close now. She put her free hand on his thigh, feeling the solid muscles. His breathing shifted, and got shallower. His eyes locked onto hers and she saw the arrogance in them. She moved her hand up, to his crotch, felt his hardness. She leaned her head close and whispered in his ear, her tongue almost touching his skin. "'The Beautiful Lady without Pity."

Realization began to seep into Vince's eyes,s but she didn't give him a chance to fully process it. She slammed the wakizashi into his thigh, just below where she was gripping him, severing his femoral artery. His warm blood flowed down the blade, over her hand. He remained hard.

She let go of him and wrapped her hand around his neck, bringing his shocked face close to hers. To anyone watching, it would look like a lover's embrace.

"You've failed," she whispered in his ear. "And you're in the wrong place."

He was trying to say something and she pressed her face against the side of his, feeling the warmth of his skin and his dying breaths caress her neck and ear. "You feel so good," she whispered.

She grabbed his coat and pulled it tight, letting his weight drop him to a sitting position, back against the crypt she'd been on. She quickly searched his pockets as the life faded from his eyes. He had one disk in his coat pocket. Number 8. She took it. She saw the 'Budweiser' insignia of the SEALs pinned to the inside lapel of the man's coat. She took that also.

She smiled. This was almost as good as getting all of Groves's disks. And much more satisfying, as she pulled the sword out of the Navy SEAL, wiping the blade off on the inside of his coat. She looked over and saw the re-enactor standing alone and forlorn inside the iron gate to the cemetery. She considered going over and ending the poor man's misery and decided against it. Let the fool suffer. He wasn't a worthy kill.

Two down of the new generation. Only Ducharme and Tolliver left.

She quickly walked out of the cemetery and onto Wall Street.

CHAPTER SIXTEEN

Ducharme had run this trail during intramural cross-country as a cadet. A rocky, precipitous route through thick woods. He emerged onto a parking lot paved with gravel and full of sports cars. This was one of the lots where Firsties—senior cadets—parked their vehicles during the week. There was a high percentage of Corvettes. Ducharme paused, catching his breath and surveying the lot. Evie would say there's a lot of compensating going on here.

Ducharme turned to the east. The upper levels of Michie Stadium were ahead. He curved to the left, toward Fort Putnam, a redoubt built to protect the rear of the post during the Revolution. He went around the base of the rock wall of the fort and then down-slope. Through gaps in the trees he saw the Cadet Chapel. He checked his watch, putting it in compass mode, shooting an azimuth to the front of the Chapel. He made his way down, moving slightly right. Checked azimuth again. He was on line. He looked up, checking the trees.

There was an old, towering oak tree directly between his location and the front of the Chapel. Ducharme scrambled down to it. He dug at the base of it facing the chapel. Six inches down, he hit something hard. He pulled up a packet. Opening it, he saw he had six more disks. He closed his eyes, remembering his uncle, picturing him digging here, burying these disks. He gripped them tightly. They had better be worth it.

Ducharme stuffed them in his pocket and began running downhill toward the impound lot.

* * *

Lily sat in the truck in the heliport parking lot, slicing her arm once more, trying to come down off the high from the killing. A Navy SEAL—a worthy opponent. And she had taken him down as easily as she had the old men— easier, in fact, than his mentor the Admiral.

She was running out of space on her forearm. She decided to continue on her thigh—no one was going to see it. After what had happened at the Academy, no one would ever see the inside of her thigh again. She was a weapon, pure and simple. She drew sustenance from blood, not sex.

She opened her laptop and looked at the information that General Parker had researched. The flow of his Google searches. The results. She focused like she used to when taking final exams at the Academy in subjects she didn't enjoy. Total. Complete immersion.

Two results.

She had no idea where *Parker's* disks were. No clues, except for the enigmatic comment that the grave was no one's and everyone's. Apparently Parker had been concerned that Groves's replacement wouldn't understand the logic flow of the Admiral's clue. She thought about it. He'd known somehow that the replacement wouldn't have the clue—which she had taken from Groves's home.

Still.

She knew the answer was there.

Right in front of her.

She went back through the information.

* * *

Burns looked at the broken window, walked over, and glanced down at the small red flag marking where the body had hit the ground. No chalk outline of the position—in all his years in the FBI he'd never seen such a thing. TV bullshit. Chalk or even a tape outline would contaminate a crime scene. That's what the crime scene photos in his hand were for.

"The American Philosophical Society," he said to Turnbull. "Sounds rather innocent."

Turnbull shrugged. "Sometimes things aren't what they seem."

"So true." Burns went over to the computer. The hard drive had been ripped out of it. Then he looked at the wall. The painting of Jefferson was sliced to bits. And there was a clean spot to the right where something else had been hanging. And a wall safe in the middle of the clean spot.

"A portrait of Hamilton hung there," Turnbull said.

"Hamilton and Jefferson," Burns mused. "Curious. Perhaps we're dealing with an art lover and hater."

"Your humor escapes me," Turnbull said.

"The safe?" Burns asked.

"Nothing in it."

"How do you know?"

"My men checked," Turnbull said vaguely.

"Are we going to the Annapolis crime scene?" Burns asked. They'd raced down from New York on the functioning Blackhawk, Turnbull wanting his opinion on the crime scene, which Burns didn't believe for a minute.

"No."

"Why not?"

"We don't need to."

"But we needed to come here," Burns said. He looked at the crime scene photos from the responding FBI units, then back at the room. "We have a problem."

"And that is?"

"The hard drive was taken after the first units got here. Its removal wasn't part of the crime. The original crime, that is. Tampering with evidence is a separate crime."

"It's not a problem," Turnbull said. "My people took it. Tried to read what was on it, but it had been wiped clean."

"What *did* you find?" Burns asked. "Where's his phone?"

"Very good," Turnbull said. He crooked a finger and a man came over with an evidence bag, which Turnbull reached into. "We've got it," he said pulling out the phone and ignoring the look of surprise from the agent at the mishandling of evidence. "Parker called four numbers and texted them all the same message just before he died." He held out the phone to Burns.

Burns took the phone and checked the numbers. Then he scrolled through the message. He went back up and looked at the numbers once more. Then he pulled out his small notebook and checked. "He texted Ducharme and Evie."

"Yes."

"Who else?"

"A Navy SEAL named Vince Simone. Body was just discovered in Trinity Church Cemetery in New York City. Stabbed in femoral and bled out. Right in front of Alexander Hamilton's grave."

"And who's the fourth?"

Turnbull nodded toward the door where a pool of blood indicated where the other body had been found.

Burns checked his small notebook. "Major Elizabeth Peters. What was her connection to Parker?"

Turnbull shrugged. "Your guess is as good as mine."

Burns decided it was just as well to ignore Turnbull when he lied.

"So we're up to seven for our killer."

Burns looked at the message again. "The killer saw this. Went to New York City for some reason."

"I think the killer made a mistake again," Turnbull said.

Burns was confused. "By killing the Navy SEAL or Major Peters?"

Turnbull shook his head. "No. I think, like at Poe's grave, she went to the wrong place. As did the SEAL."

"So they read the clues wrong." Burns straightened as the implications hit home. "You want me to read the clues right." It was not a question.

"I want you to do your job," Turnbull said blandly. "If the killer read them wrong and came up empty-handed, then she'll backtrack. If you can read them right, we can beat her to her next location."

"We could have done all this in Baltimore," Burns said.

"That irritating habit of telling me something I already know." Turnbull shook his scarred and battered head. "Very bothersome and worthless."

"What makes you think the killer will backtrack? How can you be certain the killer didn't find what she was looking for in New York?"

"Stop asking me questions," Turnbull said. "I'm the supervisor. I do the asking. So where should the killer go next?"

Burns stiffened and turned and looked at the older FBI agent. "Strange way you phrased that question."

"It's a still a question and I'm still your superior," Turnbull said.

Burns looked at the slashed picture. "Well, she went to Hamilton's grave and was wrong. Maybe Jefferson's?"

"Then let's catch her there." Turnbull turned toward the door.

Burns looked at one of the crime scene photos. "Why was Peters's ring left on her chest? The killer had to have put it there. She's *taken* trophies before, not arranged them."

"No clue," Turnbull said over his shoulder.

Burns watched him leave, and looked around at the other paintings on the walls. He glanced at the desk on the way out and paused. The mouse pad for the computer had an insignia on it. He leaned over: A helmet with two crossed rifles overlaid on it. Across the top was written USAF Honor Guard. And across the bottom: In Honore Et Dignitate.

Burns wondered about the honor and dignity of taking a header out a window. He made some notes in his pad, shook his head, and followed Turnbull, stepping around the still congealing puddle of blood that had once graced Major Peters's veins.

* * *

Evie found a small electronics store in Highland Falls, just outside the main gate of West Point. The owner scratched his head for a moment when she asked about a 8mm projector, then disappeared into the recesses of the store. She heard some banging, and then he reappeared with a dusty metal case. He opened it, revealing a projector.

"Can't guarantee it works," he warned, but she bought it anyway.

She took it back to the pickup, and then headed back to the dirt road where she had parted ways with Ducharme. She was chagrined that he was already there, leaning against the black Blazer, checking his watch. She stopped and he came to the driver's door.

"You got a projector?" Ducharme asked, looking over his shoulder into the bed of the truck.

"You got the disks?" Evie asked.

"Yes."

"Good. Know someplace where we can watch this film? It's got to be important if LaGrange put it in with the cache report directing you to the disks. He wants you to do more than just find things; he wants you to understand *why* the disks are important. Ultimately, why the Jefferson Allegiance is important. Same way McBride gave me his journal."

"Let's check it out," Ducharme said as he headed for the driver's door.

"I'm driving," Evie said.

Ducharme paused, then shrugged. "Sure." They got in and she threw the Blazer into drive.

Ducharme pointed. "Go that way."

She followed his directions and finally turned right underneath a metal sign that proclaimed: CAMP BUCKNER.

"Second year cadets—yearlings—do summer training here," Ducharme explained as they drove up to a locked pole gate. He got out, looked at the lock, then drew his pistol and shot it off.

"You might get in trouble for that," Evie noted when he got back in after pushing the pole aside.

"I'm worried."

They drove down the road until rows of long metal barracks came into view.

"Pick one," Ducharme said.

She pulled up to the closest building. Ducharme grabbed the projector and they went inside the musty building filled with metal bunk beds. Evie looked at one of the mattresses with longing, the fatigue she'd been keeping at bay nipping at her heels.

Evie set up the projector, pointing it at one of the gray-painted walls. Removing the film from the plastic case, she saw some faint writing on a label. Squinting she could make out a date and some letters: *7 August 1974. N-PS.* She swallowed hard, knowing the importance of that date, and looked over at Ducharme. She almost said something, but decided to let the film show them whatever LaGrange thought was important without prior commentary. She took the end of the film and fed it into the machine while Ducharme shut the blinds on the barrack's windows.

"You ready?" she asked Ducharme.

He nodded. "Born ready."

Great, she thought.

Ducharme turned off the light. The machine whirred, the light flickered, and then a black and white wide-angle shot of what appeared to be some sort of library/sitting room appeared along with a low, continuous hiss of sound being recorded along with the film. A shadowy figure sat in a large armchair. It was only when he leaned forward to pour himself a drink that he became instantly recognizable.

7 AUGUST 1974

President Nixon sat alone and weary in the early morning darkness contemplating non-existent options within the positive psychosis that had become his last refuge. He was in his White House private office, surrounded by legal documents, books, spools of tape, transcriptions and bottles. He'd run out of Coca-Cola sometime during the night, and was now drinking straight rum on the rocks, but the alcohol did little to dull the pervading sense of betrayal.

The room was lit only by the reflection through the windows of the exterior security lights, which cast long shadows through the room. He sat in an armchair, a set of headphones on his lap, the cord of which dangled to the reel-to-reel machine. He just couldn't understand why everyone else didn't hear the tapes the way he did; understand that he had acted in the best interests of the country.

The previous day and evening had been, in his opinion, a non-stop barrage of betrayal and cowardice. Kissinger had pleaded in person; Governor Reagan had called from California; a harsh letter had been hand-delivered from George H. W. Bush who was the National Chairman of the Republican Party; a parade of naysayers had trooped down from Capitol Hill; all pushing for him to resign. And in the midst of it all, Ehrlichman and Haldeman had been calling the White House switchboard, desperately trying to get through to ask for Presidential pardons, an even more certain sign the clock was ticking.

The media was the worst, especially those parasites from the Washington Post *who'd splashed what should have been classified information all over their pages. Phil Graham would roll in his grave if he knew how his wife and Ben Bradlee now used his newspaper. Nixon clenched his fist, furious with Bradlee, that hypocrite, who was tearing him apart daily, but had had no problem with his sister-in-law, Mary Meyer, banging Kennedy. Of course, she'd ended up with a bullet in her head and one in her heart less than a year after Kennedy took one. Not much reporting on* that *either, Nixon thought.*

The door opened without a knock, and Nixon turned his gaze toward it. A ghost of a smile touched his lips as he recognized the only person he would allow to penetrate his private sanctum: his daughter, Julie. As trouble had come cascading down on him, Nixon had been disappointed that his wife had faded away, but encouraged that Julie had taken her place to the point where the press were calling her "the First Lady in practice."

Julie had traveled across the country the past year, giving over a hundred interviews, trying to get people to see the reality of the President's position. For that, Nixon was greatly indebted to his daughter. He tilted his head up and she kissed him on the forehead before sitting down on the leather couch close to his chair.

"You've heard?" Nixon asked.

His daughter nodded sadly. "They've turned. I know I shouldn't be surprised, but I thought at least a few of them would stand with you."

"And David?" he asked, referring to her husband, David Eisenhower, grandson of the former General, and the man under whom Nixon had served as Vice President for two administrations. Just two months ago, his daughter and her husband had stood in the East Garden, and she had told the press that her father planned to fight this crisis 'constitutionally down to the wire.'

He saw a flicker of concern on her face. "He's been fielding calls all night, trying to generate support. He says you should take a break. Go to his camp," she added with a brave attempt at a joke as she referred to the Retreat that President Eisenhower had named after his grandson when he took office.

"You know Roosevelt called Camp David 'Shangri-La,'" Nixon said. "I could use a Shangri-La right now. A little escape from reality."

He caught his daughter's glance at the bottle of rum, but she said nothing about it, instead focusing on the problem. "You're right about the situation. I know you as well as anyone. I know the burden you carry. To resign now would be to admit you had done something wrong—and that simply did not happen. The President is above it all, and has to act in the best interests of the country in ways ordinary people cannot possibly understand."

Nixon nodded. "Only someone who wears the heavy mantle of the office can truly comprehend what's involved. Even the great Eisenhower, as Supreme Allied Commander had that Summersby woman, and don't forget the U-two scandal."

The President didn't see his daughter's sudden stiffening at the mention of a forbidden family topic. "And Kennedy—don't even get me started on the women and the Bay of Pigs and the other disasters the man perpetrated in his few years in office. Hell, Kennedy got us into Vietnam, and I had to get us out. I did that. And China!" Nixon's voice had a wavering edge to it. "No one talks about China. It's Watergate this and Watergate that, but never a mention of China. I split the damn Commies up. Russia and China. Opened China up to us."

"Dad." Julie Nixon-Eisenhower's voice was low, and he didn't hear her the first time she said it, so lost was he in his diatribe. "Dad."

The President paused and looked at his daughter, something in her tone getting through to him. "Yes?"

She couldn't meet his gaze. "The General wants to speak with you."

"What?"

"I'm sorry." She went over to the door and opened it, beckoning. Surprisingly she slipped out the door, and the President fought back a surge of irritation as he recognized his Chief of Staff entering.

"What is it?" Nixon snapped.

The General was a dark shadow, silhouetted against the open door, his military bearing unmistakable despite the suit he wore. *"There are some people you need to talk to, sir."*

Nixon frowned. It was four in the morning and he was facing the most difficult time of his life. The last thing he wanted was another former colleague who had turned on him. *"Who?"*

"They have something you need to read."

"I'm in no mood for—"

"You need to talk to these men," the General interrupted in a voice used to issuing orders, which caused the nominal Commander-in-Chief to half rise out of his chair, the headphones falling to the floor with a clatter.

"How dare you—"

"It's the Jefferson Allegiance, sir. I warned you." Without waiting for assent, the General turned to the open door and gestured. Four men filed in, and the General departed, shutting the door behind him. The President slumped back wearily into the chair.

"Who are you?" Nixon demanded. His hand shook as he grabbed the bottle and poured a dash of rum over the half-melted cubes in his glass. He took a quick swallow, trying to alleviate the pounding in his head.

One of the men stepped forward in the darkness, a wooden tube in his hands. He had thick, flowing white hair. *"I am the Chair of the American Philosophical Society, and with me are the Philosophers, Mister President. We have a message for you."*

Nixon stiffened as he heard the titles. *"Who is the message from?"*

"Thomas Jefferson and Alexander Hamilton, and a legal majority of Congress." The Chair opened the end of the tube and carefully pulled out a scroll, yellowed with age. He extended it to Nixon.

The President didn't take it. *"I have no time for games."* Nixon was trying to buy time, but he knew it had run out.

"This is no game, Mister President," the Chair said.

Nixon reached up and turned on the light next to his chair, barely illuminating a small circle around him. The man appeared to be in his fifties, tall and distinguished. He was not military, that much Nixon could tell.

"You work at the Post, don't you?" Nixon demanded. *"For that ass, Bradlee."*

"My job is not important," the Chair said. *"Just my duty."*

The other three men were still as statues. All were in uniform and had the same stiff bearing as the General. The three major services were represented by the uniforms: Army, Navy and Air Force. Stars glittered on the men's shoulders, but not enough to bring light to the gloomy room.

The President finally took the scroll, feeling the fragileness of the paper. He carefully opened the scroll. There were four sentences followed by numerous signatures. The first

173

sentence, Nixon immediately recognized. The following three, though, were startling to say the least, but what he had been warned about.

Nixon noted the signatures, recognizing the names of men long ago turned to dust, but whose power lived on.

The Chair continued. "We require you to resign the Presidency or face the consequences implicit in the words you've just read. The country is in no condition to go through a long impeachment, nor do we think it is good for the country to be so divided at such a dangerous time."

Nixon shook the document as if he could make the writing slide off the page.

"It's the Jefferson Allegiance," the Chair said. "It is law, sir, part of the highest law of the land. And it will *be enforced. So you have no option other than to resign." He did not wait for a reply. "Your Chief of Staff has already coordinated with Vice President Ford. You will eventually be pardoned and live the rest of your life in peace. But you must vacate this office. Your crimes against the Constitution and the country have become unacceptable."*

Nixon stared at the writing. "This can't be true."

"It is true," the Chair said, "and frankly, sir, you can't take the chance. It will harm the country greatly if we have to enforce the Allegiance, but we will. It's our sworn duty. You know you have violated the law and exceeded your powers. The country is divided and on the precipice. It is our duty to bring it back on course. You have no other option than to do what we demand."

The Chair reached out and took the document. He gingerly rolled it, then slid it into the tube, and sealed the end. "If you have not announced your resignation within twenty-four hours, the Philosophers will present the Jefferson Allegiance to the Joint Chiefs of Staff, and the generals and admirals in charge of all the major commands, who will take action."

With that, he turned for the door and left, the three military men following. The door swung shut, leaving the thirty-seventh President of the United States alone once more in the dark.

Not for long. His Chief-of-Staff, General Haig, once more entered unbidden.

"You know what they told me?" Nixon demanded. "What they showed me?"

"Yes, sir."

"Can it be enforced?"

The General took a deep breath. "Mister President, I took an oath on the Plain at West Point on Reception-Day—the very first day I was there—when I was a Plebe. The same oath every military officer takes. I didn't swear to defend the country. Or the people. Or even the Presidency," he added pointedly. "I swore to defend the Constitution of the United States."

"But the Allegiance isn't part of it," Nixon argued.

"Incorrect, sir. The Allegiance is part of the Bill of Rights," Haig countered. "And—" he paused and took a deep breath—"when I received my third star and was promoted to Lieutenant General, I was made to re-swear my oath. Except there was an addition—I was told there was a secret addition to the Bill of Rights: the Jefferson Allegiance. I wasn't told what it was, but I was informed that some day I might have to enforce it."

Nixon leaned back wearily in his seat. "So the Joint Chiefs will uphold the Jefferson Allegiance?"

"Every officer in the military will, if they become aware of it."

"That would be a coup!"

"No, sir," the General said firmly. "It would be enforcing the highest law of the land. And then the country would go back to the way it was originally designed to work."

A long silence played out, the words seeming to sink into the books lining the walls of the room.

"Leave me," Nixon finally ordered.

The General spun on his heel and departed, shutting the door.

The 37th President of the United States was alone in the dark once more; the only sound his labored breathing. That slight sound was over-ridden by the shrill ring of the phone. Another violation of the isolation Nixon had ordered. Rattled by the recent visitors, he turned on the speakerphone. "Yes?"

A voice echoed out of the small box next to the phone. "Mister President, this is Lucius. I understand you've had some visitors."

How could he know so quickly? *Nixon wondered. "They just left. What are you going to do about--"*

"I'm afraid The Society can't help you, sir."

Nixon's hand tightened on the receiver, the knuckles turning white. "You promised—"

Once more he was cut off. "You've received all the support The Society could give you, and you over-stepped the boundaries. The tapes are too damning. We cannot have the Allegiance invoked. You are now on your own. Good luck in your new life."

CHAPTER SEVENTEEN

The film went black.

"That was McBride," Evie said. "He was the Chair."

Ducharme let out a deep breath. "My uncle, the General, was one of the Philosophers. And another was Groves. I recognized him from the crime scene photos. The third must have been Parker."

"Who was Lucius?" Ducharme asked. "The person Nixon was talking to on the phone at the end?"

"The head of the Society of the Cincinnati," Evie guessed. "Named after Lucius Cincinnatus. And the General was Haig."

"Yeah, recognized that," Ducharme said.

They were silent for a while, the only sound the fan cooling off the projector bulb.

"Fuck," Ducharme finally said. "What the hell is in this document?"

"We know it's powerful." Evie filtered through the facts. "Powerful enough to force Nixon to resign, because he did the very next day—" she held out the case, showing him the date. "We know Nixon had his offices wired for sound, but no one has ever released a film before like this. It seems the Philosophers had his private office rigged for video and sound. Or Haig did. Who knows where the film came from? Maybe even the FBI. Bottom line is, we now know the Jefferson Allegiance is powerful enough to take down a president."

"Damn," Ducharme said.

Evie put a hand on his shoulder, feeling his agitation. "Things aren't as clear as everyone likes to believe. Even history. Nixon was so crazed by the time that was made—" she pointed at the reel of tape—"that the Pentagon— on Haig's and Kissinger's advice—had actually removed the real launch codes for our nuclear forces from the 'football' that was carried around by his military attaché."

"Bullshit." Ducharme said, startled.

"No bullshit. Smarter minds prevailed. For months before his resignation, Nixon didn't have the authority to launch nuclear weapons. Think about the person you saw in that film. You'd want his finger on the button?"

Ducharme ran a hand across his forehead. "What the hell is going on?"

She pointed at the film once more. "Haig—along with Kissinger—knew Nixon was unstable and drinking too much. They made the decision on their own to do that."

Ducharme rubbed his hand against the back of his head as he spoke. "Fuck."

"You could expand your vocabulary," Evie noted mildly.

Ducharme grabbed the film off the projector and headed for the door. They jumped into the Blazer, Evie driving, an implicit sign of trust by Ducharme.

Evie followed his directions and drove out of Camp Buckner, toward the Thruway so they could cross the Hudson on the Interstate and head east toward Boston.

"What are the numbers on LaGrange's disks?" Evie asked.

Ducharme checked the numbers on the inside. "We've got disks one through seven and twenty through twenty-six. We need the middle twelve."

* * *

The Blackhawk was over southern Pennsylvania when Burns saw Turnbull take a call on his satphone, and then issue orders to the pilots. The chopper banked and headed east.

Burns keyed the intercom. "We're not going to Monticello?"

"You must have been a detective in a former life," Turnbull said. "I'm suspecting you suggested Monticello as a diversion."

"Why would I do that?"

"Why indeed?"

"So are you going to tell me where we *are* going?" Burns asked.

"I've had people working on the enigma of this case," Turnbull said.

"Interesting choice of words. And?"

"They believe the next location isn't Monticello, although I am sending some people there just in case."

"So you believe them over me?" Burns asked, playing with the rim of his fedora.

Turnbull smiled, but there was no warmth in it. "Mister Burns. I've seen your file. You're a law and order fellow. One who believes that those words written in black and white and bound in leather are the answer to all of life's problems. Unfortunately, as you might have found out in your career, the world isn't that simple a place."

"I—"

Turnbull didn't let him get a second word out. "I've seen your official record, Mister Burns, and I've seen your unofficial record. Vincent Foster. You were a brand new field agent in the FBI's Washington Office in ninety-three. You got dumped in the deep water pretty quickly on that. I assume no one else wanted to touch the case, given Foster's relationship with the President, and particularly the First Lady. So you were sent out as the sacrificial goat. You even tried to do your job and find out what really happened. Commendable, although extremely naïve."

Burns took a deep breath. "I did my duty as best I could, given the circumstances."

"And it's the circumstances that I'm talking about and you seem to want to keep ignoring," Turnbull said. "One would have thought you'd learned."

"I learned." Burns hunched his shoulders. "I just haven't changed."

The smile that never reached his eyes crossed Turnbull's scarred face. "At least you have awareness of your flaw. Be careful it doesn't turn out to be a tragic one. I've always had awareness of who I am and, as importantly, of the world around me. It has stood me in good stead. Thus, I do not believe you about Monticello, and I do believe my people. The next destination of the killer, and most likely Professor Evie and Colonel Ducharme, is John Adams's grave in Quincy, Massachusetts."

Burns stared at Turnbull for several long seconds, and then nodded. "It's a possibility."

"A likely one. More likely than Monticello. Correct?"

"Perhaps."

"What's rather amusing," Turnbull said, "is that you still supported Clinton in the next election."

"I can see the bigger picture," Burns said.

"Can you? Can you indeed, Agent Burns?"

"Besides," Burns added, "it was a suicide."

"Was it really?"

Burns felt his world go black for a second. "What are you saying?"

"Nothing."

"So we're going to Quincy?" Burns forced himself to stay in the now.

"No."

"Where are we going?"

"Back to Washington," Turnbull said. "It's all playing out, and it's best if we're at the center of the storm."

"What about Quincy?"

"It will be taken care of." Turnbull turned away, back to his satphone as the Blackhawk headed east.

Burns pulled his fedora down over his eyes. He appeared to go to sleep, but he was thinking. Hard.

* * *

"Whatever the Jefferson Allegiance is," Ducharme said, "it involves officers being messed up in politics. The film showed that."

"We'll know when we find it."

"Confidence," Ducharme noted. "Not to be confused with hope."

"What's the difference?"

"Hope is often based on faith. Confidence on ability."

"'Hope is sweeter than despair.'" Evie's voice had taken on that *I'm quoting someone from long ago* tone, Ducharme was beginning to recognize.

"Thomas again?" he asked.

Evie nodded. "From the Head-Heart letter."

"Which one said that?"

"The heart."

"Figures. Thought you liked the head better." Ducharme's satphone buzzed and he turned it on. "Ducharme."

"Duke, it's Kincannon. Just got this over the terror network. Navy SEAL named Vincent Simone got cut—femoral and bled out—right near Hamilton's grave."

Ducharme glanced at Evie. "So that leaves the two of us."

"What am I? Chopped liver?" Kincannon asked. "I've got your back. You on your way to Quincy? Got the General's disks?"

"Roger that. Your location?"

"ETA Monticello in twenty miles."

"Be careful."

"I'm tired of being careful," Kincannon said. "Time for the other guys to be careful. Out, here."

Ducharme told Evie about Simone and Hamilton's grave.

"We have to assume this Surgeon has at least two disks now," she said. "Simone's and Peters's."

"Right." The Interstate to the east beckoned.

* * *

The sun was getting lower in the west, the rays reflecting off the tower at Hanscom Air Force Base as the Bell Jet Ranger flew along a taxiway toward the refueling area. Lily was alone in the back with her case of goodies, eyes closed, resting. When the chopper's skids touched down, she opened her eyes to the flashing lights of several Air Police vehicles surrounding the chopper.

"You gave them the authorization code?" she asked the pilot over the intercom.

"Yes, ma'am."

"Get the aircraft refueled." Lily took off the headset and shoved open the rear door. Two Blackhawk helicopters were parked on the ramp, weapons pods attached on either side. She saw pilots lounging in the front seat of one of them and knew it was an on-call, immediate reaction force aircraft.

A tall man in uniform stepped forward out of the surrounding vehicles. The gold leaves on his shoulder and the arrogance in his swagger immediately annoyed her.

"This is not an authorized refueling stop for FBI—" he began, but she cut him off.

"At ease, Major. My pilot gave the proper level of authorization."

"True, but we're home to the Air Force Electronic Systems Command and conduct a lot of highly classified—"

"I don't care," Lily said, stepping closer and peering up several inches at the officer.

He bristled. "Who are you?"

She grimaced as a bolt of pain shot across her brain, from the side where she'd been shot to the other. It was gone as quickly as it had started. She blinked, realizing her hand was on the grip of the wakizashi, the blade half drawn. She forced herself to slide it back down. "Do I have the proper authorization or not, Major? Or do I need to call your superior and discuss your inability to follow orders?"

The Major angrily waved at her chopper. "My people are already refueling your aircraft. I was just—"

"Being a fool," Lily said. She had a headache and this idiot wasn't improving things.

"Screw the FBI," the major muttered.

Screw the Air Force, Lily thought, remembering all the years and blood and sweat she'd put into the organization, only to be discarded like a cog that was no longer functional. If you couldn't kill for the military, what was the point? For some reason she couldn't control, a vision of her classmate lying in a puddle of blood flashed through her mind. She dismissed it as quickly as it came. "Forget about the refueling. I want that aircraft," she said, pointing toward the Blackhawk.

The major adopted a confrontational stance. "That's our Immediate Reaction Force bird. You—"

"You have a second Blackhawk," she said. "Call in its crew."

"You can't!"

"I can," Lily said. "I have the proper authorization, don't I?"

The major's silence was enough answer.

"Tell the crew to get it cranked," Lily ordered.

The major stalked away toward the Blackhawk. Lily's brief feeling of victory was interrupted by her satphone buzzing.

LOCATION?

>>>HANSCOM AFB<<<

DUCHARME & TOLLIVER HEADING TO QUINCY

Lily texted back an affirmative.

CHAPTER EIGHTEEN

Sergeant Major Kincannon stared through iron bars at the tall obelisk that marked Thomas Jefferson's grave. It was just after dusk. Pollack had dropped him off a half-mile away, doing a quick touch and go in a field, and then she had disappeared into the darkness to hover out of range of sound until he called her back. He wore night vision goggles, which presented the world to him in varying shades of bright green.

Jefferson had specified his own epitaph. For a man with so many accomplishments, it was most interesting what he had chosen to be written in stone, and what he had left out. Jefferson's wish was to be remembered for what he had done for the people, not what the people had given him. Thus, there was no mention of being Secretary of State, Vice President or President:

HERE WAS BURIED
THOMAS JEFFERSON
AUTHOR OF THE
DECLARATION
OF AMERICAN INDEPENDENCE
OF THE
STATUTE OF VIRGINIA
FOR
RELIGIOUS FREEDOM
AND FATHER OF THE
UNIVERSITY OF VIRGINIA
BORN APRIL 2, 1743 O.S.
DIED JULY 4, 1826

Kincannon stood perfectly still, scanning the iron fence surrounding the marker, even though he felt the urge to hop the fence and dig. His patience was rewarded when he spotted the motion sensor attached to the bottom of fence, almost completely covered in old leaves. Almost. The wire that ran from the sensor to the iron was a thin, dark line. Touching the fence would set it off. Disconnecting it or destroying the sensor would bring the same result: whoever had placed it there was probably not too far away.

Kincannon pressed the speed dial on his satphone, and Pollock answered immediately, the sound of the chopper engine idling providing background noise. He checked his watch, gave her orders quickly and efficiently, and then shut down the connection.

Letting the MP-5 hang on its sling, Kincannon jumped, grabbing the top rail of the iron fence. In one smooth move he was over and dropping down on the other side. He drew his knife as he knelt in front of the obelisk and probed quickly, covering the ground in a pattern. The fifth probe touched something and he dug, clearing leaves and dirt away. His hand closed on a small, hard object and he pulled it out, stuffing it into a pocket on his body armor without even looking at it.

He leapt, grabbed the top of the fence and pulled himself over. As soon as he landed, he brought the MP-5 up to his shoulder, scanning the immediate area.

Coming through the woods were three dark figures silhouetted in the rising moonlight. They were moving in perfect triangle formation, light glinting off of automatic weapons in their hands. They walked far enough apart a single grenade wouldn't take more than one out, with angles of fire that allowed any two to cover the third. And they were heading right toward Kincannon.

His finger caressed the trigger. Ducharme's admonition to not kill flickered in his head, an irritating red light. With a silent curse, Kincannon lowered the gun. With his free hand, Kincannon reached into a pocket on the inside of his coat and brought out a cluster of what looked like small, green ping-,pong balls and a clacker. He put the small grenades up to his mouth and pulled the pins with his teeth. Then with a smooth underhand movement, he tossed them toward the intruders.

While the balls were still in the air, he yelled: "Freeze. Mini-frags on my command, dead man's switch."

In concert, the three men aimed their weapons directly at Kincannon. The balls landed on the ground around the men.

The point man of the three lowered his weapon, holding his left hand in the air, palm open, a badge in it. "FBI. Who the hell are you?"

Kincannon held up his hand, the clacker in it. "The guy whose balls you're fucking with. If you don't want to lose yours, put your guns down."

The point man looked at the ground. "We're FBI."

"What's the motto of the FBI?" Kincannon yelled.

"Put your weapon down," the man countered with.

"That's not it." Kincannon held his ground, detonator in one hand, weapon in the other. The faint sound of a helicopter approaching washed over the area.

"You're inside the blast radius," the FBI point man said.

"So?"

"Are you crazy?"

"It's been said before."

The point man carefully put his gun on the ground. "We're FBI."

"You keep saying that," Kincannon said, "but I think you're lying. I don't like liars. Might just kill you on principle."

The man was persistent, if not bright or quick. "Are you Colonel Ducharme? We're here to escort you back to the Hoover Building."

"Already been there," Kincannon said. "If I want to go again, I can find the Hoover building on my own."

"Are you Ducharme?"

"Maybe, maybe not."

"Listen—"

Kincannon brought up the MP-5, finger on the trigger, the other hand still holding the clacker. "I got things to do." The chopper was closer. Kincannon slid to the left, to the middle of the road. The Huey came in fast, flaring hard, skids barely touched the ground, and Kincannon hopped on a skid and they were airborne.

As Kincannon pulled himself into the cargo bay with one hand, he tossed the clacker out of the helicopter. It released and the mini-grenades exploded, a cluster of bright lights all around the three 'FBI' men. The crack of the explosions reached Kincannon a second later, and there was no sign of the three men.

Kincannon swung into the cargo bay, sitting on the edge. He watched the lights of Monticello fade in the distance. He put on the headset.

"What the hell happened?" Pollack demanded.

"'Welcome back to the fight'," Kincannon muttered. ""This time I know our side will win.'"

"What are you talking about, Jeremiah?"

"Casablanca." Kincannon got up and leaned between the pilot and co-pilots seat. He planted a kiss on Pollack's cheek. "Nothing my dear, nothing at all."

* * *

184

The Blackhawk landed on top of the Hoover Building, and Burns held on to his fedora as Turnbull opened the side door. They got out and the helicopter lifted and disappeared into the night sky.

Letting go of his hat, Burns put on his fedora and faced Turnbull. "That's it? Investigation over? The killer walks?"

"Oh, I doubt the killer is walking," Turnbull said. "Either now, literally, or in the future, figuratively."

"Why did you have me on this wild goose chase?" Burns asked.

"You were assigned to it," Turnbull replied as they headed toward the roof door accessing the stairwell. "You had something better to do?"

"I'd like to finish the job I started."

"What job was that?"

"Catching a killer."

"Insignificant in the big picture," Turnbull said, pulling the door open.

Burns resisted the urge to throttle the higher-ranking officer.

"What is this big picture you keep referring to?" Burns demanded as they went inside. "Why don't you let me do my job?"

"Oh, you're doing your job," Turnbull said. "You do know what your job is?"

Burns clenched his jaw. "I know my job."

"I'm not sure you do," Turnbull said. "I think you've spent so many years among the trees, you've lost sight of the forest."

Turnbull led him down one flight without comment. A metal door barred access to the top floor of the FBI headquarters. In all his years working in the building, Burns had been on the top floor only once, to receive a commendation from the Director of the FBI. It had been a brief affair: a handshake long enough to have a photo snapped, then he'd been sent back down to the trenches. Such a momentary event was supposed to supply him with enough motivation to keep going for years, above and beyond the call of duty.

Turnbull pressed his palm against a reader and looked up at the unblinking eye of a security camera. The door hissed open.

"Come on." Turnbull led him down the corridor. "Law and order, that's you," he said. He paused at a set of double doors. His name was carved into the wood itself, indicating an atypical sign of permanence at a level where heads rolled on a regular basis, depending on which way the political breezes in Washington blew. "Are there levels to the law? A pecking order? A higher good?"

Burns pulled the brim of his fedora low, putting his eyes into its shadow. "There's the law."

"So simplistic." Turnbull put his hand on the lock pad and turned his face toward the small camera above the doors. The camera scanned his retina. There was a solid click, and Turnbull shoved both doors wide open, revealing a spacious office with thick, blast-proof windows at the far end. If it were daylight they'd have a wonderful view of the center of DC: White House, Washington Monument, the Potomac, all of Washington.

Turnbull turned in the middle of the open doors and pointed. "Elevator is that way."

The doors swung shut, leaving Burns alone in the corridor. As he walked away, he pulled out his satphone.

* * *

Ducharme's satphone vibrated. With his free hand he pulled it out and hit the on button. "Ducharme."

"Colonel Ducharme, this is Agent Burns."

"Need me to answer more questions?"

"You didn't answer many to start with," Burns said.

"Do *you* have any answers?" Ducharme asked.

"I'm not even sure what all the questions are," Burns said. "But I have a few."

"Caught the killer yet?"

"You know I haven't."

"How do I know that?" Ducharme asked.

"Because you saw what happened in Baltimore."

"And you know what happened in Annapolis and Philadelphia," Ducharme threw in. "And New York City."

"Yes." Burns didn't deny it or hesitate in responding, which told Ducharme something. "I've been accompanying a man named Turnbull. He claims to be a high-ranking FBI official."

"'Claims'?"

"Technically, he is," Burns allowed. "He has the badge and clearance and the office on the top floor of the Hoover Building with his name on the door."

"But?" Ducharme watched the snow-covered hills of western Massachusetts roll by on either side.

"He's working on a whole other level," Burns said. There was a pause. "You should head to John Adams's grave in Quincy."

Ducharme frowned. "Why are you telling me?"

"Because this Turnbull fellow is after something. I think the killer works for him. It isn't about the killings, it's about something Turnbull wants."

"Right."

"Are you agreeing with me or confirming what I just said?" Burns asked.

Ducharme hesitated for a moment, but then decided the odds were so high against them, it was worth taking a chance on gaining an ally. "Confirming."

"Do you know what it is?"

"Yes."

There was a sigh from the other end of the phone. "But you're not going to tell me."

It wasn't a question, but Ducharme answered anyway. "Nope."

"I just gave you some good information," Burns pointed out.

"We're already on the way to Quincy. So you gave me nothing new."

"The killing in New York City," Burns said. "Simone was Admiral Groves's aide' de camp before the Admiral retired six years ago. He'd been recalled from operations in Iraq just a few days ago, just like you got called back from Afghanistan."

"Interesting," Ducharme said.

"And General LaGrange was your uncle. Major Peters, who was killed in Philadelphia, served with General Parker in a unit here in DC—Air Force Honor Guard. And Mister McBride was Evie Tolliver's mentor. Say hi to her by the way for me."

Ducharme looked over at Evie. "Agent Burns says 'hi.'"

Her eyes got wide.

"She says 'hi' back," Ducharme said into the satphone. "Listen—" he paused, realizing he was getting ready to roll the dice—"this thing everyone's after. It's important."

"Indeed?" Even through the static of the scrambler on the satphone the sarcasm was clear.

"I'm saying it's—" Ducharme searched his mind for the words to convey what he wanted to say to Burns—"it's powerful."

"But you really don't know what it is."

"Not yet."

"How can I help?" Burns finally said.

"We need a plan," Ducharme said.

"That's a good idea," Burns said dryly.

"This Surgeon—" Ducharme began, but Burns cut in.

"Who?"

"The killer. That's what she calls herself. I think she works for your Mister Turnbull."

"No shit. And then there's General Parker," Burns said.

"What about him?"

"I'm not stupid," Burns said. "The pieces are all there. McBride-Tolliver-Poe's grave. LaGrange-You-Custer's grave. Groves-Simone-and most likely John Adams's grave. So we have Parker-Peters and what grave?"

"No idea," Ducharme said.

"'No one's and everyone's'," Burns said.

"What's it mean?"

"No idea. I figured Tolliver might do something with it."

"Who does Turnbull really work for?" Ducharme asked.

"I don't know," Burns said.

"But you can try to find out."

"I've tried and he doesn't exist."

"What?" Ducharme said.

"He didn't go to college. He didn't go to high school. He wasn't born. As I said, I think he's at another level."

"What level?" Ducharme said.

There was silence. "I've been in Washington a long time," Burns finally responded. "There's another level. I can't define it specifically, but the real power lies somewhere in the shadows, and that's where Turnbull comes from. Where did he get those choppers from? An Apache? Gunmen?"

"Then we're going to have to go into the shadows," Ducharme said.

"How?" Burns asked.

The image of the words popped into his head and he said them without thought: *"Let the enemy come 'til he's almost close enough to touch, then let him have it and jump out and finish him with your hatchet."*

"What the hell are you talking about?"

"Rogers's Rules of Rangering. I was in the Infantry for a while," Ducharme explained. "It always comes down to boots on the ground, face to face, and blade to blade. You understand the latter, don't you?"

"Yeah, I do."

"See you on the ground."

The phone went dead.

"What was that about?" Evie asked. "'No one's and everyone's'?"

"The clue to General Parker's disks," Ducharme said.

Evie sat back in her seat. "Interesting."

"You know," Ducharme said, "it would have been a whole lot easier if they'd just FedExed us the disks."

"This was the only way they could keep the Cipher—and the Allegiance—safe," Evie said.

"Great," Ducharme muttered.

* * *

Burns wearily walked to the bank of elevators. They opened before he reached them. He knew that he would never again reach this top floor unless Turnbull authorized it. The thought didn't disturb him because he had no desire to be at this level if it meant being the greedy, self-centered power seeker that 'succeeding' in Washington required.

He got in the elevator and punched in the number for the much lower floor for his office. The elevator descended and then halted. The doors swished open. Burns walked down the corridor. About a quarter of the desks in the large, open DC Section pool were occupied. He strode through, nodding at familiar faces, grabbed a cup of day-old coffee, and went into his small office. Barely big enough for a desk and chair. The reward for over two decades of selfless service.

There were no windows in the office.

Burns kicked back from the desk, the back of the chair immediately slamming into a filing cabinet. The walls felt like they were closing in on him. His eyes darted about. A wall full of plaques, photographs, and certificates. The equivalent of the tiny ribbons military people wore on their dress uniforms above their left pockets. Even adding in the plaques and their engraving, all told it was worth less than a couple of hundred bucks in cold cash when they were made, and so much less now.

Worth only what one felt about them. Burns had always been proud of his awards, his medals, his certificates. Had been.

"Fuck you, Agent Turnbull."

Burns bellied up to the desk. He pulled out his notepad. He thumbed through, reading his notes since this clusterfuck had begun. He paused at what had appeared to be a minor observation at the time: the mouse pad from General Parker's office. Burns turned on his computer and Googled "USAF Honor Guard." He wasn't surprised to see the result: the Air Force's ceremonial unit in the DC Area. Handled events at the White House and burials at Arlington. Looking down the unit's web page he saw that Parker had commanded the unit from 1997 through 1999, before retiring.

Odd that of all the units Parker had been in and all the combat missions he'd flown, the only unit crest he had in his office was that one.

Anomalies deserved further investigation.

The pieces were here, and he knew he had to put them together. Burns looked up at the ceiling and extended the middle finger of his right hand.

* * *

"Welcome back," Ducharme said to Kincannon. "What's the word on New York?"

Evie was still driving. They'd picked up Kincannon from an open field next to the service road off the Interstate. Pollack had immediately taken off in search of fuel, telling them to call her when they needed her.

"The killing in New York was covered up, just like all the other ones," Kincannon said. "Our friend the Surgeon has very powerful friends."

"What did you find at Monticello?" Evie asked.

Kincannon reached into his pocket and pulled out a small plastic case, which he opened. He retrieved a thumb drive. "Bingo."

"Hurt anyone?" Ducharme asked.

"Don't ask a question you don't want to know the answer to," Kincannon said.

Ducharme grimaced, but nodded.

Evie held out her hand. "May I have it please?"

Kincannon put it in her palm. "Can I see this cipher thing?" he asked.

Evie pulled out the rod with the fourteen disks they'd recovered so far on it, passing it to him. Kincannon took it and spun the disks, nodding. "Pretty sharp."

"Jefferson was a genius," Evie said as she pulled out McBride's computer and pushed the on button. "He invented the Wheel Cipher while serving as Secretary of State to ensure that his correspondence would be secure from prying eyes. To encode a message, a cryptographer dials up a twenty-six-letter message in a row. Then go to any other row and write those letters down and send them. To decipher the message, the receiver would set his own identical Wheel Cipher to the text and look for a message on the other lines that made sense."

"So shouldn't there be another one?" Kincannon asked.

Evie explained the concept of a Key line to set the machine and reveal the message.

"Ok, another stupid question," Kincannon said. "Even if we get all the disks—we still don't know what the twenty-six letter Key is."

"I've been thinking about that," Evie said. "Jefferson encoded the location of the Allegiance on this cipher—" she pointed at the partially complete machine. "He wasn't sending a message to another cipher, he was sending the cipher to someone in the future. If I might have the momentary conceit to think like him, then the Key line is central to finding the message."

"That's what Kincannon just said." Ducharme was irritated. "We don't have—"

Evie cut him off. "But we must have it. The code line for this cipher isn't a random list of letters."

He frowned. "What do you mean?"

"Like everything else we've been tracking down in this puzzle, there must be a logic to it. I believe the code line is something coherent, a phrase most likely, that we dial up. And somewhere else on the cipher is the location of the Allegiance."

"So what's the Key?" Kincannon asked.

"I haven't figured that out yet," Evie said. Her attention was on the flickering computer screen. She pushed the thumb drive into the USB port.

CHAPTER NINETEEN

In the rear of the Blackhawk, Lily glanced at the GPS display. A small, red blinking dot had just appeared at the forward edge of the screen. The chopper was gaining on it rapidly. Looking out the window, the twin black ribbons of the Massachusetts Turnpike slashed across the snow-covered countryside.

"Gain some altitude," she ordered the pilot over the intercom. "I don't want us to be heard by someone on the ground. And slow down."

"Roger that, ma'am."

She alternated her gaze between the GPS and the highway below, waiting until the red dot was dead center. "Go steady with the eastbound flow of traffic and offset to the south."

"Yes, ma'am."

Lily glanced out the left window. There was a line of cars on the turnpike, but she easily spotted the big black Blazer with tinted windows. "Arm your Hellfire missiles," she ordered.

The pilot and co-pilot both twisted their heads and stared at her for a moment in shock, before looking forward. "Ma'am," the pilot said tentatively. "We're in the States. What—"

"There's a vehicle with terrorists on the road," Lily snapped. "I have the authority to use deadly force to stop them."

There was a pause, and then the pilot's voice came over the intercom. "Hellfires armed."

Lily pulled out her satphone and texted.

>>>EVIE AND DUCHARME IN SIGHT. HELLFIRES ARMED. REQUEST PERMISSION TO TERMINATE.<<<

The reply was immediate.

NEGATIVE. THEY HAVE HALF THE DISKS. FOCUS ON PRIMARY MISSION. RECOVERING DISKS IS PRIORITY

Lily grimaced.

>>>DESTROYING DISKS AS GOOD AS DESTROYING ALLEGIANCE<<<

NEGATIVE NEGATIVE NEGATIVE. THE ALLEGIANCE WILL ALWAYS BE A THREAT. IT MUST BE FOUND AND DESTROYED

>>>YES SIR<<<

THREE OPERATIVES KILLED AT MONTICELLO. TIME IS OF ESSENCE

Lily stared at the words trying to make sense. Had there been disks there? Who'd killed the operatives?

The phone went dead. She turned the intercom on. "Put the safeties back on your Hellfires. Get me to Quincy, ASAP."

"Yes, ma'am." The relief was audible in the pilot's voice.

Lily ran her nails over the poorly healed cuts. Blood welled up.

* * *

"What's wrong?" Kincannon asked in a low voice, ignoring Evie who was enraptured with the computer in the back seat.

"I don't know," Ducharme said. He realized he was hunched forward, shoulders tight, hands gripping the steering wheel with just a little too much force. "Bad vibes." It felt like he was back in Afghanistan, driving the Up-Armor Humvee, waiting for an IED to go off.

Kincannon straightened in the passenger seat, looking at the mirror on his side. "I don't see anything."

Ducharme forced himself to relax. "Nothing. It's all right." He glanced back at Evie, catching her attention. "What's the relationship between Jefferson and Adams besides the fact they died on the same day?"

"Adams was a Federalist," she began, but Kincannon cut in.

"Hold on," he said. "I thought you said the Federalists hated Jefferson."

"They did," Evie said, lowering the screen. "Let me explain—and you need to understand before I tell you what McBride wrote on this—by telling you about the low point between the two of them, and how Hamilton was involved. Because I think the Allegiance is some sort of compromise. And you need to understand the way these people operated."

"All right," Ducharme said. "Go ahead."

"The election of eighteen hundred was Thomas Jefferson versus the incumbent John Adams. That election exposed one of the flaws of the Constitution. The Electoral College could only vote for President. The way the Constitution was written, the Vice President was the person who got the second largest number of votes in the election. When the vote was tallied, they ended up with anti-Federalist Jefferson versus his own Vice Presidential candidate, Aaron Burr, in a deadlock and Adams was out of it. To further complicate things, because of the tie, the vote was then given to the outgoing Federalist House of Representatives."

"Clusterfuck," Kincannon succinctly summed it up.

Evie nodded. "At first, most Federalists voted for Burr simply to keep Jefferson out of the White House in a show of support to Adams. But Alexander Hamilton hated Burr more than Jefferson. So he got a congressman named Bayard to swing a group of Federalists to vote for Jefferson and give him the election. This sowed the seeds of the most famous duel in American history four years later between Hamilton and Burr. It also led to the Twelfth Amendment in the same year, requiring Electors to make a choice between their selections for President and Vice President."

"What did Jefferson give Hamilton in return for the votes?" Ducharme asked.

Evie graced him with a smile. "You're getting the hang of the way politics really works. Back-room deals. When he became President, Jefferson left a lot of Federalists in office, when the practice was to do a clean sweep."

"And Adams?" Kincannon asked.

"He was so disgusted with all of it, he left Washington in the middle of the night right before Jefferson's inauguration."

"Not very sporting," Kincannon said. He pointed at the computer. "What's this report on?"

"History," Evie said.

"History?" Ducharme repeated. "All we've been getting is history lessons. Why is McBride's so damn important? What's it about?"

Kincannon cut in. "How 'bout we read the darn thing?"

"We need to get moving," Ducharme said.

"We need to know what we're doing, Duke," Kincannon countered. "And maybe, just as importantly, why McBride got killed. I would say he knew some things we need to know, and he put that information in his computer."

"Is it about the Jefferson Allegiance?" Ducharme asked. "And the American Philosophical Society and the Society of the Cincinnati?"

In reply, Evie leaned forward, putting the laptop on the console between Ducharme and Kincannon.

Everyone in the Blazer leaned closer to read.

Dearest Evie:

I gathered most of the information that follows from the secret notes I uncovered in the Archives of the American Philosophical Society, although the known historical information in this report is readily available.

In every country, of course, the ruler is most important. For many people around the world not blessed with a democratic republic such as the United States enjoys, 'the ruler' is not just the head of a government, often people's very lives depend on his whims. There are few philosophical kings, and even fewer 'benign' rulers. And, of course, the title "despot" implies little if any benevolence. In most countries, the people live to serve the ruler.

In the few thousand years of recorded history, the limited power of the American Presidency and government over the last two-plus centuries has represented the best of our country and is unique in history. Free elections, constitutional safeguards put in place by reasoning men at an unreasonable time, seem almost an improbability. Yet it happened in 1787.

Fifty-five men of rather dubious background carved out something unique: a document both flawed and designed to correct its own flaws- at least initially. It appeals to the logical mind that those who invented this government recognized their own limitations and put in place protections against those limitations. At the same time, they sought to achieve lofty goals for the individual, while ignoring large portions of their country's population. The same intriguing combination of logic and awareness of human limitations. They were philosophers who were very understanding of the reality and precariousness of their situation.

It is often forgotten among many Americans that the fifty-five men who signed the Declaration of Independence were breaking the law and traitors to their government and king. One could say they were extremely "unpatriotic." Five of them paid with their lives; captured by the British, tortured and executed. Two had sons killed during the war. Most lost their houses, their fortunes, and their reputations. Quite a few died in poverty; such is the gratitude of a free nation. At the very end of the Revolution, the British General Cornwallis had his headquarters in the home of one of the signers of the Declaration of Independence, who urged General Washington to open fire on it. His house was destroyed, and the man died homeless and penniless.

Perhaps it was part of the flaws inherent in their genius and what they brought forth. Still, one wonders how many Americans today would give their lives for freedom—from a tyranny imposed by their own government?

Ducharme glanced at Evie. "What did McBride mean by that?"

Evie shrugged. "Think how the signers of the Declaration of Independence would be treated today. Frankly, I believe they would be outcasts, political heretics. Much as if Jesus came to a modern church to preach, he would most likely be cast out as a heretic."

"Woman's got a point," Kincannon said. "They weren't very open-minded in my old Bible study class."

"You were a kid," Ducharme told his partner.

"I was wise beyond my years," Kincannon said. "And the one's running it were adults."

"Let's keep reading," Ducharme suggested.

Think about the Constitution and Bill of Rights. Imagine declaring all men free and able to self-govern, yet ignoring women and counting African-Americans as three-fifths of a human being? And the three-fifths applied only to use that population for representation in Congress, not to allow them to vote, thus giving the slave states a greater proportion of representatives as opposed to true voting population. Plus, the Founding Fathers, an odd choice of words, added an article vowing never to change by Amendment that slaves would continue to be imported for 20 years.

Why? To make a compromise. To appease the slave states offended by the non-slave states. But to outlaw slavery would have forced the slave states out. There would have been no union, no United States. Instead they formed a Union that would have to face the immorality of slavery in the future. The fifty-five men knew this, and that they were sowing the seeds for an inevitable civil war. But one must have a country before a civil war, and they chose country.

The fact that the twenty-year article expired and no more slaves were imported into the United States after 1808 intrigued me, and it surprised many I told it to. Most thought slaves continued to be brought into the United States right up until the Civil War. In fact, what further surprised people was that the War of 1812 with Great Britain was to an extent a result of the stoppage of the importation of slaves into the United States. A move that crippled a significant economic interest of a country that pretended to be morally above slavery. The fact that Great Britain was the country that profited most from the slave trade has made a good topic for the cocktail circuit in Washington.

During all the wrangling over the form their new government would take, the Presidency seemed an afterthought because the perfection of he who they knew would be the first president—George Washington—eased their fears for the near future. Alexander Hamilton proposed that the President and Senators be elected for life. Jefferson, Madison and others saw a grave danger in this. Thus, another compromise. And that is what the Jefferson Allegiance is all about—compromise.

The electoral college, antiquated and flawed, was also a compromise. There have been candidates for the Presidency who received the majority of at-large votes, yet lost the election because they did not 'swing' crucial states for the electoral college.

But, like slavery, the inherent flaws in the Executive branch began to show almost immediately—in fact, as you will note in the First Section of my report, it was Thomas Jefferson, the third President, who exceeded his Constitutional limits and recognized the flaw and the potential for Imperialism in the future, and brought into being the Allegiance.

That the President be above the law will be expounded by subsequent administrations, as you will see in my other Sections based on when the APS intervened. Indeed, several

Presidents have notably broken the law 'for the greater good.' Lincoln's Emancipation Proclamation was one such case. Illegal, but moral. And smartly, yet also deviously, Lincoln only freed the slaves in the rebelling Southern states, not those in border states he needed to keep in the Union.

The role of the Society of the Cincinnati was also a large issue. It was a very divisive issue among the Founding Fathers. Indeed, it was the reason the American Philosophical Society was redirected from its original purpose to counter the Cincinnatians. And, as you will see, the Cincinnatians pushed Presidents at times to break the law to further their own objectives.

So let us delve into history and see how the Jefferson Allegiance, or in most cases, the threat *of the Jefferson Allegiance kept the country from sliding completely into an Imperial Presidency, and stopped the Cincinnatians from gaining the control they desire up to the present day:*

McBride's Report: The Imperial Presidency and the Jefferson Allegiance
Section One. Jefferson & Hamilton
Section Two. Polk & John Quincy Adams (and Lincoln)
Section Three. Lincoln & Grant
Section Four. Teddy Roosevelt & Alice Roosevelt
Section Five. Franklin Roosevelt & General Marshall
Section Six. Kennedy & Hoover and Mary Meyer
Section Seven. Nixon & McBride

They finished reading the short summaries of the times the American Philosophical Society had intervened—and even the report about Hoover and the Cincinnatians.

"Damn," was Kincannon's summary.

"They only had to actually pull out the Allegiance out twice," Evie noted.

"But they sure used it like Teddy Roosevelt's big stick," Ducharme said. "And they often used someone close to the President to deliver the warning. Effective."

"Hold on a sec—" Evie. "I just realized something." She scrolled back to the Kennedy section. "Mary Meyers. She was killed around a year after Kennedy was assassinated." She looked up at Ducharme and Kincannon. "A single round at close range in the head…and another in the heart."

"A message," Ducharme said, "from the Cincinnatians."

Evie nodded. "There's more in the report," she said, scrolling down.

Nixon was put out of office by the pressure of the Jefferson Allegiance, pre-empting the need for him to be impeached (strangely, many believe, wrongly, that Nixon was actually impeached). But his legacy had profound effects on shifting the balance of power from the legislative to the executive branch, to the point where the Founding Fathers would barely be able to recognize our current form of government. He was stopped, but many of the precedents he set have lived on.

Nixon, in various ways, took more control of the power of the purse than had been envisioned when our country was founded. The Founding Fathers believed that having the Legislative Branch control the money would keep the President in check, and also keep him from allying with those who wanted the purse directed their way—i.e. the Cincinnatians. Think of the military-industrial complex as warned of by Eisenhower. Nixon began the concept of calling any who opposed his fiscal policies "un-patriotic." He used his powers to reward those economic areas he favored and hurt those he didn't. He determined the level of spending, a right reserved for Congress.

He also trampled on Civil Liberties on a level not seen since FDR. He had the FBI, CIA and NSA investigate those who he deemed threats, real or imagined, regardless of what the law said those organizations were allowed to do.

The ability of the President to make decisions without having to inform Congress, never mind gain its approval, has echoed through every President since Nixon.

I was particularly interested in the Executive Branch and its power to take the country to war. As you can see from the previous historical sections, this power has evolved over the years to a form that would have been unacceptable to the Founding Fathers. I found an interesting piece of writing by James Madison that I wish to quote, because it seems to be something forgotten over the centuries since its writing:

"In no part of the Constitution is more wisdom to be found, than in the clause which confides the question of war and peace to the legislature, and not to the executive department. Besides the objection to such a mixture to heterogeneous powers, the trust and the temptation would be too great for any one man."

Thus, it was surprising for me to learn that the last time our country went to war under the strict guidelines laid out by the Founding Fathers, was in 1941. That was the last time Congress properly declared war.

Ducharme looked up from the screen. "Wait a second. Congress voted for the wars in Korea, Vietnam, Iraq and Afghanistan."

Evie shook her head. "Read on."

For every armed conflict the United States participated in since FDR and the Second World War—and there have been quite a few—the Chief Executive has gotten Congress to vote to suspend the Constitutional requirements for Congress itself to declare war, a strange paradox making an end run around the basic law set down by the Founding Fathers. Korea, Vietnam, Iraq—twice—Afghanistan. I imagine I might have even missed some conflicts or interventions in there that were not even voted on by Congress voting itself out of voting on it—such as Grenada, Lebanon, Somalia, the Balkans, Libya etc. All were done not in the manner the Founding Fathers set forth for the conduct of war, and use military might. And there is no doubt war profiteering by Cincinnatians plays a large role in many of these conflicts.

Dangerous times, as we are still wrapped up in two un-declared wars.

"That's it?" Ducharme asked, scrolling down and finding nothing more. He knew he was being sharper than he intended, but the prospect of the coming conflict was making him edgy. And there was one glaring omission: "What exactly is the Allegiance?"

"We're going to have to find it to figure that out," Evie said as she closed the laptop.

Kincannon frowned. "All these wars since World War Two—we really didn't win any of them. And not a single one of them was fought against a direct threat to our country. You could say after the first nine-eleven we did, but we sure didn't need to invade Iraq to go after the fuckers who took down the World Trade Center and hit the Pentagon."

Ducharme stirred uncomfortably in the driver's seat because all of this was touching on things he'd discussed with his uncle, the General. "Maybe that's exactly why we haven't won any of them."

Everyone in the Blazer turned to look at him. "I don't like admitting it, being a career soldier," he said, "but we haven't done too well since World War Two. And I don't think it's the military's fault. We've had the best military in the world for a long time—best equipped, best trained, best led. Volunteers since the end of Vietnam. I've served with damn fine people.

"I think it's these people—these fucking Cincinnatians and their ilk. They've sent us to fight bullshit wars for bullshit reasons to fatten their pockets. And it's hard for men—and women—to put their all into a war they can't believe in. That they actually didn't sign up to fight in. I swore an oath to defend the Constitution, to defend the country. What the fuck did invading Iraq have to do with that? Even the 'Stan. Yeah, Bin Laden trained his people there, but we should have just gone after Al Qaeda, not the whole damn country. Hell, Special Forces took out the Taliban in a couple of months. We should have packed our bags and come home. Not hung around to try to 'build' a country no one there really wants built. But there *is* an oil pipeline there."

"Easy, Duke," Kincannon said in a low voice.

Ducharme realized he'd raised his voice. He was surprising himself as much as the others in the vehicle. The beast was ruling, surging, but in a new direction. Ducharme forced himself to calm down, even though his head was throbbing. It wasn't time yet for the beast to rule.

Evie leaned forward. "Can I ask you something?"

"Is it going to be a 'did you know?'" Ducharme said.

"No." She pointed toward his hand. "Where's your West Point ring? You said graduates took their rings seriously. How come you don't wear yours?"

Ducharme knew she was redirecting him, but she was behind the power curve. "Charlie LaGrange—the General's son—and I left our rings at his family's home outside of New Orleans when we deployed to Afghanistan. We had a little ceremony, and we agreed we'd repeat the ceremony and put our rings on when we both got back home. We didn't have that second ceremony. He made it back from the 'Stan all right—before me. I buried both our rings with Charlie at Arlington just before I met you that night."

"Why'd you bury yours?" Evie asked.

Ducharme started the Blazer and pulled out, to get back onto the Turnpike. "To be honest. I don't really know. Seemed like the right thing to do at the time, like Kosciuszko refusing the sword. Now I know it was."

* * *

Inside the Anderson House, Lucius's attention was on the chess set. Half the pieces were scattered about the board, the other half lost in conflict on the sides of the board, indicating a game in progress. He reached out and moved a black bishop three spaces diagonally with utter confidence.

"Who are you playing?" Turnbull asked.

Lucius looked up. "My opponent is a member of the Society far away from here. We have spent considerable time discussing the strategic situation in the world. If we can finally do away with the Allegiance and the Philosophers, there is much we can accomplish. How close are we to achieving that?"

"The Surgeon is ahead of them, for once. She'll get the disks at Adams's grave. But I believe they now have the decryption thumb drive for McBride's computer."

"You 'believe?'"

"Three contractors were killed at Monticello. We think the drive was buried at Jefferson's tomb."

"Not very efficient. And I'm beginning to hear rumblings. Too many deaths. Too much notoriety."

"I'll wrap it up quickly," Turnbull promised.

"Ducharme and Tolliver won't give up their disks easily," Lucius noted.

"Leverage," Turnbull said simply.

"And the last set of disks?"

Turnbull rubbed his scarred hands together. "We haven't figured it out. Don't know if they have. But if they have or they do—leverage will still be the key to forcing them to hand them over."

CHAPTER TWENTY

It was dark as Ducharme drove the Blazer past the sign indicating the town limits of Quincy, Massachusetts. Another sign proclaimed Quincy: 'The City of Presidents.'

"Before the Bushes, the Adamses were the only father-son Presidential tandem," Evie informed them as they entered the town.

"Great," Ducharme said.

"John Hancock was also from Quincy." She pronounced it Quin-zee, which irritated Ducharme.

"Fantastic." Ducharme checked the GPS.

"Are you being sarcastic?" Evie asked.

"Ignore him," Kincannon advised Evie. "He gets snarly on a mission."

Ducharme stopped the truck. "There's the church."

They all looked ahead at the old building, which claimed the triangle in the center where three roads formed the exterior.

"It's the only church that has two dead Presidents buried there," Evie said, apparently undaunted. "The National Cathedral in Washington has one: Woodrow Wilson, although Eisenhower, Reagan and Ford had their funerals there."

"Can we focus?" Ducharme asked.

"The disks aren't going to be buried," Evie said.

"Why not?" Kincannon asked.

"Because John Adams, his son John Quincy, and their wives, are in crypts in the basement of the church," Evie said.

"OK." Ducharme tapped Kincannon on the arm. "See any surveillance?"

"Negative, but I should do a sweep around the perimeter," Kincannon replied, checking his MP-5.

Kincannon was out of the Blazer and gone into the darkness.

"What kind of crypts?" Ducharme asked.

"Stone sarcophagus," Evie said.

"So we'll need something to get the lid off if the disks were placed inside," Ducharme said.

"If they're here," Evie threw in.

Ducharme paused and put a hand on her arm. "Don't waffle on me now."

"I believe my reasoning to be valid based on the data."

"You want to bet your life on it?" Ducharme asked.

"I am betting my life on it."

Ducharme rubbed the back of his head. "Relax, Evie. Let's hope it doesn't come to that. Let's separate the disks again. You keep McBride's and the rod, I'll keep LaGrange's."

"Why?"

"Because we're splitting up in a minute, so it makes sense. It's one of Rogers's rules."

"Well, we wouldn't want to disappoint old Mister Rogers." She pulled out the rod, unscrewed one end, and slid off seven disks, handing them to Ducharme. He placed them in one of the Velcro pockets on the outside of his bulletproof vest.

Kincannon appeared in front of the Blazer, the sub-machinegun tucked underneath his long coat. Ducharme lowered the driver's window.

"It's clear," Kincannon reported.

Ducharme looked back at Evie. "Stay here. We'll be back as fast as we can. You hear shooting, get the hell out of here and we'll contact you by phone; if we can."

Ducharme went to the back of the Blazer and opened the tailgate, grabbing a crowbar, which he tucked under his jacket. He headed toward the church, with Kincannon flanking him. Ducharme scanned the area, noting there was little traffic on the streets surrounding the church.

"No security?" Ducharme asked as they approached.

"Didn't see any," Kincannon said.

"I guess dead Presidents don't rate."

"Ain't like they're gonna get any deader."

Ducharme took the four stairs at the front of the church two at a time. Using one of the four large pillars as concealment, he went to a door. It was locked. He pulled a set of picks out and made short work of that.

He slid inside, pulling out his sub-machinegun. It would be some kind of irony if they were ambushed inside a church. What kind, he didn't know.

He and Kincannon made their way to the stairway to the presidential crypt. Another gate barred the way. Ducharme pushed on it and it swung wide open. He checked the lock. It had been pried open.

"Fuck," he muttered. "Someone's been here already. Came in some other door."

"Let's hope they haven't left," Kincannon said, the stock of his weapon tucked tight into his shoulder.

They entered the crypt as a team. Covering across each other's fronts, sweeping the room with their eyes, the muzzles of the sub-machineguns following, fingers on the triggers.

The crypt was empty of life.

Resting on top of John Adams's sarcophagus was a piece of paper. Ducharme grabbed it and read:

CALL FOR A TRADE

"Oh, shit," Ducharme exclaimed. He ran out of the crypt, Kincannon on his heels. Up the stairs, out the front of the church. He could hear the sound of a helicopter lifting off, and saw the dark silhouette of the aircraft flit across the stars to the west and then disappear. He ran across the street to the Blazer.

The doors were open. The Blazer was empty.

* * *

Special Agent Burns stood on the roof of the Hoover Building dusting for fingerprints. He lifted the set off the door handle, and then went to the elevator. He took it to the floor that housed the Criminal Justice Information Services Division. Finding an empty room, he processed the prints, and then fed them into the FBI's database.

Nothing.

As expected.

He dug deeper into the computer. He ran the fingerprints against the IAFIS, the Automated Fingerprint Identification System which held over 47 million sets of prints, gathered from all over the country by local, state and federal law enforcement agencies.

Nothing.

The next largest list of fingerprints outside of the FBI was not as easily accessible. He pulled a little black notebook out of his pocket and thumbed through it. A list of user-names and passwords were listed near the rear. Favors culled from favors he'd dispensed over the years.

Using one set, he accessed the Pentagon's personnel records database. He ran the prints.

A Top Secret banner popped up, barring any further information unless the user had the proper clearance. He checked his book again and found a name and a password.

He punched it in.

A Department of Defense Form 214 appeared in response to the prints. Of a Lieutenant Colonel Thomas Blake.

He scanned the form, his own brief stint in the military allowing him to make sense of the abbreviations.

Blake graduated the United States Naval Academy in 1962. Was commissioned in the Marine Corps. Served two tours in Vietnam with distinction, winning the Navy Cross. Was assigned to the National Security Council in 1969.

Blake was promoted to Lieutenant Colonel in 1974, still serving in Washington. He retired from the military in 1976. And that was it.

Burns went back to his tiny office and sat down. He Googled "Thomas Blake," and wasn't surprised at what came up. Blake's graduation from Annapolis and his time on the National Security Council were well documented. As were numerous allegations that he was involved in illegal operations involving arms smuggling, drugs and other nefarious dealings. He was indicted on numerous Federal charges.

The charges came to naught in 1977. Retired Lieutenant Colonel Blake, facing six federal indictments, died when the small plane he was piloting crashed at sea off the coast of Florida.

No body was recovered.

Burns had no doubt that Blake became Turnbull in 1977.

A player once more, with a different name and a different position, but doing the same thing.

Burns put his fedora on, pulling the brim down low over his eyes. Time to play the player.

CHAPTER TWENTY-ONE

"The Surgeon will make the next move." Ducharme slammed his fist into the steering wheel. "She'll want the damn disks for Evie."

"Ain't gonna be no trade," Kincannon said. "You know that."

Ducharme tried to figure the angles to the tactical situation. His head was pounding and he was having a hard time concentrating on the facts. He finally accepted the grim reality: there were no angles other than the disks. "We're screwed."

"We've been in tight situations before."

"Not with so much at stake," Ducharme said.

Kincannon snorted. "I consider my life pretty damn high stakes."

"You know what I mean."

"Yeah." Kincannon let out a long breath. He reached down and retrieved his sub-machinegun. He checked the magazine, pulled the bolt back slightly to make sure a round was chambered. "What now?"

"I think it's time we—" Ducharme was interrupted by his satphone buzzing. "Yeah?"

"Colonel, it's Agent Burns. Just found out that the man who's been running this op, Turnbull, is actually a former marine who worked on the JCS: Thomas Blake. Reported killed in a plane crash over deep water a long time ago."

"Let me guess," Ducharme said. "No body recovered."

"Right. He was facing six Federal indictments. And now he's supposedly an ADiC in the FBI."

Ducharme absently rubbed the scar under his eye with his free hand. "What do you have on him? Anything?"

"Besides the fact he's not interested in catching the killer and is actually the one issuing her orders?"

"Anything else?"

"No. But I'm going to keep an eye on Blake, aka Officer Turnbull. I'll let you know what he's up to."

"Good idea."

"And there's something else. I don't know if it means anything or not, but General Parker commanded the Air Force Honor Guard in the late nineties. They do the burial detail for Air Force personnel at Arlington, so maybe his disks are there?"

Ducharme considered that. "But how does it tie in to the 'no one and everyone' thing?"

"No idea. But something is going to break loose soon."

"Just make sure it isn't you," Ducharme said.

"Right."

The phone clicked off. Ducharme brought Kincannon up to speed. He listened, thought for a second, and then shook his head. "Turnbull's a spook, deep black. Not government either. This damn Society of Cincinnati is pulling all the strings."

"My thoughts exactly."

"And lots of graves at Arlington," Kincannon said.

"You don't have to tell me."

"Sorry."

Ducharme pressed his hand against the back of his head. He could see the dirt covering the grave of Charlie LaGrange. He opened his eyes and looked at the steering wheel. "'No one's and everyone's.'" He stiffened.

"What?" Kincannon asked.

"Did you know—" Ducharme stopped, and then swore.

Kincannon laughed. "It's catching, ain't it? Did I know what?"

"That the hero of Gettysburg, Colonel Joshua Chamberlain, was a college professor just like Evie, before the Civil War?"

"'Evie'?"

Ducharme ignored the comment. "He wanted to enlist, but the college he taught at felt he was too valuable. So they gave him a two-year leave of absence to depart the country and go overseas to study foreign languages. So he promptly enlisted."

"My kind of guy," Kincannon said, laying the sub-machinegun across his lap.

"Yeah, he was. The governor of Maine offered him command of a regiment, but he declined, saying he kind of wanted to start a little lower and learn the business of war first."

"Weird thinking there," Kincannon said dryly. "Very un-officer-like."

"Anyway," Ducharme said, ignoring the sarcasm, "he eventually took command of the Twentieth Maine, and ended up holding the far left of the Union line on Little Round Top at Gettysburg. They got attacked hard by the Fifteenth Alabama. Things were looking bad for him—and the Union. His own flank got pushed back so far, his line ended up being in a Vee and his men were about out of ammunition."

"Essentially, he was screwed," Kincannon summarized.

"Which is the point of my story," Ducharme said. "You know what he did then?"

"Nope."

"He had his men fix bayonets and charge," Ducharme said. "The Confederates were exhausted from attacking so hard all day, that it took them by surprise and broke their will and saved the left flank and, in essence, the entire Union line. And ultimately the Civil War."

"So we're a gonna fix bayonets," Kincannon said.

Ducharme smiled grimly. "When the time is right."

"And then charge."

"Yes."

* * *

"Ducharme is going to hunt you down and—"

"Shut up," the Surgeon snapped, slapping Evie across the face with the flat side of the wakizashi. Blood filled her mouth. Her body still twitched from the Taser. Her hands were cuffed behind her back, the chain looped through a cable along the back seat of the helicopter.

The Surgeon was facing her, sitting on a plastic case right behind the pilots. She slid the gun back into its holster, and then held up the rod with seven disks on it. Evie watched her unscrew one end and slide the six recovered from John Adams's crypt onto it. Then she slid another one on.

"One through fourteen," she said. "Over halfway toward my goal. How many does Ducharme have?"

"Fuck you," Evie said, punctuating the statement by spitting blood at the Surgeon.

"Such bad language," the Surgeon said. "How many disks does Ducharme have?"

"Fuck you," Evie repeated.

The Surgeon smiled coldly. "I can cause you great pain." She looked at Evie, eyes roaming, as if trying to decide the best cut of meat in a butcher shop. She made up her mind, aiming the blade when her satphone rang. With a regrettable sigh, she lowered the sword and put the phone tight against her ear to hear over the sound of the helicopter.

* * *

"Yes?"

Ducharme recognized the Surgeon's voice and steeled himself. "What's the trade, missy?" He could hear a helicopter in the background.

"Colonel Ducharme," the Surgeon replied. "I have a friend of yours."

"What makes you think she's my friend?"

"I get irritable when my time is wasted, and then I put blood on my blade."

"Not my blood."

"Not yet."

"So you're an optimist?" Ducharme asked.

"A realist."

"The reality is I am going to kill you."

"Can we get beyond this bluster to the details of what you're going to do *for* me?"

Ducharme pulled the satphone away from his ear for a moment, took a deep breath, then brought it back. "Go ahead, missy."

The response was quick and hard. "Are you insulting me?"

"I don't even know you. Tell me what you want?"

"How many disks do you have?" the Surgeon asked.

Ducharme glanced at Kincannon who was listening in. The Sergeant Major shrugged. They both knew what was coming.

"I can make the lady experience considerable pain," the Surgeon added.

"Seven."

"So all we're missing are General Parker's five remaining disks," the Surgeon said. "Any idea where they are?"

"No," Ducharme said.

"I think you're lying."

"You can think all you want."

"I can do more than think. Do you want to hear her scream?"

Ducharme gripped the phone tight. "I will rip the life right out of you. I will snatch it—" Kincannon pressed a nerve in Ducharme's shoulder, causing him to stop talking and loosening his grip on the phone. The Sergeant Major grabbed the phone and put it on speaker.

"Honey darling?"

"Who is this?"

"Someone else you're going to have to spend every minute of what remains of your life looking out for if you hurt Tolliver."

There was a moment of silence. When the Surgeon spoke again, her voice was tight. "We meet. I give you Tolliver back. You give me your seven disks."

"How?"

"I'll send a helicopter to pick you up," the Surgeon said.

"Negative," Kincannon said. "We've got our own pilot and chopper."

There was another short pause. "All right."

"How can we trust you?" This earned him a roll of the eyes from Ducharme.

"I was an officer and a gentlewoman," the Surgeon said. "I also was bound by an honor code."

"Right," Kincannon said. "That took."

"I'm going to enjoy—" the Surgeon caught herself. "I'll meet you and Ducharme—"

"We'll decide where to meet," Ducharme said.

"You don't—"

Kincannon's voice was like steel. "We've got what you have to get. And you need the disks more than we need Professor Tolliver. We're professionals. It's the disks that are important. Right?"

"Where?" the Surgeon asked.

Kincannon looked at Ducharme, letting him answer.

"Washington. I'll direct the pilot to the exact spot once we get close. Just be in the area."

"All right."

"I'll see you soon," Ducharme said.

"Looking forward to it," the Surgeon said.

"You shouldn't."

CHAPTER TWENTY-TWO

Lily turned away from her captive in the rear of the helicopter and typed into her satphone.

>>>HAVE DISKS 1 THROUGH 14. HAVE TOLLIVER. MEETING DUCHARME IN DC TO GET HIS 7 DISKS<<<

There was a short pause before a response came on-screen.

WHERE ARE LAST 5?

>>>DON'T KNOW<<<

WHERE ARE YOU?

>>>EN ROUTE TO DC. WHERE SHOULD I LAND?<<<

There was a long pause.

THEODORE ROOSEVELT MEMORIAL. ISLAND WILL BE SEALED OFF

>>>ROGER<<<

The screen went blank. Lily moved forward and leaned between the pilot and co-pilot's seats. She told them where to go, and for a moment she thought they were going to argue with her, but they acquiesced, punching up the destination on their flight computer. Lily pulled out her satphone and accessed Google Maps. She typed in the Roosevelt Memorial and put the resulting map on hybrid, zooming in. She nodded as she saw the result.

Isolated. A perfect place to finish things.

* * *

Kincannon pointed up and then to his ear. Ducharme could hear a helicopter approaching the Quincy Hospital heliport.

Ducharme walked to the edge of the helipad with the Sergeant Major. "How are you feeling?"

"Most fun I've had in a while," Kincannon said.

"Sorry to drag you into this mess," Ducharme said.

"Ain't nothing but a thing," Kincannon said.

"What exactly does that mean?" Ducharme asked as the lights of the Huey appeared in the night sky, coming in low and fast.

"No idea," Kincannon said, cheerful at the prospect of action. "But I like the way it sounds."

Ducharme sighed. "Sometimes, I wonder if it's worth it. Catching Charlie's killer, yeah. But the people pulling the strings—they're so powerful. What good can we do?"

"We can get this Allegiance," Kincannon said. "It's got to be pretty strong stuff. Enough to scare the string-pullers." The chopper was getting closer, lights flashing in the darkness as it came in. "Evie pointed out this Mary Meyers woman who was connected to Kennedy got a head and heart double-tap. But the Cincinnatians didn't take over the country then. Somebody fought them. And the Philosophers were still around to confront Nixon."

Kincannon put a hand on Ducharme's shoulder. "Listen. From Casablanca: 'You might as well question why we breathe. If we stop breathing, we'll die. If we stop fighting our enemies, the world will die.' Don't go Rick on me. Go Lazlo."

Ducharme smiled. "Someone's got to stand fast, right?"

"Not just stand fast, but fight back."

The chopper touched down, Pollack at the controls. Ducharme and Kincannon threw their gear in the cargo bay, and then climbed in, sliding shut the cargo door. The chopper was airborne within seconds, and heading southwest.

* * *

Burns followed Turnbull out of the Hoover Building. The senior agent got into an armored Town Car with darkly tinted windows. Burns grabbed one of the 'ready' cars parked in front of the building after flashing his badge.

The keys were in the ignition. There wasn't much traffic this late, and Burns had no problem following.

He quickly caught up to Turnbull's car on Constitution Avenue, but dropped back as four black Suburbans abruptly swung onto the road, falling in behind the Town Car—not FBI. Spooks of one sort or the other, government or more likely contractors. Who the fuck knew, and at the moment it didn't matter to Burns.

Burns kept Turnbull in sight through Washington to the on-ramp for the Theodore Roosevelt Bridge. Traffic was a bit heavier now as they were on I-66. Then Turnbull's car immediately swung off onto a little used exit. There was no way Burns could follow and not be spotted. He slowed down, staying parallel, earning the ire of drivers behind him, keeping pace with the Suburbans and Town Car on the service road to the right.

A sign indicated it was the exit for the Theodore Roosevelt Memorial.

Brake lights flashed in the night. Right next to the footbridge that led to Theodore Roosevelt Island in the middle of the Potomac. Burns sped up as men in black piled out of the Suburbans. The island was uninhabited, lots of trees and walking trails, and a plaza with a Memorial to the former President. An easy place to keep secure.

Burns continued on the GW Parkway and took a left exit, and then another left, driving until he was opposite the stopped vehicles, with the GW and Jeff Davis Parkways separating them. He parked illegally, went to the trunk and pulled out a set of night vision goggles. He walked into the trees until he could see a vantage point. He took off his fedora and pulled on the night vision goggles. He could see the Suburbans, Town Car and armed guards at the footbridge. A line of dark figures was crossing the bridge onto the island.

Burns settled in to wait.

* * *

Evie opened and closed her fingers repeatedly, trying to keep the blood circulating. She knew asking to have the pressure of the cuffs reduced would be a fruitless exercise. The Blackhawk was somewhere over Maryland. The Surgeon was seated facing her. Her short sword was across her knees. The air of confidence she projected pissed Evie off.

"He'll never give up the disks," Evie yelled over the sound of turbine engines and blades cutting through the air overhead.

The Surgeon looked at her. "You underestimate yourself."

"I do?"

"Men are foolish creatures," the Surgeon said. "Your Colonel is not thinking straight."

"You're wrong," Evie insisted, but she had a moment of doubt, remembering how Ducharme had acted at times. It wasn't about hormones like the Surgeon thought, but because of his brain injury. Then again, she thought . . .

"You people keep telling me I'm wrong," the Surgeon said, "but I have fourteen of the disks."

"You could have all the disks," Evie said, "and it still won't be enough to find the Allegiance."

The Surgeon shrugged. "But having them will stop you from finding it. Just as killing you and Ducharme would achieve the same thing. I already took care of the other two."

"You'd have destroyed the disks and killed me if you believed that. Whoever's controlling you wants the Allegiance. You're just a puppet being used by the Cincinnatians."

The Surgeon gave a cold smile. "No. I'm using them for my own purpose."

"Right." A vision of Ducharme drawling the same word in his unique accent flashed through her mind. "You have no idea what you're messing with. It's--" Evie stopped speaking as the Surgeon lifted her sword.

The steel flashed toward Evie's face and she flinched, expecting to feel the sharp pain of sliced flesh. Instead, the flat side of the sword slapped against the side of her face once more.

Evie glared at the other woman. "Easy to hit someone who is chained up."

The Surgeon nodded. "You're quite correct. And I couldn't care less about the Cincinnatians."

"What?" Evie was confused. Then she saw the look the Surgeon's eyes, and realized that all of this was just part of some twisted sickness in the woman's head. She'd seen the same in some of the CIA field agents—the ones who reveled in places like Abu Ghraib rather than be repelled by them.

The Surgeon hefted McBride's briefcase. "Should I read what your Chair wrote on his computer?"

"It doesn't say what the Allegiance is."

The Surgeon shrugged. "I couldn't care less." She tossed the briefcase to the floor with a thud, and Evie flinched as much as she had when the sword had been coming for her. Looking past the Surgeon, Evie could see a bright glow on the horizon. The Washington Monument, well lit by ground lights, appeared out to the front left. The helicopter arced around the restricted flight zone of Washington until it was over the Potomac near Georgetown.

The pilots dropped altitude to just above the water. Evie could see the lights of downtown Washington to the left and the headlights of cars on the GW Parkway to the right. A line of trees suddenly appeared in front, and the aircraft lifted slightly, clearing them. And just as quickly, descended to a paved plaza in the midst of the trees and landed.

A ring of armed men dressed in black surrounded the helicopter and beyond them, a statue, one hand raised.

"Teddy Roosevelt," Evie said, as the whine from the turbine engines wound down and the blades slowed overhead.

The Surgeon slid open one of the side doors. Then she un-cuffed Evie. "Let's go," the Surgeon said, pointing with her sword toward the men gathered in front of the 17-foot high statue of the former president. There were four stone monoliths surrounding the plaza.

"Do you know," Evie said, "what it says on one of those stones?"

"I don't care," the Surgeon said, gesturing once more with the sword for her to get off.

"You should care," Evie said. "Roosevelt said: *'If I must choose between righteousness and peace, I choose righteousness.'* I think Colonel Ducharme is going to bring some righteousness down on you shortly."

CHAPTER TWENTY-THREE

Pollack was flying low and fast, staying off radar and making up the time they'd lost refueling at Fort Dix. Ducharme checked the GPS. They were fifteen minutes from Washington. His satphone buzzed and he pulled it out, pressing it tight against his ear in order to hear over the sound of the helicopter.

"Yeah?"

"It's Burns. Are you chasing a Blackhawk to DC?"

"How'd you know?"

"I saw it land on Roosevelt Island. There's a shitload of contractors there, too. Along with Turnbull. I wouldn't advise going there."

"I don't plan on it. Did you see who was on the chopper?"

"Negative. They landed at the Memorial, and trees block the view. The only way onto the island is via a footbridge and it's well guarded."

"I'm going to force them to move to Fort Myer. Make a trade."

There was silence for a little while. "A trade?"

Ducharme glanced over at Sergeant Major Kincannon, who was leaning back against the back wall of the cargo bay, weapon on his lap. "Yeah. Listen, we might need some back-up."

"I'm your man."

"Let me know when and how they move."

"All right."

Ducharme turned off the phone. He moved closer to Kincannon. "Sergeant Major?"

"Yes, sir?"

"We're going to meet this Surgeon at Fort Myer to set up an exchange of our disks for Evie."

"'Evie'?" Kincannon smiled, and then shook his head. "You thinking straight? There's gonna be no exchange. They're going to come in guns blazing."

Ducharme nodded. "That's where we need some help if you don't mind making a call or two."

After telling Kincannon his plan, Ducharme opened one of the plastic cases and pulled out a military issue computer. He accessed the Defense Department's Interlink. He needed intelligence on the target and the layout of a building.

* * *

The presence of the contractors made Lily uncomfortable—she preferred working alone. And Turnbull had taken charge of the prisoner as soon as she got Tolliver off the chopper. He had her near the central fountain in the plaza under heavy guard. She had left the briefcase in the chopper, a possible bargaining tool if Turnbull turned on her like he had the contractors.

"Sir." Lily tried not to stand at attention, but she knew no other way to approach someone of higher rank.

Turnbull turned his ice blue eyes on her. "Yes?"

"Are you really going to give Tolliver to Ducharme for the disks? We can destroy the Philosophical Society once and for all tonight."

"And what purpose would that serve?" Turnbull asked.

Lily was surprised. "We would finish off our enemies. It's a maxim of military strategy to—"

"This is not a military problem," Turnbull interrupted. "This is a political issue. The disks are more important than the people."

"Yes, sir, but—" she stopped as her satphone buzzed. She turned it on. "Yes?"

"Hey, missy."

She squeezed the phone the way she'd like to squeeze Ducharme's neck, but she kept her voice level. "I'm waiting for you."

"Don't want to keep a lady waiting," Ducharme said.

"Bring the disks to—"

"You don't listen very well."

She stifled a sharp retort, feeling Turnbull's eyes on her. "What do you want?"

"My friend."

"Give me the disks."

"I will."

"Come to Roosevelt Island and—"

"You really don't listen," Ducharme cut her off. "You're sitting there with a bunch of gunmen, waiting for me to stick my head in the trap."

She looked about. They had a traitor in their midst. Or Ducharme had just made the logical deduction. She rubbed the side of her head. "Where, then?"

"Get in your helicopter with Tolliver. Everyone else stays there. Once you're airborne, I'll give you the grid coordinates where we'll meet."

"You need Tolliver back," Lily said.

"I *want* Tolliver back," Ducharme said. "You *need* to do what I say." The phone went dead.

"Yes?" Turnbull asked.

"Ducharme wants me airborne with the prisoner," Lily said. "He'll give me the coordinates of the meet once I'm airborne. He knows your men are here. He wants none to leave. He might have someone watching us."

Turnbull inclined his battered head ever so slightly. "Ah. Officer Burns. Very enterprising. Go. Do the meet. Negotiate. Don't worry about what he wants. Take six men. Haggle over Tolliver. Can you do that?"

She stiffened at being talked to in such a manner. "Yes, sir."

"Go."

* * *

The Blackhawk lifted just as the satphone buzzed. "Burns."

"Chopper in the air?"

He recognized Ducharme's voice. "Yeah."

"The merks moving?"

Burns looked at the bridge and the vehicles. "Negative. Not yet at least, but I couldn't see who got on the chopper."

"Turnbull will be sending muscle on it. Keep an eye on him. Can you?"

"He's got a lot of firepower, but I'll do what I can."

"Thanks."

Burns watched the footbridge through the night vision goggles. "Where is the meet?"

"Fort Myer. Ord and Wietzel Drive. There are some old warehouses off to the right. Go past them and there's a field adjacent to Arlington. That's where the party will be."

"You sure it's going to be a party?" Burns asked.

"It's time to fix bayonets."

Burns saw people crossing the footbridge toward him. "Yeah, it is." He drew his pistol and headed toward the highways separating him from his 'supervisor.'

* * *

216

The Huey touched down in a snow-covered field, leafless trees surrounding it. The blades created their own minor snowstorm, which subsided as the chopper powered down.

Ducharme leaned between the seats and tapped Pollack on the shoulder. "Get ready to start up quick. Also, can you get clearance from military air traffic control to go up to twelve thousand feet? Offset from DC's restricted airspace, right on the northwest edge."

She nodded, casting an anxious glance toward Kincannon who was stepping off, sub-machinegun in hand.

"I'll watch out for him," Ducharme promised.

"And who's going to watch out for you?" Pollack asked.

"He will," Ducharme said. "We're a good team."

She lifted her hand off the cyclic and extended it. "*We're* a good team."

He grasped her hand in his. "We are."

* * *

"Officer Burns." Turnbull put away his satphone.

A half-dozen heavily armed men in black surrounded Burns, but he focused on his nominal superior, who acknowledged the pistol in Burns's hand with a single arched eyebrow. "Going to take us all on?"

"If need be," Burns said. "I am the law. I have no idea what you are, and I know they—" he indicated the mercenaries—"aren't the law."

"The gun won't be necessary," Turnbull said. "Things will be solved peacefully."

"They haven't been so far," Burns said. "Body count keeps rising."

"Not my fault," Turnbull said. "One can only control a free agent so far."

"You're saying the Surgeon doesn't work for you?"

"You know her code name." Turnbull didn't seem impressed. "We've tried to keep her under control, but I'm afraid she's gone off the grid."

The FBI agent went still. Even though he had feared it, the confirmation of betrayal still struck deep. "You want me to do your dirty work."

"I want you to do your duty," Turnbull said. When he got no response, he added: "What do *you* want?"

"To keep you from interfering with the trade."

"So you've thrown your hand in with Ducharme," Turnbull said. He shrugged. "I have no plans to interfere with the trade. I *want* the trade to happen as much as Ducharme does."

"Who is on the Blackhawk with the Surgeon?" Burns asked, pulling out his satphone.

"Professor Tolliver, as requested."

"And how many of your hired guns?"

"Six," Turnbull said. He opened the driver's door of the Town Car. "Why don't you use my car and join Ducharme and his friend Kincannon? Give them a hand." He stepped away from the car. "I'll be right here, waiting to hear what happens."

Burns hesitated, but got in. The keys were in the ignition. He cranked the engine and headed away, punching in a speed dial on his satphone at the same time.

* * *

"You've got six mercenaries on board the Blackhawk along with the Surgeon and Tolliver." Burns's voice was strained.

Ducharme threw an infrared chem light out into the field, in front of the Huey, to mark the landing zone. "Figured as much."

"I'm en route to your location by ground."

"And Turnbull?"

"Says he's waiting to hear what happens."

Ducharme paused from checking the magazine in his sub-machinegun. "That doesn't sound like him."

"Actually," Burns disagreed, "it sounds exactly like him. He's playing this from every angle, letting everyone else get their hands dirty."

"What's the angle he wants?"

"The disks," Burns said.

"He's—" Ducharme heard the sound of an incoming helicopter. "Got to go. See you shortly."

He glanced to his right where Sergeant Major Kincannon stood tall, weapon at the ready. The landing Blackhawk sent a flurry of snow in their direction. As the large helicopter's engines wound down, a single figure dressed in a long black cloak stepped out of the left side cargo bay door.

Ducharme kept the muzzle of his weapon lowered, and took a few steps forward. "Close enough," he called out when the Surgeon was about ten feet away.

"The disks?" the Surgeon demanded.

"Tolliver?"

The Surgeon flicked her hand up and the other side door on the Blackhawk opened. A figure was roughly shoved out, followed by six heavily-armed men. Evie struggled to her feet, hands cuffed behind her back, receiving no help.

"I have what you want," the Surgeon said, "*and* I have the power to *make* you give me what I want."

"You're wrong," Ducharme said.

The Surgeon's hand drifted inside her coat, going toward the handle of her sword. "Give me the disks and take your woman."

218

They both turned as a set of headlights carved down the dirt road leading to the clearing. Three of the merks turned their weapons in that direction while the other three kept theirs trained on Ducharme and Kincannon. An armored Lincoln Town Car pulled up, forming the third point in a deadly triangle. Agent Burns exited the driver's side, his pistol at the ready.

"We still have the firepower," the Surgeon said. "Give me—"

Her head swiveled back and forth as a half-dozen figures in camouflage, holding M-14 rifles, stepped out of the surrounding trees.

"Mine's bigger," Ducharme said. "This is Army turf."

The Surgeon remained still.

He took a step closer. "Un-cuff Tolliver."

The Surgeon gestured and one of her men who did as he was told.

"Now," Ducharme spoke slowly, sensing the Surgeon was on the edge. "Give the rod and disks to Tolliver."

The Surgeon took a step toward Ducharme, hand still inside her cloak. He brought the muzzle of his weapon up. "I *will* put a round straight through your eyeball and blow your fucking brains all over the inside of that hood."

She stopped, breathing hard, practically hyperventilating.

"The disks and rod to Tolliver," Ducharme ordered.

The Surgeon's other hand moved and from an interior pocket, she pulled out a leather bag. She held it up.

"Switch hands," Ducharme ordered, needing to get the bag in her sword hand. Disappointment crossed her face, but she did so.

"Don't get in my line of fire," Ducharme warned Evie. She hurried forward. Burns also headed over. Evie took the bag, and Ducharme's finger caressed the trigger, but the Surgeon did nothing.

"Took you long enough." Evie looked about. "Who are the soldiers?"

"Third Infantry." Ducharme kept his focus on the Surgeon and her men. "Weapons on the ground."

They reluctantly complied.

"Master Sergeant," Ducharme called out. The same senior non-commissioned officer who had confronted him on his visit to Arlington stepped forward.

"Sir?"

"Secure these people. I'm sure Agent Burns will be back for them. As soon as you have them secure, leave some guards and follow."

"Roger that."

"Did you bring what I asked?"

The Master Sergeant gestured, and a soldier came forward carrying a large kit bag.

"Put it on the helicopter," Ducharme ordered. As soon as it was on, the Huey took off, disappearing into the night sky.

"Where are we going?" Evie asked.

As the 3rd Infantry soldiers cuffed the Surgeon and the six mercenaries, Ducharme finally lowered his sub-machinegun and looked at her. "What happened to your face?"

"It's not important," Evie said, but her hand went to the red skin on her cheek and rubbed it.

"Do you know where the last five disks are?"

"'No one's and everyone's,'" Evie said. "I've been thinking about it, but it's kind of vague. I don't have a historical reference."

"They're here," Ducharme said.

"'Here'?" Evie looked about. "You mean Arlington."

Ducharme nodded. He looked from her to Kincannon, to Burns. His motley team trying to save the country. He turned to his right and headed toward the trees separating them from the National Cemetery. "Let's go get them."

CHAPTER TWENTY-FOUR

"They're moving, sir."

Turnbull got in the passenger seat of one of the Suburbans and looked at the GPS display on the dash. A small red dot, representing the bug he had planted on Tolliver during the few minutes he'd had her, was moving from Ft. Myer into Arlington. He nodded. "Very good. Let's roll."

* * *

Ducharme led them out of the trees onto a road. Arlington House was to their left. Evie was at his side, and Kincannon was on one flank with Burns on the other.

They made their way deeper into the cemetery. Gardens of stone appeared on both sides. They reached an intersection. According to the signpost, the road they were on, Wilson Drive, made a sharp left. The road continuing straight was now named Memorial Drive.

There was a glow about a hundred yards to the left front. *Memorial.* Ducharme continued straight. A large circular structure appeared. A series of colonnades compromised the outer rim. Ducharme led his team through the entrance into the Amphitheater. Rows of benches lined the interior, facing a small covered platform.

They went down the center aisle and to the side of the platform. Exiting the Amphitheater there was a broad series of steps down to a brightly lit plaza with a single marble sarcophagus and three marble slabs in front of it. Marching in front of it was a soldier in dress blues with an M-14 at shoulder arms.

"The Tomb of the Unknowns," Evie whispered.

Ducharme glanced at her. "It's the perfect place to hide something you want protected. Since nineteen thirty-seven the Tomb has been guarded non-stop, twenty-four-seven, three hundred and sixty-five days a year."

"But *someone* is buried there," Evie said.

The Sentinel came to the end of his twenty-one paces—equal to the twenty-one gun salute. He halted and turned, facing the tomb, remaining perfectly still for 21 seconds. Then he turned back the way he come, went to shoulder arms on the side facing away from the grave, remained still for the same amount of time, and then began his next twenty-one steps. There was a deep simplicity and gravity to it.

"Not in all the graves," Ducharme said.

* * *

The 3rd Infantry had left two men as guards. A sign of over-confidence in Lily's opinion. Her hands were cuffed behind her back, and she was seated on the metal edge of the Blackhawk's cargo bay. She waited until the guards' focus was outwards, and then jammed her left hand between the edge of the co-pilot's seat and the frame of the helicopter.

She took a deep breath, and then abruptly leveraged her arm, cracking the bones in her hand. The tearing of flesh and splintering of bones shot pain up her arm, refreshing her. A couple of the mercenaries heard and turned to stare at her, shocked expressions on their faces—they certainly weren't getting paid enough to do that. Pausing only to take another deep breath, she pulled her right hand, with all her strength while forcing the left to hold in place. The metal cuff scraped skin, compressing broken bones, cracking them further, and then the loop of metal freed her left hand.

Checking to make sure the Army guards were still looking toward the surrounding woods, she strode over to the pile of weapons and retrieved her wakizashi. Her left hand was on fire and dangling uselessly, but her right gripped the handle of the sword and drew it. She was on the first guard, sliding the blade across his throat before he was aware there was a threat.

His dying gasp caused the other one to turn. She swung her sword. His head tumbled into the snow as blood still pumped out of the severed stump of his neck and the body slowly collapsed.

Tucking the bloody sword under her arm, she pulled the cuff keys out of his combat vest and turned to the mercenaries.

* * *

"Halt! Who goes there?" The sentry swung his weapon from shoulder arms to at-the-ready.

"Colonel Ducharme, Sergeant Major Kincannon and Special Agent Burns from FBI." Ducharme stepped onto the Plaza. The guard seemed uncertain what to do. Not many infiltrations on the Tomb of the Unknowns.

A voice called out authoritatively from the left. "At ease, Sergeant."

Ducharme recognized the voice of the Master Sergeant from the 3rd Infantry and so did the sentry, who lowered his weapon and snapped to a position of port arms. The Master Sergeant came up to Ducharme. "I've gone along with you this far, but I can't allow you to violate the grave of one of the Unknowns."

Ducharme nodded. "I'm not asking you to violate a soldier's burial place. I need to look in an empty grave." The Master Sergeant understood right away, but still hesitated.

Kincannon stepped forward. "This is important."

The Master Sergeant looked doubtful, but nodded. "All right, sir. Do no damage."

"Thank you," Ducharme said. He walked toward the sarcophagus, Evie following. There were three marble slabs laid even with the plaza spread in front of it. He knelt in front of the center one. Kincannon hung back with the others.

"The Unknown from World War One is buried underneath the sarcophagus." Ducharme then nodded toward the slab to his left. "That's the Unknown from World War Two." He gestured to his right. "The Korean War."

"And this one?" Evie asked, pointing at the one directly in front of him.

Ducharme reached down and ran his fingers across the words etched in the marble. "It reads: 'Honoring and Keeping Faith with America's Missing Servicemen.' It used to read 'Vietnam' along with the dates of that war."

"'Used to'?" Evie asked.

"The Unknown from Vietnam was exhumed in nineteen ninety-eight, and the DNA was tested. He was identified and returned to his family. The tomb was left empty."

"'No one's and everyone'," Evie said.

"Exactly." Ducharme pulled a short crowbar out of his vest and slid the edge underneath the lip of the marble. He caught the edge and then put all his weight onto it. The slab didn't move. Evie knelt next to him and added her weight, her body pressing against his. Stone rumbled and the slab lifted. Hooking his fingers underneath, Ducharme grunted as he lifted the slab higher and held it in place. An empty crypt.

Except for a black bag.

"Grab it," Ducharme told Evie.

Evie didn't hesitate, trusting that he would hold the heavy stone. She reached in and retrieved the bag. Ducharme carefully lowered the slab back into place. Still kneeling, he turned and faced Evie who had the leather bag open. She pulled out five disks. Retrieving the rod and disks from the suitcase, she unscrewed one end. Checking the numbers, she slid the five remaining disks on and replaced the end. She looked up at Ducharme.

"We have the Jefferson Cipher."

CHAPTER TWENTY-FIVE

Lily deployed the six merks among the colonnades of the Memorial Amphitheater, weapons at the ready. She plugged in the headset for her satphone and pressed the earpiece in her right ear—her broken hand precluding text messaging. She hit the speed dial, and the phone was answered immediately.

"Yes?"

"Mister Turnbull, I have Ducharme, Evie and the others in my sights. They've retrieved the last disks of the Cipher. We can take them out now."

"I want the Allegiance," Turnbull said.

"If we get the Cipher, we can get the Allegiance," Lily argued. "And we can finish off the next generation."

"We're still missing a piece," Turnbull said. "There's a Key phrase to set the Cipher. Hold off. We're close."

Cursing to herself, she used her bad hand to signal for the six merks to hold in place, enjoying the pain, hating the order. Her good hand twitched on the handle of her sword.

* * *

Evie got to her feet, holding the Cipher tight to her chest. With Ducharme at her side, they walked over to the others. Everyone was in the shadow of the Amphitheatre. A solemn tableau in a solemn place.

Evie held up the rod and disks. "The complete Jefferson Cipher."

"And?" Kincannon asked dryly.

Evie was startled. "It's an original. Thomas Jefferson made it. It holds the secret to finding the Jefferson Allegiance."

"It only holds the secret," Kincannon said, "if we can use it."

225

"Well—" Evie paused, her burst of pride subsiding—"we need the phrase to Key the—"

Ducharme put an arm across her shoulder. "Can I have a smoke?"

Evie swiveled her head and stared at him in surprise. Of all things to be asking right now. "I don't smoke anymore and—"

"A smoke, please," Ducharme said. "Please, Evie."

Evie reached into her pocket and pulled out her cigarette case. "It's just gum."

Ducharme smiled at her, his arm still around her shoulder. "Read me the saying on the case once more."

Evie didn't have to read it. "'A blood of patriots and tyrants.'"

"A mistake by the engraver, right?" Ducharme didn't wait for an answer. "Except it isn't a mistake. How many letters are inscribed?"

Evie swallowed hard as she counted, already knowing the answer. "Twenty-six."

"That's your Key," Ducharme said.

With shaking fingers dialed up the saying.

ABLOODOFPATRIOTSANDTYRANTS

She turned the Cipher in her hands, searching line by line, her stomach twisted in a knot, and then she halted.

UNDERWESTSIDEJEFFERSONSTONE

She handed it to Ducharme, a wave of relief washing through her body as it all came together.

"'Under west side Jefferson stone?'" He looked at her. "What stone? The Jefferson Memorial?"

"No." She pointed to the east, toward the bright lights of Washington DC. "The center of the country."

Ducharme's face tightened. "You go with Kincannon. Get the Allegiance. I have something to do."

Evie was surprised. "What?"

"We need to make a clean sweep of things. Once and for all."

She blinked. "Lucius?"

Ducharme nodded. "Lucius. I trust you to get the Allegiance." He disappeared into the dark.

CHAPTER TWENTY-SIX

The Huey landed next to the Amphitheatre, and Ducharme climbed into the cargo bay. It took off in a flurry of light snow. He grabbed a headset. "Twelve thousand feet."

"Roger that," Pollack replied.

Ducharme unsnapped the kitbag the 3rd Infantry had brought and began to get ready.

* * *

"Status?" Turnbull asked.

Lily immediately replied. "It looks to me like Tolliver knew the Key phrase. She dialed something up."

"Get it from her. I'm almost there."

Lily was going to add that Ducharme had left, but the line was already dead. She heard the chopper power up and then fly away. Ducharme could be dealt with later—Lily put that in the background, a dessert to be savored.

* * *

"We've got company," Kincannon announced.

Evie looked up from the Cipher. Silhouetted between the colonnades of the Amphitheatre were a half-dozen armed figures. And stepping into the light featuring the Tomb was a short, slender figure carrying a sword.

"Our friend, once more" Kincannon muttered, bringing his MP-5 to the ready as the Old Guard readied their M-14s. "This ain't gonna be pretty. Some itchy fingers all around. Someone tries to scratch an itch, we're gonna have a blood bath."

"Hold your fire," Evie said.

"No shooting," the Surgeon yelled over her shoulder, but she kept coming. The merks who had begun moving forward, stopped, keeping a tactical separation. The weapons were trained on the members of the Old Guard. It was a relatively even standoff for the moment. Except for the Surgeon's insanity.

The Surgeon had her Japanese sword in her right hand. The left dangled uselessly, deformed. As she got closer, Evie could see the deranged look in her eyes.

* * *

Ducharme passed the last strap between his legs and snapped it into place. Then he squatted, tightening the harness as much as he could. He took a deep breath and glanced out the window in the cargo bay door. Washington DC was twelve thousand feet below and offset several miles, the Washington Monument brightly lit, a clear point of reference. To the east, from this altitude, the first hint of dawn was on the horizon.

He glanced once more at the computer screen, committing the target to memory.

* * *

The Surgeon was heading straight toward Evie, arm rising, the lights shining toward the Tomb making her seem to grow in stature as her shadow lengthened.

"Our killer," Burns said, stepping next to Evie. Kincannon also stepped forward.

"Get back," the Surgeon snarled, her focus on Evie and the device in her hand.

"Ma'am," Burns said, tipping his Fedora with his left hand. "You're under arrest for murder. You have the right—"

The Surgeon halted, pointing her sword toward him. "Shut up or die."

"Let's add in resisting arrest," Burns said, as Evie heard a distinct click. Burns's right hand snapped forward in an underhand throw. Evie dropped the Cipher Wheel and began charging forward as soon as Burns's arm moved. The Surgeon swung the sword, and there was the clink of metal on metal as her blade hit the switchblade he'd thrown, knocking it aside. Evie was on top of the Surgeon a split second later, grabbing the arm holding the sword and applying pressure to the nerve.

The sword fell to the ground as the Surgeon shoved Evie away. The Surgeon took a quick glance at the sword on the ground, and then shifted into a defensive position, arms up, mangled hand dangling.

"Come on," the Surgeon said, a look of anticipation on her face.

* * *

"All right," Ducharme said into the intercom. "I'm out of here."

"Good luck," Pollack said.

Ducharme took off the headset. He slid open the cargo bay door. Freezing air swirled in and he felt the bite of the cold.

He stepped out into the darkness.

* * *

"You're mine," Evie said, getting up on the balls of her feet and approaching the Surgeon. Everyone around them was frozen, waiting for this to play out.

The Surgeon charged, snapping a kick at Evie's jaw. She deflected it with a middle block and, anticipating, blocked the punch from the Surgeon's good hand. Evie kept the momentum from the second block, swinging a backfist toward the Surgeon, connecting on the side of her head and following it with a turn kick into the woman's side.

The Surgeon staggered back, gasping in pain and even more so in surprise.

* * *

Ducharme free fell, arms and legs akimbo for a thousand feet, and then pulled the ripcord. The chute deployed, snapping him upright. He grabbed the toggles and quickly oriented himself to the grid of downtown Washington. He found the convergence of roads on Dupont Circle. He pulled on a toggle, turning in that direction.

The building was easy to spot. Large and H-shaped. Ducharme squinted as he silently passed through one thousand feet. He couldn't see his landing point. He was losing air. He turned, searching, time running out.

Then he spotted the small rectangle on the roof. He dumped air, heading straight for it. At the last moment, he pulled on both toggles, abruptly slowing his descent, pulling his feet and knees tightly together, rotating his elbows in front of his face to protect it.

He smashed through the skylight, feeling a piece of glass cutting into the side of his right leg, then slammed into a hard floor. He jumped to his feet, hitting the quick releases on the parachute harness, and then bringing the MP-5 up at the ready.

Just in time as a pair of guards came running into the room.

Ducharme fired rounds as fast as he could pull the trigger, just as he'd been trained and done in combat. Right into the men's foreheads.

* * *

The Surgeon charged again, and Evie retreated. Not fast enough as the Surgeon spun, and side-kicked, hitting Evie hard in the stomach.

Just what Evie wanted.

She tumbled to the ground as if badly hurt, rolling as the Surgeon brought her boot down to stomp. Evie dodged the boot and thrust upward with all the strength in her legs, hands leading right for the Surgeon's throat.

The Surgeon came to an abrupt halt. The handle of Burns's switchblade stuck out, exactly in the small space where the collar of the Liquid Armor Cloak allowed an inch of clearance at her throat.

The Surgeon blinked in shock. Her good hand reached up to her throat, fingers curling around the handle. She pulled it out, staring at the red on the blade in momentary confusion as arterial blood pumped out of her neck. Evie backed up.

The Surgeon dropped to her knees. The look had changed. There was something dark and salacious in them as she watched her own blood spurt out.

"Everyone stay calm!" Kincannon yelled, moving forward. "No shooting."

The Surgeon's mouth was moving, trying to say something, but no words came. She collapsed forward and was still.

* * *

An alarm bell was ringing as Ducharme ran down a hallway lined with portraits. Nearing the heavy looking door at the far end, he fired at the lock. The rounds ricocheted off, the lock not so easily defeated.

Reaching into his vest, Ducharme pulled out a small charge and slapped it on the door over the lock, arming it. He ran back ten feet, and then pressed the remote detonator. There was a sharp crack and the door blew inward.

Ducharme staggered forward as a bullet hit him right in the middle of his back, slapping his body armor. He rolled and twisted, firing a sustained burst and taking down the cluster of guards crowding into the narrow hallway. Then he was on his feet running toward the open door, dropping the magazine from the sub and slamming a new one in just as he entered the room beyond.

An old man sat behind a large desk, calmly staring at Ducharme, holding a chess piece in one hand. "Colonel Ducharme?"

"Lucius." Ducharme strode forward, MP-5 tight to his shoulder, muzzle centered on the old man's forehead.

* * *

"No firing," commanded a new voice that easily carried through the sudden, tense silence. Turnbull walked to the front of the mercenaries and halted, not deigning to look down at the body of the Surgeon at his feet.

"*Agent* Turnbull," Burns said as he reached down and retrieved his knife, wiping the blood off on the Surgeon's cloak. The sound of sirens approaching filled the air. The mercenaries disappeared into the darkness, running away among the cemetery markers.

Evie realized she was almost hyperventilating and brought her breathing under control. Turnbull nodded at Burns. "You've done your duty, Agent Burns. You have your murderer." He looked over his shoulder, and a sheen of nervousness appeared on his scarred forehead despite the cold air. "You can't touch me. Give me the Cipher."

Evie held up the Cipher like a trophy. "Yes and no. You can be touched now, because your precious Lucius won't be there to protect you any more. And you will never get the Cipher or the Allegiance. You've lost."

"You'll never get to Lucius," Turnbull declared even as Burns snapped the cuffs on him.

* * *

"Now, now, Colonel," Lucius said. "Can we talk about this?"

"Sure," Ducharme said. "Who did you have kill Charlie LaGrange?"

"That death was avenged," Lucius said. "As a matter of fact, your friend the Surgeon took those contractors out."

"But you ordered it."

"Not exactly. I gave my subordinate a mission statement. The actual mission execution turned out to be extreme. The truce can be restored. There is no need for such extreme measures now."

"Actually, there is." Ducharme fired, a small black hole appearing in the center of Lucius's forehead, blood and brain splattering onto the books behind as his body flew backward.

The gun hidden in Lucius's other hand dropped to the floor with a clatter as Lucius's lifeless head slammed forward onto the desktop, scattering chess pieces.

CHAPTER TWENTY-SEVEN

"The Jefferson Memorial is to the right," Kincannon noted, as he drove them over the bridge into DC.

"Take Constitution Avenue," Evie said. "Toward the Zero Milestone."

Kincannon drove her around the Lincoln Memorial. Looking to the side, she saw the gash in the earth of the Vietnam Memorial. As they crossed 17th Street, Evie glanced left, past Kincannon's grim profile. A solitary figure was standing there, dressed in black.

Kincannon slowed and Ducharme slid into the back seat.

No one had to ask.

Evie reached a hand between the seats and Ducharme took it. Squeezed tight. Relaxed the pressure, but didn't let go. He noted that there was blood on her hand.

They drove in silence until Evie broke it: "Stop here," she ordered when they were due south of the White House—and the Zero Milestone.

Kincannon pulled over to the curb. When Evie got out, Ducharme and Kincannon followed.

"This way," Evie said, pointing to the south, away from the Zero Milestone and in the direction of the brightly lit Washington Monument. The mall was empty this early. There were more sirens in the distance, in the direction of the Anderson House blocks away.

Evie walked in a straight line, boots eating up ground. Ducharme was at her side and Kincannon a dark shadow, off at a tactical angle.

"What's the Jefferson Stone?" Ducharme asked.

"When Washington DC was first laid out by Pierre Charles L'Enfant, there was much discussion about establishing a prime meridian for the new country. Jefferson pushed for it. He thought the United States should be scientifically and geographically 'free' from Europe as well as politically. He

232

wanted the new prime meridian to run through the center of the President's house. So a stone was placed out here—" she pointed ahead—"to be that meridian. It was actually used for a long time before the United States joined the international community in accepting the Greenwich Meridian."

"I've never heard of this Jefferson Stone," Ducharme said.

"Most people haven't," Evie said. "Actually, the marker disappeared for a little while around eighteen seventy-two when the Corps of Engineers was cleaning up the area around the un-finished Washington Monument."

"The Jefferson Stone?" Ducharme pressed.

"We're getting there," Evie said as they passed by the Monument.

They approached a short, worn stone set in the ground.

The stone was a square block, about waist high. There was writing etched in the stone—midway down there was a gouge across it.

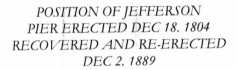

POSITION OF JEFFERSON
PIER ERECTED DEC 18. 1804
RECOVERED AND RE-ERECTED
DEC 2. 1889

Then there was the gouge, followed by:

DISTRICT OF COLUMBIA

"What happened to it?" Ducharme asked,

"It was used as a pier and barges were lashed to it when the water in the canal ran close to here."

Kincannon came up to them, watching the perimeter. "What now?"

Evie knelt down and beginning digging in the almost frozen ground with her bare fingers.

"Hold on," Ducharme said, pulling out his knife. "Let me." He dug until the blade hit something solid. Then he probed with his fingers. There was a flat stone blocking his way. He removed it. With a final tug, Ducharme pulled a black wooden cylinder out of the hole below the stone. It was a foot long and four inches in diameter.

"The Jefferson Allegiance," Evie said. "Shall we?"

"Should we?" Ducharme responded.

Evie paused, her hand on the cap. "What do you mean?"

"Do we even want to know?" Ducharme tapped the side of his head. "We read that, then the knowledge is in our heads. Makes us targets."

"Uh," Kincannon said, "I think we passed that one already."

Evie put a hand on his chest—rather, his body armor. "We have to know. We're the new Philosophers. We have to know what power we hold."

Ducharme said nothing further as she unscrewed the lid and pulled out a piece of parchment. Delicately she unrolled it. She turned so that the reflected light from the Washington Monument illuminated the words.

"It's the Second Amendment," Ducharme said as he began to read.

"It's a revised Second Amendment," Evie corrected. "Read the last sentences."

A well regulated militia being necessary to the security of a free State, the right of the People to keep and bear arms, shall not be infringed. The Army and Navy of the United States, and the militia of the several states, at the direction of the American Philosophical Society, shall remove from power any Federal official who, having openly violated his oath of office or the decreed balance of power, has not been impeached or otherwise checked by the will of the people. At last resort, every Federal official will be removed from office; a Constitutional Committee will be formed by democratic vote in each state, and a new government will be established under a new Constitution. The responsibility for such removal shall be the sworn duty of the General Officer Corps of the Army and Navy of the United States.

"It's signed by a sufficient number of members of Congress at the time it was ratified," Evie pointed out. "And President Jefferson. Thus, it is *law* and part of the Constitution."

She rolled it and put it back in the wooden tube.

"What now?" Ducharme said.

"What do you suggest?" Evie asked.

"What do *you* suggest?" Ducharme said.

Evie looked around. The Washington Monument loomed over them. The White House was to the north. Capitol Hill loomed to the east. They were literally in the political epicenter of the United States. "We have to reconstitute the Philosophers."

Ducharme nodded. "We need two more military. Navy and Air Force. I can do that. I know good people—high-ranking officers who were friends of General LaGrange. Men who can be trusted."

"In the meantime," Evie said, kneeling, "we put the Allegiance back." She slid it into the hole, replaced the stone and pushed the dirt back on top. Ducharme swept a covering of light snow over it.

Evie stood. "We need to hide the Cipher until we reform the APS and break the disks back out again among the members for each to hide their set."

Ducharme nodded. "I know what to do with the Cipher for now." He looked over at the tall figure of Kincannon, standing guard. "Sergeant Major, we're heading back to Arlington."

234

* * *

Emergency lights were flashing around the Tomb of the Unknown Soldier, and Ducharme figured Burns had his hands full trying to explain things. Too many people with too much power needed this entire thing hushed up, so Ducharme wasn't overly concerned about publicity.

"We can't put part of the Cipher in the Tomb," Evie said.

"We're not going there."

Kincannon and Evie followed Ducharme through the cemetery, away from the flashing lights, into the calm of fields of dead. Dawn was lighting up the eastern sky and the tombstones cast long shadows in the early morning chill.

Ducharme halted. "Here."

Evie looked at the newly emplaced headstone:

CAPTAIN CHARLES LAGRANGE
BORN NEW ORLEANS 6 MAY 1972
DIED 3 JANUARY 2011
DUTY-HONOR-COUNTRY
SILVER STAR

Ducharme knelt at the foot of the grave where new turf had been laid. A raw grave was to the right: the General. Ducharme pushed his knife into the loose soil and probed for a few moments. He struck something and pulled out the leather pouch he'd buried. He opened it and the two rings tumbled into his palm. He slid one onto his finger. Then he took a third from a pocket—General LaGrange's, which Evie had retrieved from the Surgeon's body. He put it in the pouch next to the General's son's ring.

Ducharme buried the rings back in the hole, pressing them down deep.

Then he held out his hands to Evie. "Let me have the Cipher."

Evie removed the rods and disks. Ducharme unscrewed the end and removed 19 of the disks. He handed the rod and 7 remaining disks back to her. "You hide your seven wherever you want. Make sure it's a place where whoever you appoint as your successor can unravel the clues to finding it by knowing you. I'll hide the rest until we name the next two Philosophers. Then I'll give each one their six."

Ducharme turned back to the General's grave. He slid his commando knife into the dirt and covered it.

"Won't you be needing that?" Evie asked.

"I hope I won't need my knife. Not quite Kosciuszko's sword, but you get the idea. We need to move beyond the sword. I think the words of the Jefferson Allegiance are more powerful than any knife or sword."

Evie nodded. "They've proven to be so far. It's our duty to make sure they continue to do so."

THE END

COMING 5 NOVEMBER 2013
THE KENNEDY ENDEAVOR

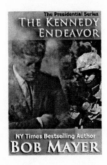

No one looks for something that isn't supposed to exist.

For 13 days in October 1963 the world came the closest to nuclear Armageddon. On 22 November 1963, President Kennedy was assassinated. On the 25th of November, as Kennedy's body lay in state at the Rotunda in Washington, Anastas Mikyoan, Khrushchev's top adviser, presented the Premier's condolences to Jacqueline Kennedy. She took Mikoyan's hand in both hers and told him: "I am sure that Chairman Khrushchev and my husband could have been successful in the search for peace, and they were really striving for that. Now you must continue this *endeavor* and bring it to completion."

On 12 October 1964, a Washington socialite named Mary Meyer was shot in the back of the head and through the heart at point-blank range. She had been married to a high-ranking CIA agent. More importantly, she had been carrying on an affair with President John F. Kennedy and was one of his most trusted friends, at his side through the Bay of Pigs and the Cuban Missile Crisis.

Mary Meyer kept a secret diary.

On 13 October 1964, the day after Mary Meyer's murder, the Soviet Politburo forced Nikita Khrushchev to resign from power and put him under house arrest.

What was in Mary Meyer's diary that caused her murder and Khrushchev's resignation?

Paul Ducharme learns that someone is searching APS Archives for information about Kennedy and Khrushchev, looking for details of a secret deal made between the two after the missile crisis that has significant repercussions to this day—that in fact, could spell nuclear destruction for the United States.

To find out what those two world leaders did, Ducharme must unravel the mystery of Kennedy's assassination, the murky history of the CIA, and what role the Society of the Cincinnati played in all of those. And, most chilling of all, what role his own American Philosophical Society played.

ABOUT THE AUTHOR

NY Times bestselling author **Bob Mayer** has had over 50 books published. He has sold over four million books, and is in demand as a team-building, life-changing, and leadership speaker and consultant for his *Who Dares Wins: The Green Beret Way* concept, which he translated into Write It Forward: a holistic program teaching writers how to be authors. He is also the Co-Creator of Cool Gus Publishing, which does both eBooks and Print On Demand, so he has experience in both traditional and non-traditional publishing.

His books have hit the *NY Times, Publishers Weekly, Wall Street Journal* and numerous other bestseller lists. His book *The Jefferson Allegiance,* was released independently and reached #2 overall in sales on Nook.

Bob Mayer grew up in the Bronx. After high school, he entered West Point where he learned about the history of our military and our country. During his four years at the Academy and later in the Infantry, Mayer questioned the idea of "mission over men." When he volunteered and passed selection for the Special Forces as a Green Beret, he felt more at ease where the men were more important than the mission.

Mayer's obsession with mythology and his vast knowledge of the military and Special Forces, mixed with his strong desire to learn from history, is the foundation for his science fiction series *Atlantis, Area 51* and *Psychic Warrior.* Mayer is a master at blending elements of truth into all of his thrillers, leaving the reader questioning what is real and what isn't.

He took this same passion and created thrillers based in fact and riddled with possibilities. His unique background in the Special Forces gives the reader a sense of authenticity and creates a reality that makes the reader wonder where fact ends and fiction begins.

In his historical fiction novels, Mayer blends actual events with fictional characters. He doesn't change history, but instead changes how history came into being.

Mayer's military background, coupled with his deep desire to understand the past and how it affects our future, gives his writing a rich flavor not to be missed.

Bob has presented for over a thousand organizations both in the United States and internationally, including keynote presentations, all day workshops, and multi-day seminars. He has taught organizations ranging from Maui Writers, to Whidbey Island Writers, to San Diego State University, to the University of Georgia, to the Romance Writers of America National Convention, to Boston SWAT, the CIA, Fortune-500, the Royal Danish Navy Frogman Corps, Microsoft, Rotary, IT Teams in Silicon Valley and many others. He has also served as a Visiting Writer for NILA MFA program in Creative Writing. He has done interviews for the *Wall Street Journal*, *Forbes*, *Sports Illustrated*, PBS, NPR, the Discovery Channel, the SyFy channel and local cable shows. For more information see www.bobmayer.org.

OTHER BOOKS BY BOB MAYER

"Thelma and Louise go clandestine." *Kirkus Reviews on Bodyguard of Lies*

" . . .delivers top-notch action and adventure, creating a full cast of lethal operatives armed with all the latest weaponry. Excellent writing and well-drawn, appealing characters help make this another taut, crackling read." *Publishers Weekly*

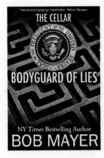

"Fascinating, imaginative and nerve-wracking." *Kirkus Reviews*

THE PRESIDENTIAL SERIES BY BOB MAYER

COMING 5 November

THE GREEN BERET SERIES

"Mayer has stretched the limits of the military action novel. Synbat is also a gripping detective story and an intriguing science fiction thriller. Mayer brings an accurate and meticulous depiction of military to this book which greatly enhances its credibility." *Assembly*

"Will leave you spellbound. Mayer's long suit is detail, giving the reader an in-depth view of the inner workings of the Green Machine." *Book News*

"Mayer keeps story and characters firmly under control. The venal motives of the scientists and military bureaucracy are tellingly contrasted with the idealism of the soldiers. A treat for military fiction readers." *Publishers Weekly*

"Sinewy writing enhances this already potent action fix. An adrenaline cocktail from start to finish." *Kirkus Reviews*

HISTORICAL FICTION BY BOB MAYER

SHADOW WARRIOR SERIES

"Sizzling, first rate war fiction." *Library Journal*

"A military thriller in the tradition of John Grisham's The Firm." *Publishers Weekly*

"The Omega Missile comes screaming down on target. A great action read." *Stephen Coonts*

"What a delicious adventure-thriller. Its clever, plausible plot gives birth to lots of action and suspense." *Kansas City Journal Inquirer*

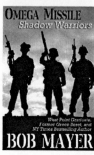 

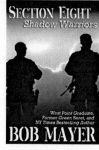

THE ATLANTIS SERIES BY BOB MAYER

"Spell-binding! Will keep you on the edge of your seat. Call it techno-thriller, call it science fiction, call it just terrific story-telling." *Terry Brooks, #1 NY Times Bestselling author of the Shannara series and Star Wars Phantom Menace*

PSYCHIC WARRIOR SERIES

"A pulsing technothriller. A nailbiter in the best tradition of adventure fiction." *Publishers Weekly.*

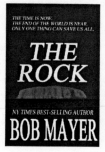

AREA 51/NIGHTSTALKERS SERIES

"Bob Mayer's *Nightstalkers* grabs you by the rocket launcher and doesn't let go. Fast-moving military SF action—just the way I like it. Highly recommend." *B.V. Larson*